Praise for

By the Book

★ "In this refreshing first novel, Sellet manages the large cast of characters well, while portraying the protagonist's big family, her small circle of friends, and her first romance with considerable wit and insight. As Mary struggles with the practical and emotional troubles arising from her many mistakes, her rueful, self-deprecating narrative is sometimes impossible to read without laughing out loud. A smart, engaging romance."

—ALA *BOOKLIST* (STARRED REVIEW)

"Delightful . . . Amid the brief diary entries and opulent prose, Sellet manages to hide a clever and biting social commentary in Mary's point of view. One doesn't need intimate familiarity with the classics to enjoy *By the Book*, but the more you know, the more you'll laugh."

—NPR

"A sweet story with a focus on family and friendships."

—*KIRKUS REVIEWS*

"Put in the hands of readers who love a smart and precocious cast of characters, reminiscent of Amy Heckerling's film *Clueless*."

— *SCHOOL LIBRARY JOURNAL*

"This debut sparkles! A heroine to root for, Mary Porter-Malcolm leaps off the page. Sellet has crafted a story of friendship, first love, and family dynamics that absolutely sings."

—EMMA MILLS, AUTHOR OF *FIRST & THEN* AND *LUCKY CALLER*

"At once clever, hilarious, and poignant."

—MIRANDA ASEBEDO, AUTHOR OF *A CONSTELLATION OF ROSES*

"*By the Book* is a true delight — a bibliophile's dream."

—MARY O'CONNELL, AUTHOR OF *DEAR READER*

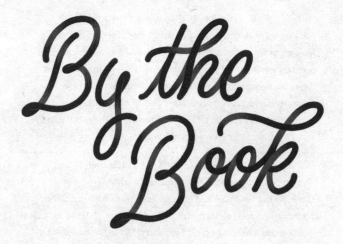

By the Book

A Novel of Prose and Cons

Amanda Sellet

CLARION BOOKS
An Imprint of HarperCollins*Publishers*

Clarion Books is an imprint of HarperCollins Publishers.

Library of Congress Cataloging-in-Publication Data
Names: Sellet, Amanda, author.
Title: By the book : a novel of prose and cons / Amanda Sellet.
Description: Boston : Houghton Mifflin Harcourt, [2020] | Includes
bibliographical references. | Summary: "A teen obsessed with
19th-century literature tries to cull advice on life and love from her
favorite classic heroines to disastrous results—especially when she
falls for the school's resident lothario." —Provided by publisher.
Identifiers: LCCN 2019020307 (print) | LCCN 2019022286 (ebook)
ISBN 9780358668084 (pbk.) | ISBN 9780358156642 (ebook) |
Subjects: CYAC: High schools—Fiction. | Schools—
Fiction. | Dating (Social customs)—Fiction.
Classification: LCC PZ7.1.S42 By 2020 (print) |
LCC PZ7.1.S42 (ebook) | DDC [Fic]—dc23
LC record available at https://lccn.loc.gov/2019020307
LC ebook record available at https://lccn.loc.gov/2019022286

Typography by Andrea Miller
22 23 24 25 26 PC/LSCC 10 9 8 7 6 5 4 3 2 1

First paperback edition, 2022

To my big family and my little one.
You're all in here somewhere.

Dear Diary,

Here's a secret I've never told anyone: Sometimes I pretend my life is happening inside a book. I'm the main character, and there's a narrator following me around, describing everything. **Her piercing cerulean eyes gazed wistfully into the distance as an errant breeze caressed her lustrous auburn tresses** . . . Et cetera.

Obviously I'm the good kind of heroine, not someone whose poor life choices will lead to her dying of consumption while still in her teens. And I'm wearing a long dress, and maybe there's a handsome stranger in the distance. Beyond that, the story is vague. Possibly because my real life has always been light on plot development — until today.

M.P.M.

CHAPTER 1

The beginning of the upending of my life took place on a sweltering August afternoon, the summer before my sophomore year of high school. I was lying on the couch, immersed in the story of a genteel family with too many daughters and not enough property. The slow rotation of the ceiling fan ruffled the pages of my book. If I held perfectly still, it was possible not to sweat.

"Mary," said my mother's voice, summoning me back to the present. "Can I see you in my office?"

There was no clap of thunder or eerie howling in the distance. The sun continued to blaze down from a cloudless sky —or so I imagined, not having been outside. Apart from the mild annoyance of being interrupted in the middle of a crucial scene, I had no presentiment of doom. After fumbling for my bookmark, which had slipped between cushions, I levered myself upright.

When I hobbled into the office on limbs stiff from too many hours in the same position, I was surprised to see my father seated at one end of the desk. Usually he (and Mom) preferred it when he worked in a different room.

"What's up?" I asked, lifting a stack of literary journals from the threadbare armchair so I could sit.

"Mary." Dad leaned forward on his stool, hands cupping his knees. "How would you like a new . . . lunchbox?"

Mom winced.

"The one I have is fine. Why?" Being observant by nature —reasonably skilled at reading a room, deciphering subtext, sniffing out the nuances of human behavior—I had an inkling there was more to come.

Dad blotted his temple with the back of his wrist. "Well. As you know, there are things in this life that endure, and others that are more—" He paused, squinting at a framed poster of the Bloomsbury Group, as if one of them might supply the missing phrase. "Transitory."

"And you think my lunchbox is going to stop existing?" I looked to my mother for enlightenment.

She inhaled as if preparing to plunge into the watery deep. "What your father is *trying* to say is that you have to change schools."

Dumbfounded, I struggled to make sense of her words. I'd been at the same school since I was three, a ramshackle on-campus facility catering mostly to the children of professors. It was small, and smelled like old shoes when it rained, but it was also a second home. I knew every rip in the carpet and limp beanbag. "Are you serious?" I finally managed to ask.

"The school's grant wasn't renewed." Among my mother's

gifts was the ability to pack a world of disapproval into the briefest of utterances.

"And they just figured this out? Summer's almost over."

The two of them exchanged a furtive glance.

"The possibility presented itself some time ago, but the situation wasn't definitive until quite recently." Dad gestured vaguely. "A month or so—"

"Two at the most," Mom cut in. "We thought it best not to upset you while there was still a chance the issue could be resolved. Plus we had the symposium in Chicago, and then the twins were getting ready for the Shakespeare festival, not to mention Cam's tournament." Her eyes slid to me, clearly hoping for some version of *Oh wow, you're right, that* was *hectic,* but I was more concerned by the revelation that they'd known about this in the *spring.*

"But what am I going to do? This changes everything." A vision popped into my head: setting off on the first day only to have one of them call after me, *By the way, Mary, your school no longer exists.*

My mother squared her shoulders. "There was very little choice involved. Private school isn't an option for us. It was Millville High or the circus."

While we weren't paupers, all of us understood that a family of seven had to observe certain economies to get by on an academic pay scale. That didn't excuse leaving me in the dark for so long.

"What about Jasper?"

She rolled her eyes, a gesture reminiscent of the sibling in question. "No doubt your brother will be delighted."

"You haven't told him yet." The part of me that kept a running tally of which sibling got what was relieved. It was important to make sure the privileges of birth order were respected, even when the rest of the universe was falling apart.

"Jasper is enough of a contrarian to think middle school will be fun." Mom huffed through her nostrils, in case we'd missed the sarcasm.

"And so will Millville High," Dad said with forced cheer. "Especially with your sister there to take you under her wing."

Despite this assurance, I found it hard to imagine Cam playing nursemaid. She was going to be a senior, and captain of the field hockey team, with a busy life of her own. I could go to her in dire straits, or if I needed to intimidate someone, but it wasn't as though we spent a lot of time hanging out together now. I didn't bother explaining this to my parents. There were too many other things to worry about.

"So I'm going to Millville High in—a week?" I glanced at the calendar on the wall, each month featuring the idyllic childhood home of an English novelist. "And I'll know one person, and everyone will look at me and wonder why a sophomore can't figure out where her classes are or how to open a locker or anything else that happens at a normal high school?"

"Pooh pooh." My father was the only human being I knew who actually said those words, instead of using them as a verb. "Of course not. Anjuli will be there, too."

That brought me up short. "She will?"

Dad scratched his head. "Did we not mention that?"

"You led with the lunchbox," Mom reminded him.

I hardly listened to the ensuing back-and-forth about which of them was the more skilled communicator. What mattered was that I wouldn't be alone in the wilds of Millville High. Anjuli and I had spent most of our lives in the same classroom, the only girls in our grade. We hadn't actually spoken since the last day of school, but that was fairly typical of our summers. She traveled the world visiting family, while I stayed in Millville, rereading. Perhaps this dramatic shift in our lives would bring us closer?

My expression must have brightened, because Dad pointed triumphantly at me. "You see? I knew Mary would rise to the occasion. When you think about it, this has the potential to be an exciting adventure, rather than a catastrophic loss!"

Mom patted his hand. "Well put, dear." She stood, rolling the exercise ball she used as a chair under her desk. "We should give Mary space to process." Her hand rested briefly on the top of my head as she moved toward the door.

"The lunchbox offer still stands," my father whispered as he followed.

I watched the door close, feeling a twinge of wistfulness that I'd let them slip away instead of drawing out my time in the spotlight. But that would have required me to pitch a fit, and histrionics were beneath my dignity—particularly if I wanted to be taken as seriously as my older sisters.

Besides, the first wave of trepidation was already receding.

In its place my pulse thrummed with a sense of newfound possibility. A plot twist of this magnitude had to signal *something*. A fork in the road. The start of a fresh chapter. It was like the part of the book where the heroine receives an invitation to visit someone's country estate. There would be people to meet, a chance to see and be seen, organized socializing. Though probably not croquet or masquerades.

All my life I'd been waiting my turn to be the one with important stuff happening. Maybe this was it at last—my time to take center stage. I wasn't sure exactly what that might entail, but one thing was certain: a fetching new lunchbox was only the beginning.

Dear Diary,

The good thing about Millville High is that it's not a germ-ridden penal colony masquerading as a boarding school, à la **Jane Eyre**. I'm pretty sure I can cross corporal punishment and starvation rations off my list of worries, not to mention waking up next to the corpse of my only friend.

Although if Anjuli **had** succumbed to a picturesque nineteenth-century illness, it would explain why she's not returning my calls. I had to find out from her mom that the only class the two of us have together is lunch, which is disappointing, but at least means I won't have to brave the cafeteria alone.

M.P.M.

CHAPTER 2

My first impression of Millville High was kaleidoscopic. Fragments of color and sound swirled around me, the new faces and snatches of conversation overlaid with an aroma best described as Overcrowded Candy Store: bouquet of fruity chemicals and nervous sweat.

It may seem chaotic, I told myself as the sea of humanity swept me in the direction of my next class, *but there's bound to be an underlying logic.* Perhaps it would take a few weeks to learn the steps of this new dance. All I needed was to bide my time until I figured out how to join in without tripping over my own feet.

When the bell rang for lunch I hurried to the cafeteria, eager to compare notes with Anjuli. After several fruitless surveys of the cafeteria's outer ring, I finally spotted her, sitting at an otherwise empty table. That part didn't surprise me. What caused my steps to falter was that she'd positioned herself at the very center of the room. I might be a babe in the woods when it came to the social politics of Millville High, but a morning had been sufficient to notice a distinct class structure. Not so much in the sense of freshman, sophomore, and so on; this was a hierarchy of position. And right now, the crème de la crème had assembled at the heart of the cafeteria.

To insert ourselves among the upper crust on our first day felt presumptuous at best. At worst it would look like we were putting on airs. Getting ideas above our station. Begging for a swift comeuppance. Against this I weighed Anjuli's rigid posture. I imagined her arriving early to secure us a spot, followed by tense moments alone as she waited for me to appear. Her left arm was crooked protectively around the nearest chair, as though she feared it might be snatched away. Even her hair was on the defensive, the neat braid she'd worn since second grade replaced by a curtain of flowing locks that shielded her face from view.

"Oh," she said dully when I set my backpack on the table. "Mary." Her brow knit as she looked me up and down.

As greetings went, this one was more *huh, it's you* than *reunited at last!* Perhaps she'd given up hope, resigning herself to a lonely vigil. Either that or it was a subtle way of letting me know I was late.

"I didn't see you at first, in all the hullabaloo."

Anjuli's mouth compressed, suggesting my explanation left something to be desired. I reached for the chair she'd been guarding, but she yanked it away. "Not there."

Personal space, I theorized, edging around her to take one of the four other vacant seats. Or maybe she was using that chair for storage. I'd briefly considered carrying all my school supplies with me in lieu of braving the dreaded locker combination.

I felt her watching as I unzipped my lunch. "It's nothing exciting," I warned, in case the new bag had given her false hopes. "Same old sandwich." I didn't mention the apple or granola bar; Anjuli knew my family's health-conscious pantry as well as I did.

She went back to scanning the room. Which seemed odd, now that I was there, unless she was on the lookout for potential threats. A burst eardrum maybe, given the noise level.

"It's a lot to absorb, isn't it?" I whispered.

Her eyes flicked to me. "I have no idea what you're talking about."

"The size of the building, the sheer number of people, the mysterious group dynamics. This is a completely unfamiliar milieu."

A muscle twitched in Anjuli's jaw. "Do you have to talk like that?"

"I'm just saying, they have a *cafeteria*." I tipped my head at the line of people carrying orange and yellow trays. At our old school, you could have fed the entire grade with a single pizza, provided it had a gluten-free crust and vegan "cheese."

"Ooooh." She fluttered her fingers. "I'm so weirded out by the vats of canned vegetables. How will I survive?"

Before I could muster a counterargument, Anjuli's expression softened into a tentative smile. I waited for the words that must be coming: *You're right, Mary. It* is *intimidating. The stress is making me testy.* Then I realized the warmth in her gaze wasn't directed at me.

"Pittaya," I exclaimed, tipping my head back to see all of

him. Our erstwhile classmate had grown several inches over the summer. "I didn't know you were going to be here."

He dipped his chin, conveying *hello* and *yes* and *I didn't know you didn't know* with characteristic economy of words.

"I saved you a seat," Anjuli informed him, pointing to the chair I'd been denied.

Objectively I could see how Pittaya would be a higher-status lunch companion, what with the unkempt black hair and brooding mien, qualities that had inspired my mother to dub him *Heathcliff Junior*. Yet even with the newly impressive height, Pittaya would always be Pittaya to me. The same kid who'd dealt with frequent childhood nosebleeds by dangling streamers of bloody Kleenex from his nostrils.

"How did it go this morning?" Anjuli asked. That the question was intended for Pittaya was evident in the unblinking gaze she trained on his face.

He blushed, a typical Pittaya response to being singled out. "Fine."

"You would love my New Media class." Her voice deepened as though trying to match his bass rumble.

"That sounds fun," I put in, thinking to spare Pittaya the ordeal of a response.

Anjuli scowled at the interruption. "It's not your kind of thing, Mary."

"I know." The word *new* was enough of a clue. "Still, it's too bad we don't have any classes together."

For the first time since Pittaya's arrival, she looked directly at me. "We've been stuck in the same room for twelve years."

I swallowed a bite of sandwich that should have been chewed more. "True," I choked out. "And at least we'll see each other at lunch."

She grunted something I chose to take as an affirmative.

"What else are you taking?" People usually perked up when given the chance to talk about themselves.

Anjuli snapped a carrot stick in half. "We're not seriously going to sit here and talk about our classes, are we?"

"It seemed relevant." I spoke the words mostly to my water bottle. "This *is* a school."

"News flash. There's more to life than academics. Everyone knows the overachiever lifestyle is a trap. Haven't you been reading all the articles about how toxic stress and anxiety are for teens? The pressure to be perfect, blah blah blah?"

"I guess I missed that."

"Yeah, well, they were written in this century, so." A faint huff accompanied this remark, not quite a laugh but close enough to sting.

"Other centuries have a lot to offer. When you think about it." It sounded tentative and mealy-mouthed. The temptation to kick myself was strong. *Way to be scintillating, Mary!*

Anjuli gave a dismissive hair toss. "I'm about the now. No doilies for me." Pittaya glanced between us, a faint pucker to his forehead. "That's why I'm taking Modeling and Design."

It took me a second to place the name, given how quickly I'd breezed past it in the list of elective options. "Isn't that the class where you build stuff?"

"Yes, *Mary*. I'm going to get my hands dirty and actually

create things instead of living in the abstract." Her slender (and perfectly clean) fingers brushed the back of Pittaya's wrist. "You understand. As an artist."

I blinked at this tableau, wondering if I'd accidentally slept through the first six months of my sophomore year and missed certain developments. Like the one where my name now doubled as an insult.

"So what kind of stuff will you make?" I asked, hoping to shift the conversation onto less contentious ground. "Is it about putting together birdhouses and whatnot?"

"I'm not in *jail*. This is a maker space, for skilled artisans. It's part of how I'm redefining myself."

"All right if I take this?" an unfamiliar voice cut in.

A boy in blue gestured at one of the unoccupied chairs. Grateful for the distraction, I started to say *please do* . . . only to feel the words wither on my tongue. The dark-blond curls were a little longer, the jawline a shade more defined, but the eyes remained bright as ever, a near match for the shade of his shirt. *I know you,* I thought, as our gazes collided.

"I told you we could share," whined a pink-clad girl who had appeared beside him, tugging ineffectually at his elbow. I didn't realize I was frowning until his brows drew together.

"Come on," his companion urged.

"You only want me for my tater tots," he teased as he dragged the chair back to their table.

Anjuli waited until the pastel pair were seated to address me. "What was that?"

"Nothing." As in, *nothing I want to discuss.*

14

Chin in hand, she stared at the overcrowded table that had spawned our chair thief. Every last one of them sparkled with teenage joie de vivre. It was like peeking through the window of a London drawing room to watch the aristocrats strut and pose. I felt like a scullery maid by comparison, lurking in the background until someone needed their fireplace cleaned.

"Talk about a lost opportunity." Anjuli emptied her juice pouch with an angry slurp.

"It really wasn't." By now he would have forgotten our existence, *if* he'd noticed us in the first place.

"A cute guy walks up—"

"Don't be taken in by the pretty face. Handsome is as handsome does."

"What does that even—you know what, never mind. The point is, we could have had a moment."

"While he stole one of our chairs?"

"And instead of being friendly," she continued as if I hadn't spoken, "you looked at him like he was a bowl of dog food."

I snuck another glance at the beautiful people, a flicker of doubt tightening my chest. Had I been rude? He was talking to a different girl now. Whatever he'd said must have been charming; the shoulders of the dark-haired girl's companions shook in a chorus of giggles. Growing desperate, the girl in pink shoved a tater tot past his lips, forcing him to look her way or asphyxiate.

"He's not exactly suffering." When I turned back to Anjuli, thinking she might concede the point, her eyes were closed and her fingertips were pressed to her temples.

"I saw some girls today." She spoke without opening her

eyes. "I'm pretty sure they made their own clothes. Really long skirts. They were talking about slow cooker recipes."

I glanced at Pittaya, but he appeared equally clueless. "Why are you telling me this?"

"They might be your kind of people."

My pulse whooshed in my ears. "I don't care about slow cookers. Or sewing."

Anjuli's eyes opened, but instead of looking at me she studied her hands, bedecked with several new rings. A daisy, a skull, some kind of animal . . . it was hard to tell what aesthetic she was going for. "They like old-fashioned stuff."

"Thanks for the tip." I tried to keep my voice light, but even to my ears it sounded shrill. "I'm sure there are plenty of people at this school who share my interests."

Turning hopefully to the teeming hordes around us, I searched for a likely candidate. It was hard to tell that kind of thing from the outside, but I doubted the guy dribbling chocolate milk onto his neighbor's hamburger was a kindred soul. Or the person gouging a tabletop with her ballpoint.

My gaze hopped sideways, inadvertently landing on the boy in blue. He must have been in a brief lull between flirtations, because he looked back at me with raised brows. I shook my head, wishing there was a telepathic way to convey that the eye contact had been accidental. He could scratch my name off his list of admirers. If he actually *knew* my name.

Which he did not.

"Did you talk to anyone in your classes?" Anjuli asked, not bothering to hide her skepticism.

"It's the first day. My sisters said—"

"Your sisters had *cool* interests." Anjuli speared a segment of mandarin orange from the plastic cup in front of her, pointing at me with the dripping fork. "I guarantee there's no such thing as a Moldy Old Books group at this school. Nobody here wants to sit around drinking tea with their pinkie sticking out."

"My pinkie just does that. It's not an affectation. And you read, too." On the rare occasions we'd socialized outside school, most of our time had been spent reading together—or rather, in the same room.

"Yeah, sci-fi, which is full of cutting-edge discourse."

I thought dubiously of the covers of her paperbacks, with their skintight spacesuits and phallic ray guns. "My books have a lot of deeper meanings. Moral lessons. Et cetera."

Sighing, she glanced at her watch.

"Is lunch almost over?" Pittaya asked hopefully.

Anjuli shook her head. "Some people from EFS said they might stop by."

"*Effs?*" I echoed.

"Experimental Film Society." From her long-suffering tone, you would have thought I'd asked how to tie my shoes. "Nonlinear, nonnarrative, avant-garde cinema. It's *very* political." She bit her lip. "They should have been here by now."

I knew Anjuli well enough to read the anxious creasing of her brow: Maybe they weren't coming at all. She'd been stood up. Snubbed. As a friend I should have shared her dismay, but a secret part of me was relieved.

Despite my ambivalence, I was struggling to come up with

a neutral-yet-sympathetic response when a trio of strangers approached. Ordinarily my curiosity would have been piqued, but I was too startled by the change in Anjuli to pay them any mind. In an instant she'd gone from clouds to sun, her body language unfurling like a flower.

"Hey!" Where a moment ago every word had emerged weary and annoyed, her voice now crackled with energy. "This is Pittaya, the one I told you about. He's an amazing painter."

Greetings were mumbled. I waited for Anjuli to introduce me, but she was focused on the empty chairs. Later I would find it impossible to say how much time elapsed in tortured silence before it clicked: two chairs, three people. Anjuli barely looking at me throughout lunch. Her attempt to fob me off on random stew-making seamstresses. The simmering undercurrent of irritation.

How could I have been so foolish? She hadn't been waiting for *me* to show up; she didn't want me there at all.

I pushed my chair back. "I have a . . . prior engagement." The words were barely audible, addressed to no one in particular.

Pittaya gave a microscopic nod. Anjuli pretended not to hear, laughing with one of her new friends at some inconsequential remark. I wouldn't have been surprised to look down and find that I'd become ghostly and insubstantial. Invisible to the naked eye.

Gathering the scraps of my dignity, and my lunch, I fled.

Dear Diary,

I wonder if the popular crowd in high school will be as ruthless as the society mavens in an Edith Wharton novel. Probably that dynamic exists in any stratified society, with the upper echelon cutting people down to maintain their own power and position.

The good news is that I have no desire to be part of the ruling class or their cruel games. Give me a simple life with interesting companions, far from the movers and shakers. I'd rather be safe than sorry any day.

M.P.M.

CHAPTER 3

When at last the final bell signaled the great stampede toward the parking lot, I snuck out a side door and cut across the sloping green lawn that always made my mother grumble about water shortages. I had decided to detour through downtown to reduce the risk of crossing paths with Anjuli. The charms of Millville's quaint shopping district, the flower boxes and sidewalk cafes, were lost on me; I was seeking sanctuary, not an overpriced sandwich. The entire concept of sandwiches had been poisoned in the wake of the Shunning.

As I walked, my thoughts continued to circle the fateful lunchroom encounter, rewriting it in my head. *Et tu, Anjuli?* That would have been a good parting salvo, and not just because we'd read *Julius Caesar* last year. It felt like a stabbing. She'd opened a hole in my side, and now everything was leaking out. Not blood and guts, but all my comfortable assumptions about the world and my place in it. My idea of interpersonal conflict was a discreet verbal jab: *I take no leave of you. I send no compliments to your mother.* Not silently repudiating your oldest friend.

And okay, maybe on some level I'd been aware that things between us had been strained of late, but it was like hearing an odd noise in the middle of the night. A reasonable person pulled the covers over her head and pretended everything was fine, because what were the odds of assassins creeping up the stairs . . . or sitting next to you in the cafeteria?

If this were a novel, I would have staggered around moaning and wailing with the shock of betrayal. But you couldn't do those things in real life, at least not where people from your high school might see. I was already an outcast; no point making things worse. The most I could allow myself was to slow my steps to a trudge, staring numbly at storefronts I'd seen a thousand times before.

A flurry of movement caught my eye. Someone was gesturing at me from inside Toil & Trouble, one of Millville's many used bookstores. That was one of our town's claims to fame: too small for big box superstores, yet bursting with booksellers and coffee shops. Or in the case of Toil & Trouble, a bookstore/café combo.

Momentary panic seized me at the thought that the person trying to get my attention might be Noreen, Toil & Trouble's sour and oversharing proprietor, who assumed every customer had come in search of detailed accounts of her medical history. But no, it was Marco, one of my father's grad students. I started to wave back before realizing he was beckoning me inside.

Soothing flute music heralded my entrance, the mingled scents of coffee, incense, and mildewed paper rising in welcome. It was a few degrees cooler inside, away from the direct heat of the sun. My spirits climbed fractionally. Why not hide out here instead of going straight home, where someone might ask about my day? I was heading for the fiction aisle when Marco edged in front of me.

"How's it going?" he asked, stroking his overgrown beard. Viking chic was all the rage among English majors these days. His eyes darted to the door before returning to my face.

"Okay." I had the strong impression he wasn't really listening, despite the nod.

"You busy right now?"

"Not really." Surely he wasn't about to ask me to hang out. My mind dismissed the possibility as soon as it arose, which wasn't quickly enough to arrest the heat I could feel rising into my cheeks.

Another furtive glance at the exit, and then his feet. "Listen, I really need to run to campus and talk to your dad, but his office hours will be over by the time I get off."

I looked at him blankly, not unsympathetic but unclear as to how I could help.

"If you could just sit up front until I get back, that would be excellent." He pulled a white hand towel out of his waistband and handed it to me. "You don't have to do anything. I usually get some reading in."

"What if someone wants to buy something?"

"Highly unlikely. Check it out," he said, leading me to the front counter. "Cash register, coffee machine, phone." Marco pointed at each item in turn, already backing toward the door.

"But—"

"I owe you big time," he called out, breaking into a run as soon as he hit the sidewalk.

Silence settled over the bookshop. No doubt Marco was right; all I had to do was sit here and await his return. Downtown brushed right against the edge of campus, so it wasn't even a very long walk. Climbing onto the wooden stool behind the counter, I pulled my backpack onto my lap. The biology worksheet didn't appeal, and I felt I'd been punished enough without subjecting myself to Algebra II. Social studies would have to do.

I had just opened the battered textbook when the bell over the door jingled.

The bad news hit me in stages: Customers.

Plural.

And they went to my school, a place I'd hoped to erase from my consciousness until tomorrow morning.

Worst of all, there was a chance this trio of girls had actually witnessed my humiliation. The one in the lead had candy-red hair, a shade so distinctive I immediately recalled where I'd seen it before: at the table of glistening, giggling, popular kids. The who's who of High School High Society had just walked through the door of Toil & Trouble. And they were headed straight for me.

I closed my book and set it aside. Maybe they were lost and had merely stopped in for directions. Any request I could answer by pointing should be within my capabilities.

"Hi," said the one I mentally dubbed the Crimson Contessa. There was a subtle air of sophistication to her tortoiseshell sunglasses and crisp white shirt, not to mention the textured leather bag resting in the crook of her elbow. As often happened with new people, I imagined how she would be described in a book. Long-limbed and narrow, with pencil-thin brows and a severe bob, she stood with an air of . . . waiting for me to respond to her greeting.

I inhaled too deeply, choking out a hello.

She smiled warmly before turning her attention to the chalkboard menu on the wall behind me. "How's the Mystic Mayan?"

Using the contextual clues, I figured out she was talking about a coffee drink. "I've never tried it," I said sheepishly. "More of a tea person."

The Contessa's cheerfulness was undimmed. "Okay. I think I'll go for that one. Why not?" She bounced to one side, making room for the next girl, who had her back to me as she spoke to the third member of their party. This one was smaller in stature, with a softly rounded figure and an evident preference for pastels. Her long ash-blond hair was held back with a cheerful headband. The overall effect was sweet and feminine —the nineteenth-century ideal of womanhood. *I'll call her the Milkmaid,* I thought as she turned.

It was all I could do not to take a step back. The look on her face wasn't unfriendly, exactly, but the hawk-like brown eyes issued a clear warning. *Don't try any funny business.* The adjective that came to mind was *no-nonsense,* because clearly all nonsense had been glared into submission until it backed from the room on its knees, gibbering apologies. She slapped both palms onto the scarred wooden counter.

"Iced mocha," she announced, and her voice matched her expression: forceful and businesslike, with a hint of rasp. Not a simpering Victorian milkmaid at all. She should be called Madam Something—Madam CEO, perhaps.

I was on the point of explaining that I had no idea how to make a mocha, iced or otherwise, when the third girl stepped forward. My eyes widened. She was so *winsome* and *gamine*, with high rounded cheeks tapering to a daintily pointed chin and huge brown eyes fringed in luxuriant lashes. Her black hair was abundant and wavy, falling around her shoulders like a dark cloud.

"I know," the Contessa said, catching my eye. "She looks like a princess."

My thoughts had been more along the lines of Natasha, the ingénue from *War and Peace,* but we probably meant the same thing. The Beauty looked at the floor, her perfect cheeks burning, and I had the revolutionary idea that it must be uncomfortable to be stared at all the time, even if everyone was doing so out of admiration.

"What do you want?" Madam CEO asked her shy friend, indicating the menu on the wall. This time I looked at it too, both because it was equally new to me and to give the Beauty a respite from being gaped at.

"Do you have any cookies?" She scanned the shelves of coffee accoutrements with a hopeful expression.

"No sweets, I'm afraid. Noreen — who owns this place — can only serve beverages. Her ex got the baking rights when they split." In my family, this episode was known as the Great Used Bookstore Schism.

"Her ex runs a bakery?" Madam asked.

I shook my head. "Another bookstore, right across the street. Tome Raider."

"Dramatic." The Contessa looked impressed. "So is this like your afterschool job?"

It took me a second to realize she was talking to me. "I don't work here."

She gave me a funny look.

"I'm covering for someone," I explained, earning a chorus of *ohs*. It would have been nice to end on that moment of perfect understanding, but the Contessa had already pulled out her wallet.

"How much do we owe you for the drinks?"

"Actually —" *The machine is broken. We're out of coffee. The city shut off our water supply.* Excuses flitted through my consciousness, but in the end, I wasn't bold enough for an outright lie. "I've never made coffee before. I could help you find books?"

I expected laugher, or at least mocking looks. Had Anjuli been there, her worst suspicions about my backwardness would have been confirmed.

"Well," said the Contessa, "we were mostly looking for a quiet place to talk."

"You're welcome to stay." I pressed my lips together, worried that had sounded too eager. Was I already turning into a lonely recluse, desperate for any vestige of human contact? "Or there's a Starbucks on the next block," I added, in the interest of fairness.

"We already tried there. It was packed. Not like this place." The Contessa made Toil & Trouble's lack of business sound like something that had been deliberately cultivated. "Hey, you know what?"

I shook my head.

"My cousin Stephanie's geometry tutor was a barista."

"Ah." I tried to pitch it somewhere between *I see* and *huh?*

"She always brewed a bunch of shots ahead of time for iced drinks. It might be worth checking." She nodded at the mini-fridge behind me, smoothing her fiery hair.

Inside, I found a carafe helpfully labeled "coffee," as well as several quarts of milk, a bottle of chocolate syrup, and a can of aerosol whipped cream. A few minutes later, following a steady stream of advice from the other side of the counter, I had filled three tall glasses with a murky brown concoction.

The Contessa took a careful sip. "Delicious," she pronounced, beaming at me. I flushed with pleasure as she nudged Madam CEO with her elbow. "I told you this place looked interesting. Very mellow vibe."

"In my defense," Madam countered, "the name sounded like a really extreme CrossFit place."

"'Double, double toil and trouble. Fire burn and cauldron bubble.'" I realized a little more context might be required. "From *Macbeth*. That's where they got the name. Because of the cauldron and, you know, coffee. Not that they brew it in a cauldron. As far as I know." The name also reflected Noreen's general outlook on life, but that seemed like inessential information.

"Ooh," said the Contessa. "Fancy." She raised her drink toward the tiny seating area. "Okay if we sit there?"

I shrugged. Competition wasn't exactly fierce.

She slid a ten and a five across the counter. "Keep the change," she said, sparing me the shame of explaining I didn't know how to operate the cash register either.

After tucking the money into a drawer, I put away the drink-making paraphernalia and wiped down the counter. Even though I wasn't an actual employee, the presence of customers made me self-conscious about twiddling my thumbs. Tantalizing snatches of conversation drifted from the other side of the room like a distant strain of music.

—You had no idea?

That sounds like something he would—

—I would have died. You are so lucky.

No, I know. He's completely—

It was frustratingly opaque, especially since the Contessa was so animated in her speech, face in constant motion as she leaned toward the other two. I was sure they must be discussing something scintillating. What I did manage to glean was that the redhead and the blonde had been friends much longer. They spoke over each other like siblings, whereas both took pains to be polite with the Beauty, drawing her into the conversation with a series of questions.

Questions about what, though? I edged closer. My hands made a pretense of returning pens to the chipped mug next to the phone, straightening a stack of mail, brushing dust off a shelf. It wasn't spying so much as trying to piece together a story. Nor was it only the mystery that drew me in. I was a moth to their flame, fascinated by the brightness they gave off. How would it feel to be part of a group of friends who were genuinely excited to spend time with you? To have things to talk about, and people to discuss them with who didn't roll their eyes every time you asked a question?

"Alex Freaking Ritter," the Crimson Contessa sighed. Absorbed as I had been in a fantasy of hanging out with my own illusory friends, a second passed before I processed the words. My body went rigid as the Contessa spoke again.

"Your first day at MHS and the hottest guy in school asks you out." She raised both hands, fingers fanned, as she fake-bowed to the Beauty. "You are *en fuego*! Did I say that right?"

I'd never thought of myself as a gasper, but I must have gasped then, because all three girls turned to stare. A sticky silence ensued, flooding the room with tension despite the soporific flute music still playing in the background.

"Is everything okay?" the Contessa asked at last.

A few hours ago I would have hesitated to draw attention to myself, but I was a different person now. World-weary. Battle-hardened. The sting of my own rude awakening was too fresh to permit another innocent to have her hopes dashed.

My eyes met the Beauty's. "You're the one he was flirting

with." *Really* flirting with, as opposed to randomly glancing at while absconding with a chair. I should have recognized the back of her head. "Alex Ritter."

"And?" the Contessa prompted. "Is there a problem?"

I let out a long breath. "You could say that."

Madam CEO frowned. "Meaning what, exactly?"

"Trouble," I replied.

"What kind of trouble?" asked the Crimson Contessa.

There was no point prevaricating. "The kind that ends with somebody getting run over by a train."

Dear Diary,

I'm sure someone (maybe Van?) told me **Anna Karenina** was a love story. To which I say: thanks A LOT. If that's what passes for romance, I'll happily stay single forever. I'd describe it as a train wreck but that would be a really bad pun.

Talk about a relationship that was doomed from the outset. As anyone with half a brain would have known. Poor Anna may be nice, but she's not the sharpest tool in the shed. And don't even get me started on Vronsky.

M.P.M.

CHAPTER 4

The blonde clunked her glass onto the table. "Excuse me?"

The Contessa waved the other girl to silence, her eyes never leaving my face. "Do you know him — Alex?"

Summoning my courage, I took a step closer. "Kind of. I know *of* him."

"Alex Ritter." Madam CEO repeated. She looked me up and down, face taut with suspicion. "Who are you anyway?"

"Mary Porter-Malcolm." Whenever possible I gave my whole name, because *Mary* by itself was sorely lacking in gravitas. "But that's not important right now." I turned to the Beauty. "Alex Ritter may seem charming, but he's dangerous."

"Oh," the Beauty breathed. "One of those."

Madam's frown deepened. "One of what?"

"Like a gentleman strangler," the Beauty replied. "Handsome but deadly."

That wasn't quite what I'd been trying to convey. Clearly it was time for the gloves to come off. "I'm sorry to say that he's a Vronsky."

The Crimson Contessa gasped, fingers flying to her mouth in a flurry of jade green polish.

Madam looked from her friend to me. "A what now?"

"Not what," I corrected. "*Who.*" From their silence, I gathered they were having difficulty digesting the news.

"Maybe you should sit down," suggested the Contessa.

Feeling only slightly more out of place than I had behind the counter, I pulled out a chair.

"I'm Arden," the Crimson Contessa informed me. "And that's Terry." She pointed to the Beauty.

"Teresa Larios," the dark-haired girl supplied, pronouncing it *Te-RAY-sa* rather than *Te-REE-sa* and rolling the *r* in both names. *Teresa,* I silently repeated. That was much more fitting. She needed a name that danced on the tongue, like Beatrice or Titania. I spared a moment to wish *Mary* had a longer, more mellifluous form.

"Lydia." Madam CEO extended an arm. Her small hand squeezed mine like a vise, but that wasn't the part that surprised me.

"Your name is Lydia?"

Her eyes narrowed. "Why? Did you hear something about me too?"

"No, you just don't seem like a Lydia."

"Meaning what?"

Flighty. Gauche. Prone to ill-advised elopements. Something told me this wasn't the right time to bring up *Pride and Prejudice*. "You were asking about Alex Ritter."

Lydia adjusted her headband, making it clear she was only accepting the diversion because it suited her purpose. "We're listening."

I took a deep breath. "A guy like that is completely wrapped up in his own drama, all the Sturm und Drang, 'have mercy, my heart is bleeding.' He never stops to consider the other person's needs. If you ask me, it's the pining he cares about, not the pine-ee."

The pause that followed this speech gave me plenty of time to reconsider my word choices, not least because I'd made it sound like he had a thing for conifers.

"And in English this time?" said Lydia.

"Getting involved with a Vronsky is a recipe for disaster," I replied, cutting to the chase. "You're setting yourself up for misery."

"What's the deal with the train?" Arden asked in a hushed voice.

"You know—like Anna K."

They looked at me blankly.

"How she abandons her family to carry on a torrid affair with him, and they have a baby, but slowly the weight of society's disapproval chips away at her sanity until one day she's at the train station and that's it." I walked my fingers to the edge of the table before plunging them over the side.

Lydia held up a hand. "Are you saying his baby mama offed herself?"

I endeavored to conceal my surprise. How could they forget that part of the story? It was one of the most famous endings in literature. "Yes."

Arden shook her head. "I can't believe I never heard about this."

"Maybe your school read *War and Peace* instead?" I suggested, trying to make her feel better.

"Instead of what?" Lydia asked.

"*Anna Karenina*." I paused to look around the table. "The Tolstoy novel. With the famous hay-mowing scene?"

Lydia squinted her eyes into slits. "What does that have to do with Alex Ritter?"

"Or hay," Terry put in. "Does someone get mangled by one of those big machines with the spinning blades?"

"Ah, no. The mowing part is more about 'isn't it great to live in the country and commune with nature.' No one dies." I turned to Lydia. "As for Alex, what I mean is that Vronsky is the archetype. Alex is a modern version of the same kind of bad behavior."

"Except one of them is made up," Lydia countered.

Arden put a hand on the other girl's arm. "That's not what she's saying, Lyds. The point is we don't want Terry to end up brokenhearted at the train station."

"We don't have a train station. She'd have to go Greyhound."

"You know what I mean." Arden smiled encouragingly at me. "Tell her, Mary."

"It's about certain universal truths of human nature. You

can't trust a person who never gives a second thought to the consequences of his actions because no one's ever going to blame *him* for anything."

Lydia pushed her empty glass to one side. "Based on what evidence?"

"She's going to be a judge," Arden told me, holding her hand in front of her mouth as if it were a soundproof barrier. "Not the cheesy TV kind."

I thought of the scene I'd witnessed at lunch, Alex giving that come-hither look to all and sundry. Flirting for tater tots, or his own twisted amusement, while the wreckage of my friendship with Anjuli smoldered in the background. He was what he'd always been, a destructive force wrapped in a deceptively appealing package.

"Here's the thing about Alex Ritter," I began.

"The one in real life?" Lydia cut in.

"Yes. Two years ago—"

"When he was a sophomore," Arden supplied.

I nodded, accepting her math, though he'd seemed much older to me at the time. "It was during rehearsals for *Antony and Cleopatra*. The play," I added, to forestall the possibility of further confusion.

"He was Antony?" Arden guessed.

"He would have been, but everyone was worried he'd upstage Cleopatra in the looks department, so they made him the understudy. Unfortunately, that left a lot of free time for him to hang around backstage."

"Uh-oh." Ice cubes rattled as Arden swirled the dregs of her drink.

Lydia gave her a look. "Like you know where this is going."

"Hush." Arden put a finger to her lips. "Go ahead, Mary."

"First the stage manager and the girl playing Octavia got into a huge screaming match. The next day it was the attendants, Charmian and Iras. Every time he talked to someone, they came away thinking Alex was in love with them. It was madness. Even the Clown got involved, despite the fact that she had a very serious boyfriend. Who happened to be running lights for the show." I raised my eyebrows, letting them imagine the fallout from that little wrinkle.

"Wow." Arden rested her chin in her hand. "What else, Mary? I can tell there's more."

She was right, but part of the story involved me being foolish and ignorant, which was not the image I wanted to present. Even the fact that I remembered the whole thing so clearly was probably a sign I needed to get out more, and yet the mental snapshot stubbornly refused to fade.

Let me guess, you're Juliet. That had been his opening line.

Most afternoons that fall had seen me hanging around the theater, fetching and carrying for my sisters. It was inevitable our paths should cross; what I didn't expect was for him to engage me in conversation.

Naturally I lit up like a candle. It was the first time a boy had paid attention to me in that playful, noticing way. He thought I was not only an actress but *Juliet*? The thrill dimmed slightly when it occurred to me why he might have singled me out. It wouldn't be the first time an actor had attempted to improve his casting by currying favor with the twins — or a member of their immediate family.

"I'm afraid you're not the right kind of Romeo," I gently informed him. It was no secret the next Baardvaark production was going to be *Romeo and Juliet*. Fewer people were privy to the fact that it was slated to have an all-female cast.

He pressed both hands to his chest, mock groaning. "Stabbed in the heart."

"Actually, Juliet's the one who stabs herself. Romeo takes the poison." I mimed drinking from a vial.

It was only after I'd been called away on an errand that I realized he'd meant something else. By then it was too late to explain that a) I hadn't meant he was the wrong kind of Romeo for *me* personally and b) I was a glorified stagehand, not the leading lady. And while the twins sometimes solicited my opinion on casting decisions, I would never throw my weight behind someone just because he'd tried to butter me up.

The next time I saw him, he was bantering with my sister Addie. I passed within five feet of them and he looked right through me, without so much as a flicker of recognition. Like maybe I'd imagined our whole interaction, or else he chatted up so many girls it was impossible to keep track of them all. The whole thing was so mortifying I'd never spoken of it to another soul — until now.

But how to convey all of that in a few nonembarrassing words?

He's the kind of guy who has the effrontery to act like he's going to sit with you when all he really wants is to steal one of your chairs.

He's the kind of guy who flirts for personal gain then drops you like a rock.

He's the kind of guy so indiscriminate in his attentions he'll trade one sister for another in the blink of an eye.

"He hit on my sister," I said in a rush. "I think maybe he thought she was my other sister. The one who directs."

Arden made a tsking noise with her tongue. "That's just rude."

"Why would he think your sister was your other sister?" Lydia asked.

"Face blindness?" Terry suggested.

I shook my head. "They're twins."

"Aha," Lydia said. "Then it doesn't mean he's for sure a player."

I made a vague noise in the back of my throat, privately resolving to ask my brother Jasper about the precise connotations of the term, since he was the most au courant member of the family when it came to slang. Although fairly certain I got the gist, I'd been wrong about such things before. (In my defense, "twerking" did sound like a rude gesture involving teeth.)

"Wait a sec." Arden studied me intently. "You're talking about the twins who put on the plays?"

I nodded.

"They were in my brother Morrison's year! He had a huge crush on one of them, Allie or something—"

"Addie."

"Yes!" She slapped the table with her palm. "I used to hear about them all the time. Super smart and artsy, which is completely Morrison's jam. Apparently one of them came to school in thigh-high boots—"

"Part of a costume," I said quickly. "For Baardvaark. That's the name of their troupe. All Shakespeare, all the time."

"Isn't this great?" Arden squeezed Terry's wrist. "You're getting so much background info. She just transferred from Sacred Heart, so I'm helping her get up to speed." The last part was clearly for my benefit. "It's hard when you don't know many people."

I tried to smile as though I had a vague and largely theoretical understanding of such a predicament, but the result must have looked more like a grimace.

"Freshman year is awesome," Arden assured me. "Totally low-stakes. I miss those days. It's not like tenth grade, when everyone expects you to have it all figured out. Seriously, can we talk about the SAT after I get my license? One thing at a time, people."

"I'm actually a sophomore."

"Hey!" Arden shoved me in the shoulder. "Us too. How come I haven't seen you before? Did you just move here?"

She seemed so intrigued I was loath to disappoint her. "I've lived in Millville all my life. I just haven't gone to public school until this year."

"Homeschooled?" asked Lydia.

"No. Though my school was in a house—on campus." My head tipped in the direction of the college. "It was run by a bunch of grad students from the School of Education. Sort of an experimental research program, until they shut it down."

This description seemed to give them pause.

"Not because there was anything weird going on," I said quickly. "It was mostly unstructured time and talking about your feelings."

"Sounds very evolved," Arden said.

I shook my head. "Our feelings about whatever pedagogical method they were using that week. But on the plus side, we got to do a lot of independent study. Reading and such."

"So that's how you know so much," Arden mused.

"Mostly about nineteenth-century novels. That was my area of concentration."

"Yeah, but there's so much wisdom in books." Arden tapped her forehead. "And you have it all up there, ready and waiting. *Super* useful."

"Oh boy," Lydia sighed. "Here we go."

"What?" Arden was the picture of wounded innocence.

"You sure you want to jump on this bandwagon? I'm still traumatized from when you made me KonMari my underwear."

"I'm just saying it's interesting, is all."

Interesting. I savored the word.

"Did any of your friends come over from your old school?" Terry asked.

I hesitated. "No. I—there's no one." When I looked up, expecting to see derision on their faces, Arden's eyes had a sheen of wetness.

"That is so sad. You went through your whole first day

alone?" She pressed her hand to mine. "I would have *died*. You are so brave, Mary."

Whatever response I might have made was interrupted by the buzzing sound emerging from Lydia's bag. "My mom's running late," she reported, glancing at her phone. "I have to walk Muffin."

"I'll tell Morrison we're ready for a ride." Picking up her own phone, Arden tapped out a message. "One more week and he'll be back in his dorm. It's going to be so nice when a bag of tortilla chips lasts more than ten minutes at our house." She looked up from the screen. "What's your number, Mary?"

"I . . . don't have a phone." My parents weren't technophobes, exactly, but they had informed us in no uncertain terms that they couldn't afford data plans for a family of seven. That wasn't the sort of information I felt like volunteering.

"Thanks for the advice," Terry said with a shy smile.

Lydia jerked her chin at me. "Yeah. Allegedly, and all that, but you made some good points."

The bell over the door jangled as a red-faced Marco staggered inside, a tower of books balanced between his arms.

"I made it," he panted, stashing the reading material behind the counter. He straightened slowly. "Whoa. Customers." He looked questioningly at me. "Friends of yours?"

I hesitated. Saying no would sound like I was repudiating them, while claiming them as friends would be presumptuous —however much my heart swelled at the thought.

"Yep," Arden answered for me, with another of her easy smiles. "Coming, Mary?"

Dear Diary,

When my parents decided to name all their kids for someone from the life and works of Virginia Woolf, I'm guessing they didn't expect to have four daughters. **Mary** is clearly an afterthought — the kind of name you give someone when you've already used up the good ones.

Sometimes I worry it marked me for life. Why couldn't I have been the firstborn, or a twin, or as tough as Cam, or the only boy? A name like Jasper Orlando is wasted on my little brother.

M.P.M.

CHAPTER 5

Dinner that evening was a sweaty affair. The windows had been thrown open to admit the purple dusk and chanting cicadas, and also because my parents didn't believe in air conditioning.

All seven of us were home, filling the long oval table. Mom and Dad sat at either end, with my four siblings arrayed around them: twins Addie and Van, the Shakespeareans, now in their second year at Millville College; athletic Cam, whose hair was the same burnished gold as the twins' but worn short so it couldn't be used against her on the field hockey pitch; and my brother Jasper, the baby of the family. The din of so many forks and knives made it easy to retreat into the privacy of my own thoughts, which were currently stuck on the incident at Toil & Trouble.

I was still bemused by my own daring in following Arden and the others to her brother's car. It was as though she'd said, *Lifeboat, Mary?* and I'd leaped at the chance, even though I could easily have walked the few blocks home.

Hopefully I'd acquitted myself in a reasonably normal fashion when we parted ways. At the time, I'd been too caught up in seeing my house through their eyes. The peeling paint on the porch, the patchy lawn: they'd seemed so much starker in the harsh light of afternoon. While Arden in particular had exclaimed over the quaintness of the neighborhood's cobblestone streets and whimsical pastels, I wondered if that was a euphemism for *poor*.

Not that the disparity of our financial situations really mattered, compared to the gulf in social standing. What had been an epic encounter to me was likely a minor blip to girls like that, who met new people all the time.

Using the edge of my fork, I nudged the chicken and broccoli closer to the mound of brown rice, hoping to imbue the gooey mass with a little flavor. This was a typical late summer meal: a little *too* good for you, as our parents tried to compensate for all the times during the academic year when they had essays to grade and lectures to prep—the hummus months. I thought I was doing a good job rendering myself invisible without being too conspicuous about it when Jasper suddenly piped up.

"What's up with you, Mary?" Although he'd spoken through a mouthful of rice, the words seemed to hover in the thick air, drawing everyone's attention.

"Nothing," I said stiffly, shoving a bite of chicken into my mouth.

"Nothing as in *nothing*, or nothing you want to share?"

All at once I was grateful for the stifling temperature, which meant my face was already flushed. Had Jasper heard about the Anjuli incident? I couldn't think of a way to find out without showing my own hand, and I had no intention of discussing the subject with my family, despite the fleeting satisfaction it would have given me to tell my parents how very wrong they'd been. Piling their pity on top of my humiliation would be too bitter a pill.

"Can you pass the salt, please?" Addie asked our mother, who was seated closest to the shaker.

"Try behind the dresser," she replied without lifting her head.

"Thanks, Mom," Jasper said. "Very helpful."

She gave a vague *mm-hmm* in answer. Jasper waggled his brows in my direction, an invitation and a dare. I wasn't feeling especially playful, but pride demanded I make an effort.

"We're only going to read books by men in English this year." When there was no reaction, I added, "*White* men."

The room fell silent, all of us watching our mother.

"Addie and I are thinking of branching into musicals," Van announced, picking up the baton. "From the greater Disney canon. Lots of princesses and uncomfortable shoes. Retrograde fantasies about marrying up. Magical domestic objects."

"Is that so," Mom murmured, aiming a forkful of broccoli in the general direction of her mouth. A second later, we heard the telltale rustle of a turning page.

Since Van had spoken for both the twins, as was her wont, Cam launched the next volley. "I broke my leg at practice." She slid a glance at our mother, whose expression remained placid. "The bone is jutting out of my thigh."

Dad tried to frown at us, though from the way his mouth squeezed in and out like an accordion it seemed he was having trouble mustering the necessary solemnity. He leaned as far sideways as the narrow-backed chair allowed a man of his girth. "What are you reading, dear?"

"Hmm?" Mom blinked at him, lifting the magazine from her lap and flipping it around so the rumpled cover faced us. "The new *New Yorker* came. I didn't want to get behind."

"That's from 2007," I pointed out.

Her lips pursed. "Must have been a good one."

As if we ever got rid of any printed matter. No doubt she'd stumbled across the magazine on her way to dinner, fingers reaching for it without thought, like scratching an itch.

"So Mary, you were telling us about your first day of real high school," Jasper drawled. My brother was like a dog with a bone when he had an agenda. Since I had no idea why he was pressing this particular issue, aside from an uncanny instinct for human weakness, I settled for giving him an all-purpose scowl.

"Is it the full teen movie experience?" he continued, unmoved. "Football and cheerleaders? Getting pumped for the big dance? People randomly breaking into song?"

"Honestly, Jasper," our mother chided. "You're rotting your brain with that tripe."

"Give me some credit," he said, waving his fork. Grains

of rice scattered, and I mentally double-checked it wasn't my night to clear the table. "I also play video games."

"I always thought of high school as more *Macbeth*," mused Van, who liked to talk about that part of her life (two whole years ago) as though it were a sepia-toned photo in a dusty album. "Speaking of which, you're still going to help with auditions next weekend, right, Mare-Bear? Not too busy with your new life?"

"Ha," I said weakly. "Of course I'll be there. But . . . what do you mean about high school being like *Macbeth*?"

"Spineless men, conniving women, political infighting, a creeping sense of dread — all that jazz," Van replied with an airy flap of the hand.

Addie gave a delicate shudder then cast a worried look my way. "There were a lot of great things about it, too."

"Millville High is an excellent school," Dad observed, as though we'd been discussing its academic reputation. I slanted him a doubtful look, which he failed to notice. It would be a long time before I trusted my father's opinions about high school again.

"And Mary's so easygoing." Addie sounded too chipper, overcompensating for her twin's bluntness. "All that angst will be like water off a duck for you."

I goggled at her. A swan would have been one thing. And what did that make everyone else? Humans, presumably, enjoying their complicated lives on dry land while I paddled in circles, quacking to myself. Maybe one of them would throw me a few crumbs. With a sinking feeling, I realized I must be the only member of the family who thought of me as a main character in her own story, as opposed to a background figure in the lives of more exciting Porter-Malcolms.

"It comes from being the middle child," our mother opined, stroking the underside of her chin. "That's why I wasn't worried about Mary starting a new school."

"But I'm not the middle child," I said when no one else pointed out the fallacy of this argument. "Four is not the middle of five."

Then again, perhaps tellingly, there wasn't a name for my place in the pecking order. Penultimate? That was only marginally better than *second-to-last*.

"It's a state of mind," said my father. "You've always been even-keeled. Content to go along with the crowd."

Jasper dabbed a few grains of salt from his plate before licking them off his finger. "She doesn't seem that chill to me."

"Of course she is," Addie protested. Next to our dad, she was the family member most likely to smooth ruffled feathers, whereas Van more closely resembled our acerbic mother, and Cam and Jasper shared a certain unflappable cool. I was . . . not quite in any of those camps.

"Not that you should feel tied down," Mom said with the too-casual air of someone pretending not to tell you what to do. "People grow and change during adolescence, as they should. To be honest, I'm not sorry you've been pushed out of the nest. It was time for a challenge."

"I thought she should have transferred last year." Van stifled a yawn. "Broaden her horizons."

"Mary doesn't have to do things the same way we did," Addie countered. "She made her own choice."

"Or did she?" our mother asked, wagging a finger.

Addie shrugged. "All her friends were staying behind. It's completely natural for Mary to want to be with them."

"Sometimes past associations hold us back. Nostalgia can be a trap. Don't confuse loyalty and sentimentality," Mom spoke in her most oracular tone, as though dispensing obscure bits of wisdom from a mountaintop grotto, but we all knew she was talking about Anjuli.

I fought the urge to bang my forehead against the table. "That won't be an issue anymore."

"Out with the old, in with the new." Dad raised his glass to me.

The problem was that the *old* in this equation was me, since I'd been jettisoned like so much trash. My family's helpful advice only served to remind me of that fact. It was like the time I'd had my wisdom teeth removed. I wanted to pack the wound with gauze and forget it was there, not poke around to find out exactly how much it could hurt.

Jasper cracked his knuckles. "I'm going to go nuclear when I get to Millville High. This year is just a warm-up for the real action."

Sadly, I suspected he was right. Between the curls and the big dark eyes, he'd always gotten away with murder around people who didn't know him well enough to be on their guard. Plus, he had a cool name, which probably counted for a lot. No one would spurn *Jasper* on his first day.

"And we all live in fear of that day," our mother chided. "Did you find the copy of *Death in Venice* I left you?"

"The one on my pillow? Yes, yes, I did. Even though I'm just a boy, it turns out I'm not blind *and* dumb."

Dad raised both hands in a conciliatory gesture. "Jasper, you know we have faith in your intellectual potential. A number of men have made important contributions in serious fields of study. If you work hard, there's no reason you can't keep up with the girls." Dad pretended not to see our mother's dubious expression.

Yarb the cat, whose name came from our father's favorite Gogol novel, yowled from the next room, a long and variegated complaint.

"I'll let him out." I jumped up before anyone could revisit the subject of my ex-friend, new school, or social prospects therein.

Dear Diary,

Confession: I never reread the depressing parts of books. The first time I'll make myself slog through the wretched childhoods and tragic mishaps, but once I know about the floods and bankruptcy and scarlet fever, I skip straight to the first signs of hope, like when the orphan gets a bit of bread, or the hero and heroine exchange meaningful glances.

I wish there was a way to do that in real life. Flip a few pages and boom! Everything's better.

M.P.M.

CHAPTER 6

I t's a big place.

No one knows who you are.

As long as you keep moving, who's to say you don't have scores of friends waiting around the corner?

This was my internal monologue as I walked to my locker the next morning. Meanwhile, another voice sang counterpoint:

Everyone else has friends.

The reek of loneliness is rising off you like a noxious cloud.

People are staring.

The internal clamor made it difficult to concentrate on anything else, including the sound of my name. In the time required to pause, play back the tape in my head, and confirm that yes, someone had been calling "Mary," my brain conjured a vivid fantasy. Anjuli, waiting with a penitent expression. When I turned around, however, it wasn't my former friend.

"Arden," the other girl reminded me.

As if I could have forgotten, even without the scarlet locks. It was almost funny that she thought me less likely to remember *her* than she was to remember *me*. Not that I was in the mood to laugh.

"Guess what?" she asked, with an air of barely suppressed excitement.

I could only shrug.

"We watched the movie." Arden held out her phone; with a flick of the finger, the image on screen sprang to life. Figures in ball gowns and filigreed uniforms advanced and retreated, spinning in circles. I spotted Anna and Vronsky right away. She was all in black and he was staring wolfishly at her.

Another tap of the finger and the scene froze. "You were so right. Starts off super-hot, turns into a major downer." She glanced both ways to be sure no one was listening. "Just like certain guys *at this school*."

I smiled faintly, part of me still on tenterhooks. Was that all she'd wanted to say? As she slipped her phone back into a slim vermillion purse, I regretted the dowdiness of my back-pack, which until that moment had seemed de rigueur for a high schooler.

"Anyway, we wanted to know what you're doing for lunch."

"Lunch?" I parroted, as though I'd never heard the word.

"We were thinking somewhere downtown." Arden leaned toward me, lowering her voice. "Since we can't speak freely here."

"Sure," I said, feigning nonchalance. One advantage of growing up with three older siblings was that I'd had lots of practice pretending to know what people were talking about.

～

We ended up at a pocket park between the yarn shop and a Himalayan restaurant. Since Terry and I had packed our lunches, Arden and Lydia grabbed pita wraps to go. Sitting on facing benches in the dappled shade, the humid air lightly perfumed with the scents of cooking oil and spices, I resisted the urge to pinch myself in case the whole thing was a mirage. I'd fully expected to spend this part of the day huddled between shelves in the school library, utterly alone.

"So," Arden began, dabbing at the corner of her mouth with a paper napkin. "We've been thinking. It's a new year. The perfect time to make some changes."

I waited for the axe to fall. *Actually, Mary, we've decided you're an idiot, who knows nothing.* What were the odds of two lunchtime rejections in a row? I wasn't sure why they'd felt it necessary to invite me here to sever a connection that was tenuous at best, but at least they'd had the courtesy not to dump me in front of the entire school.

"This is a pivotal moment," Arden continued, oblivious to my inner turmoil. "Do we want to lead totally superficial lives? No way. We have to stop accepting everything at face value, like we did with Alex Ritter. 'Oh, he's the most crushed-on guy at this school since Joe Lefort graduated, let's just fall down and worship him.' Or like, 'Let's keep eating lunch at this generic popular table because everyone wants to sit there, even though it's super crowded.'"

"And loud," put in Terry.

"Extremely," Arden agreed. "It's time to start living more intentionally, making conscious choices so we can manifest our own future—" She broke off at Lydia's forceful throat-clearing.

"The thing you need to know about Arden is that she reads a lot of those 'hey loser, fix your life' books," Lydia informed me, flicking one of her long blond braids over her shoulder. "How to revolutionize your existence in five minutes. Step one, buy this book. Step two, check out my line of yoga mats and water bottles. That kind of thing."

"Excuse me," said a clearly affronted Arden. "Some of us didn't plan our entire career at the age of seven. We're still searching."

Lydia gestured at me with her can of sparkling water. "I'm just explaining to Mary what she's getting into."

I wasn't sure what my face was doing, but my shoulders might as well have been carved from a block of stone.

"It's nothing bad," Arden hastened to assure me. She took a deep breath before releasing a rush of words: "I hope you won't be offended, but I have a feeling you might be our good luck charm?"

"No," I replied, after mastering my surprise. "That's not offensive." I could think of *much* worse things to be called.

"Oh, good." Arden shifted forward on the bench, clearly relieved to have that behind us. "Because I was thinking about yesterday, and how close we came to disaster. I mean, I was ready to push Terry right into you-know-who's arms. The only thing that saved us was you."

Heat rushed into my cheeks. I had no idea how to respond. Fortunately, Arden wasn't finished.

"What kind of person does something like that?" she asked. "Stepping up to help people."

I shrugged, hoping the answer wasn't *a busybody*.

"The kind of person you want to have in your corner. A *quality* person." Arden lifted her brows in a significant manner. "If you get what I'm saying."

I opened my mouth and then closed it again. I did not, in fact, get it.

"Am I coming on too strong?" Arden glanced from my face to Lydia's. "I don't want to smother you, Mary, so tell me if this is too much too soon. I like things to be super clear, so I'm just putting it all out there."

"She wants you to be our *fwend*," Lydia baby-talked.

"Sorry, did I not say that?" Arden shook her head, the sun bringing out glints of magenta in her hair. "It's just, you have the kind of energy we want in our lives. I like to be around people I can learn from, who are on an upward journey. Trying to figure out what it all means."

"Getting a little woo-woo," Lydia murmured.

"Okay." Arden pressed her palms together. "Bottom line. I think we'd be good together. The four of us." She looked hopefully in my direction.

I swallowed hard. "That sounds really good to me." This may have been the understatement of the century.

"Fantastic!" Arden blew out a long breath. "Whew. I am *sweating* right now. That was like asking somebody out, times ten." She fanned her face with the paper bag from her lunch. Terry passed her an extra napkin.

"So." Lydia played with her necklace as she considered me. "Old books. That's your fandom?"

"Yes." It would have been silly to pretend otherwise.

"And is there a lot of death?" Terry asked, dark eyes eager.

"See, I pictured them being more about relationships," Arden put in. "Like love stories, only messed up."

I screwed the cap back on my water bottle while I thought it over. "It's all that, but other stuff too. Like power, and who has it and who doesn't, and how oppressive society can be with its rules and restrictions, especially for women. Class conflict. Being judged by appearances. How one mistake can ruin your life."

"Pretty much the story of our lives, am I right?" Arden poked Lydia in the shoulder.

Lydia's nose wrinkled. "I don't know how excited I can get about a time that was basically, Men Control Everything, They Do What They Want. Oh wait, make that White Men. Even more than now. It's like, 'Yay, let's be more oppressed!' No offense," she added, glancing at me.

"Actually, a lot of them are women's stories, written by women." I tried not to sound like I was disagreeing with Lydia, who was by far the most intimidating of the three. "They're the heroines. And even when they get shafted by society, the books make you see how tragic that is, because they have these rich inner lives. It gives them a voice."

"Exactly!" Arden pointed a potato chip at me. "Maybe they couldn't fix all their problems, because patriarchy, but *we* can.

It's about taking control of your destiny. We can learn from the past. 'Heads-up, don't get owned.'"

"That's how I think about it." My heart raced. Was I courting public ridicule all over again by talking about these things? "I don't want to be a victim, or a villain, so I try not to make any of the mistakes I already know about."

"Or let your *friends* make them," Arden added, with a significant look at Terry. "Like dating the wrong people."

"There are plenty of those," I agreed.

Arden's eyes widened. "At MHS?"

"In books. But maybe also at our school. I don't really know anyone else, so it's hard to say."

"But we do. Know people, I mean. Or people who know people." Arden flung out a hand. "Wait. I'm having a brain wave. That should totally be our goal, don't you think, Lyds?"

Lydia squinted at her. "Having brain waves?"

"To show Mary the ropes," Arden corrected. "See the sights, meet new people, try all the things they didn't have at her old school. Give her the complete Millville High experience."

"What about Terry?" Lydia asked.

"Terry's new, but not *new* new. She's coming from a different school, but it's like Mary's from a different century." She offered me a quick smile. "In the best way possible."

"Uh-huh," said Lydia, who did not seem to find this analogy as pleasing as I did.

"I have a really good feeling about this," Arden assured her.

"You have feelings about a lot of things."

"Yes, I do, Robotica. But this one's bigtime. And you know how much I like having clearly defined goals."

"Arden's mother runs an event business," Lydia informed me. "The urge to plan is genetic."

A fluttery feeling migrated from my stomach to my throat. "It sounds almost like a *season*."

"I guess we could make it a fall thing." Arden's furrowed brow suggested this was a significant scaling back of her plans.

"Not that kind of season," I said. "There used to be a tradition where a young woman would make her debut, usually at a ball."

"Like a *debut*-tante," Arden put in.

"Exactly. After that she'd officially be 'out.'"

Terry's mouth opened in an O of surprise. "Out as in—?"

"Letting down her skirts, changing her hairstyle, going to grown-up social events. Once you made your debut, you were eligible for courtship, so your chaperone would plan a 'season' to introduce you to everyone, mostly in hopes of finding you a husband."

"So pretty much like high school," Arden said.

Lydia raised a hand, index finger extended. "Except for the teen bride part."

"Obviously," Arden retorted, rolling her eyes. "That's just how they did it back in the day. They were probably in a hurry to lock it down before they lost their teeth. We can focus on other things. Personal growth. Fixing your skirts, like Mary said. Which I totally love, by the way. It feels"—she cupped her hand as if summoning the right word—"classy."

Lydia stood and began gathering her things. "You know what's not classy? Pit stains. We better start walking so I don't sweat all over myself."

"I can't wait until Thursday," Arden sighed as we began the return journey. She must have seen the consternation on my face. "It's my birthday. Sweet sixteen. And I think we all know what that means."

"Limousines and a DJ?" Lydia teased. "A sheet cake with your face on it? Renting out a hotel ballroom?"

"Yeah, no. Great-Aunt Aggie's birthday is the same day, so we're going to her house for dinner. It's a whole thing. But on *Friday* I get my license." She waggled her brows. "Just in time for the party at Kaitlynn's."

Lydia pinched the pink fabric of her T-shirt away from her chest, fanning it for air flow. "So we're going?"

"I think we should. It's the first big event of the school year, and everyone will be there. What better way to kick off the *season?*"

There was a beat of silence before Lydia spoke. "What's with the TV announcer voice?"

"I'm in my feelings, okay? This is going to be epic."

"It's not going to be that epic," Lydia tossed over her shoulder, to where Terry and I were walking side by side. "My curfew is eleven."

Arden shushed her, thumb and fingers clamping together like a sock puppet. "Don't spoil the moment."

Dear Diary,

Parties at my old school: The same minuscule guest list every time. Allergen-free snacks. If things got wild, magic tricks.

Parties in books: Gossip and games of whist. Piano ballads. If things got wild, rolling back the carpet for a quadrille.

Parties at Millville High: ???

M.P.M.

CHAPTER 7

The thumping bass seemed to emanate from inside my bones. The sternum, to be exact. It was Friday night, and we were standing in front of a two-story house on an otherwise quiet cul-de-sac, preparing our souls for what lay on the other side of the door.

Arden looked nervously from me to Terry. "Um, yeah, so I thought it would be a little more chill." Her smile lacked its usual wattage. "But don't worry. If it's a nightmare, we can leave. I have *lots* of other things on my list for Lady Mary's season. You don't mind if I call you that, do you? Like from Downton Abbey?"

I shook my head, dazzled by the prospect of such a glamorous nickname. Or any nickname bestowed by someone outside my family.

"Great! Okay then." Arden paused in the act of turning to the door. "Listen, once we start meeting people, if any of them are bad news, pass it on. Dark secrets, evil tendencies, a twisted past. Whatever." She gave me a conspiratorial wink before raising her hand to knock.

The door flew open before she made contact. The noise from the stereo punched the night, followed by a chorus of hyena-like shrieks. A guy in a dripping T-shirt staggered past, clutching a large athletic shoe (in addition to the two on his feet).

The music cut off abruptly. A few seconds later, a slower, smoother beat took its place.

"Right." Arden straightened her shoulders. "Maybe it's starting to calm down."

"You're a real glass-half-full kind of person," Lydia murmured, following her across the threshold.

With Arden in the lead, we wedged and twisted ourselves along the front hall. The crush of bodies was borderline claustrophobic, and I felt at least one other person's sweat slick the bare skin of my arm. At the same time, part of me thrilled at the unaccustomed sensation of being in the thick of things, especially when no one looked askance at me or demanded to know what I was doing there. Even Terry slipped past without undue notice, likely because she was looking at the floor, and all anyone could see was the part in her hair.

The hallway opened onto a living room. There was enough space now that I could lower my arms. Arden made a beeline for a girl with a nose ring and lavender highlights. The two of them embraced, Arden holding on to the girl's shoulders as they took turns speaking into each other's ears.

"That's Kaitlynn," Lydia explained. "She and Arden were

in some kind of club together. Or maybe it was a camp. The possibilities are endless." The three of us had settled into a pocket of empty space beside a leather love seat. A few feet away, Arden squeezed the other girl's arm before working her way back to us.

"Okay," she said, swirling a finger in the air. "Let's circulate."

I was afraid she meant separately, but when no one else peeled off, I followed them up a step into a formal dining room, where the only refreshments appeared to be a forlorn plate of celery sticks. From there we passed through the kitchen, a smaller room with a large-screen TV where we were nearly deafened by video game explosions, and into another hallway. Arden paused beside a half-open door. The music pulsed from the other side like a living organism.

Terry shook her head. "No basements."

Arden blinked. "Oh. Well, that's where the dancing is, if you want to check it out later."

As we started moving again, Terry edged closer to me. "Horror Movie 101," she whispered.

More shoving and squeezing brought us back to the living room. This time Arden led the way to a secluded spot against the wall, between a floor lamp and a potted palm.

"At a party like this, it's good to do a lap first," she explained. "See who's here. And who *isn't*."

I got the feeling this was supposed to be a *dun dun duuun* moment, but the implication was lost on me.

Lydia shrugged. "You knew Miles wasn't coming. He never does."

"Thank you for the reminder, Lyds. That's very helpful."

"Who's Miles?" Terry's question relieved me of the worry that I was the only one who didn't know.

"My bae."

"Your what?" I asked.

"Bae," Arden repeated. "My man. Significant other. Honey bear. All that."

"You mean your *beau?*"

"It's pronounced boo, actually," Lydia corrected.

Was this another of those words I'd only ever read on the page, leading me to invent my own pronunciation? I made a mental note to check later; for now, the more important revelation was that Arden had a boyfriend. I was immediately curious, both about the courtship experience in general and the specific identity of her paramour. "Is he a sophomore too?"

"Miles goes to Memorial, in Waterford. He's pretty much the star of their debate team." Arden tossed her hair in a way that said she was trying not to brag but couldn't help herself. "But if we could focus for a second on someone who is *not* bae material, I was trying to tell you that *Alex Ritter*" — her voice lowered to a whisper — "isn't here. Kaitlynn said he showed up about an hour ago with Megan G., but then she saw him head out the door with Eva Moskowitz."

I wondered if either was the girl who'd been hand-feeding him at lunch the other day, or if these were new conquests.

"Wow." Lydia's tone was grudgingly impressed. "You weren't kidding, Mary. Dude gets around."

"I told you." Arden patted my arm. "Mary is very wise.

She's looking out for us. Did my own brother tell me any of this important information? No, he did not. But like I said, we don't have to worry about you-know-who bothering us tonight. We can people watch in peace." With a sigh of contentment, she settled her shoulder blades more comfortably against the wall. Terry moved sideways to make room, tucking herself partway behind the plant.

"What do you think so far?" Arden gestured at the loose groupings that filled the room. One knot had formed around a game board, but most were engaged in conversation, a dozen different stories unfolding at once.

Lydia leaned across Arden. "She means have you spotted any creepers yet." Her brow creased. "Is it just me, or does it feel like we should have night vision goggles and then Mary does the voice-over like, 'Here come the cheetahs, gathering at the watering hole'?"

The last part was delivered in the gravelly British accent common to nature documentaries. Unfortunately, I hadn't spent years observing the nocturnal habits of teenage wildlife. My face must have betrayed my qualms, because Arden gave my forearm a reassuring squeeze.

"No pressure. We're just soaking up the atmosphere."

"And the reek of body spray," Lydia said, not quite under her breath. She glared at the guy walking past us in a cloud of cologne. His long shorts and bleached bangs seemed designed to give off an improbable surfer vibe, considering our land-locked location.

"Are you seeing what I'm seeing?" Lydia's gaze was still

fixed on the pseudo beach bum. As we watched, he approached a girl with a deep tan and lip gloss so shimmery it looked like crushed pearls. She fluttered her lashes; he leaned close enough that his hip bumped hers.

"That's Preston Hicks," Arden explained. "He's been dating Allison Grant for ages."

I nodded slowly, though in truth I wasn't sure why an intimate tête-à-tête between a guy (however overscented) and his longtime girlfriend had so thoroughly scandalized Lydia and Arden. Surely that sort of thing was par for the course at high school parties?

"That's not Allison." Lydia jerked a thumb at the shiny tan girl, whose neck smelly surfer boy was now nuzzling.

Terry sucked a breath through her teeth.

"I know, right?" Arden shook her head.

"It's so brazen," I said.

"Super shady," Lydia agreed. "One summer of protein shakes and Proactiv and he thinks he's God's gift to womankind. And poor Allison is probably sitting at home all lonely and sad, because from what I hear in band, he's still stringing her along while he tries to upgrade."

"Who's she?" Terry asked, indicating not-Allison.

"Rachel James. Her father owns a car dealership, which apparently makes her Princess Chevrolet." Lydia rolled her eyes.

"So she's rich, and the other girl is poor?" I asked.

Arden tipped her hand back and forth. "Allison is average, like Preston. Both of them worked at the smoothie place over the summer."

I didn't need to hear any more. "It's like *An American Tragedy*."

"I don't know if I'd go that far," Lydia said. "Yes, it's a total dick move —"

"That's the name of a book," I explained.

Arden pulled out her phone, swiping several times before looking up at me. "I'm ready."

Lydia frowned at her. "What are you doing?"

"Taking notes. Go ahead, Mary."

"It's about this guy named Clyde, who's really into this rich girl but figures she's out of his league because he's working class, so he gets together with someone from the factory where he works. Only then the rich girl does notice him, but when Clyde tries to dump his poor girlfriend, she tells him she's pregnant."

"Dang," Arden whispered, pausing in her typing.

"That's not all. Horrible, wishy-washy Clyde takes the poor pregnant girl sailing, and she ends up *drowning*."

"He murdered her, didn't he?" Terry asked.

"That part is sort of ambiguous. In his mind it was an accident, but Clyde isn't the most self-aware guy on the planet. He spent the first part of the day thinking how great it would be if she wasn't around anymore, and the second part not trying very hard to save her when she fell overboard."

Lydia narrowed her eyes at Preston, the Perfumed Philanderer, who was demonstrating his virility by hoisting his non-girlfriend in the air. "Tell me he didn't get away with it."

I drew a finger across my neck.

"Somebody cut his throat?" Terry asked.

"Electric chair." To the best of my knowledge, there was no way to mime that particular fate.

Arden's lips pursed. "I might need to drop a warning in Allison's ear."

"Ix-nay on the water sports," Lydia intoned, crossing her arms in a forbidding manner. "Or we could pull the plug on Preston right now."

I felt the blood drain from my face. Discussing such matters in the abstract was one thing; the idea of confronting wrongdoers in the flesh had never crossed my mind.

"Remember what you told me when we were in sixth grade, Lyds?" Arden patted Lydia's arm. "Vigilante justice is a double-edged sword." Her expression turned thoughtful. "Which one do you think is worse, death by train or death by drowning?"

Terry didn't hesitate. "Drowning is way better. It's right up there with hypothermia for a peaceful way to go."

"You could say it was death by other people's selfishness," I mused. "Both times."

Arden pointed at me. "Yes. I like that." Her fingers flew across the screen of her phone. "First a train, then a boat. All we need to round out the trifecta is one that happens on an airplane."

Lydia gave her a look.

"Which is obviously not going to happen in one of Mary's books. Duh." Arden flicked herself in the forehead.

"There were some carriage rides that definitely took a turn for the worse," I offered by way of consolation.

Arden's lips parted. I could practically see the question hovering, but before the words emerged a boy wearing a glow-stick headband trotted up to Lydia. He spread his arms wide as if about to fold her into his embrace. Which was strange, as I would not have pegged her as the hugging type.

"Lydia!" He raised his arms even higher, palms up.

"Danny," she replied, poker-faced.

He shimmied his shoulders. "Do you know what time it is?"

Lydia's coolness melted into a grin. "Let's do this." She held out her hand, allowing him to tug her into motion. The two of them disappeared without a backwards glance.

"Is that her boyfriend?" I asked. Another question hummed underneath: *Do you* all *have boyfriends?* Surely Terry would have mentioned that fact vis-à-vis Alex Ritter's attentions.

"Lydia will dance with anyone," Arden explained. "Good luck getting her to make a more serious commitment, though." She glanced at me. "I think you're going to be really good for her."

I pointed to my collarbone. *Me?*

"If you tell her someone's worth her time, she might actually listen. Let down her guard for once. Take a chance on love — or at least like."

There was an edge to her voice I would have liked to explore further, but at that moment our lavender-haired hostess reappeared, beckoning urgently to Arden.

"Either she wants me to make snack mix, or somebody spilled something and she needs a stain removal consultation.

Those are my two superpowers." Arden's brows drew together. "Will you guys be okay?"

"Sure," I said, though part of me was tempted to grab her by the ankle and hold on.

Terry and I exchanged a look. It was the first time we'd been alone, without Arden's effusiveness or Lydia's strict focus to keep the conversational ball rolling. A lot of people assume two introverts will automatically be comfortable with each other, but sometimes it's the opposite, due to a double helping of awkward silence.

"Did they have parties like this at your old school?" I asked, before the quiet could grow too entrenched.

"Maybe." She glanced my way, gauging whether I would accept this as an answer. "I didn't have much of a social life."

"Really?"

"It was a bad year." She looked down. "I kind of split up with my friends."

An unspoken *you too?* trembled on my tongue. "What happened? I mean, if you don't mind talking about it."

Terry played with the clasp of her purse. "Puberty, I guess? I started wearing contacts, because glasses make my nose sweat, and then I got my braces off and . . . stuff."

I heard the words she wasn't saying: *I turned beautiful.* To some it would have sounded like a Cinderella moment. What more could a woman want from life than to win the beauty lottery? But I'd read plenty of stories in which prettiness was more of a curse, like wearing a target on your face. Helen of Troy, anyone? Not exactly an aspirational lifestyle. Far better to have a noble brow, or graceful figure, or some other subtly striking feature for the discerning admirer to notice, preferably after they learned to appreciate your strength of character.

"I went through something similar," I told Terry, in an effort to bolster her spirits. "Not the transformation part"—I circled a hand in front of my face—"but with a person from my old school." My brain shied away from the word *friend*.

"Really?"

She sounded interested, or at least desirous of a distraction, so I gave her the broad-strokes version of the Shunning.

"People suck," Terry said when I finished.

"Yeah." I felt my shoulders relax. Reliving the memory didn't carry the same sting, especially with such a sympathetic audience. "Is that why you transferred?"

"Partly. They also have a better science program here, and I need that for what I want to do."

"Doctor?" I guessed.

"Forensic pathologist."

It was like hearing Snow White aspired to a career in bare-knuckle boxing. "That's very, ah, specific."

"Me and my mom watch a lot of crime shows." Her eyes slid briefly to me. "We read, too. Mysteries, true crime—stuff like that."

"Cool." Generally speaking, Porter-Malcolms were not genre snobs.

"I was actually thinking tonight is kind of like an Agatha Christie," Terry observed.

Since I didn't recall stepping over any corpses, I raised my eyebrows in question.

"We're getting picked off one by one. Now it's down to you and me, which means either of us could be the killer. Unless someone faked her own death to throw us off the scent."

"That's a very layered analysis," I said admiringly.

I would have liked nothing more than to continue this line of conversation, but an unfamiliar form slammed between us, forcing Terry and me to step farther apart.

"'Sup, ladies," said the deep-voiced stranger. He leaned closer to Terry. "My friend thinks you're hot."

I waited, assuming there must be more, but no: that was the whole speech. Not exactly "You pierce my soul. I am half agony, half hope." And okay, there were probably very few high-schoolers who could approach the level of Captain Wentworth's passionate letter at the end of *Persuasion*. Still, this guy ought to have been able to manage a simple, *Hi, my name is So-and-So, do you mind if I join you?* What did he expect Terry to do, fall to her knees in gratitude? His slack-jawed grin conveyed very little, aside from a certain smug blankness.

"Would you excuse us?" I said, because someone had to raise the tone of this encounter. I cut my eyes at Terry, indicating that she should join me.

"Do you know him?" I asked when we had stepped out of hearing range.

She shook her head. The look on her face was trusting, as if I were about to take care of everything. Which would have been a lot easier if there were clear social rules to follow in a situation like this. Even though I had no desire to live in an era of corsets and chaperones and zero career prospects for women, it was hard not to feel nostalgic for old-fashioned civility. In those days, a young man wouldn't have been allowed to accost us until he'd been formally introduced.

Since that convention had gone the way of white gloves and calling cards, I lifted my chin, determined to handle this my own way. As I approached our would-be swain, Terry fell in behind me. "Please tell your friend that we received his message, which I'm sure he meant to be flattering—"

"We have half a case of Keystone in back," the guy interrupted, directing the words to Terry. (No prizes for guessing where the missing half had gone.) "You want to check it out?"

The leer that accompanied these words made it clear he was proposing more than a look-at-my-beer expedition.

Terry tugged on my sleeve. "Are you thinking what I'm thinking?" she whispered.

"Maybe?" The way I saw it, there were several possibilities, ranging from *He's drunk* to *When hell freezes over.*

"Dissociative identity disorder," she pronounced, not bothering to lower her voice. "I'm pretty sure the quote-unquote *friend* doesn't exist."

"Hey," said the guy, and for a moment I thought he was objecting to the diagnosis. Then his hand clamped onto my hip.

I half jumped, half spun out of his grip. "What are you doing?"

Far from being chastened, he completed a slow inspection

of my body — or at least the part from knee to neck. "You're cute."

There it was again, the air of noblesse oblige, like he was doing us a favor. My nostrils flared. "No."

"For real. You have kind of a" — he waved his hand as though cleaning a mirror — "decent little body."

It took me a second to realize we were speaking at cross-purposes. "I wasn't disagreeing with you." Though given my druthers, I would have chosen a more impressive adjective than *cute*. The larger issue was that he assumed his opinion mattered to me. "I meant no as in 'no thank you.' Not interested."

His face gave no indication my words had registered. On the contrary; his arm reached out as if to grab me again.

"I have pepper spray," Terry said, brandishing her purse.

He grunted a laugh.

"Pretty sure she's not kidding." I let a warning note enter my voice. The situation seemed to be heading south rather quickly, but I still had faith in the power of words. "Don't you think it would be better to walk away? This whole thing is getting unnecessarily awkward."

Mr. Uncouth looked at me as though I'd issued a violent fart instead of a diplomatic suggestion that would allow him to save face.

"Whatever." He stormed off as abruptly as he'd arrived. If I hadn't jerked aside, he would have shoulder checked me out of the way.

I resisted the urge to make a rude gesture at his retreating back. "Charming."

A new voice, male and amused, spoke from behind me. "I prefer 'unnecessarily awkward.'"

The muscles in my back seized, an instinctive response to danger. With a mounting sense of dread, I forced myself to turn.

Not again. The words sounded in my head like clanging cymbals; talk about a fire-to-frying-pan scenario. Poor Terry, subjected to constant attack by importunate males. A spark of outrage lit me from within. "Unbelievable."

"He is, isn't he? I don't know what people see in that guy," Alex Ritter observed, as though picking up the thread of an ongoing conversation. Shifting slightly, he smiled a greeting at Terry.

Oh no you don't. "Who's to say the two of you aren't in cahoots?"

His lids lowered in a slow, catlike blink. "Cahoots?"

"That's right." I lifted my chin. Although he wasn't encroaching on our space like the other guy, a hint of scent teased my nostrils: something soapy and a little bit green, like a forest. I didn't know enough about the male toilette to guess whether it came from his hair or clothes or skin.

He lifted one hand, shifting the curl artfully draped across his forehead. "You really think I'd ask someone like Chad to be my wingman?"

"Why not? After him, anyone would look good."

"Actually, I thought you might need a rescue." His voice was low and laced with humor. "From the smooth moves of Chad."

Playing the hero; how opportunistic of him. "We had it under control."

Terry nodded agreement. I waited for his attention to swing back her way, but he continued to study me, head tipped to one side.

"You look familiar," he said at last. "Have we met?"

I frowned, almost disappointed he would resort to such a clichéd line. Frankly, I'd expected more suaveness from a rake of his stature.

"Should I take that as a no?" Alex asked.

"You tell me," I replied, sidestepping the question. The last thing I wanted was to remind him of our long-ago run-in and see the utter lack of recognition in his eyes—again.

"I'm Alex."

"I know."

He extended a hand, which I had no choice but to shake. I would have preferred to keep him at a safe distance, like a character on a page, instead of feeling his warm hand grip mine. And now I was blushing, which he was sure to misinterpret, when all it really meant was, *I am uncomfortable right now.*

"Mary," said a familiar voice. "What are you doing?"

Dropping Alex's hand, I took a hasty step back. "Cam. Hi."

My sister had made zero concessions to the party atmosphere. Despite the grass stains on her jersey and scabbed knees, she appeared utterly at ease—a lioness in nylon shorts. We stared at each other in mutual consternation until I realized she was waiting for me to answer her question.

"I came with friends," I said, trying not to sound defensive. Was it really so strange to think that I had secured an invitation to the party?

Cam's expression didn't change. (It seldom did.) "I thought you were helping the twins."

I shook my head. "Auditions aren't until tomorrow."

Her attention shifted to Alex Ritter.

He inclined his head in a mock bow. "Cam."

"Alex."

He made a show of trying to see something behind her. "Where's your shadow?"

In the doorway, I glimpsed a broad-shouldered young man watching Cam intently, as though she'd abandoned him mid-conversation. Were they here together? Like on a date?

"I need to talk to my sister," Cam said, her gaze never leaving Alex. "My very young sister."

A slow smile bloomed as he looked from Cam to me, clearly delighted at having solved the mystery of my identity. "I guess I'll go—before it gets *unnecessarily awkward*." I refused to make eye contact, certain that if I did he would wink at me. "See you around, *Mary*." He raised a hand in a general farewell.

Terry watched him melt into the crowd before pushing off from the wall. "I'll give you guys some privacy."

Cam held up a hand. "That was for him. You can stay." My sister gave me a considering look. "You'll be there tomorrow. For the play?"

"*Othello*," I supplied. "And of course I will. Just like always." Going to one measly party didn't mean I was lost to all sense of responsibility.

"Did you say *Othello*?" Arden had materialized with a silver mixing bowl in one hand, trailed by a red-faced Lydia.

"Sorry, I'm being rude." She held the bowl out to Cam. "Snack mix? I made it myself."

"These are my friends," I said to Cam. "Arden, Lydia, and Terry."

My sister's assessing gaze lingered on each of them in turn before she nodded a greeting. Only then did she help herself to a handful of snack mix. "It's good," she told a visibly relieved Arden before returning her attention to me. "You don't need a ride?"

"We've got her covered," Arden promised, linking her elbow with mine.

Before turning to go, Cam sent me a loaded look. "Be careful."

"I'm a very safe driver," Arden assured her.

I suspected the warning had more to do with Alex Ritter. As if I didn't know any better; I was fifteen, not five.

"So." Arden leaned into me. "Tomorrow. The play."

"It's just auditions. The performances are in December."

"Are you trying out?" Lydia asked.

"Me? No. I always help out behind the scenes."

"You're a volunteer," Arden translated. "Which means you're basically doing community service." She handed the bowl of snack mix to Lydia, freeing both hands to grab hold of mine. "And *that's* flipping perfect, because guess what else is on my list of activities?"

"Um, community service?"

"Bingo!" Arden squeezed my fingers. "Technically I had it

down as 'padding your college application,' but it's basically the same thing. And you know what *that* means?"

Lydia, who was clearly more accustomed to this type of leading question, answered first. "We're going to watch a bunch of people try out for a play."

"Yes," Arden agreed. "But also, Mary's season, scene two!" She paused, nose wrinkling. "No pun intended."

Dear Diary,

Maybe it's a touch melodramatic, but the part in **North and South** where Thornton sees Margaret with her brother at the train station and assumes it's a tryst but decides to keep her secret because he loves her so much kills me. That's what I call a romantic moment.

Usually it's the opposite scenario — a secret lover someone tries to pass off as their platonic acquaintance despite the damning circumstances, because people are shameless.

M.P.M.

CHAPTER 8

Arden snuck a glance at the nearest cluster of auditionees, who were loitering amid the faded grandeur of the Millville College theater lobby. Some were monologuing under their breath, while others stretched or stared at their phones.

"Do you think they think we're in college?" she asked, barely moving her lips.

"Either that or a gang of jewel thieves." Lydia smoothed the front of her navy tunic, which she had paired with leggings of the same shade. It had been Arden's idea for everyone to wear dark colors, the better to blend in with all the thespians.

The doors of the auditorium swung open. A hush fell over the lobby as the twins emerged. Van's expression was tense and slightly abstracted, as though she had the weight of the world on her shoulders. I put it at about 70 percent genuine, and the rest performative: the great director at work. Behind her, Addie wore a less showy air of preoccupation, which gave way to a smile when she spotted me.

"Mary." Van waved a peremptory hand, despite the fact that I was already moving in their direction. "We need you."

"You are such an insider, Lady Mary," Arden breathed behind me.

"My friends are here with me," I explained to the twins.

"How can we help?" Lydia's brisk tone exuded competence.

Van regarded them with new interest. "We can use you at the first checkpoint. I'm not saying actors are like cattle, but they do respond to herding."

Addie frowned, lips parting as if about to protest, but Van had already marched back into the auditorium, drawing the rest of us in her wake. The heavy doors closed with a *whoosh* behind us.

Van pointed to a long table leaning against the wall, legs folded. "Check-in is there." She moved her arm to indicate a spot at the back of the theater, between the last row of seats and the main doors. "We need them to sign in and fill out a contact sheet, and then you can give them a packet with the scenes we'll be reading from." Bending, she lifted a box from the floor and passed it to Lydia. "Are we clear?"

"Crystal." Lydia executed a sharp turn and headed for the table.

"Not you," Van said, when I took a step in that direction. "Anton needs you backstage."

"He's the costume and makeup person," I explained, in response to Arden's look of interest.

Addie checked her watch. "You can open the doors in ten

minutes," she instructed my friends. "And thank you," she added, smiling warmly.

I glanced worriedly over my shoulder as I trailed the twins down the center aisle, wondering if the other three regretted their impulsive decision to accompany me this afternoon. To my relief, they looked more excited than put-upon. Lydia even went so far as to flash me a thumbs-up.

On the other side of the curtain, the first person we encountered was Karen, Baardvaark's stage manager. As usual, she wore a full headset, despite the fact that there was no one running lights or the sound board with whom she would need to communicate.

"That's how she gets orders from her alien overlords," Anton whispered in my ear.

I turned to hug him, the nubby wool of his cardigan a familiar prickle against my cheek. He was by far my favorite member of the company, with the obvious exception of my sisters.

"Be gentle. Uncle Anton is feeling fragile today." He touched a hand to his temple, in case the sunglasses indoors weren't enough of a clue.

"They need to see me first," Karen boomed at us. Anton winced. "I'm taking Polaroids, because you know half of them won't have headshots. I'll send them to you after, if there's time."

"I live to serve," Anton said with patently false humility. Turning to me, he raised his travel mug of coffee. "Let's go to our corner."

In the costume area, he collapsed into a tattered wingback chair that must have been the remnant of a non-Baardvaark production. Something depressing about family conflict in suburban America, at a guess. "You're on point today, precious. I love your sisters, truly I do, but why they insist on starting so early is a mystery to me."

"It's almost two o'clock," I pointed out, though I was accustomed to Anton's nocturnal habits, which went hand in hand with his vampiric pallor.

"Easy for you to say, Baby Fresh Face." He lowered his glasses, peering at me over the chunky plastic frames. "What is this look?"

I was wearing an old Baardvaark T-shirt (black, from a production of *Titus Andronicus*) and my darkest jeans. "It's Saturday, and I'm here to work."

With a long-suffering harrumph, he heaved himself out of the chair and crossed to a rolling rack of clothing. "Here," he said, whipping something black from a hanger and holding it out to me.

I slid my arms into the sleeves of the jacket before looking down at myself. "Is this from a tuxedo?"

Anton adjusted the collar of the borrowed coat. "We have a reputation to uphold. Someone on this team has to bring the glam." He shot a pointed look at Karen before grabbing my ponytail and pulling it over my shoulder for closer inspection.

"Are you checking for split ends?"

"I'm thinking about making a hairpiece. You have enough for both of us." One of the great sorrows of Anton's life was his hairline, which he monitored obsessively for signs of thinning. "You've been conditioning," he said approvingly, running the ends of my hair against his palm.

A floorboard creaked. "Time to work," Anton said, releasing my hair. He pressed a tape measure into my unresisting hand before spinning me around.

I froze, staring at the new arrival. "What are you doing here?"

"What are *you* doing here?" Alex Ritter countered.

I opened my mouth to protest before remembering that he *knew* I was here to help my sisters; he'd heard Cam asking me about auditions last night. And I'd stupidly announced they were happening today, which meant his presence was my fault.

"Did you sign in?" I was hoping for some clue as to whether he'd already spotted Terry. I assumed she was his main reason for being here. Unless he intended to flirt *and* try out for the play, so as to wreak maximum havoc. The twins did occasionally cast upper-level students from Millville High, though surely they'd learned their lesson in his case.

"Darling, let's do our job. He can worry about the paperwork later." Anton had resumed his seat, leaning back at an angle with his long legs crossed in front of him. He picked up a notebook and pencil from an adjacent side table. "Ready when you are."

I took a deep breath. Just because Alex Ritter was an agent of chaos didn't mean I had to let him throw me off my stride. "Hold your arms out," I instructed. "Like a scarecrow."

The request seemed to take him by surprise, but after a

moment's hesitation he complied. I stepped closer, wishing for the first time that I had opted to assist Karen. Pictures could be taken from a safe distance. Getting someone's measurements was a different story.

Holding my breath, I reached around him with the tape measure in one hand. My goal had been to minimize physical contact, but the plan backfired when I left too large a space between us, causing me to stumble forward as I tried to wrap the tape around his waist.

"Sorry," I mumbled, removing my face from the pocket of his shirt before calling out the number for Anton to write down.

"It's my cologne," Alex Ritter replied. "It has that effect on people."

It's a well-known fact that as soon as someone mentions a smell, it's impossible not to sniff. I thought I'd inhaled stealthily, until Anton weighed in.

"How is it, Mary? Spicy? Piquant? More of a musk?"

"He smells like syrup," I said tightly.

"Pancake Saturday," Alex confirmed. "Best day of the week." He sniffed the back of his hand, *hmm*ing appreciatively. "My blood is probably twenty percent Log Cabin right now."

I cleared my throat. "Where was I?"

"You're just getting warmed up," Anton quipped from the comfort of his chair. "Better double-check that chest measurement. Once more unto the breach, and all that. Let me know if you need an extra pair of hands."

I reached around Alex again, careful to keep my balance this time. This was a job, no different from painting scenery—although plywood and canvas didn't give off body heat or stare back at you when you were doing your very best to avoid eye contact.

"I'm flexing," he said, as I brought the ends of the tape measure together over the buttons of his shirt. "Can you tell?"

I shook my head, meaning *I'm not going to answer that.*

"Ouch," said Alex. "Stone cold."

"Bulging pecs are overrated," Anton volunteered.

Ignoring both of them, I wrapped the tape measure around Alex's neck. He shivered when my fingers brushed his nape. "That tickles."

My embarrassment was now at such a critical level that my body seemed to move independently of my mind. Shoulder to wrist. Armpit to hip. The length of his back. Even so, the part of me watching the scene from the outside couldn't help noting how often it looked as though we were caught in a torrid embrace.

"I do remember you," he whispered, during one such moment.

"From last night? Impressive."

He shook his head. "Before that."

I gave a skeptical *humph.* It landed somewhere between his shoulder blades. Maybe his memory extended as far as the first day of school, but I doubted it. Before he could speak again, I stepped back to call a number to Anton.

"What if the other leg is longer?" Alex asked, when I moved to one side of him to measure the distance from his waist to the floor.

"Then you have bigger problems than your costume," I answered shortly. We had reached the most intimate stage of the process, and my mind was scrambling for a way to avoid what came next. "Do you happen to know your inseam—like in pants?"

Alex crossed his arms, tapping his bottom lip with one finger. "Thirty-two? No, maybe it's thirty-four."

I frowned at him. "You're not that tall."

"You give me life, Mary!" Anton called. "So much sass behind that sweet face."

Alex glanced from Anton to me, and I felt heat suffuse my cheeks.

"There you are," said a sultry voice.

I took a quick step back. Although the person who'd spoken sounded like a nightclub singer, she had the cascading ringlets of a pre-Raphaelite painting, and the body-conscious clothing of a yoga instructor. She sidled up to Alex, her delicate shoulder giving him a playful nudge. "I thought you came to hang out with me."

My mind skittered from one revelation to the next: He's here with *her*—a College Student. Which means he didn't come to woo Terry. Unless he's really, really debauched.

"There was a door propped open, so I walked in and these two grabbed me." Alex made it sound as though Anton and I had wrestled him to the ground like a pair of thugs, when all that really happened was that—I squeezed my eyes shut, striving in vain to suppress the memory of draping a tape measure around every section of his body.

"I figured they were going to shake me down for my lunch money," Alex added.

Anton ignored this exchange, tipping his sunglasses up to stare at the new arrival. "Do you model?"

She flashed a coquettish grin, all lowered chin and fluttering lashes. "A little."

"Let's see the walk." Anton all but rubbed his hands together in anticipation, headache temporarily forgotten.

The girl—or rather, woman—threw her shoulders back and shook out her hair. She stomped a straight line from where she was standing to Anton's chair.

"So you're not auditioning?" I hissed at Alex while his special friend spun around to begin high stepping back our way.

"I never said I was."

I ground my teeth, annoyance twisting the knife of my embarrassment. His significant other rejoined us.

"Hold this, will you?" She handed her bag to Alex, then used both hands to coil her long hair into a magazine-worthy bun. Not even with a wall of mirrors, oceans of hairspray, and battalion of bobby pins could I hope to replicate such a feat.

Pressing both hands to her abdomen, she inhaled deeply through her nose, lips puckering on the long, slow exhale. "Are you going to watch?" she asked Alex, before commencing the next round of exaggerated breaths.

"I'll be in the front row," he assured her, laying on the supportive boyfriend act with a shovel.

"Then you'll be staring at her feet." I hadn't intended the

words to carry, but Anton licked his finger and made a sizzling sound.

Alex favored me with a slow grin. It seemed highly inappropriate for him to look at anyone that way with his girlfriend standing right there. "Where are you sitting?"

"I'm not. I'll be running around. Doing things."

"No rest for the wicked," Anton quipped.

Belatedly I realized that if I set Alex loose in the auditorium, he would almost certainly run into Terry. "You can watch from the wings." Feeling the need to sell the idea, I added, "It's a really cool view."

"So cool," said Anton. "The coolest." For someone who claimed to be on the brink of death, he was remarkably quick with the commentary.

"Which way?" Alex asked me.

I pointed.

He turned to the Older Woman. "Ready, Phoebe?"

She rolled her head in a half circle, stretching her neck muscles, before resuming her perfect posture. "Okay."

"I'll see *you* later." Anton blew her a kiss.

We watched the two of them saunter out of sight, Alex's arm draped across her shoulders. Crossing to Anton's chair, I slumped onto the armrest.

"You really think she'll get a part?" I asked.

"Oh yeah. But that's not what we need to talk about." He gave my knee an encouraging pat. "Tell Uncle Anton everything."

"What do you mean?"

Anton tipped his sunglasses down the bridge of his nose. "What's the story with you and that boy?"

I shrugged. "He's the school Don Juan."

"And?"

"There's no story." It would have been too complicated to explain the Vronsky intervention, so I opted for a change of subject. "How's your head?"

"Terrible."

"Want me to ask Karen for aspirin?"

"You'd do that for me?" He pretended to wipe away a tear. "Back to the issue at hand. You're holding out on me. I may not be in peak form, but I saw the way he looked at you."

"He looks at everyone that way. It's his nature."

"Hmm." He did not sound convinced. "Someday Uncle Anton is going to explain the difference between good-bad and bad-bad when it comes to boys."

"I think I'll stick to good-good."

Anton feigned a yawn. "Sounds a little dull—which that one definitely was not."

Usually I enjoyed his teasing, but on this subject, Anton had pushed far enough. "You know he has a girlfriend," I admonished. "At *least* one."

"Does he?" Anton sounded surprised, which made me want to check his forehead for fever. He really was out of it if he'd failed to register what was going on with *Phoebe*.

The scuff of footsteps drew our attention to a stocky young man with a stubby ponytail. "Hi," he said, shuffling to a stop. "Is this where you get measured for a costume?"

Anton held up a hand. "Wait there." To me, he said, "If that's the case, I revoke my approval. You let Uncle Anton know if he tries to toy with your emotions again."

Tape measure in hand, I stood. Perhaps I lacked the elegant posture and charming first name of a Phoebe, but my sense of self-preservation was fully functional. "Trust me. That's not going to be a problem."

Dear Diary,

I'm not saying I want to eat kippers or kidneys or any other strange animal products, but I do like the sound of a "breakfast room" with an array of tempting items arranged on the sideboard. Usually our sideboard is covered with books and student essays and piles of half-opened mail.

Plus, Mom is way too invested in ancient grains to let us step off the cereal bandwagon any time soon.

M.P.M.

CHAPTER 9

After auditions, Arden drove us to a minimart near campus. Our purpose was twofold: to fill her car with gas and undertake the essential teen experience of scrounging an entire meal from convenience store provisions.

While they explained to me the major food groups (crunchy, cakey, slushy, and sticky), I recounted the happenings backstage — chiefly the part about Alex Ritter's paramour. The incident with the tape measure wasn't really worth repeating, as it had been more of an embarrassing gaffe on my part, whereas the fact that he'd hit on Terry while already in possession of a girlfriend had direct bearing on his character. Naturally my friends were scandalized.

We carried our plunder to a nearby park, where two teams of sweaty boys were playing soccer. As the sun set, tinting the sky pink, the four of us chatted about classes, homework, the indignities of PE, TV shows I hadn't seen, and whether soccer thighs were preferable to swimmer shoulders.

Did I like soccer thighs? The question had never crossed my mind. It felt slightly crass to discuss such things until I recalled the Regency fashion for strutting around in skintight pantaloons, which had been all about guys showing off their assets.

What I *did* like was being asked my opinion, and not just as a precursor to telling me why I was wrong. They seemed genuinely curious about what I had to say, something I'd never experienced with Anjuli. The words flowed among us without a single strained silence or sullen eye roll until the lights came on at the park and we realized it was time to go home.

◦⌣◦

The next morning, I stayed in bed reading until a grumbling stomach drove me downstairs. In the dining room, I found my father surrounded by uneven stacks of books and papers, as well as no fewer than three oversize mugs. There was a bare patch just large enough for my cereal bowl at the far end of the table. After pulling in my chair, I peered at the scribble-covered legal pad next to his hand.

"What are you working on?"

"That remains to be seen." He pushed his glasses farther up his nose. "I'm noodling for now."

Dad's thought processes were famously nonlinear. *Almost Woolfian in their circumlocutions,* our mother liked to say of his stream-of-consciousness style. It sounded like a compliment, but I got the feeling Mom was trying to convince herself, when in fact she wished he would empty the clean plates from the dishwasher *before* upending a half-full cup of tea over them.

"Where is everybody?" I asked around a mouthful of whole-grain nuggets. The house was unusually quiet.

"Your mother's at yoga." Dad's mind always turned to Mom first. "I believe Adeline and Vanessa are still slumbering." His forehead crinkled as he looked at me. I would have thrown him an oar but wasn't sure which mystery had him confounded: the name of his missing daughter, or her whereabouts.

"Cam's at practice?" I guessed.

Dad tapped the table, his version of *aha!* "She did say something about that, though it may have been yesterday." He shook himself, tufts of salt-and-pepper hair jutting in all directions. Most people never guessed he was younger than our mother by several years, since Dad tended to be bear-like and shambling while Mom was a health-food-powered dynamo of petite proportions.

"What are your plans for the day?" he asked, surprising me. My father was not a Keeper of the Social Calendar type.

"Homework, mostly." And maybe a phone call to Arden, who'd asked me to update her with any casting news.

Dad sat back, threading his fingers and resting them on his belly. "No parties on the horizon?"

I rubbed the sleep from my eyes. "Parties?" It seemed like even more of a non sequitur than usual.

"Your sister told me," he said gruffly. "About seeing you out on the town."

"Oh." I set down my spoon. "That kind of party."

His brows drew into a worried line. "Is there a reason you didn't inform us of your plans, Mary?"

"I did tell you. You were sitting in the living room with

Mom and I said, 'By the way, I'm going to a party' and she nodded, and you said, 'Indeed.'"

"Well." He cleared his throat. "It's possible I mistook your meaning."

I decided to let that one slide, especially as Jasper walked into the room at that moment, followed closely by his best friend Bo, son of the anthropology professors two doors down. (His full name was Boas, after the pioneering social scientist Franz Boas.) Judging from the state of their hair, they'd just woken up, grabbing a cereal box and pair of mixing bowls en route to the dining room.

"Mary would never sneak out without telling you," Jasper said sleepily. Although ostensibly speaking in my defense, his tone was a tad insulting.

"Who's sneaking?" Bo looked from Jasper to me. "You're not talking about Mary?"

"Yep. Believe it or not, Mary was out after dark. At a *party*." Jasper shook a little more cereal into his bowl. If no one intervened he would go on this way—a little more cereal, a little more milk—until the last dusty grains had been consumed.

"A high-school party?" Bo whispered, in a tone usually reserved for words like *chlamydia* or *cyanide*.

"Just a regular party," I said, poking at my cereal.

"With those new girls you're hanging with?" Jasper asked between crunches.

I stared at him, spoon frozen above my bowl. "How did you hear about that?"

He shrugged. "Social media, baby. You're all over Instagram."

"How would you know?"

He smiled, a trail of milk dribbling from the corner of his mouth. "We have our sources."

I was still grappling with this revelation when two sets of footsteps presaged the arrival of the twins. Van swept through the door first, staggering dramatically toward a chair. "Bring some for me, will you?" she called after her twin, who had headed straight for the kitchen.

"Some what?" Addie asked without turning.

"Whatever you're having. Toast is fine. With marmalade. And tea."

Addie returned a moment later, setting down the butter dish with slightly more force than necessary.

"Late night?" I asked. Addie opened her mouth to answer, pausing when her twin yawned loudly.

"Exhausting," Van groaned. "But productive. Some exciting new faces in the mix."

I glanced at Addie, who had shifted as if about to speak. Then the kettle whistled, and she walked back into the kitchen instead.

"Did you make the final cast list?" It felt strange to have to ask. Usually I stayed until the bitter end, listening to the twins debate which actor fit this or that part, but yesterday I'd begged off so I could leave with my friends.

"We're still pondering a few possibilities," Van said, with what I suspected to be a deliberate air of mystery.

Addie walked back in from the kitchen carrying two mugs. "She likes the one with the hair and the"—she flapped a hand at her own torso—"bodysuit for Iago." It was clear from Addie's expression that this wasn't a conviction she shared. The twins took a liberal view of cross-gender casting, so that couldn't be the issue. A petty part of me enjoyed the thought that sheer physical attractiveness wasn't enough to make up for what must have been an otherwise lackluster performance.

"Phoebe," Van supplied, not even pretending to search for the name. I'd noticed Alex Ritter's lady friend chatting with my sister during the break, listening with rapt attention to whatever Van was saying. It smacked of sucking up to me. I wondered if Alex had given her the idea. "But not for Iago. I'm thinking Desdemona."

I could tell from the way she spoke that Van was uncertain of her twin's approval.

"What? No." Addie set one of the cups in front of Van before dropping into her own chair.

"Why not?" Van countered. "She looks the part."

"It's too much—the confidence. It feels showoffy. 'Look at me, look at my body.' When Iago starts casting aspersions, instead of thinking, 'Oh no, poor maligned Desdemona,' everyone's going to say, 'She is a bit of a wanton, isn't she?'"

"I think it would be an interesting dynamic." Van very carefully added two sugar cubes to her tea. "And why shouldn't she express her sensuality? Phoebe trained as a dancer. Of course she's comfortable with her body."

That explained the way she held herself, shoulders wide and

back as though she'd never heard the word *slouch,* even when she was pressed to Alex Ritter's side. Part of me had wondered what it would feel like to be her: an arm around my shoulders, rib cages touching, flirtatious banter. Not with someone infamous like him, of course, but a serious, responsible boyfriend, appropriate for a person like me.

"That's great for Phoebe," Addie said, eyeing the mug in her hands, "but should it be the first thing anyone notices about Desdemona?"

"What, you want her to walk around holding an astrolabe, so people know she's smart? Or no, we'll put her in *glasses.* That'll be original." Van was always at her most acidic when she felt threatened. "Anyway, Anton liked her too."

"Anton wants to dress her," Addie corrected. "It's not the same thing."

Van grabbed the box of cereal, frowning as she shook it. "This is empty."

Jasper slurped the last of his milk straight from the bowl before grinning sloppily at her. "Now you can be a real starving artist."

Van threw her head back, hands over her eyes as if she couldn't bear to look at any of us. "Can we just stop for bagels on the way?"

"You asked for toast," Addie reminded her. "Which I put in the toaster for you."

Van jerked a hand at Jasper. "He can eat it."

"Fine." Addie stood, taking her mug with her as she

departed. A few seconds later we heard it thud against the kitchen counter.

"Well," said our father. Picking up his own mug, he attempted to drink. Finding it empty, he frowned before hoisting himself from the chair and heading for the kitchen, leaving all three empty cups behind.

Van glanced at the cuckoo clock on the wall as she gulped a few swallows of tea. I could tell her mind had already left the room, followed in short order by the rest of her.

"That was intense," Bo said.

I nodded. It wasn't that the twins never disagreed. Like the rest of us, they had occasional differences of opinion, but this had felt more like the kind of argument that led to hair-pulling and slaps.

"Speaking of relationship drama," Jasper observed oh so casually, "you didn't finish telling us about your new *friends*."

I knew I should ignore him, but one of my brother's superpowers is that he's almost impossible to brush off. "Why do you say it like that?"

"How did I say it?"

"I heard the italics."

"I wasn't *italicizing*. Invisible air quotes, maybe."

"What's your point?"

"I'm glad you asked, Mary." Bo leaned his elbows on the table. "We do have some concerns. First you drop your old friends and now you're chasing the popular crowd. It's not like you."

I shook my head, not wanting to know how they'd acquired their information, however erroneous. "That's not how it happened."

"And what's in it for them?" Jasper put in, as though I hadn't spoken.

"We get along." Did that sound defensive? "It's fun to hang out with them. They're nice, and interesting, and they . . . seem to like me too. We have things in common."

Bo nodded slowly, as if he were a shrink with a notepad and I was lying on his couch describing my delusions. "Such as?"

"Well, we all like order and planning. Analyzing things. None of us want to live an unexamined life."

Jasper lifted his silky eyebrows, as seal-dark as his hair. "Have they asked you for anything? Copying your homework, a little help with an essay, just this once?"

"We're not even in the same classes—"

"Of course not," Bo said soothingly, shooting Jasper a warning look. "Listen, Mary, if I were a teenage girl, you'd be at the top of my list. But we don't know these people."

"Aside from following them on Snapchat," Jasper put in.

"We've seen these situations before," Bo continued, "and they don't always end happily. You need to watch your back. Don't be their Carrie."

"As in *Sister Carrie*? You think I'm going to move to the big city and become someone's kept woman?"

"As in pig's blood in the shower and a prom night massacre when your telekinetic rage finally breaks free," Jasper replied.

"Have you considered the possibility they're stringing you along as part of an elaborate prank?"

I stared at him for the space of several thundering heartbeats. "Your faith in me is touching."

"It's not you, Mary," Bo crooned. "It's the world. The city streets are dark and dangerous. And let's face it, you're an innocent."

I wanted to tell him that *some* people found me sophisticated and worldly, but I knew Jasper would laugh. Taking my silence as encouragement, Bo reached across the table to gently stroke the back of my hand. "We worry about you all alone at that blackboard jungle, where we can't watch over you."

"I'm two years older than you," I reminded him. "And you guys have been at public school exactly as long as I have."

"Some things you're born with. Savvy is my middle name."

Jasper snorted. "Your middle name is Jaap. And I'm pretty sure the Dutch are known for tulips and wooden shoes, not street smarts."

Bo's family tree included Japanese, Filipino, and African offshoots, in addition to the aforementioned Dutch. What most people noticed about him, however, was his adorableness. Even now that he was growing from baby-faced to gawky, strangers smiled indulgently at Bo, sighing over his long lashes as though his good looks were a favor he'd done the world.

"You need to be sure these people appreciate you for the right reasons." Bo put a hand to his heart. "The way I appreciate you."

There was no point trying to explain the difference between being used and being *useful*. Just because Jasper and Bo saw me as plain old Mary, the least interesting of the Porter-Malcolm sisters, didn't mean other people looked at me the same way. To the larger world, I could be someone new and exciting.

Sitting at that picnic table in the park last night, I'd felt the glow of my friends' approbation even through the sugar buzz. The three of them had chosen me—almost as if I'd auditioned for the part and been found worthy. Maybe I was a babe in the woods when it came to Real High School, but I had things to contribute, thoughts and ideas of my own. And if my new friends deemed me cool enough to be part of their group, who was I to argue? They were the experts, after all.

"Probably you should let us inspect these girls, before you get in over your head," Jasper suggested.

I gave him a look that said, *In your dreams*. "We're friends. There's nothing weird or underhanded about it." Picking up my bowl, I started for the kitchen.

"Running away?" Jasper asked. "Things getting too hot for you?"

"I have a phone call to make. To a *friend*. Whose name is Arden," I added, worried my exit line had sounded suspiciously vague.

"You do you, Mary," Bo called after me. "Don't let them change you."

Dear Diary,

I never paid much attention to the age difference between heroines and their love interests until the twins became teenagers, at which point I realized how creepy it would be if a middle-aged guy wanted to marry one of them.

Now that I'm almost sixteen, I can't believe anyone my age would ever want to be married at all, much less to a person old enough to be someone's dad. With or without the madwoman in the attic.

M.P.M.

CHAPTER 10

A few days later, I was shoving a biology textbook into my locker when I sensed a presence behind me.

"Hey—" I started to say as I turned, expecting to see Lydia or Terry, because Arden would have been bouncier. The rest of the sentence evaporated as though I'd shoved a paper towel in my mouth.

Alex Ritter stood behind me, head cocked at a questioning angle. My heart galloped, up and then down again. "You were saying?" he prompted.

I shook my head.

He eased backwards until he was propped against the wall. Today's shirt was Wedgwood blue, which brought out the dark ring around the paler hue of his irises. Surely he planned these things for effect.

"What?" He looked down at himself. "Why are you looking at me like that?"

"I'm trying to decide if you're a fop."

"Excuse me?"

"Dandy, popinjay, coxcomb. Fancy man." I broke off, realizing my mouth had sprinted ahead of my brain. His whole attitude was so *familiar,* as if we were intimately acquainted, that I'd fallen into the trap of talking to him the same way. *You did measure his hips,* I reminded myself.

"I'm guessing you'll ace the vocab section of the SAT."

I braced myself against a rush of warmth; there was bound to be an ulterior motive behind the flattery. "Did you want something?"

He nodded. "You've read *Jane Eyre.*"

It was a statement, not a question. I blinked at him, nonplussed. He wanted to talk about the Brontës?

"Phoebe says everyone in your family is like a walking library," he continued, filling the space where a normal person would have joined the conversation instead of gawping at him like a rube.

"Of course," I finally managed to say. Honestly, did I *look* like a philistine?

A girl in tasseled ankle boots grabbed his hand as she passed. "See you tonight, Alex?"

His answering smile sent her off with a spring in her step. "What did you think about what happened at the end?" he asked me, without missing a beat.

"You mean when the ghostly voice is calling 'Jane, Jane' across the moors? As in, do I think it was a paranormal event or some kind of Freudian delusion?"

He scratched his chin with a thumbnail. "What about what happens after that?"

"When she goes back to Thornfield and it's a burned-out husk?"

"Hmm. It's not what you'd call a happy ending, is it?"

"What? No, it's beautiful. How she finds him again and sort of hints he's not totally blind—"

"Who's blind?"

It shouldn't have surprised me that Alex Ritter was not a close reader. "Rochester. From the fire," I reminded him. "When he tried to save his first wife from the burning building, but she leaped to her death instead? Which is tragic, but also handy for Jane because, goodbye, bigamy!"

He was staring as though I'd spoken a foreign language. With painful slowness, my brain pieced together the puzzle.

"You have no idea what I'm talking about, do you?"

"Didn't quite make it that far," he admitted without the faintest trace of shame. "To recap, house burns down, he goes blind, she comes to find him, and then?"

"They get married." I reported this with the robotic inflection of someone who has been shocked into a catatonic state.

A slow grin spread across his face. "That's exactly what I needed to know."

I swallowed, unsure where to direct my gaze. The force of his attention was like standing in a spotlight. "It is?"

"Essay test next period."

"How could you not finish *Jane Eyre*? It's so . . . juicy." I had been on the point of saying *romantic,* but pulled back in time.

"Busy week," he replied, with the insouciant air of someone

accustomed to charming his way out of trouble. "I got to the part where that creepy family takes her in. Seemed obvious she was going to marry the boring preacher guy and settle in with the sister-wives for a life of tea and embroidery."

"That is so incredibly wrong."

"I know." He leaned closer, lowering his voice to a confidential murmur. "Thanks to you."

Heat simmered beneath my skin, a red tide of outraged sensibilities. His laissez-faire attitude—in literature *and* love —offended me almost as much as the fact that I'd been unwittingly embroiled in his cheating.

"Wait," I said, as he turned to go. "Don't you want to know about the *very* end?"

He raised his brows in question.

"There's an epilogue. It turns out Bertha—the homicidal first wife—isn't really dead."

"After jumping off the roof?"

"She's pretty messed up," I improvised. "Extremely bedraggled. And she's kind of . . . singed. And limping."

"Sounds twisted."

"It is. Especially when she breaks into their house at night —Rochester and Jane's. And then there's a big fight, but since Rochester is still mostly blind it's up to Jane to save the day."

"And does she?"

I nodded. "Nobody messes with Jane. She stabs Bertha. With a kind of . . . dagger." Though I was tempted to embellish the description, it seemed wiser not to push my luck.

"Wow." He looked back at me with an expression I couldn't decipher. Hopefully it wasn't suspicion. "I guess I should have kept reading."

"Mm-hm," I agreed, smiling sweetly.

⁀

"Finally!" Arden exclaimed when I made it to lunch. Before I could explain the nature of the delay, she nudged her phone across the table, watching me with barely contained glee. "Check it out."

A patchwork of pictures filled the screen, but my eye went to the words unfurling in ornate script across the top. "Bad Guys from Books?" I read aloud.

"It's a working title. I'm open to suggestions." Arden flashed me a tentative smile. "What do you think?"

I studied the images more closely. They were black-and-white, or nearly so, with hazy effects near the edges, but all featured the same, vaguely familiar subject: a young man in formal dress with an intense expression.

"It's *him*," Arden informed me. "From the movie. Scroll down."

Farther down the page, in a smaller font, another line of text appeared: Is Your Guy a Vronsky?

"You made this?" I asked.

Arden nodded, biting her lip.

"It looks very professional."

She waved off the praise, though I could tell she was pleased. "I had some time last night, and I thought it might be a good idea to share what we've learned. Like a public service."

"We could call it the Loser List." Lydia took a meditative bite of carrot stick. "Or the D-bag Dictionary. Encyclopedia of Creepers?"

"Dangerous Dudes?" offered Terry.

Arden's lips pursed in thought. "If you had to summarize why a *certain party*, who wanted to date Terry even though he already had a girlfriend, was bad news, what's a word for that?"

"Irresponsible?" I was thinking of his reading habits, among other things. "Feckless? Or maybe libertine? Rogue? Scoundrel?"

"Ooh, *scoundrel*. I like that." Arden's thumbs danced across her phone. "Let's call it 'The Scoundrel Survival Guide.' Okay." She looked up at us. "What's rule number one?"

Terry raised her hand. "Always check for a criminal record?"

"I was thinking more specific to the type," Arden said diplomatically. "But that's a *great* general principle."

"Never trust a guy who has better hair than you?" Lydia suggested.

Arden looked entreatingly at me.

What *was* the crux of the issue? You couldn't really say *too attractive*, because the way Alex Ritter looked wasn't entirely his fault. "Watch out for guys who are too charming? And flirt with everything that moves? And fall in love at the drop of a hat?"

"Yes," Arden said as she transcribed.

I peered at the screen of her phone. "Is this going to be online? For anyone to see?"

"It's totally anonymous," Arden assured me. "Like a blind item in a gossip column."

"We're okay in terms of libel laws," Lydia added. "Technically we're not even talking about anyone real."

"Exactly. It's about guys in books who happen to suck in ways we can all relate to." Setting her phone to one side, Arden picked up her bag of chips. "Who are some others, Mary?"

"Scoundrels?"

She nodded. "The really famous ones. Super skeevy."

I took a bite of leftover spring roll, chewing as I reflected. Where to start? "There was a man who claimed to love this woman because she was such a free spirit, passionate and intelligent and not afraid to speak her mind, but when push came to shove, he was like, 'Sorry, I'm going to marry your passive-aggressive cousin instead because she's better at faking it to fit in.'"

Arden smacked Lydia in the arm. "Remember Jimmy, Morrison's friend? He used to date this girl Maggie, who was completely wild, in a totally adorable way. So funny, you never knew what was going to come out of her mouth. But then he dumped her senior year for this girl who basically never laughed. Ever. I don't even know if she had teeth. Seriously, wouldn't you rather be embarrassed a couple of times than bored out of your mind every single day?"

I nodded sadly. It was rare to find someone who truly valued the unique or original. Most people wanted to have what everyone else wanted, as if forming their own opinions was too mentally taxing. "There's a famous one where a guy is mad at this other guy for calling him on his bad behavior, so the first guy dates the second one's way younger sister and tries to get her to elope."

"Revenge dating," Lydia said at once. "I've heard of that."

"What about murderers?" Terry asked.

"Well," I began, thinking fast. "There's the person who was obsessed with his adopted sister, and they basically ran wild together until one day he overheard her saying something unflattering about him and he had a hissy fit and ran away. When he finally came back, he was so furious that she'd married their namby-pamby neighbor, he went and married the wussy guy's sister. And then he was so horrible to everyone they basically died of sheer misery."

Arden stared at me wide-eyed.

"I know. And there are people who think *Wuthering Heights* is a classic romance, even though the so-called hero has the emotional maturity of a two-year-old."

"But somebody takes him down in the end, right?" Lydia asked.

"His childhood love comes back to haunt him after she bites it." I gave a grudging shrug. "That part is actually pretty cool. But I don't know if it relates to anyone here."

Arden patted my hand. "Don't worry. We're going to get out there and meet more people very soon. In fact, I thought we might tackle another item on my list this afternoon. Add a little more *seasoning* to your life. If you get what I'm saying."

Lydia placed the cover on her lunchbox, snapping the corners into place. "What are we in for this time? I need to mentally prepare myself."

"It's a totally fundamental experience. Fanciness, luxury, and excitement, all under one roof!"

"For the record," Lydia announced, "I am not getting my eyebrows waxed. Or anything else."

"It's nothing like that." Arden self-consciously smoothed her own slender brows.

"The DMV," Lydia guessed.

"No, we're not taking Lady Mary to wait in a really long line." A smidgen of testiness had crept into Arden's voice. "It's way better than that."

Lydia turned to Terry. "Help me out here. What am I missing?"

"Black-market organ smuggling?"

Not even Arden had a response to that one.

"I saw it on an episode of *Underground Forensics*. This girl went to a party at a warehouse, and she thought the drinks tasted a little funny. When she woke up the next day she felt rough stitches in her lower back." Terry pressed a hand to one side of her spine. "It turned out they'd stolen one of her kidneys."

Lydia nodded as if this were a possibility that merited consideration.

"They say people pay more for young organs." Terry's already soft voice trailed off when she saw the look on Arden's face.

"The mall," Arden said through gritted teeth. "It was supposed to be a surprise, but I'll just tell you. No one's getting cut open. We're going to the freaking mall!"

"That's cool," said Lydia. "I need a new sports bra."

Dear Diary,

I've never been to Italy, but I feel like I've gotten a taste of it in books, like traveling to Florence with Lucy Honeychurch in *A Room with a View*. Someday I'll visit places like that in real life — touch the ancient stones of famous buildings, eat amazing food, wander the glorious countryside.

Just the thought of the great big world waiting out there makes me excited to grow up and have thrilling adventures in exotic locales.

M.P.M.

CHAPTER 11

Technically this wasn't my first trip to Gatewood Mall. I'd tagged along once or twice when Cam needed equipment from the sporting goods store. Our mother vociferously opposed further incursions into the sprawling emporium on the grounds that we should support smaller merchants in Millville—and also because the mall was "a soul-sucking hellhole."

I didn't mention that part to Arden, who seemed anxious for everyone to have fun. She began the tour by narrating the parking options, with recommendations according to both weather and shopping priorities. Because the early September afternoon was sticky with heat, we opted for a covered lot near one of the fancy department stores.

Stepping inside the gleaming interior, with its glass-fronted displays and expensively dressed mannequins, I felt a frisson of panic. Forget visiting the village milliner to buy a new ribbon for your bonnet; there was no way I could afford so much as a barrette in this place. My only source of pocket money was pet-sitting for Bo's family during their travels, and I'd already spent most of last summer's earnings on snack runs.

"This is more of a grown-up-lady store," Arden whispered, linking her elbow through mine. "We're just doing a stroll-through, to soak up the atmosphere, though it is excellent for special occasions."

My neck muscles released some of their tension. Living beyond one's means was a frequently fatal condition for young women in classic literature, on par with malicious gossip or falling in love with the wrong person.

We traveled up an escalator, past the children's department, and into the thick of women's wear. The stretchy sheen of what Arden called athleisure soon gave way to an entire section of ball gowns.

"Oh wow." Arden had stopped in front of a mannequin wearing a blindingly red dress. Sequined flowers climbed all over the bodice. She spun to face us. "Do you guys want to try things on? Just for fun."

Lydia checked the price tag. "No."

Ignoring this, Arden appealed to me. "Which one do you like, Mary?"

"The blue one is pretty." I pointed at a misty confection of silky skirts with a gauze overlay.

"Totally." Arden slid two off the adjacent rack and handed the hangers to me. "Sometimes the sizing is wonky for gowns, so you're better off trying a couple of different ones." She narrowed her eyes, studying the other displays. "Let's see. For Lydia, I'm thinking—"

"Dusty rose," Lydia interrupted, raising her arm to point. "That one."

We followed her deeper into the formalwear section, where she grabbed a flouncy pink dress with a bow. "I'm only trying this on because I already have the bra for it."

"Very practical," Arden agreed. "Now, Terry can probably rock anything, but if you want my opinion"—she paused, giving Terry time to nod—"I think purple is your color."

As we weaved in and out of the racks in search of a purple dress, Arden trailed the tips of her fingers along the diaphanous fabrics. "I bet they got to wear dresses like this all the time in the olden days," she said dreamily.

Not exactly like this, I thought, contemplating the exposed midriffs and thigh-high slits.

When the four of us assembled in front of the triptych of mirrors in all our finery, the results weren't quite as transformative as I'd hoped. The hem of Terry's dress pooled around her feet. Lydia's was the right length, but the straps didn't fit over her shoulders. The waist of the blue dress hit me mid–rib cage, as if I'd grabbed a child's size by accident.

"Anton would pass out if he saw this." I made a futile attempt to smooth the waterfall of fabric shooting out half a foot above my hips.

"Too bad we didn't get to meet him," Arden said, pouncing on the mention of Anton. "Have you known each other long?"

"A couple of years."

"And is he dark-haired or blond—"

"Just ask her," Lydia cut in, before Arden could finish. "Mary, are you into this guy or what?"

"Um, no. He's like a big brother. Who is also gay. And he was in the Peace Corps before college, so he's pretty old. As in *twenty-four*."

"Gross," Lydia grunted, holding up the top of her dress as she strode back down the carpeted aisle. "It would be like hooking up with Gandalf. Not that Gandalf is a scoundrel. I'm sure he's great if you're super old and don't mind being left alone a lot. The elves are a whole other story," she called through the dressing room door. "Those bitches need to be taken down a few pegs."

"Okay. I get it." Arden rolled her eyes. "Just trying to keep an open mind."

"Your dress looks great," I told her, both because it was true and as a sop to her pride.

"Yeah?" She took a few selfies from different angles before checking the time on her phone — something she'd been doing at regular intervals since our arrival.

"Are we done here?" Lydia called over the door of her changing room.

Arden sighed. "Fine. It's just nice to look ahead sometimes. Think about the future. You never know when a special occasion is going to present itself. A little pre-shopping can go a long way."

It sounded awfully specific for a general rule of thumb, but then again Arden often spoke that way.

Terry emerged from behind her own swinging door in

record time. It probably helped that she'd kept her jeans and shoes on under the dress. "Where to next?"

Arden checked the time on her phone again. "Let's start making our way to the food court."

Once we emerged onto the second floor of the mall proper, storefronts stretched to infinity ahead of us, with annexes branching in multiple directions. It felt a little like I imagined one of those really tall hedge mazes on a country estate, only without the fresh air and natural light to ease the sense of entrapment. We made a slow circuit of the upstairs, looking into the stores we passed but never entering. All the while, Arden kept surreptitiously glancing at her phone.

"Why are we going so slow?" Lydia asked from behind me. "I think those mall walkers just lapped us."

"Mary needs time to soak up the atmosphere," Arden scolded.

Actually, I was afraid that much more time spent under the onslaught of artificial scents and distorted echoes of sound would reduce me to a quivering bundle of nerves, but I couldn't tell Arden that. It was easier to focus on the people: grownups pushing strollers, ladies in work clothes, a noisy tangle of boys Jasper's age, all clutching jumbo paper cups that seemed in imminent danger of spilling their lurid contents onto the floor.

That was probably why I noticed him, the young man sitting on a nearby plastic bench, eyes narrowed as he watched the junior hooligans tussle and guffaw. He was pale and sharp-featured, though part of that might have been the expression of distaste pulling his cheekbones into relief. I wasn't exactly an expert on men's fashion, but his clothes seemed to convey an air of sophistication, or at least expensiveness.

Arden's hand tightened on my arm. "The people watching is pretty good around here, am I right?" As we drew even with the bench, she stole a glance at the well-groomed stranger. "Note to self," she murmured. "Mary likes them clean-cut. Good to know."

I worried she might be bold enough to drag us over and strike up a conversation. Then her phone buzzed, and we were triple-timing it away from the stranger, toward destinations unknown.

⟨⟩

"Voilà," Arden said, two escalator rides later. "The food court."

Although there wasn't so much as a fountain in sight, something about the humid, chemically perfumed air made me think I was standing near a pool.

"Are we eating?" Lydia asked, peering at a display of dried-out pizza slices.

"In a minute," Arden replied, pulling me along beside her. She was scanning the mauve and turquoise seating area with methodical focus.

"There's plenty of room," Terry pointed out.

"Oh, I know." Arden's laugh was not entirely convincing. "I'm just looking for the perfect spot."

Lydia squinted at her. "Something's going on. What did you do?"

"I told you, we're having the complete mall experience." Arden avoided Lydia's gaze.

"People used to do this in old books all the time," I said. "Not the fast food, obviously, but promenading around so they could look at each other. At the park, or sometimes just in the drawing room after dinner."

"They would wander in circles?" Lydia asked. "For fun?"

"It's not like they had Netflix," Arden reminded her. "Oh, look!"

The exclamation suggested relief as much as surprise. With rapid steps, she cut through a group of tables, heading for one occupied by a lone young man in khakis and a navy polo with an embroidered crest to one side of the buttons.

"Miles is here?" Lydia asked, though it was clear she meant, *What is Miles doing here?*

Arden didn't reply. She was intent on reaching Miles, who had risen from his seat. Now that he was standing, I saw that he was several inches shorter than Arden and half again as wide, with wire-rimmed glasses and a gently rounded belly. Would they kiss? Fly into each other's arms? I'd never seen Arden in girl-friend mode, but she definitely tended toward the touchy-feely.

"Where is everybody?" she asked Miles in an urgent under-tone—not the most sentimental of greetings. "Did you guys drive separately?"

His cheeks puffed as he exhaled. "About that."

"No." Arden waited in vain for him to contradict her. "They didn't. They wouldn't."

"It's the first tournament of the year. We're not where we

124

need to be." He put his hands in his pockets. "Especially me, trying to break in a new partner."

Arden flinched. "Is it that big of a sacrifice, taking an hour off?"

"It's the timing—" he started to say, breaking off at the sight of the three of us hovering nearby. "Hey, Lydia." He held up a hand to me and Terry. "I'm Miles."

Arden performed the introductions with a reasonable facsimile of her usual cheer, though I could tell she was making an effort.

"Are you guys getting something to eat?" Miles cast a hopeful glance at a burger restaurant.

Placing her hands on his cheeks, Arden gently turned his head away from temptation. "How's your blood sugar?" He looked at his shoes. "That's what I thought. You better go do your thing, because otherwise you'll be stressed. And eat something healthy."

He leaned in for a quick kiss. "I'll call you later."

"What was that about?" Lydia asked as soon as Miles was out of earshot.

Arden lifted one shoulder. "He was supposed to bring some guys from the debate team to hang out with us."

"Like an ambush," Lydia said.

"No, like an iconic experience for Mary," Arden corrected. "Flirting with guys at the mall. Only better, because they wouldn't be total strangers."

"You still wouldn't want to get into a car with them," Terry said. "Never let them take you to a secondary location."

"Sure," Arden agreed with an abstracted air. "Also, you know they're capable of dressing up. If there ever happens to be an occasion where that might come in handy."

"Yeah, if we ever need a bunch of guys who look like they're cosplaying their golfer grandpappies we're all set." Lydia pretended to tighten an invisible tie.

"Mary happens to like the conservative look. You saw the way she was scoping out the guy upstairs, with the fancy shoes!" Arden cocked her head to one side. "Maybe he's still here?"

"Dude." Lydia put a hand on her arm. "Relax. We had fun. I'm sorry it didn't end up with a group wedding or whatever, but it's all good. Right?"

Terry and I made noises of assent.

Somehow, Arden managed to smile and sigh at the same time. "So is this like something from a book? We can add it to the list of warning signs."

It took me a moment to look beyond the immediate environs of the food court—loud, greasy, and artificially bright—to the deeper issue. "There is a book where a girl accidentally goes to the wrong church on their wedding day, and her fiancé thinks he's been stood up, so he takes up with another woman, only the one he was supposed to marry was pregnant and ends up dropping dead."

"What's the lesson?" Terry asked.

"Don't freak out if your plans get messed up?" Lydia suggested. "All they had to do was try again the next day. Maybe get a better map. Work on their communication."

"There *are* other places we can go to practice our social skills," Arden allowed.

Lydia tapped the back of her hand. "I bet you have six or seven of them on your list."

"At least."

"That's the spirit." Lydia shouldered her bag. "Now let's get out of here before this lighting gives me a stroke."

Dear Diary,

If I ever become a writer like George Sand, with or without a nom de plume, I hope people remember me for my books, and not because I had an affair with a sickly pianist.

Although it is romantic imagining Chopin trying to impress her with his beautiful playing while she concentrates on her novels. That's what Arden would call a power couple.

M.P.M.

CHAPTER 12

The next item on Arden's list was destined to remain shrouded in mystery a little while longer. A merry-go-round of afterschool commitments kept my friends busy the rest of that week and well into the next, which was how I ended up walking home alone on a windy September afternoon, hefting both my backpack and Cam's, since my sister had an away game that evening. At least the heat had abated, the first hints of yellow appearing on the trees like a promise of fall.

"They have these things called e-readers," someone said from behind me as I stepped from the school parking lot onto the sidewalk. I froze, which had the unintended consequence of allowing Alex Ritter to draw even with me. "That way you don't have to carry the whole library with you." He reached for the strap of Cam's bag.

"What are you doing?" I meant, *Why are you stealing my sister's backpack?* but he blithely ignored my protest, slinging it over his own shoulder.

"Taking a walk. What are *you* doing?"

"I'm going home." Mentally I kicked myself for falling into the Little Red Riding Hood trap. But that was silly. It wasn't as though he had any intention of following me through the woods. Or neighborhood, in this case.

"Great," he said, falling into step at my side. "Aren't you going to ask how I did on my test?"

I bit my lip. The jig was up. He knew I'd invented an action-hero finale for *Jane Eyre*.

"A ninety-six." He paused, watching me for a reaction. "Also, 'Excellent, exclamation point.' Ms. Milano even read some of it to the class. She particularly liked my revisionist slant."

Was I a tiny bit impressed? Perhaps. But I had no intention of telling him that. "Imagine how well you could have done if you'd read the whole book."

He leaned closer, his shoulder brushing mine. "But I like the way you tell it."

Even though I recognized this as the type of remark he must use with anyone of the female persuasion, it *almost* caused a fluttery feeling in the pit of my stomach. "I'm going this way," I said, pointing toward downtown.

"What a coincidence. So am I."

"Don't you have places to go? People to see?" It would have been one thing to tease me in passing, but we were way off school property now.

"Where else would I go? Who would I rather be with than you?"

I pretended to think it over. "I don't know, maybe *Phoebe*?"

"Eh." He lifted a hand, dismissing the idea. "I see plenty of her." My eyes widened. It was impossible to tell whether he was being risqué or merely callous. "Where are your friends today?" he asked, unflappable as ever.

"Here and there."

His eyes flashed with amusement. "Are they robbing a bank? Because that sounded pretty suspicious. Take it from someone who's talked his way out of a lot of sticky situations."

I had no doubt what sort of situation he meant. Stopping in the middle of the sidewalk, I turned to face him. This had gone on long enough. "Listen. Alex."

"So serious," he murmured.

"If this is about Terry—" I paused, hoping he might betray his true feelings, but he merely lifted his brows, waiting for me to go on. "Then you should know it's futile."

"What is?"

"Using me to get to her. It's never going to work. She's not interested. In going out with you, I mean." I held my breath.

Alex shrugged. "I know."

"You do?"

"Yeah. You don't see me following *her* home."

I was still digesting that piece of impertinence when a loud *ahem* sounded from my left. Absorbed in the exchange with Alex Ritter, I hadn't noticed we were standing outside Toil & Trouble, from which Noreen had emerged, spray bottle in hand. The cheery tropical print of her shirt stood in stark contrast to her menacing demeanor.

"Are you bringing your date in or what?" she asked, scowling at both of us.

"He's not—we just—no," I stammered.

"You see how she is?" Alex shook his head sadly.

For the first time in my life, Noreen looked at me with something like approval. "Make him bleed," she said, before scuttling back inside.

Alex blinked at the closed door. "She seems fun."

I had no desire to discuss Noreen, or anything untoward she might have implied. "About what you were saying—"

"Before you turned me down cold?"

I sighed to show I wasn't amused. "You seem okay about it." Although we both knew he had at least one other girlfriend, I'd expected pouting at the very least.

"I'm crying on the inside." He drew a finger down his cheek. "Quite contrary of you, Mary."

There was a joke I'd never heard. "I was talking about *Terry*."

"Maybe I was a little surprised." He'd started walking again, tossing the words over his shoulder.

I hurried to catch up. "Why, because no one ever turned you down before?"

"No, because that wasn't the message she was sending."

We stopped at the corner to wait for the Walk signal. "You can't possibly think she was encouraging your advances."

"Then what was all this?" Alex ducked his chin, sending me a sidelong look through fluttering lashes.

The impression was annoyingly on point. If one didn't know better, I could see how *some* of Terry's mannerisms might read as coy. "She's shy."

"Is that why she didn't tell me herself?"

"She was working up to it. Anyway, it was strongly implied."

The light changed, and I hurried into the crosswalk.

"What was it?" he asked when we were safely across.

"What was what?"

"That she didn't like about me."

My shoulders tensed. What was the diplomatic response? *It's not you, it's her. She took a vow of chastity. Her parents have already arranged marriage to a Carpathian prince.* Meanwhile, the truth lodged in my throat: *I told her not to date you.*

"You're not her type," I finally managed. It seemed that wasn't enough of an answer, because he continued to regard me expectantly. "She's a very quiet person. Whereas you're more" — I circled a hand in the air, trying to conjure a better word than *promiscuous*. "Friendly."

"Friendly?"

"Yes. You know, sociable. Free with your attentions."

He reached out to grasp me lightly by the elbow. Reluctantly, I turned to face him. "You think I should sew an *A* on my shirt?"

Staring at the point above his heart indicated by a fingertip, I struggled to follow his train of thought. "Like a monogram?"

"As in *The Scarlet Letter.*"

Again with the unexpected literary references, though there was no guarantee he'd read to the end of this one either. "I'm just trying to be helpful," I said primly. "Prevent any misunderstandings."

Alex shook his head. "I think you just slut-shamed me."

"No!" I looked around in alarm. "And I hate that word."

"Do you have a better one? How about 'strumpet'?"

"Don't be ridiculous." *Casanova,* maybe. Or *louche,* though he would probably think it was a compliment. He raised his eyebrows, letting me know he was still waiting for a response.

"She's a Cecile, okay? Not a Marquise de Merteuil. From *Dangerous Liaisons,*" I added helpfully. "By Pierre Choderlos de Laclos. They made a movie out of it."

"For people like me who struggle with big words?"

"No!" Who knew scoundrels were so sensitive? "I just don't assume people like the same things I do."

"What *do* you like, Mary?" In an instant, his tone turned playful and intimate, as though he'd flipped some internal switch reverting to his default setting. I might have been fatally unnerved had I not noticed we were about to turn onto my street.

"Oh, you know," I said vaguely, holding out a hand for Cam's bag.

He made no move to relinquish it. "I don't know, which is why I asked. I think we should finish our conversation. You can say more foreign words."

"I'm pretty sure this is where our paths diverge." I shaped a V in the air between us, pressing the heels of my hands together.

"I'll walk you to your door."

I started to decline, but then the full meaning of his words hit. "Wait, how do you know where I live?"

"I'm considering branching into some light stalking. I thought I might put you on my route." He paused to examine his thumbnail before grinning at my gobsmacked expression. "Phoebe had me drop her off once. For 'rehearsal.'"

He gave me a significant look, as though we shared some

secret understanding, but my mind was otherwise engaged. "And you just decided to walk home with me?"

His hand closed around the strap of Cam's bag. "It looked like you could use the help. And since you were so generous with my English assignment, it only seemed fair."

I flushed, shifting guiltily. "You know what they say. All's well that ends well."

"I thought it was 'all's fair in love and war'?" He grinned at my discomfiture before glancing past me, in the direction of my house. "Are you going to invite me in?"

"Um," I began, grasping for a polite denial. He *had* carried Cam's heavy bag all this way, not to mention taking a sporting view of my *Jane Eyre* sabotage.

"I'm kidding," he said, throwing me off-balance yet again. "My piano teacher lives over there." His thumb indicated the yellow house on the corner.

I knew Mrs. Madden taught piano, but it had never occurred to me that someone like Alex Ritter might be coming to her house every week. On *my* street. It was hard to believe I hadn't felt the crackle in the air that signaled his presence. If the windows were open, I could have listened to him banging out stormy sonatas while long white curtains billowed in the breeze.

I shook off the image. Probably I was giving him too much credit. "Are you any good?"

"That's a very personal question, but I should be used to that by now, coming from you." He let me squirm a few seconds. "Yes, as a matter of fact I am. I do a mean 'Twinkle, Twinkle, Little

Star,' 'Pop Goes the Weasel' if I'm feeling ambitious. But my favorite" — he lowered his voice — "is 'Mary Had a Little Lamb.'"

I shook my head. "You're messing with me."

"Tempting, but I have a lesson in five minutes." He glanced at his watch. "Make that two."

"Oh." How foolish to have believed he was angling for an invitation to come over. It was another of his little games, nothing more. "Well, have fun."

The corner of his mouth twitched. "I'll try."

Our hands brushed as he passed me Cam's bag. I flinched, which made me want to kick myself — especially since Alex probably hadn't noticed the contact at all.

⁓

Later that evening I was in my room, alternating twenty minutes of algebra with ten of reading. It took longer overall but increased the odds of retaining my sanity. When the phone rang, I leaned back in my chair, rubbing my eyes. For a moment I listened in vain, hoping to hear my name called. Then I decided to go downstairs anyway and make myself a cup of tea.

Jasper was leaning against the side of the refrigerator with the receiver cradled against his face. He spoke in a confidential murmur, as though I had any interest in eavesdropping. After filling the kettle with fresh water, I set it on the stove and turned on the burner.

"Hold on a sec," I heard Jasper say as I rummaged through the tea cupboard. "Mary. It's for you."

I turned to stare at him. "Are you serious?"

He cupped a hand over the receiver. "It's Arden."

There was no time to ask how or when the two of them had come to be on a first-name basis. I was too busy choking on the sudden fear that Arden somehow knew I'd walked home with Alex Ritter.

Jasper waved the phone in my face. "Earth to Mary. Time is money."

I held it to my ear. "Hello?"

"Hey!" said Arden's voice. "Oh my gosh, I am so excited. Not to toot my own horn, but I have seriously outdone myself this time. Hashtag nailed it. Prepare to have your mind blown."

A long silence ensued, during which I waited for her to share the explosive tidings. "I'm ready," I said at last.

"I meant on Friday," Arden explained. "That's when it's going down—the next big event."

"What is it?" For some reason I whispered the question, though Jasper had departed, jumbo bag of white cheddar popcorn in hand.

"I don't want to spoil the surprise. This is just a heads-up so you can start planning your look."

"I need a special outfit?" My mind leaped to the formalwear section at the mall.

"No, no. Just dress to impress."

"You mean literally a dress?"

"Mm, I wouldn't. Think weekend chic. Classy, but comfortable. Something that makes you think, 'Damn, I have it going ON' when you check yourself out."

"Oh. Right." I couldn't actually summon a memory of that feeling, but I knew exactly who to ask for advice.

Dear Diary,

They used to talk about a young woman being "accomplished," which meant she could do all the ladylike things: singing, drawing, dancing, pouring tea. Maybe speak a smattering of pretty foreign words, learned from a governess since girls didn't get a formal education.

Nowadays the list of things you're supposed to master is a lot longer. Be pretty! And smart! And sporty! They call it being well-rounded, but sometimes it feels like they're saying the same thing as in the olden days: Pretend to be perfect in every way!

M.P.M.

CHAPTER 13

On Friday, I dressed in the blouse Anton had sent home via the twins, accompanied by a note explaining that it should be worn with jeans to keep the look young. He'd also drawn a diagram to guide my makeup application, complete with color palette.

The black shirt had a high neckline, but the Respectable Widow effect was offset by semi-sheer lace panels and cap sleeves. When I regarded the results in the mirror, I wasn't sure they quite reached the level described by Arden, so I ran up the stairs to the twins' room for a final consultation.

"Very vintage chic," Addie pronounced, sweeping a section of my unbound hair forward so that it hung in front of my shoulder. "Brings out your chestnut highlights."

Shaking her head, Van set down a bound copy of the script and rose from her bed to brush my hair back the way it had been.

I was too busy savoring the word *chestnut* to care where my hair fell. Perhaps it lacked the poetry of *titian* or *raven,* but it was infinitely better than plain old brown, which had always been my secret dread.

Van heaved a theatrical sigh. "Our little Mary, all grown up. I didn't think it would happen this fast, did you?"

"Mary's her own person. Who among us ever really plumbs the depths of another's heart?" Since Addie had moved on to braiding a small section of my hair, I both heard and felt the tension behind her words, delivered in a series of sharp yanks.

Van came to inspect the results. "I like it. Simple and charming without being too jejune."

Addie humphed. Another time I might have wondered about the discord scenting the air like overripe laundry, but my mind had already leaped ahead to the evening with my friends. With a hasty thanks, I slipped out the door, ready for my next adventure.

෴

When Arden parked the car behind Millville High, my spirits deflated. We were one amid a sea of vehicles gathered for the weekly field hockey match. And while the lights were bright and the percussion section of the school band was pounding out a jaunty rhythm, this was not exactly uncharted territory. Cam's games were a regular feature in my life, which was why I hadn't felt bad about missing this one. I was also acutely conscious of being overdressed.

Arden linked her arm through mine. "Are you excited?"

I summoned a smile. "Yes."

It wasn't really a lie; I was excited to be there with my friends. That would be different from sitting with my family, trying to keep my mother from cursing too loudly when she didn't like the officiating. "I guess you must have had 'sporting event' on your list?"

"Something like that." Her mouth curved in a distinctly Cheshire cat fashion.

Lydia gave a skeptical huff. "I hope we're not about to walk into something weird." She considered Arden for a moment. "You know flash mobs are not a thing anymore, right?"

Arden merely shrugged. The rest of us hurried to keep up as she pranced through the gate and past the concession stand, not slowing until we reached the bleachers. Pulling me to a halt, she surveyed my appearance.

"Shake out your hair," she instructed. "Okay. Now look over there."

I turned, doing my best to make the movement appear natural. The crowd was a patchwork of half-familiar faces, blurring into a general impression of Millville High students. I was beginning to worry I'd missed Arden's big surprise when an anomaly caught my eye.

It was the guy I'd noticed at the mall; the well-groomed, disapproving one. He appeared even more out of place in this context, where no one else had seen fit to polish their shoes. I felt a lot better about my own outfit.

"Ta-da!" Arden hummed in my ear. "Ask and you shall receive!"

Of the many questions buzzing around my brain, I chose to pose the most baffling. "How did you find him?"

"His host dad plays racquetball with my uncle," she said, as if that explained everything. "Will Arnheim, German exchange student at Jefferson High — which is why his shoes are so extra. He's only going to be here one semester, so we better hurry." Placing a hand at the small of my back, she shoved me forward.

"Wait, what are we doing?" I asked in an urgent whisper, digging in my heels.

"Going to talk to him. Obviously."

I stole another glance in his direction. He really did look the part, mysterious and dashing in his dark sweater and sleek haircut. It was a level of elegance seldom witnessed at Millville High, where being sharply dressed meant tying both your shoes. I could easily picture him brooding in the corner of a drawing room while listening to classical music, or whatever was on NPR at the time. Was this the moment I'd read about so often, when two strangers caught sight of each other across a crowded ballroom? The connection would be instantaneous, drawing us together like magnets — as soon as he put down his phone.

"Ready," I said.

Arden snapped her fingers at Lydia and Terry, signaling them to fall in behind us. My heart hammered as we closed the distance to where Mystery Guy — *Will*, I reminded myself — was sitting. From a chance sighting at the mall to a meaningful encounter on the sidelines of a field hockey match, the hand of destiny seemed to be nudging us together. With a little help from Arden, who cleared her throat before addressing the young man who had yet to acknowledge our presence.

"Hey," she said brightly, dropping onto the bleacher at his side. "Will, right? How's it going?"

At last his pale, sharply defined chin lifted. While waiting for him to notice me, I attempted a coquettish pose, glancing down through my lashes without being too obvious about it. His piercing hazel eyes rose. They moved across my face—

And kept going, until they landed on Terry. The double-take, that sudden inhalation of surprise and interest, his newly intent stare: it all happened exactly as I'd imagined. Unfortunately, it wasn't happening to *me*. While Terry tried to cringe her way to invisibility, Arden's surreptitious hand movement urged me to take up a position on Will's other side.

"It's so great you're having a totally American experience," she said to Will, who sat ramrod straight between us. "*Friday Night Lights*."

"Except it's supposed to be football, not field hockey," Lydia pointed out.

"The school board was worried about traumatic brain injury," I volunteered, showing off a heretofore undiscovered knack for banter. Let's talk more about concussions!

"Where are my manners?" Arden smacked herself on the forehead. "We haven't even introduced ourselves." She left my name for last, which might have been a reasonably subtle tactic if she hadn't followed it up by adding, "Mary actually comes from a family of geniuses. Both her parents are professors at the college, and she knows *all* about Millville, if you ever need a guide to the local attractions."

His eyes flicked to Terry at the word *attractions*. Leaning past me, he repeated her last name in a caressing tone. "*Larios.*" This was followed by a stream of rapid-fire Spanish, of which I caught the obvious *you speak Spanish?* and Terry's reluctant *of course.* As for the rest, I suspected it was along the lines of *you walk in beauty like the night,* because Terry blushed and looked away.

"So, Will," Arden cut in. "Do you have any hobbies?"

He frowned at her.

"Sports? Clubs? Extracurriculars?"

"I like to ride my bike."

Arden looked hopefully at me; I shook my head. No spandex shorts for me. When Will started to speak again, she brightened, clearly encouraged to see him taking an active role in the conversation.

"This country has no respect for cyclists," he said in his clipped accent. "Your bike lanes are a disgrace."

"Interesting." Arden propped her chin on her hand. "You must have a unique perspective. What are some of the things you like?"

"Some of the people are charming," he said, with another betraying glance at Terry.

Arden bit her lip; I could tell she was worried on my behalf. I also knew she was too much of an optimist to give up on her vision of how this evening was supposed to unfold without a fight. My feelings were more fatalistic. The dream of romance was like a butterfly that had been savagely pinned to a specimen board. If Terry and Will were meant for each other, far be it from me to stand in their way.

"You don't paint your face like some girls," Will murmured approvingly to Terry. "Why do they do that in this country?"

Terry shook her head, unable (or unwilling) to answer. Arden widened her eyes at me, urging me to seize the opening.

"At least it's not lead-based, like they used to wear in the eighteenth century." I laughed nervously. "People aren't rotting their faces off."

Although Terry appeared intrigued by this tidbit, Will's lip curled in disgust.

On the field, the cheer team began shouting out a chant. The fans clapped in time, stomping the metal bleachers until the whole stadium shook.

Will winced. "So much yelling."

Arden laughed as though he'd made a joke. "That's kind of their job. You want me to teach you the words? You can impress all your friends at home."

"We don't do this where I'm from." He sniffed in distaste. "Even the women are loud here." His eyes strayed to Terry. "Most of them."

"I need candy," Lydia announced, jumping to her feet. "Anybody want anything?"

"Americans and their sweets," Will said, with a scornful huff. "You eat like babies."

"Nom nom nom," Lydia deadpanned. "Coming, Mary?"

I didn't need to be asked twice.

❧

"No offense, but I'm pretty sure I hate him," she said when we were out of earshot. Instead of continuing on to the snack bar, Lydia led the way up the stairs into the next rank of bleachers.

"I thought you wanted candy."

She shook her head. "You know how Arden gets. She was just going to keep beating that dead horse."

We climbed until we were near the top of the stands. Lydia edged into a mostly empty row, leaving plenty of space on all sides. I exhaled, feeling the tension of the last several minutes subside. From the corner of my eye I noticed Lydia checking out my purse, resting on the aluminum bleacher beside me.

"No book?" she asked.

I shook my head; I'd fallen out of the habit of carrying one with me. These days I was most often with my friends, and not in need of other entertainment.

Lydia pulled a silver-and-pink tube from her own bag, coating her lips in a frosty peach gloss that perfectly matched the color of her sweatshirt. "I read too, you know." She cleared her throat. "Not as much as you, obviously."

Despite the stiffness with which she relayed this information, I felt a rush of delight. "What kind of books?"

"It's not your type of stuff. That's why I mostly read on my phone, so no one can make fun of the covers."

In my head, I tried on various possibilities. Lydia the secret romance reader. Lydia the lover of spy novels. Legal thrillers seemed the obvious possibility, given her professional ambitions . . .

"I like fantasy." The words were barely above a whisper. Steeling herself, she added, "Preferably epic."

I confined my surprise to a few rapid blinks. "That's cool. There's a class on Literature of the Fantastic I want to take when I go to college."

"You'll go here?" She nodded in the direction of the Mill-ville College campus.

"Probably. Free tuition."

"That's no joke," she agreed, more confident now that we were discussing pragmatic concerns.

A whistle blew, and a player from the bench took the place of someone on the field.

"Do you have a favorite?" I asked.

She kept her eyes averted. "I have a thing for dragons."

Before I could muster a response — something like, *I get it, dragons are tough but also noble, like you* — a tall figure loomed into view.

"Now this one looks interesting," Lydia murmured.

I blinked up at the new arrival. "Pittaya?"

He gestured at the bench, mutely requesting permission to sit. Lydia looked from me to him and back again, eyebrows at the alert.

"Lydia, this is Pittaya. We went to school together. Before."

"Scoundrel?" she asked, barely moving her lips.

"Not as such," I whispered back. "But he was there that day."

Recognition flickered in her eyes. "Becky with the good hair. The one who —"

"Ditched me, yes." It never got more fun to admit that.

Once I'd told Terry about the Shunning, it seemed weird to keep it from Arden and Lydia, which was how Anjuli had ended up on our list as a Becky Sharp, the callous social climber from *Vanity Fair*. It wasn't a perfect fit; I may have exaggerated Anjuli's culpability for dramatic effect. I was also anxious to gloss over the part where she found me boring and replaceable.

Lydia looked Pittaya up and down. She was small and fair, yet deeply menacing, like an Easter egg with fangs. "You have some nerve showing your face around here."

I wanted to tell her she was barking up the wrong tree. Pittaya wasn't going to explain himself. He was a pillar of silence, staring at his hands as though they were chess pieces and he needed to contemplate the next move—

"I apologize."

My eyes widened. I'd forgotten how deep his voice was.

"I'm not good with conflict," he continued. "Also, you had the position of strength."

"What are you talking about?" My memory of that day mostly involved cowering.

"You like people, and they like you." He nodded at Lydia. "But Anjuli—"

"Is a cold-hearted snake," Lydia supplied. She gave Pittaya another once-over. "That doesn't let you off the hook. You should've had Mary's back."

I bit my lip to keep from grinning like a fool. It was thrilling to have Lydia on my side. It also made me want to tear up a little.

Pittaya nodded solemnly. "I should have left with you. Even if it made things worse with Anjuli."

"What do you mean?" Lydia sounded dubious.

He swallowed, obviously uncomfortable. I'd never seen Pittaya squirm before.

"Because Anjuli has a crush on you," I said as realization struck. "If you'd stuck up for me she would have really gone berserk."

He lowered his head in acknowledgment. "Not that I think of you that way."

"Likewise," I assured him, my mind already flying in another direction. Was this the real cause of the falling out with Anjuli: Not a desperate urge to make pretentious movies, but the desire to eliminate a supposed rival? It was almost flattering to think she considered me a threat in that way, until I remembered the unmistakable flavor of her annoyance. The sighing and seething, like every word out of my mouth grated on her nerves. My charms obviously weren't *that* potent.

"I stopped speaking to her," Pittaya informed us. "After."

My first thought was, *Does she know you're giving her the silent treatment?*

Lydia looked grudgingly impressed. She pulled five dollars from her wallet and held it out to me. "Mary, would you do me a solid and get me a candy bar? Hook yourself up too."

I hesitated. "For real this time?"

"Yeah." Her eyes were locked on Pittaya. "I'm going to have a little talk with your friend."

After a brief consultation with my conscience, I decided Pittaya could hold his own.

We both could.

Dear Diary,

I love the moment in a story when the love interest first appears on the scene. The heroine doesn't always like him right away, but there's still a zing that makes you sit up and think, *Aha! This guy is going to be important.*

If the narrator spends a lot of time talking about his clothes, or describing his facial features in excruciating detail, that's usually a sign you're looking at the hero.

M.P.M.

CHAPTER 14

Standing at the back of the serpentine line for the snack bar, I rose onto my toes in an effort to see the menu.

"I see you found someone who meets your standards," said Alex Ritter's voice.

Turning as well as I was able in such close confines, I gave him a mystified look. "What are you talking about?"

"The guy who looks constipated." When I continued to look at him blankly he added, "Sitting next to your friend."

"Pittaya?"

A crease appeared between his brows, which were several shades darker than his hair. "I thought his name was Will."

"Ohhh. Him."

"Yes, him." His eyebrows lifted in challenge. "Apparently he got the green light."

"What?"

Alex blew out a breath, as if my slowness both amused and frustrated him. "He's not too *friendly* for her?"

My throat had gone dry. "They're just hanging out."

"Pull the wool over your own eyes, Mary Porter-Malcolm." He paused, gaze roaming over my face. I saw him notice the black shirt, studying it with the same focused attention he was devoting to every detail of my appearance. Maybe this was his secret weapon, beyond the way he smelled, or the perfect hair, or how his shirts brought out the blue of his eyes: he made you feel *compelling*.

"I'm surprised they didn't give you all *M* names," he murmured. "It really trips off the tongue."

"My family isn't big on alliteration." His eyes narrowed as I spoke. "Repeated consonant sounds—"

"I know what it is. I was wondering about the look on your face."

I glanced away. "It's a sensitive subject."

"Alliteration?"

"No."

"Your family?"

"No! My *name*."

"But—"

"I don't want to talk about it."

"Okay." He held up both hands in surrender. The line shuffled forward a few paces.

"Rebecca Rowena Randall."

Alex looked questioningly at me.

"*That's* a good name, if you want to get alliterative. She was a character in a book named after characters from a different book."

He whistled. "That's much better than my idea."

Don't ask; it's what he wants you to do. I held out for a full five seconds. "What was your idea?"

"Mary Christmas. It's so cheerful."

I maintained a frosty silence.

"That Will guy probably doesn't make jokes," he continued, as though thinking aloud. "Was that the attraction?"

"Actually, he can make jokes in *several* languages."

"He could, but does he? I'm going to go out on a limb and guess *nein*."

From where we were standing it was just possible to glimpse the less than boisterous grouping of Will, Terry, and Arden. As we watched, he angled his phone above himself and Terry. She started to smile, but a glance at Will's pained expression nipped that in the bud.

"Does he think they're in a perfume commercial?" Alex whispered, bending close to my ear.

"He's probably very artistic," I retorted. "Look at how he dresses, and his . . . deportment."

"Yeah. You could take a guy like that anywhere. Libraries. The opera. Funerals."

"You're just—" I bit back the word *jealous*. That hit a little too close to home, though I felt I'd behaved with admirable magnanimity in ceding the field to Terry.

"Please." He swept a hand through the air. "Enlighten me."

"He's a better match for her, okay? I'm sorry if that wounds your ego."

Alex glanced across the bleachers. "You think those two make a good couple?"

"There's potential." At the very least they'd look good in stark black-and-white photos.

He shook his head. "No way."

"Excuse me if I question your objectivity." That was easier than asking myself how I'd ended up on this side of an increasingly ridiculous argument.

"Suit yourself." He shrugged as if it didn't matter to him. "But when it all falls apart, remember I called it first. No spark."

I crossed my arms, looking away. "We'll see."

"Zero chemistry," he murmured, standing near enough that my fingers would have brushed his shirt if I hadn't been clenching them so tightly. "If she was interested in him, she wouldn't keep looking over here."

I darted a glance at Terry, but she was listening to Will, who had unbent sufficiently to use hand gestures as he spoke.

"Maybe she wants me to get her some candy."

"Are you sure that's all it is?"

"As opposed to what?" It sounded like he thought Terry was looking at *him*.

His eyes glinted in an extremely disreputable fashion. "The two of you might be, you know —"

It was the eyebrow twitch that tipped me off. "Having a torrid affair involving lots of pillow fights in our skimpy pajamas?"

"I was going to say, 'plotting something,' but I like your version better. What kind of jammies are we talking about? Those little short sets or a nightie?"

"You're incorrigible. Has anyone ever told you that?"

"I can honestly say you're the first, *Mary*." It was a testament to his Vronsky-ish ways that he made even my name sound suggestive. He could probably give a word like *mucilage* a saucy twist.

"Answer me this," I said with as much dignity as possible. "Would you tell your best friend to date you?"

"Absolutely not. Jake's a pig. I don't think he even knows where his toothbrush is. There's no way I'm letting that tongue in my mouth."

I closed my eyes. "You know what I mean. How about your sister? And obviously not the literal you, because that would be incest, but someone *like* you."

"Which sister? I have three."

My eyes flew open. "You—" I swallowed the urge to compare notes or ask if by chance he had an annoying little brother too. "It's a hypothetical question."

He hit me with the slow blink. "Don't knock it until you've tried it."

Whatever riposte I might have made fell by the wayside when the boy in front of me moved and a harried parent volunteer said, "What can I get you?"

I rattled off the order. After a momentary hesitation, I turned to Alex. "Do you want anything?" He'd been standing in line a long time, ostensibly for a reason other than needling me.

"I hope you don't expect something at the end of the night just because you bought me Skittles."

"*Skittles?*"

"Are you mocking my taste in candy?"

155

I shook my head; what could you say to someone so lost to all reason?

The woman behind the counter set a bag of Skittles next to the candy bars. "Is that it?"

Alex squinted at the menu, pretending to consider.

"He's fine," I told her, handing over the money.

"Oh, I know, honey." She slid the change to me with a wink.

"See how you are?" I hissed when we'd edged away from the concession stand.

His expression was all innocence. "What did I do?"

"Maybe it's unconscious. A reflex." I'd been speaking mostly to myself, but Alex looked intrigued — not surprising, given that he was the subject of my ruminations.

"What is?"

"The way you act." I waved a candy bar at him. "Those looks you're always giving people and the hair—"

His hand flew to his head. "What's wrong with my hair?"

"You can't pretend you wake up looking like that. How long does it take you to style yourself every morning?" His mouth opened; I pointed at him to show I wasn't finished. "And the way you smiled at that lady, who by the way is someone's *mom*—"

"I was thanking her."

"You were giving her heart palpitations."

"Really?" Alex grinned. "How do you figure?"

He wanted me to admit that I'd been affected too, but I had no intention of revealing any such thing. It was bad enough I could feel myself blushing. My eyes cast about for an escape.

The band kicked into an up-tempo number, signaling the end of the first quarter.

"There's my sister," I said, as though I'd been looking for her all along. Hurrying to the low chain-link fence bordering the playing field, I waved at Cam, who was chugging from a water bottle. Alex didn't follow, nor did I look back, though the prickling between my shoulder blades suggested he was still watching.

"How's it going?" I asked her, trying to sound normal and winding up closer to *crazed fan*.

Cam swiped her forearm across her sweaty forehead. "We're winning," she said dryly.

I nodded, racking my brain for a more informed remark about a match I'd barely watched. Cam's almost-smile faded.

"I need to go," she said abruptly. Turning on her heel, she marched over to the coach, saying something I couldn't hear.

From the corner of my eye, I spotted a tall figure staring in the same direction. A quick glance led to another, and then a third, as a vague sense of *he looks familiar* shifted to *Oh! It's that brawny guy*. The one I'd noticed lurking near Cam at the party. It was the breadth of the shoulders that gave him away. Well, that and—

"I didn't know you were into man buns," Lydia whispered, sidling up next to me. She pointed to the back of her head, lest I mistake the kind of buns she meant.

"What?"

She held up both hands, palms out. "No judgment. I'm sure he's more fun than what's-his-name—Herr Skeletor."

"I think we should go back there."

Lydia turned so that we were both looking at the scene on the bleachers. Will was regaling Terry with what appeared to be a long and involved story. Arden was absorbed in her phone.

"Why?" Lydia asked, pulling out her own phone. "I could just text her, tell her where to meet us."

"They might need our support. And it's possible he's not as bad as he seems. Some people get nervous in unfamiliar settings." All of these were plausible excuses, and much better than confessing my desire to prove Alex Ritter wrong.

"Fine," Lydia sighed. I handed her a Snickers, to soften the blow.

As we approached, Will was holding forth about American literature, dropping names and titles as if scattering seeds on virgin soil. From what I could tell, his tastes ran mostly to stories of neurotic white guys lamenting their self-inflicted tragedies while the women and people of color dealt with real problems somewhere off stage.

It never would have worked, I thought, bidding adieu to the last trace of regret at being overlooked in favor of a more beautiful friend. I held my M&M's out to Terry, so she'd know there weren't any hard feelings.

"You eat these?" Will's tone would have made more sense if Terry had started nibbling on her toenails. Lydia's eyes narrowed.

"You guys!" Arden jumped in. "What a coincidence! We were just talking about books." Her smile was strained. "Will was, anyway."

"Mary's a serious reader," Terry said. I got the feeling both she and Arden had been trying to interject for some time.

Will glanced at Lydia, sniffing with amusement. "What, the vampire books?"

"I'm Lydia." She bared her teeth. "That's Mary."

He appeared to find this a trifling distinction. "You are such a puritanical culture. Obsessed with sex, but too much like children to call it that, no, it has to be teeth instead."

"Holy cow," I said, staring at him.

His lips curved patronizingly. "You never realized what it means when the fangs penetrate and the girl bleeds? Sorry to melt your bubble."

"Actually, that's pretty basic. I mean, gothic literature has been around for centuries." If someone was going to sneer at me, they could at least have the decency to scrape up something better than bargain-basement symbolism.

"Excuse me, but I am German. I think I know more about what is gothic than —" He gestured mutely at me.

"Than what, a girl?"

He shrugged, as if to say, *Close enough.*

How had I ever found him handsome? Features I'd considered sculpted now struck me as pinched. "'You're the sort who can't know anyone intimately, least of all a woman,'" I quoted. "That's from *A Room with a View*. Maybe you've heard of it?"

He rolled his eyes. "I don't watch your teenager beach house reality shows."

"It's a novel," I corrected. "By the great English writer E. M. Forster."

"The British!" He made a sound of disgust at the back of his throat. "So repressive, with their manners and their tea-cups. I prefer something real, not this, 'Oh, I must wave my handkerchief.'"

I heard a roaring in my ears. Had he just dismissed the entire tradition of English literature? Lydia rubbed her hands together. "Go ahead, Mary. Don't hold back."

"I think it's time for us to go," I said in my most dignified manner.

"Yes, okay," he snorted, "keep hiding in your Hollywood chewing gum world, instead of opening your eyes to reality."

"Right," said Arden, standing up. "That's all the reality I can handle. Ready, Terry?"

Will frowned at Terry. "You're leaving with *them*?"

"I—yes," she said. "I'm going with my friends."

Crossing his legs, he angled his body away from us. We were officially beneath his notice.

It was much less painful to be snubbed as part of a group, I reflected as we made our escape. It also helped to know that the person doing the disdaining was a total prig, as opposed to a friend you'd had since childhood.

Not that I aspired to become a connoisseur of such things.

Dear Diary,

The purpose of the Scoundrel List isn't to point out the obvious villains: guys who steal your inheritance or lock you in a tower or invite their mistress to move into the guest room. It's about finding the ones who conceal their treachery behind a smiling façade. That's the kind of nefariousness you have to watch out for.

M.P.M.

CHAPTER 15

As the flies and mosquitoes had vanished with the coming of cooler weather, forgotten and unmourned, so too did the memory of Mall Guy dwindle in the following weeks. There were plenty of distractions: homework, helping the twins with play prep, trying to keep track of Arden's many and varied afterschool commitments. The only lingering sting was my unspoken worry that the incident reflected poorly on my judgment. Fortunately my friends were too generous for recriminations, placing the blame squarely on Will (whom we did not mention by name).

One afternoon when even Arden had no extracurricular obligations, the four of us met in the parking lot after the final bell for another excursion. All I knew about the agenda was that it involved food, followed by what Arden termed *housekeeping*. Which was almost certainly code for something far more enticing.

"I'm feeling salty," Arden announced as she fastened her seat belt.

"Also the title of my memoir." Lydia tapped out a rimshot on the dashboard.

We drove to the less picturesque part of town, where our destination proved to be McDonald's. I could practically hear my mother's squawk of horror.

Arden slowed the car to a crawl as she negotiated the narrow lane between parked cars. "It's packed." Her shoulders had hiked until they nearly bracketed her ears.

"The good McDonald's is always crowded." Lydia pointed through the windshield. "What about over there?"

"Are you kidding? I'd have to *parallel park*."

"I don't see anything else," Terry murmured as we rounded the building.

A second later, Arden stepped on the brake. "Oh no."

"What?" Lydia asked.

"That's Aaron Masterson's car."

Lydia leaned forward in her seat to inspect the offending vehicle. "Crap."

He was on the Scoundrel List as a card-carrying Willoughby, the faithless paramour from *Sense and Sensibility* who forsakes Marianne for being poor, then gets maudlin about how she was the perfect woman once she finds someone better to marry. Aaron's version was showing up whenever his ex-boyfriend (whom he had dumped) went out with a new guy. Apparently he thought it was romantic to stare longingly at the person whose heart he had broken, when in fact he was being a fickle jerk.

"I told Thomas I would be extremely disappointed if he got

back together with him," Lydia said, trying to peer through the windows of the restaurant.

"She did," Arden confirmed. "It was intense. I was shaking in my boots."

Lydia gave a modest shrug. "I do what I can."

"Okay, but we can't go in there now. He's even worse if there's an audience." Arden gripped the steering wheel with both hands.

Terry nodded. "A lot of sociopaths have an exhibitionist streak."

"What's option B?" Lydia half turned in her seat, directing the question to all three of us.

Arden lowered the volume on the stereo. "It can't be pancakes. That's late-night food." Not for the first time, I was amazed by the arcane knowledge my friends possessed.

Seconds ticked past. When it appeared no one else was going to speak up, I cleared my throat.

"I know a place." But was it the right kind of place? I tried to think of a way to describe it that wouldn't raise their hopes too high. "They have angled parking."

"Works for me," said Arden, flicking on her blinker.

༄

"Freaky place for a café," Lydia observed as we descended the stairs to Tome Raider—or, as it was known in my family, Shaggy Doug's.

"When Doug and Noreen split up this was all he could afford," I explained. "He bases all his baked goods on famous children's books."

Terry tried to peer through the dingy glass of the front door. "Like what?"

"It's different every day. I'm not big on the Turkish delight, like the White Witch gives Edmund in the Chronicles of Narnia, but everything else I've tasted is great." Pulling the door open, I ushered them inside.

We settled at a small wrought-iron table in the corner, a relic from someone's garden. The only other furniture was a sagging couch the color of Dijon mustard, currently occupied by Cadbury, Doug's tabby cat.

"Would you like to see a menu?" asked Doug, who had crept from behind the nearest bookshelf so stealthily we all jumped at the sound of his voice. His thinning hair was pulled into a straggly ponytail. Unlike the top of his head, the rest of Doug's body was thickly furred; hence the nickname.

When I nodded yes to the menu question he blinked owlishly at me. "Hello — not one of the twins."

"Mary," Lydia prompted.

Doug snapped his fingers. "Right. I knew you weren't Cam."

That was me: the *other* Porter-Malcolm daughter. Old what's-her-name. I forced a smile as he set down a single sheet of lined paper, edge still ruffled where it had been torn from a spiral notebook. His cursive was surprisingly neat, like that of an elementary school teacher.

"The Wonderland Sampler," Arden read aloud. "What's that?"

"A selection of *eat me* cakes and *drink me* elixirs in cute little vials." He held his fingers and thumb a few inches apart, indicating the size. "All the colorings are natural. Fruit concentrates."

Natural or not, it was clear from Terry's expression that she had no intention of drinking anything served in a vial, especially not in the subterranean lair of a scruffy middle-aged man.

"What's the scone of the day?" I asked, glancing at the coppery streaks of spice decorating his apron.

"I'm experimenting with something new for the holidays." He turned pink with excitement. "I call them Tiny Tims."

"Because they have . . . ?" I waited for him to fill in the blank, hoping the answer wasn't *goose,* or worse, *limping little boys.*

Doug lowered his voice to a confidential whisper. "Plum pudding."

"Yes," said Terry, with uncharacteristic decisiveness. "That."

"Fantastic!" Doug clasped his hands together, looking so ecstatic I thought he might burst out with a *God bless us every one!* He cleared his throat. "It'll take a few minutes. I'll bring you some juice boxes while you wait."

"Did he say juice boxes?" Lydia asked when he was gone.

"He can't serve any hot drinks," I explained. "Or brown ones. That's Noreen's domain." She had been careful to close the chocolate milk loophole.

After Doug dropped off the juice, we busied ourselves unwrapping straws and piercing foil. I was acutely conscious of the tomb-like atmosphere, especially compared to the hue and cry we would have encountered at McDonald's. "It's a lot less bustling here," I said, tacitly apologizing.

"No, this is different," Arden agreed, surveying the haphazard decor.

"More of a secret hideout," Lydia suggested.

"In the olden days, ladies used to reserve a separate parlor at an inn, because it wasn't proper to hang out at the bar." I sipped my grape juice, afraid to make eye contact lest I surprise one of my companions in a look of extreme disinterest.

"I like that." Arden patted me on the arm. "We can come here when we need peace and quiet. Lady time."

I smiled in relief. "Far from the madding crowd."

She nodded, setting down her juice box. "It's actually good we have privacy. We can talk about something serious."

The words were freighted with portent. Judging from their wary expressions, neither Lydia nor Terry had any clue what she was hinting at either.

A rattling sound erupted from the kitchen, followed closely by Doug. "Enjoy," he said, setting down the scones. A sweet, gingerbready aroma wafted from the plate. Terry's eyes closed in bliss.

When he'd shuffled back into the kitchen, Lydia looked expectantly at Arden. "Spill."

"As I'm sure you've all noticed," Arden began, chasing her mouthful of scone with a sip of juice, "the semester is flying by. Halloween is almost here, and then bam! Everything happens. Papers! Exams! Holiday shopping! Special events!" She brushed her hands off before pulling out her phone. "We've made a lot of great progress, don't get me wrong." Her index finger made a blur of the Scoundrel Survival Guide, scrolling past artsy photographs overlaid with dire warnings about male perfidy.

"The Messed-Up Ex. Drowning Guy. Closet Misogynist. Becky the Back-Stabber," Lydia recited, counting them off on her fingers. "And Greedy Guts, who only wanted the big payout, except not in money."

"From *Washington Square*," I reminded her. "Where he dumps the heroine when he can't get her inheritance." In our real-life version, the currency in question had been a lot more carnal, to put it delicately. It was almost a direct reversal of the old rules of conduct, under which a woman had to remain virginal or risk being cast out of society. Nowadays young women were apparently supposed to count being a sexual dynamo among their accomplishments—a far riskier avocation than embroidery or playing the harp.

From damned if you do to damned if you don't: the story of women's lives.

Lydia nodded. "And the OG, Alex Ritter."

"Vronsky, you mean." It seemed important to make that distinction.

"There's the one who drinks arsenic," Terry added. Before I could point out that it wasn't that part of the story that applied to our list, Arden jumped in.

"Makenna Brown, also known as the Worst." She tapped her bottom lip. "What was her book name?"

"Madame Bovary. A person who messes up people's lives for entertainment."

"You said she had a condition?" Terry looked questioningly at me.

"Ennui. It's like boredom, except you think it makes you interesting."

"And let's not forget Sissy Whatever," Lydia said. "The snobby one."

"Cecil Vyse. From *A Room with a View*." That was how we'd categorized Will the Exchange Student: as the full-of-himself fiancé who has no interest in actually knowing a person as long as she makes an attractive accessory.

"It's a good list." Arden smiled, but we all heard the note of doubt.

"But what?" Lydia prompted.

Arden took a bite of scone, chewing thoughtfully. "As much as I love what we've done so far, I don't think we can keep going like this."

I felt a chill of dread. Were they sick of hearing about books?

She flipped her phone over. "What if we're looking at it from the wrong angle?"

Terry covered her full mouth with one hand. "Like when someone with a fresh pair of eyes comes into the incident room, and they spot connections that break the investigation wide open."

"Mmm," said Arden. "Like that, but less murdery. I'm saying maybe we should try thinking positive for a change."

"Is this where you make us say our affirmations?" Lydia mimed stabbing herself in the eye.

Arden shook her head. "I'm *saying* it's time to be proactive. Instead of ruling people out one by one, we could actively search for someone *good*. Like, who are the best guys you've ever read about, Mary?"

Caught off guard, my mind jumped to the book I'd been reading the night before. "Well, there was a guy who only stole the cursed jewel his betrothed had been given for her birthday because he was under hypnosis. Otherwise he was pretty upstanding. *Way* better than the rival for her affections, because the embezzling cousin really was after her money."

Lydia held up a hand. "His cousin or hers?"

"Hers."

She turned to Arden. "So we should be looking for someone who isn't a blood relative? 'No incest' seems like kind of a low bar."

"I'm sure Mary has lots of other examples." Arden smiled encouragingly at me. "Maybe someone in real life, like from her classes, who seems like hero material?"

"Um," I began. Had they forgotten I was the one who'd found Mall Guy intriguing?

"What about Pittaya?" Lydia asked.

I blinked at her. In my mind, he was part of the past, divided by an invisible line from my new life. At the same time, his apology had been heartfelt, and I appreciated the bravery it had taken to speak up. Maybe he would be an okay suitor for one of my friends. The obvious choice was Terry, since they shared a tendency toward ruminative silence.

Arden looked sharply at Lydia. "Who's that? What did I miss? You know this person?"

"I know a lot of people." Lydia broke off a piece of scone and popped it into her mouth.

"Why didn't you say something? I can get his class schedule, and we'll arrange to accidentally run into him a few times, invite him out for a coffee, level up to dinner and a movie—"

Lydia made a T with her hands. "You need to cease and desist, okay? When did this go from hanging out and showing Mary a good time to a freaky obsession with our love lives? Just because you and Miles are going through something—"

"No, we're not." Arden's face flushed. "I'm fine with his new date partner." She slurped angrily from her straw, squeezing the juice box until it crumpled.

Lydia grabbed Arden by the wrist. "His what?"

"He has a new debate partner," Arden answered with a trace of impatience. "You know that. Angelica from Connecticut." She made air quotes around the last word, as if the existence of such a place was pure conjecture.

"You said *date* partner," Terry pointed out.

"Oh." Arden pressed her lips together. "I meant debate. Obviously. She's just a girl who's probably a genius and likes the exact same things as Miles and has an exotic East Coast vibe." She gave a brittle laugh. "And wears a private school uniform. Why should I worry?"

Lydia leaned forward, resting her elbows on the table. "Listen, Miles is great, and I say that as someone who has zero interest in boning her best friend's boyfriend. But he's not exactly a ladies' man."

Arden opened her mouth to protest, but Lydia shook her head. "Let me finish. There's no way Miles is cheating on you, because that would mean he's scum, and then I would have to take him out, and no matter how brilliantly I represented myself in court there's always a chance it wouldn't go my way. Therefore, it's not happening. That's just logic."

I wasn't sure whether she was referring to Miles' hypothetical philandering or the legal ramifications of revenge killing but deemed it best to nod.

"I know." Arden swiped at the end of her nose. "Everything is perfectly fine."

"Good." Lydia sat back. "Then we can all relax and stop trying to force people to couple up whether they want to or not."

Terry gave an emphatic nod of agreement.

Arden sighed. "That throws a rock in front of my skateboard."

"Why?" asked Lydia.

"Because I'm building to something, okay?" Arden traced a mint-green fingernail across the uneven surface of the table. "This is all part of a bigger plan."

Terry looked to me for enlightenment, but I could only shrug.

Lydia's brow furrowed. "What are you talking about? Are we doing some weird fix-yourself challenge we don't even know about? Because I don't get how we went from showing Mary around and calling out scoundrels to *The Bachelor, Millville High Island*."

Arden tipped her head back, eyes squeezing shut. "*Winter Formal*. Okay? Everything is supposed to lead up to the big dance, a.k.a. the perfect way to cap off Mary's season. And for that you need certain things, like dates, and fancy dresses, and pretty feet!"

"Feet?" Terry whispered.

"Pedicures. That was next on my list." Arden blew out a frustrated breath. "So much for the big reveal."

"Like a ball," I said, trying to picture it.

Lydia fake-coughed.

"It's as close as we're going to get around here," Arden shot back. "And besides, even if it's just in the gym, going to a dance is still an iconic high-school experience."

"Same in the olden days," I agreed.

"Okay, but you don't technically need a date to go to the dance," Lydia said, in a more conciliatory tone.

"I know that." Arden shifted in her chair. "I just thought Mary might want to do the whole thing. Get dressed up, wear a corsage, take lots of pictures —"

"Awkward slow dancing," Lydia suggested.

The corner of Arden's mouth twitched. "Exactly. A night to remember."

Lydia sat back sharply. "Tell me that's not the theme."

"No." Arden rolled her eyes. "They used that for prom last year. They're not going to repeat the same thing. That would be sad."

"Sadder," Lydia said under her breath.

"What is the theme?" Terry asked.

"The Cold War. Since it's *Winter* Formal."

Lydia stared at her, wide-eyed.

"Ha! Got you." Arden patted herself on the back.

"That would actually be kind of cool though," Terry said. "Kind of grim and eighties."

"They could decorate the gym like the Berlin Wall," Lydia suggested.

"What's the real theme?" My question was partly intended to keep Arden from having an aneurysm, but I was also keen to know.

"Winter in Paris. Isn't that romantic?"

"Do I have to wear a beret?" Lydia asked.

"Of course not." Arden shook her juice box, frowning at its emptiness. She reached for a scone instead, ripping off the tip. "You don't have to carry a baguette around either. Though I'm pushing for macarons on the refreshment table."

Lydia grabbed the remainder of Arden's scone. "So the only accessory I need is a date?"

"Ideally." Arden darted a glance at Lydia's face, as though hardly daring to believe she'd given in so easily. "It doesn't have to be your soulmate or anything, just someone you can have fun with for a couple of hours."

"And it doesn't matter how or where we find them," Lydia pressed.

The *yes* was already forming on Arden's lips when she hesitated. "Are you talking about a *Pretty Woman* thing?"

It was Lydia's turn to stare in consternation. "No, I'm not planning to *pay* someone to be my date. Which, not even speaking of the legal issues, why would you assume I need an escort service?"

"I don't. I'm trying to figure out where your brain is on this." She tapped the side of her head.

"I'm just saying it's getting a little Cinderella up in here. Someday my prince will come." Lydia stuck out her tongue.

Arden's eyes widened in understanding. "I don't care whether you go with a prince or a princess or whatever. I'm operating with the information I have, okay? I saw how Mary was checking out Mall Guy, and then Terry almost went out with you-know-who, and now you're talking about this other person—"

"Pittaya," I supplied.

"Who is a boy." Arden held out a hand to me for confirmation and I nodded, thinking about how she'd been observing us all along, figuring out what we liked and trying to make it happen. Lydia and Terry noticed things too, in their crime-spotting way, and I'd always considered myself a student of human nature. For a moment, the connection among the four of us felt like a tangible thing, an invisible cord tying us together. Maybe we were destined to meet.

"Unless there's something you want to tell me?" Arden directed the question to the table at large. "Personal preferences, stuff I can work with?"

Terry and I shook our heads in unison. *Nothing to see here!*

Lydia made a slashing motion with the side of her hand. "A

human, with a pulse. Or a really top-shelf AI. You can put that on my profile."

"And no criminal record," Terry added.

"Right." Arden held out a hand to me, eyes shining with confidence. "And Mary will make sure they're not *relationship* criminals. It's basically a foolproof plan."

My stomach somersaulted, and not from eating too many scones.

Dear Diary,

There are a lot of things I wonder about food in books. What does ratafia taste like? Or blancmange? How about mutton, which I imagine being a little like corned beef? As for "white soup," is there any way it isn't gross? Because it sounds like a pot of flour and water to me.

Of course, if you try to discuss any of these things at the dinner table, Jasper just yells "spotted dick!" and cackles hysterically. Granted, that is a pretty unfortunate name for a dessert.

M.P.M.

CHAPTER 16

The October breeze carried a delicious crispness through the still-open dining room windows. Mom must have sensed the incipient change in weather because she'd spent the afternoon butchering butternut squash. There would be leftovers for days, but tonight it felt like an occasion: the first squash soup of the fall, served with a loaf of seeded bread from the hippie bakery downtown and slices of sharp cheddar and Granny Smith apple.

I waited until everyone had filled their bowls and Dad was finished fulsomely complimenting the soup's velvety texture before broaching the subject uppermost in my mind. Despite Arden's assurances that a date for the dance needn't be a soulmate, I was anxious not to repeat the Mall Guy debacle.

"So how do you know if someone is right for you?" I asked, stirring a dollop of Greek yogurt into my soup. "A good match."

"Are we talking chess? Tennis? Swapping kidneys?" Jasper asked around a mouthful of bread.

"More like in a personal sense."

There was a brief silence as my family looked back at me with varying degrees of consternation. "Does someone have an admirer?" Van asked archly. She turned to Addie, as if to share the joke. "I did not see this coming. Did you?"

"There are more things in heaven and earth, Horatio, than are dreamt of in your philosophy," her twin replied without looking up.

"But is there any way to tell from the beginning?" I persisted, before everyone could start quoting *Hamlet*. "Whether it's going to work out."

"Some sort of test, you mean?" Dad said.

"They do those quizzes in *Cosmo*," Jasper suggested.

Addie dipped a piece of bread in her soup. "Send them on a quest. To test their devotion."

"No, she should disguise herself as a boy." Van's face took on a faraway look, and I knew she was envisioning Shakespearean hijinks: mistaken identity, moonlit revels, a song or two. Apparently she'd forgotten that Millville High was a whimsy-free zone. "See if they like you for you, or just because your physical attributes fit some accepted gender norm."

I shifted uncomfortably. "For the record, this isn't about me. I'm asking for a friend."

Jasper snorted.

"Does this friend have a loom?" my father inquired, brushing crumbs from the stubble on his chin. As a rule, he forwent shaving on days he didn't teach, as well as the days he was supposed to teach but forgot until the department secretary called.

"Brilliant." Mom beamed at Dad. "The faithful Penelope, weaving by day, only to unravel the cloth at night."

"Odysseus's wife," Addie explained for Jasper's benefit. He grunted, meaning either *even I know that* or *who cares?*

"When he didn't come home from the war she told all the guys who wanted to marry her that she had to weave a burial shroud for her father-in-law first," Van added, not to be outdone. "Only every night she undid all her work, so it was never finished."

I felt my original question slipping further away, soon to be lost forever in the sands of my family's rambling. "I'm not sure the burial shroud excuse will carry the same weight in this century."

"Your friend should show strength and independence. That would scare anyone off." Cam scowled as though the observation gave her no pleasure.

"If you want my opinion, that ship has sailed." Mom leaned back in her chair. "If he hasn't succumbed to her wiles by now, he never will."

I paused with a glass halfway to my mouth. "Who's not falling for which wiles?"

"Anjuli and Pittaya, of course."

My mother could be alarmingly astute, often when you least expected her to be paying attention. I wondered how long she'd known about Anjuli's interest in Pittaya, so recently revealed to me.

"Speaking more generally." I cleared my throat. "How important is the . . . physical side of things?"

"Oh, sweet." Jasper's spoon clattered as he dropped it into his bowl. "Is this where you explain the birds and the bees to Mary?"

I sent him a withering look. "I'm talking about *chemistry*." It pained me to quote Alex Ritter, but I couldn't think how else to describe it. "Whether there's a spark or not."

"Well," my father began, clearly struggling to keep his voice even, an effort belied by the beads of sweat that had broken out at his hairline, "there are certainly cases wherein the 'spark,' as you call it, fails to manifest."

"Either it's there or it isn't." Van bit into a slice of apple. "Sometimes it takes you by surprise." She looked like she was gearing up to say more, but Addie cut in first.

"You shouldn't base a relationship solely on physical attraction, though. There needs to be a degree of like-mindedness. You wouldn't want to be with someone who wasn't your intellectual equal."

Van looked at her sharply. "What's that supposed to mean?"

"We don't have to be at the mercy of our passions," Cam burst out, startling all of us.

The screen door screeched, followed by Yarb yowling to announce his arrival. The patter of paws was accompanied by hurried human steps. "Sorry I'm late," said Bo, strolling into the dining room with an apologetic smile.

"Pull up a chair, Boas." My mother extended a welcoming arm. "There's plenty of soup."

Bo sniffed the air. "Is that your signature squash bisque?"

he asked, as though he hadn't been hanging around the house all afternoon, listening to the chopping and sizzling.

"Autumn's first harvest." My father beamed at their shared good fortune. "Season of mists and mellow fruitfulness."

Once Bo was seated with a bowl of his own, he turned to the rest of us. "What's the latest on Planet Porter-Malcolm?"

"Mary's learning about her changing body," Jasper said, making both me and Bo choke.

"We're discussing the nature of love," Mom corrected.

"Two-second recap. Do you have to be attracted to someone or can you just have the hots for their brain, blah blah blah, stuff about books," my brother summarized.

"That's not—" I stopped myself midprotest. That *was* pretty much it, in a nutshell. What did it mean when you had someone like Mall Guy, who looked every inch the romantic hero, from the solemn expression to the tasteful shoes, yet turned out to be the farthest thing from swoonworthy?

"Maybe it takes some people longer to discover that kind of connection," I ventured.

"Absolutely," Bo said at once. "Or one person could be powerfully in touch with their feelings and just patiently waiting for the other person to notice."

"I pursued your mother for more than a year before she relented," Dad volunteered.

"I'd planned to devote myself to the life of the mind." Mom smiled nostalgically, as if we'd never heard this story, or the related anecdote about the love letter our father had written her, listing all the happy families in Virginia Woolf's fiction. "It seems I wasn't cut out for celibacy."

"And I'm out." Jasper shoved his chair back from the table with both hands.

"Then I guess you won't be needing this." Van's arm snaked out to grab his plate.

They slapped at each other's hands a few times, until Jasper licked his palm and pressed it on top of his half-eaten slice of bread. Van wrinkled her nose in disgust.

"Mary."

I looked up at the sound of my mother's voice.

"What do I always say?" she prompted.

"Um, turn off the lights when you leave the room? Don't stand in front of the refrigerator with the door open? Put away your laundry? Did anyone feed the cat?" I could have gone on but paused to see whether any of those had been the right answer.

Her lips pursed. "I was thinking along less mundane lines. When you're on the horns of a metaphysical dilemma, the best course of action is to—" She peered at me over the rim of her glasses.

"Do your research."

"And what's the first step in a successful campaign of study?"

"Consult the experts." I was on the point of complaining that I didn't know any experts in this particular field when a light bulb went off. There *was* someone I could ask—an undisputed authority in the area of romance.

Dear Diary,

Another Scoundrel alert: a boy named Braden offered to tutor a girl in Terry's geometry class, but it turned out he was correcting all her answers so that when he told her what he'd done, she'd feel obligated to go out with him. And then for extra creepiness he threatened to turn her in for cheating if she said no. Which is pretty much what Gus Trenor did to Lily Bart in **House of Mirth**, only with math homework instead of the stock market. And no gambling addiction or tragic use of sleeping pills.

I know Alex Ritter is the reason we started the Scoundrel Guide in the first place, but on balance, he's not the worst of the bunch.

M.P.M.

CHAPTER 17

The better part of a week passed before I could put my plan into effect. After making excuses to my friends, I hurried home on foot. There was no sign of Alex Ritter, though I knew this was the day of his piano lesson.

Despite my trepidation at the task ahead, I relished every crunch of leaves underfoot, the bursts of red still on the trees, watery golden sunlight softening the crispness of the air as it washed over my skin. It was a perfect fall afternoon, the sky so clear it felt like being cradled inside a giant blue marble. There should have been a name for days like this, but all the ones I could think of — halcyon days, salad days — referred to summer, which struck me as unfair. Who needed the obvious charms of June when you could have the burnished richness of autumn?

After stashing my backpack in my room, I crept back down the stairs and out the front door, careful not to let the screen door slam behind me. Since I wasn't sure how long piano lessons typically lasted, it seemed wisest to get into position early.

A row of hydrangeas bordered the yellow house. Squeezing between the shrubbery and the porch, I settled in to wait.

Muffled strains of music drifted through the walls. It sounded like the same few bars played over and over, with brief interludes of silence. I was beginning to regret not grabbing a snack, and a sweater, when footsteps thudded toward the front of the house. The door opened.

Peeking through the porch railing, I confirmed the identity of the student before hissing, "Pssst."

Alex Ritter started, fumbling the book of sheet music in his hand.

"Over here," I whispered.

He took a tentative step toward the edge of the porch, squinting down at me through a pair of wire-rimmed glasses. "Mary?"

I nodded, distracted by the eyewear. The effect was very different from his usual look: less perfect, more vulnerable.

He glanced over his shoulder before turning back to me. "No thanks. I'll pass."

My mouth fell open. He was turning me down already? "I haven't even told you what I want—"

"I'm getting a very strong 'drug deal' vibe. Contrary to what you seem to think about my personal habits, I'm actually a pretty clean-living guy."

"I'm not trying to sell you anything!" I stepped closer to the railing. "I need your help."

The suppressed laughter fled his expression. "Are you okay?"

"I'm fine." He was still studying me intently, checking for injuries, I presumed. "You wear glasses?"

"My contacts were bothering me." His hand moved to his hair, but he stopped short of touching the curls, sliding a self-conscious glance my way as his arm fell to his side.

"I shouldn't have said that about your hair. Obviously I'm not one to talk about styling products and all that." I flapped a self-deprecating hand at my ponytail.

A gust of wind sent leaves scudding along the sidewalk.

"Is this like when my sisters describe someone's outfit by saying she 'tried really hard'? I have the feeling next you're going to tell me I seem like a 'very sweet person.'"

"I wasn't going to say that."

His lips twitched. "That's a relief."

"I always wanted curls," I continued, determined not to be maneuvered into insulting him again.

He tapped the music book against his thigh. "Do you know what my sisters called me when I was little?" I shook my head, unwilling to hazard a guess. "Little Orphan Allie."

It wasn't hard to imagine him as a little boy with golden ringlets and winsome blue eyes. Possibly in a blue velvet sailor suit and knee socks. "My sisters called me Uriah Heep," I admitted, matching his confidence with one of my own.

"Excuse me?"

"From *David Copperfield*. Because I was always spying on them and touching their stuff."

He gave a huff of laughter, but I didn't mind. It was still better than his nickname.

"My hair sucks," he said a moment later, staring into the distance. "If I don't put anything on it I look like Albert Einstein. And I can't shave it off because my skull is too lumpy."

"People used to think you could tell things about a person from the shape of their cranium. Phrenology. It was a pseudoscience."

"Do I even want to know how you know that?"

"*Moby Dick.*"

"And here I thought it was about whales." He peered down at me. "I guess you used your spying skills to find me here, Uriah?"

I nodded. "I wanted to ask you something, if you have a minute."

"Should I come down, or do you want to keep doing it like this?" He waved a finger between us. "Because I'm pretty sure the neighbors think I'm talking to myself right now."

"Or maybe—" I clamped my lips together, cutting off what I'd been about to say. This was nothing like the balcony scene from *Romeo and Juliet,* and only a blithering idiot would suggest otherwise. "Yes," I said instead. "Good idea."

We met on the sidewalk. He looked expectantly at me.

"I guess we can go to my house." I pointed in that direction, trying to mask my uncertainty with a purposeful air. My mental to-do list consisted of one bold-print item: Ask Alex Ritter for Romantic Advice. I hadn't thought beyond that to the practical details, including where such a dialogue should take place.

The sidewalk wasn't quite as wide as I could have wished,

but it would have been weird to walk behind or ahead of him, so I resigned myself to the tight quarters, clasping my hands behind my back after my fingers accidentally brushed his.

Alex cleared his throat. "Is this about the dance?"

I stumbled, staring at the cracked pavement as if it were to blame. "How did you know?"

He shrugged and looked away. His body language suggested he was too polite to answer.

"Oh my gosh," I exclaimed as the penny dropped. "You think I'm about to ask you to go with me. Why on earth would —" Halfway through, the question answered itself. No doubt there was a line of girls eager to solicit his company for Winter Formal. He probably needed one of those big red number dispensers they had at the deli counter to keep track of them all.

"Trust me, that is *not* what I wanted to talk to you about," I assured him. "First of all, it's not about me, *per se*. It's more of a group thing."

"You want me to go with all of you?"

"What? No. This is something totally different. Mostly. But still serious and respectable."

"I would expect nothing less from you, Mary."

I couldn't tell whether this was a genuine compliment, so I held my tongue as I led him around the side of my house and unlatched the gate leading to the backyard. Leathery leaves blanketed the grass, crumpling underfoot. The Porter-Malcolms were not as vigilant as some of our neighbors when it came to raking.

Seating options were limited, now that we'd taken down

the reading hammock for the season. Not that a hammock would have been in any way appropriate for the two of us. That left only the wrought-iron bench, which seemed very small, once we were standing in front of it.

Brushing if off, I gestured for him to sit. "Would you like some tea?" The words sounded stiff and formal, like I was pretending to be an adult, and an elderly one at that. It was hard to strike a balance between thank-you-for-doing-me-this-favor and I-swear-I'm-not-trying-to-woo-you.

"And crumpets?" he asked.

"We don't have crumpets."

"Curds and whey? Blackbird pie?"

I frowned at him. "Black*bird?*"

"Four-and-twenty blackbirds baked in a pie." He smiled his lazy smile, patting the bench beside him. There was barely room for me to sit without pressing against him somewhere; I opted for knee-to-knee contact as the least embarrassing. "You have that storybook quality, Mary." He took his glasses off and stuck them in the pocket of his shirt.

"Don't you need them?" I asked.

"I can see *you*." He was doing that thing again, his eyes traveling slowly over my face and hair, a deliberate perusal that made me feel intensely visible. It was only natural to look back at him with equal focus, noting how the autumn sunlight gilded his hair, and the slight freshness of the breeze brought a hint of pink to his cheeks. If he was handsome in the hallways at school, out here, on a day like today, he could have been a fairy prince, amusing himself by toying with mortals.

An idea danced at the back of my mind, spurred by the gleam in his eyes, the half smile lurking at the corners of his mouth. Could it be that this light made everyone lovely, including me? That would explain his rapt attention, and the stillness that seemed to envelop the two of us. It felt like the universe was holding its breath, waiting for something to happen.

Or maybe that was just me.

"You wanted to talk?" he prompted.

I gave a jerky nod to hide my confusion. "I need your help, actually."

"Anything for you, Mary."

The familiar teasing came as a relief. At least now I knew he was joking, unlike the silent . . . whatever that had been of a moment before.

"It's about what you said the other night," I began. "At the game."

"You're still looking for a good nickname?"

I shook my head. "The part about chemistry. Spark. Finding someone you actually like, who's also a sensible dating option. A nice, safe romantic object . . . person."

"Safe as in boring?"

"No! Definitely not someone *blah*. Or annoying. But not a criminal either," I added, thinking of Terry. "I know about the big stuff, like evaluating their moral fiber—judging whether someone is a reprehensible human being and all that."

"That's good," he replied with mock solemnity.

"And I also know it can't just be about physical attraction," I continued, ignoring the aside. "Because appearances can be deceiving. A person who *seems* intriguing might turn out to be really condescending and full of himself, for example."

He brushed at the front of his sweater, a navy-blue cable knit. "I hate it when that happens."

"I'm asking how you can be sure you're making a smart choice — going for someone whose company you'll actually enjoy? Obviously I know love at first sight is unrealistic."

"Obviously." He tapped his chin. "They don't cover this in your books?"

"It's not quite the same situation. There were a lot of other factors back then."

"Such as?"

"Bloodlines, property, who has enough cash in her dowry to keep the ancestral estate running. That kind of thing."

"Romantic."

"Yes, well. That was the era of arranged marriages. It was basically a financial transaction. But it's not really *that* different from now, when you think about it."

He waved at me to go on.

"It seems to me high school is all about the social hierarchy. Everyone's trying to figure out their rank, only nowadays it's not just a question of having an aristocratic title. There are other status symbols."

"Shoes," he suggested.

It was probably a joke, but I nodded anyway. "The right clothes, how you look, who your friends are, any kind of public notoriety. It all gets taken into account. And then you look for an eligible partner, meaning someone on your level, or slightly above."

Alex shook his head.

"What?"

"No one is walking around calculating who to date." He pretended to scrawl numbers on the palm of his hand.

"Maybe not *literally*, but I bet you there's an underlying logic to it." I opted not to mention the obvious example of him and Terry, his equal in beauty.

"It's not that complicated." He tapped my arm. "How did you and your girl gang hook up?"

"Oh. It's kind of a long story." Which I had no intention of sharing. Especially the part involving him.

"Okay, but at some point you realized you like hanging out with each other. The conversation flows. You make each other laugh. There's good energy." He looked expectantly at me.

"Yes, but there has to be some difference, or else everyone would go around kissing their friends."

"That would be rude. Unless they were into it." He wagged his eyebrows like a mustache-twirling villain in a black cape. "Seriously, though. It starts with that same kind of connection."

A light bulb went off in my head. "Like in *Howards End*!"

"I don't do porn, Mary."

I sent him a quelling look. "It's a *book*. There's this really famous line — 'Only connect.'" I waited for him to make some expression of amazement.

"That's it?"

I gave a sheepish nod. The truth was that I'd always found it a bit opaque myself. Was it supposed to be a person-to-person thing, or something vast and philosophical? I glanced hopefully at Alex. "What do you think it means?"

"In your book or . . . ?" He circled a palm between us, presumably indicating the world at large.

"With real people. Like you were saying. When it's more than platonic."

He rubbed a hand over the back of his neck. "It can be a lot of things. You might like the way a person laughs, or how they think, their smell—anything that makes you want to cross a room to talk to them."

"And then?"

He shifted on the bench, bringing his hip and thigh into contact with mine. "You get to know them."

Moving away would have been awkward, so I held perfectly still. "And?"

"And then you feel something, or you don't."

My voice dropped to a whisper. "Like what?"

He didn't answer right away, as though there might be some other layer to my question he needed to decipher first.

"Like your day is better when you see them," he said, looking steadily at me. "And you think about them when they're not around. Or make excuses to get close, because you wonder if their skin is as soft as it looks. That kind of thing."

I swallowed. "Oh."

"Why do you ask, Mary?" He stretched his arm along the back of the bench. "Are you having feelings?"

"It's for my friends," I said hastily.

"You have feelings for your friends?"

"No! Not kissy feelings, anyway." I blew out a breath before starting over. "I mean they're counting on me to help them find dates for Winter Formal. Except Arden, of course. She's all set."

"What about you?"

"I'm not worried about that."

"You already have someone in mind?"

"Me?" I gave a nervous choke of laughter. "I barely know anyone."

Alex gestured at himself. "What am I, chopped liver?"

My gaze fixed on the leaves at our feet, but not quickly enough to hide my blush. "I'm still new to all this. I don't have your vast experience with affairs of the heart—" *Crap.* "I mean *expertise.* Which is why I asked you for help." His expression remained dubious. "Like how an FBI agent might consult someone from the other side of the law to help with a tricky investigation."

"So I'm a serial killer, and you're using my inside knowledge to catch a different murderer?"

My shoulders slumped. It had sounded so persuasive when Terry talked about her crime shows. "I just remembered how you knew that Will guy was a dud."

He snorted under his breath.

"Yes, well, it may have taken some of us a little longer to figure it out."

"That was the accent, probably. Happens to the best of us." With the arm draped along the back of the bench—the

195

one I'd been pretending not to notice, while secretly enjoying its warmth — he patted me on the back. "What you need is the opposite of him. Someone fun. Easygoing. Capable of smiling without spraining his jaw." He tugged the end of my ponytail.

"Of course," I breathed, stunned by the undeniable brilliance of his suggestion. "If Will was a Cecil Vyse, then obviously the antidote is to find a George Emerson!"

Alex frowned. "You lost me."

"It's from a book," I explained. "Cecil is the snobby upper-crust fiancé, and George is the one she ditches him for, because he's authentic and passionate — the kind of person who goes skinny-dipping in the woods with some other guys and kisses Lucy in a field of violets."

"So he swings both ways?"

It was my turn to frown. "I *think* the swimming scene is about being at home in nature and not bound by propriety and suffocating social strictures, but it's possible I missed some subtext." There was no time to worry about that now. Leaping to my feet, I offered Alex my hand. "Thank you."

His warm palm pressed against mine. When he didn't let go, I tugged lightly, pulling him to his feet. My gaze traveled from our clasped hands to his face. "I should go in and do some . . . things," I said faintly, swallowing against the sudden dryness in my throat.

The pounding of my heart measured out the time as I waited for him to reply. The look in his eyes was impossible to read. Inside the house, the phone rang.

"You probably need to get that."

It felt like there was a different question layered under that one, but I had no idea what he was asking or how to answer, so I nodded dumbly.

Alex released my hand. I watched him disappear through the gate. Only then did I walk slowly toward my back door, and a phone that had long since stopped ringing.

Dear Diary,

It's crazy how much personal grooming has changed over the centuries. Back when respectable young women couldn't show so much as a glimpse of ankle, or leave the house without gloves, or do anything to their faces beyond the pinching of cheeks, there was no reason to shave or exfoliate or moisturize or trim your cuticles — never mind the concept of "contouring," which I still find too daunting to try, no matter how many videos Arden shows me.

Obviously I'm glad corsets have gone the way of the hoop skirt, but sometimes I think it would be easier to keep more of yourself under wraps, at least from a skin care perspective.

M.P.M.

CHAPTER 18

Arden waited until my bare feet had been submerged in a bubbling basin of magenta-tinted water to drop her bombshell. "Mission accomplished."

Lydia lowered her magazine. "The mission of getting us to pay someone to paint our toenails? Even though it's not sandal weather?"

Halloween had passed, and the weather was chilly enough to make my feet flex with relief in the warm water. A little color and sparkle would not go amiss now that the world had taken on the brown and gray palette of late autumn. Even if that hint of brightness would mostly be hidden by socks.

"I found him," Arden said, ignoring Lydia's jab. "Our George." She paused to confer with her nail technician about which shade of turquoise she'd settled on. "The opposite of Will, who was really a what's-his-name," she explained, lifting one foot from the water and propping it on a towel.

When I called to explain the idea, Arden had leaped immediately into planning mode, pausing only long enough to congratulate me on this stroke of genius. It seemed simpler not to muddy the waters by introducing Alex Ritter's name.

Lydia still looked confused.

"Since Mary said we needed more of a Nature Boy type," Arden reminded her.

A picture formed in my head of one of those feral wolf children with the really long fingernails and matted hair.

"Where did you find him?" Terry's voice vibrated with the pummeling of the massage chair.

"It was right after school. I happened to be walking past his car. Nature Boy's, that is. Which of course was a Prius—"

"Where was I?" Lydia interrupted.

"Talking to your mom." Arden held her hand to her face like a phone. "So he's at his Prius, and I notice a big bag in back."

Terry leaned forward in her chair. "Were you worried?"

"Not really? It was just a bag."

"You never know," Terry pointed out, in her most reasonable tone. "It could have been full of ropes and duct tape." The young man towel-drying her foot paused to stare.

Arden shook her head. "I know it wasn't anything weird because when we were talking he mentioned he was going to play disc golf in the park."

"You talked to this rando?" Lydia cut in.

"He's not a rando. My brother's friend Tony used to play soccer with Jeff—a.k.a. Nature Boy—before he hurt his knee."

This explanation did not satisfy Lydia. "Didn't he think it was weird having you suddenly chat him up for no reason?"

"I *did* have a reason," Arden informed her. "I was inviting him to our party."

"What party?" I asked, afraid I'd missed something.

"The one I was going to plan if he said yes. But he was like, 'Parties are not my scene.'" Arden relayed this in a rumbling bass before switching back to her normal voice. "I told him they weren't necessarily our thing either. We just go to be sociable." She smiled at her own cleverness. "Not bad, eh?"

Lydia gave her a look. "That he's not coming to your pretend party?"

Arden waved this off. "There are plenty of other places we can hang out with him. For example, you know how Jeff is really into the environment?"

The three of us glanced at each other before shaking our heads.

"Remember, like the guy who swims naked outdoors? He's all earthy and natural?"

"Tell me you didn't invite him to go streaking through the forest," Lydia said, giving voice to my private fear.

Arden sighed. "Give me some credit. While we were talking, I noticed that his car is covered with bumper stickers about saving the animals and clean water and 'oh no, the trees'—that kind of thing. That's where I got the idea, which by the way has *nothing* to do with public nudity."

The nail technicians weren't even pretending not to hang on every word.

Lydia fiddled with her remote control, turning up the setting on her chair. "What *does* it have to do with?"

"Our club."

"We're not in a club," Lydia pointed out.

"Yes, but Jeff doesn't know that. Trust me, I made it sound convincing, but also casual. *Oh hey, if you're not doing anything Thursday, maybe you can stop by our amazing save-the-world club.*" She fluttered her lashes aggressively.

It took Terry several tries to regain control of her jaw, which had fallen slack. "Is that the actual name?"

"I kept that part vague," Arden assured us. "We can fill in the details later. He looked like he was trying to figure out how to say no, so I was like, 'It's just a few blocks away, at Mary Porter-Malcolm's house.' And it totally worked, because he got quiet for a second—probably thinking about baby seals—and then he was like, 'What time?' I said four o'clock," she added, before we could ask. "Also, joining a club is totally on my list for Mary's season." She blew on her fingernails before pretending to buff them on her sweater. "That's what you call multitasking."

"Sounds like you thought of everything," Lydia muttered.

Arden chose to ignore what sounded suspiciously like sarcasm. "All you have to do is make the flyer," she told Lydia.

"Our imaginary club needs an actual flyer?"

"Just throw something together—pictures of animals, that kind of thing. Keep it vague. It doesn't have to be your best work."

The look on Lydia's face said she was about to object.

"Or we could go to the coffeehouse where he plays guitar

on Thursday nights," Arden mused. "Apparently he's working on a song cycle called 'The March to Extinction.'"

"Over my dead body," Lydia snapped.

Arden's smile was just visible above the rim of her paper cup of tea. "Mary's house it is."

Dear Diary,

It's not unusual to incorporate some degree of subterfuge in the courtship process, whether you're talking about Cyrano writing love letters under someone else's name or everyone in Shakespeare pretending to be their brother/cousin/uncle, etc. Basically, it's a time-honored romantic tradition. Like Anton says, what's more fun than a little cross-dressing?

M.P.M.

CHAPTER 19

On Thursday afternoon I rushed home to start preparing while the other three printed copies of Lydia's flyer for our alleged club, Concerned Citizens. Official slogan: *For a Good Time, Do Good.*

I had time to push in chairs, straighten stacks of magazines and papers, and turn on the lights in the dining room before the doorbell rang. With a burst of laughter and rustling grocery bags my friends hurried inside.

We put out bowls of sesame sticks, cashews, and wasabi peas, which Arden decided to combine into snack mix. There was seltzer for those who wanted it, and a plate of organic date rolls. Against my better judgment, Jasper and Bo had been prevailed upon to swell our numbers to something more club-like. Bo insisted on mood music, which he defined as "either Ella or Billie; I'm not picky." Jasper found a compilation of Billie Holiday's greatest hits.

The snacks, the smooth jazz — it reminded me of something.

"Feels like a faculty dinner party," Jasper said, reading my mind. "Minus the cheap wine."

"And the old people making passive-aggressive comments about each other's research," Bo pointed out.

Lydia held up a hand for silence. "Did you hear that?"

We dashed to the front windows, peeking from behind the curtains as a male figure — presumably Jeff — bent to lock his mountain bike. Even from behind I could tell he was shaped differently from most of the guys at our school, his torso broadening into sculpted shoulders that strained against the confines of his T-shirt. I'd never pictured myself with someone buff, but I would do my best to keep an open mind. Assuming he even noticed me, rather than being instantly smitten with one of my friends.

"At least he doesn't look like he needs iron supplements," Lydia muttered.

No, Nature Boy wasn't a Cecil Vyse. And while it was too soon to pronounce him Millville High's answer to George Emerson, he at least appeared capable of climbing a tree, should the occasion arise. Then he straightened.

"It's *him*," I said, as the back of his head came into view.

Arden gave me a funny look. "Did you invite anyone else?"

I shook my head, opting to play dumb rather than explain I hadn't meant, *Oh look, it's Jeff!* but *Oh look,* Jeff *is Man Bun, a.k.a. the guy who's been following Cam around!*

"If we could get that cowrie shell necklace off him we might have something," Lydia observed as he took a long drink from the water bottle attached to his bike.

Arden elbowed her. "Maybe Mary likes his necklace."

"Yeah," Lydia scoffed. "She can get one just like it when he takes her to Burning Man."

We scurried away from the window as Jeff mounted the porch steps. When the knock sounded, Jasper slid toward the front door in his socks. My slight-framed brother looked Lilliputian next to our brawny visitor, who was gazing around the living room as though committing the details to memory. *They're bookshelves*, I wanted to say. *Full of books.* Well, that and a pile of dirty field hockey gear, which Cam had brought home to wash on her off day from practice. Possibly I should have straightened that up.

"Why don't you sit here, Jeff?" Having led the way into the dining room, Arden indicated the chair she had in mind. "Help yourself to some snack mix. And Mary, you can sit right next to him."

"What about me?" Jasper asked. "Where should I sit?"

In a different room. Sadly, my throat had gone too dry to translate this thought into speech. I tried to think of something else to say, but the only conversational gambit I could come up with was, *What's the deal with you and my sister?*

A door slammed overhead. Jeff's head snapped up. After a moment of frozen stillness, he rose from his chair and moved toward the stairs as if pulled by a hooked line.

The rapid staccato of footsteps identified the person descending as Cam. She hurtled three-quarters of the way down before noticing Jeff. The moment seemed to swell, a bead of water expanding until it was too heavy to do anything but drop.

"Cam," he said. I shivered, never having heard my sister's name spoken quite that way.

Tearing her gaze from his, she cast a quick glance around the dining room, registering our presence.

"What are you doing here?" she asked him, hands fisted at her sides.

"I wanted to see you." He made no mention of Concerned Citizens. Apparently it had been as much a ruse for him as it was for us. Which was . . . only fair.

Cam inhaled sharply. "No," she said, sounding almost childlike in her defiance as she slipped past him.

"Cam—" He reached for her, then seemed to think better of it. His arm fell to his side. "Please."

She stopped with her back to him, shoulders hunched. I'd never seen Cam shrink from anything in my life, including the perpetually enraged Doberman on the next block. Jasper and I exchanged baffled looks, eyebrows at maximum extension.

Jeff walked slowly around Cam until he was facing her again, placing his weight as cautiously as though he were approaching a wild animal. Lowering his head, he tried in vain to catch her eye. "Can we talk about this?"

Instead of taking him out with a reinforced elbow, Cam hesitated. The rest of us held our collective breath.

"That's all I'm asking," Jeff said quietly. He must have sensed the glimmer of opportunity. I could practically hear the pounding of his heart, in time with the heaving of his muscular chest. Though he wasn't on his knees, his attitude was definitely one of supplication.

My sister relented so far as to look at him. Her complexion darkened. On anyone else, I would have called it a blush. She opened her mouth.

Instead of speaking, she lunged for the door. A second later she was barreling down the front steps.

"Cam!" Jeff shouted, giving chase. The screen door slammed behind him.

We hurried to the window in time to watch them round the corner and disappear, running full out. I thought of what Alex said about crossing a room to talk to someone. To me it had sounded like a conscious decision-making process, but this felt a lot more visceral than that. Maybe *attraction* wasn't just something that happened in your mind. It could be entirely literal; a physical compulsion.

"Wow," Arden sighed as we drifted back to the table. "That was something."

Lydia popped open a can of seltzer. "Yeah, a disaster." She gestured at the window. "Nature Boy chose option D. None of the above."

"But wasn't it *epic?*" Arden tugged the bowl of snack mix from Jasper's greedy hands before he could finish it off. "I forgot what it's like. There's so much passion at the beginning of a relationship. You want to spend every second together, just *staring* at each other. You wouldn't dream of canceling plans at the last minute or waiting four hours to answer a text."

Jasper dragged the plate of date rolls to his side of the table. "Tell us more."

"Don't," I warned her. "He'll use it against you later."

Terry's hand darted out, snagging the second-to-last date roll. "I don't blame him for liking your sister. She's so bold and strong and—" She gestured mutely with one hand.

"Formidable?" I suggested.

"Scary?" Jasper countered.

Terry managed to shrug and nod at the same time.

"The chemistry was off the charts," Bo chimed in. "So much tension in that scene. I would have set it in the middle of a rainstorm, though. Like *Breakfast at Tiffany's*."

Arden clapped her hands together. "Or *The Notebook*!"

"If you want to go contemporary," Bo conceded.

I found myself in the unaccustomed position of waiting for someone else to explain a reference. "What's that?"

"You haven't seen *The Notebook*?" Arden sat back, looking stunned, before visibly gathering her resolve. "That's it, we're going to my house right now. It's totally based on a book," she assured me, reaching for her purse.

"Aren't you forgetting something?" Lydia said.

"Of course we'll help clean up first." Arden reached for one of the untouched glasses.

Lydia shook her head. "Are you up for this, Mary?"

"It's Ryan Gosling," Arden pointed out, as if that answered the question for me.

Lydia rolled her eyes. "Maybe she's disappointed? Since we built up this whole Nature Boy thing and now"—she blew a raspberry—"we have nothing?"

"Not nothing," Arden protested.

"Excuse me, I forgot the valuable lesson we all learned."

Lydia pretended to make a note. "Don't try to get with a guy who has the hots for your sister."

"It's fine. Really." The prospect of romance had been gossamer as a soap bubble, here and then gone. The odds of unrequited pining for Jeff, whom I had barely met, seemed slim.

"Trust me, this is the perfect movie for when you're having all the feels." Arden raised her index finger, in the universal sign for someone about to make a point. "I'm having another brain wave. Let's take this to the next level. Tomorrow, my house, movie night *and* a slumber party. A two-for-one special." She consulted her phone. "We are blazing through my list."

"What list?" Jasper asked.

"None of your business." The last thing I wanted to discuss in front of him was my induction into Normal Teenage Life. The mockery would never end.

"Tampon, maxi pad, cramps." Arden's incantation sent Jasper and Bo fleeing, hands over their ears.

"Nice," said Lydia.

Arden winked. "Works every time."

ᖶᓂ

After dinner, I spread my books out on the dining room table and dived into the morass of homework. That was another difference between Millville High and my old school: due dates were a lot less negotiable.

When I finally looked up, rubbing tired eyes, the rest of the house was dark. Yawning, I rolled the kink out of my shoulders before depositing my tea cup in the sink. Then I gathered my things in a messy bundle and crept up the stairs, avoiding the creaky spots. As I passed Cam's room I heard a series of rhythmic thuds and grunts, as if she'd installed a punching bag. Somehow she had returned to the house unobserved, suggesting either supernatural stealth or the tree outside her window. After a moment's hesitation, I knocked softly.

"Yeah?" she called.

I pushed open the door. Cam was on her back on the braided rug, legs bent at the knee and arms crooked behind her head.

"You're doing sit-ups?" On the face of it this was a stupid question, but Cam seemed to understand the unspoken *now?*

"I couldn't sleep." She wiped her forehead with the hem of her T-shirt.

"And . . . sit-ups help?"

She shrugged, looking away.

It seemed I would have to introduce the subject of the Incident, but how? It felt silly asking my fearless older sister if she was okay, though perhaps not as embarrassing as inquiring whether she now had a boyfriend, and if so what that was like.

"Jeff said your friend invited him over." Cam's words emerged reluctantly, but I was still grateful for the opening.

"I didn't know," I said quickly. "That the two of you had, you know, history. I mean, I saw you together a couple of times —"

"You did?" she interrupted, startled into looking up.

I nodded. "At that party. And your game." Her eyebrows climbed fractionally, which by Cam standards was practically a double-take. "I'm a younger sister," I said modestly. "We notice things."

Belatedly, I recalled that Cam was also a younger sister. Strange that I'd never thought of her that way. "Is there a reason you didn't want to talk to him?" I asked delicately, leaning against her dresser.

Cam reached for her water but didn't take a drink. "I don't know."

None of the usual objections seemed to apply. She and Jeff didn't come from different social classes, or warring clans. Besides, those lines were a lot more fluid in this century. Short of being royalty or blood relatives, there weren't many barriers to a relationship between willing parties.

"You just don't like him?" I finally asked, though that had not been my impression.

Her laugh sounded more like a sigh. "I wish."

"Why?"

"Because I don't want to become a person I don't recognize. *Jeff's girlfriend.* Half of a couple. I like this me." She thumped her thigh with a fist. "I don't want to lose myself."

"Is that what happens?"

She tipped her head back, leaning against the unmade bed. "How should I know? That's how it looks from the outside." Cam blew out a breath. "Since when is a high school guy mature enough to respect my autonomy?"

"He certainly *looks* mature."

The ghost of a smile played across my sister's face. She knew I was talking about Jeff's manly physique.

Ignoring the blush I could feel creeping up my neck, I summoned a serious expression. Seeing them together this afternoon, I would have sworn the matter was a fait accompli. The emotion between them had felt so real, beyond anything I'd imagined existing in the realm of High School Relationships. Surely there could be only one outcome.

"You could always take a risk and see what happens?" The irony of saying this to the sister whose derring-do was the stuff of family legend wasn't lost on me. Then again, in this one area, her bravery seemed to have a blind spot. "It wouldn't have to be a lifelong commitment. Since you're seventeen and all."

She cocked an eyebrow at me. "You think it might be okay?"

Cam, the most resolute of my family members — possibly of *anyone's* family members — soliciting my opinion? I would have to record this moment for posterity later.

"I do." If Arden were here, she would already be plotting their next encounter. Almost I could hear her voice, speaking through me. "You could start small. Something low-pressure, like coffee or lunch?"

"Lunch," Cam repeated, expression thoughtful. "What's the worst that can happen?"

In the interest of discretion, I opted not to answer.

Dear Diary,
Today I'm going to see a movie without reading the
book first.
Mea culpa.

M.P.M.

CHAPTER 20

Located in a gated modern subdivision lined with neatly manicured lots, Arden's house was decorated in the same palette as her beloved coffee drinks: not quite brown, not quite beige, but with hints of each swirled into the creamy background fluff. Terry called it *dulce de leche*, and said it made her want cake. To someone raised in a warren of lamp-lit rooms scaled to the tastes of a previous century, the newness was endlessly fascinating, as was her pantry full of the kind of snacks that get advertised on TV. I didn't see the words *superfood* or *non-GMO* anywhere.

After hauling our colorful bags of junk food to the basement, we sank into the mammoth L-shaped couch facing the flat-screen TV.

"Are you ready?" Arden asked me, remote pointed at the screen.

I nodded solemnly.

She closed her eyes as a shiver passed through her narrow

frame. "I can't believe this is your first time. It's like the one classic you don't know."

I pasted a pleased smile to my face as the movie began, ready to be amazed. But what was all this dappled sunlight? Whence the rowboats and waterfowl and old people? It reminded me of a greeting card, and not the fancy letterpress kind. *This is what happens when you don't read the book first,* whispered a critical voice inside my head.

Once the action moved to the past I felt more in my element. The old "rich girl, poor boy" scenario; the picture was coming into focus. I settled more deeply into the cushions, box of chocolate sandwich cookies at my side.

～

When the final credits rolled, Arden reached for the remote to mute the sound. "Gets me every time," she said, wiping her eyes with the back of her hand. "What a relief."

"The way it ended?" I ventured. "Or just that it's over?"

"I needed a good cry." She blew out a long breath. "That's what's so great about movies like that. Once you start crying, you can cry about anything." She turned to me with a watery smile. "What did you think?"

"It was definitely intense," I said, borrowing a term from her. She nodded eagerly, the look on her face saying, *And?*

"I was a little confused about one thing. Why was the other guy—her fiancé—no good?"

"Same," said Lydia. "What's wrong with having a steady job and getting your hair cut on the regular?"

"But that's the whole point." Arden gestured at the silent television. "There's nothing really *bad* about him except that he's not Ryan Gosling, and, you know, destiny. That's why it's so bittersweet."

And just a tad unconvincing, I silently added. "Then the theme is basically—"

"Follow your heart," Arden said at once. "Don't be afraid to put yourself out there."

"Go with the guy who supports your career," offered Lydia. We paused to give Terry a chance to weigh in.

"Do crosswords and stuff? It keeps your memory sharp."

"Valid point." Arden patted her hand. "Then he wouldn't need to tell her the whole story every day. They could travel."

On the coffee table, Arden's phone lit up. She lunged for it, sighing as she read the incoming message.

"What?" Lydia asked.

"I thought it was Miles. He was supposed to call me when he got back to the hotel. Maybe they're still at dinner." Her smile lacked conviction.

Lydia took a careful sip from her water bottle, eyes never leaving Arden. "You're still worried about what's-her-face?"

"Not all the time. I've been keeping busy, you know, concentrating on other things—"

"Like Winter Formal." Lydia did not sound entirely approving.

Arden rubbed her forehead with the heel of one hand. "In case you haven't noticed, we are up against the wall, time-wise. It's the same thing every year. As soon as the weather gets colder, everybody's like, 'Okay, fantasy time is over, who can I realistically expect to go out with me?' And now they're scrambling to seal the deal. If we wait much longer, every eligible person at our school will be taken! Plus there's Thanksgiving to worry about."

Terry and I exchanged a quick look of consternation. "What happens then?" she asked.

"We lose almost a week of school. Which means no one is asking anyone to go anywhere!"

"That's true. Good point." Lydia's voice had taken on a soothing tone I'd never heard before. "But I still think it might be a good idea to give it a rest, just for a little bit. Take a break from all this who's-dating-who stuff. Think about something besides people's love lives."

Arden stared at her, crumpling a tissue in her white-knuckled fist. "Why? Because Miles is going to dump me? Is that why you want me to stop caring about love—because my heart is about to be ripped out?"

"No!" Lydia's eyes widened. "I just thought maybe you were putting too much pressure on yourself with all this"—she held her hands to the sides of her face, suggesting the shape of a tunnel—"extreme focus. It happens, it doesn't happen, it's okay."

Terry and I nodded.

"As for Miles," Lydia continued, choosing her words with care, "isn't it always like this when the debate season kicks into high gear?"

"I don't know," Arden said bleakly. "It feels different this time. Worse." She turned to me. "Was there ever something like this in a book?"

"An elite debate team?"

She shook her head. "Where it seems like the other person might be losing interest. Or even possibly . . . cheating."

Talk about a minefield! There were dozens of depressing examples I could have shared, but it was hard to see how that would be helpful to Arden.

"Most philanderers are pretty obvious," I said slowly, grasping at a positive spin. "Like this horrible count who marries a young American named Isabel for her money and then tells her, 'Oh, we have to hang out with my old friend, she should vacation with us,' and obviously the lady is his mistress, which everyone *but* Isabel figured out in seconds, only by then it's too late because she's already stuck raising her husband's love child."

"See?" Lydia pointed at Arden. "Miles would never do that to you."

"Or this other guy whose wife came up to him in the garden one night and he started kissing her passionately and she was like, 'Oh good, maybe he's going to stop being such a jerk to me.' Then she said something, and he jumped back like, 'Helen! What are you doing here?'"

Terry clucked her tongue. "He thought she was someone else."

"And that's when she figured out he was cheating?" Arden whispered.

"Pretty soon after that," I hedged. "She was a little slow."

"Okay," Lydia said briskly. "*Those* are warning signs. Miles is not one of those guys. He's not a drama magnet, and he is definitely not sneaky. You have to be rational about this." She leaned forward, elbows on her knees. "This is Miles we're talking about, okay? Not some sleazy cheater. You know who Miles isn't?" She extended a hand in my direction.

"Alex Ritter," I said, recognizing my cue. His name left a sour taste on my tongue. This was a rotten way to repay him for his help, but I shoved that thought aside.

"I rest my case," said Lydia. "If there was a problem you would know, because Miles would tell you instead of running around behind your back. You guys are rock solid."

Arden flopped backwards, arm crooked over her eyes. "Unless there's a landslide."

Lydia stretched out a socked foot to kick her in the shin. "Where is the real Arden and what have you done with her?"

"I'm just saying love is a risk." Her chin jutted stubbornly. "It makes you vulnerable."

It would have been easier to argue if she didn't have centuries of literary tradition on her side.

Grabbing the remote, Lydia switched off the television, which had reverted to a still of the star-crossed lovers wrapped in each other's arms. "Enough of the gloom and doom. Let's talk about something else. What's next on our social calendar? *Besides* the dance."

"I was thinking music." Arden dabbed at her nose with the rumpled tissue. "Like an all-ages show, so we can dress up like rocker chicks and get our hands stamped and dance around."

"Sounds awesome," Lydia said with uncharacteristic perkiness. "When is it?"

"I don't know," Arden admitted with a sigh. "I haven't even

looked up concert listings. I'm sorry, you guys. I'm totally falling down on the job."

"Nope," said Lydia, holding up a hand. "No more tears. We're going to figure this out together. Anybody know a good show coming up?"

"Not really," Terry said, with a shrug of apology. Lydia sent me a desperate look.

"Um, there's Improv Opera?"

"Huh." Lydia scratched her head. "Is that—pretty much what it sounds like?"

"People making up operas on the spot? Yeah." I looked down, regretting the suggestion more keenly with every breath. An evening of arias about women dying of lovesickness: Good call, Mary! That'll cheer everyone up.

"I think it sounds very elegant," said Arden, supportive even in the throes of her own misery.

"I just feel like we need something to get our blood pumping. Leave it all on the dance floor." Lydia made a growling sound, pretending to claw the air with her hand.

"Oh!" I bolted upright, forgetting my resolve to never make another suggestion.

"What is it?" Lydia clenched her fists in anticipation.

"Trivia Night. It's *hardcore*," I assured them. "All the different college departments have a team—"

"College?" Arden interrupted. "As in, college *students*?"

I nodded. "Also faculty, staff, family, alums. Anyone with a connection to the college. There's a townie team, too."

Arden waved this off. "Back to the students."

"Dude. They're all going to be over eighteen." Lydia looked to me for confirmation.

I felt bad about dashing Arden's hopes, which must have been why I added, "Except for Neill."

"*Neill,*" Arden repeated, eyes gleaming. "Tell me more."

"Technically he's a junior, but he skipped two grades in elementary school, so he's only seventeen." As he would happily inform anyone within hearing range. Unlike Neill himself, I refused to use the word *prodigy.*

"And?" Arden prompted. "What does he look like?"

"Dark hair, kind of stocky—"

"So he's built," she translated.

I shrugged, never having paid much attention to his physique. "Supposedly he does martial arts. He volunteered to choreograph the fights for *Othello.*" I didn't add that Jasper and I suspected he'd made up his own style of fighting in order to be the undisputed expert.

"Think how impressive it would be to go to Winter Formal with a college student," Arden mused. "Everyone would be talking about it."

Anjuli's face danced across my thoughts.

"We could shop for dresses together! Definitely a different store this time. You might even inspire these two"—Arden swept a finger between Lydia and Terry—"to step outside their comfort zones and live a little. And then we'd all be there together, and it would be the Best Night Ever."

For a moment, I could see it: the flowing gowns and sparkling jewels, couples spinning gracefully around the dance floor. If I squinted at it sideways, the picture didn't even include Neill. "I guess I could *try*. He'll definitely be at Trivia Night."

Arden picked up her phone, swiping until she reached the calendar. "When and where does this trivia business go down?"

"Third Wednesday of the month, at Mung the Merciless," I said. "It's a vegetarian restaurant. Kind of a sci-fi theme."

"Drat." Arden clucked her tongue. "I have my Malaysian cooking class." She looked hopefully at Terry.

"I do Jazzercise with Mami on Wednesdays."

"And my mom is addressing her Rotary Club that night," Lydia informed us, setting down her phone. "She wants the whole family there."

Arden's lips pursed. "Lady Mary will just have to get the ball rolling on her own."

"Right." I took a deep breath. "How would I do that exactly?"

"First, you strike up a conversation," Arden began, counting off the points on her fingers. "Then you find out if he's single. If he is, ask if he wants to hang out sometime. Simple, right?" She smiled at me.

I nodded uncertainly.

"Think about it this way. Even if we can't get him to the dance, it's still a great chance to practice your social skills — which is totally on my list for your season." Arden waved her phone at me.

A chime sounded, and the screen lit up. "It's Miles," she announced, jumping to her feet. She clutched the phone to her chest. "Everything's coming together!"

I forced a smile, wishing I shared her confidence.

Dear Diary,

My cousin Meg said something once about how at school you have to downplay how much you know, so no one gets annoyed. That's when I realized there are still people in the world who would think less of a young woman for being a so-called bluestocking, whose nose is always in a book.

You never have to worry about being called a know-it-all among the Porter-Malcolms — especially at Trivia Night.

M.P.M.

CHAPTER 21

When the appointed evening arrived, I ran back upstairs at the last minute, rethinking my ponytail. It had never occurred to me to take pains with my appearance for Trivia Night, but maybe a less girlish coiffure would help Neill see me as a peer, as opposed to his usual habit of treating me like a semiliterate child.

I yanked open the bathroom door. The rest of the family was ostensibly downstairs and ready to go, which made it that much more startling to find Addie standing in front of the mirror.

She yelped. I seconded the exclamation, hopping into the air for good measure.

"Shhh!" She lowered the hand that had waved me to silence, exposing a thin, curving mustache drawn above her upper lip.

"Um," I said, staring at that point on her face.

"I know it's a little on-the-nose."

"That is not what I was going to say."

"It helps me get into the mindset." Addie circled both

hands in the air, as though drying her nail polish. A series of words had been inked in ballpoint on her palm.

"For Trivia Night?" I guessed, even though part of me knew that wasn't the answer. Addie quivered with a strange new energy. I could practically hear the hum rising from her skin, like the time Jasper snuck a two-liter of Mountain Dew at a faculty picnic.

She leaned past me, confirming the emptiness of the hallway before whispering, "Iago."

It took me a few seconds to put the clues together. "You're doing Iago?"

She nodded, glancing guiltily at her hand before fixing her gaze on the frayed pink rug underneath the sink. I was missing something. Addie often acted various parts when she and Van were blocking a scene or hashing out their interpretation of a speech. There was no reason to be self-conscious, or shut herself in the bathroom, unless . . . A radical possibility struck me between the eyes.

"You mean for real? In the show?" The twins had turned so snappish of late no one in the family had mustered the courage to ask how *Othello* was coming along.

"We needed an understudy. Just in case." Addie considered her reflection. "I doubt anything will come of it."

Her tone had gone flat, leaving me in the dark about her true feelings. Did she want to strut and fret upon the stage, or was she dreading the possibility? Was this why she'd been so out of sorts lately, especially with Van? Licking the tip of her finger, she rubbed at one end of the mustache. A smear of black spread over her cheek.

A honk sounded from outside.

"You better go," Addie said.

I hesitated. "What about you?"

She pointed to her face. "I have to wash this off."

⁓

When I slid into the back seat of my parents' car, Bo made a show of inching toward the middle without actually moving anything but his shoulders. The weather was chilly enough that I didn't mind the tight squeeze, though had it been Jasper sitting next to me I would have elbowed him out of my territory on principle.

Mom threw the car into reverse. She had donned what Jasper called her game face, ready for the competition. There was just enough room for me to remove the rubber band from my ponytail and shake out my hair. It was too dark to check my reflection in the rearview mirror. I would have to hope the effect wasn't too slatternly.

"It looks nice," Bo said, leaning into me as we turned a corner. "You should wear your hair down more often." I smiled my thanks, ignoring Jasper's snort.

The parking lot behind Mung's was packed, a phenomenon unique to Trivia Night. The familiar aroma of bean water, sweating onions, and cumin greeted us as we entered.

"Professor Porter-Malcolm," Neill said breathlessly, stepping in front of my mother. "And Professor Porter-Malcolm," he added, acknowledging my father with the exact same degree

of deference. Van had once described Neill as an equal opportunity suck-up. "Right this way."

We followed as he shouldered into the crowd, thrust-
ing and twisting as though hacking a trail through the rain-
forest. It occurred to me that I could see the top of Neill's head.
Somehow, I hadn't remembered him being quite so vertically
challenged.

Plain wooden tables lined the walls, bordered by matching benches. It wasn't a candlelight-and-flowers kind of place;
the only adornments were gummy bottles of hot sauce and the
signs indicating team placement.

"Here we are," Neill announced, in case we'd lost the ability
to read.

Our official team name was Let's Get Lit. Other sobriquets
included Oh, the Humanities!, Psy Fry, and Bougie Nights, the
last of which uneasily accomodated both Noreen and Shaggy
Doug as well as several other local business owners, including
Steve, the ropy-limbed proprietor of Mung's. Each team was
permitted to field five players at a time, with up to four alternates. In later rounds, the bench was occasionally allowed to
weigh in on a group question, but for the most part subs (like
myself and Neill) were charged with keeping the first-string
supplied with green tea and raw pumpkin seeds, and cheering
when one of our own scored a point.

My plan, such as it was, consisted of asking Neill a few
leading questions between rounds. I'd taken the precaution of
writing them down on a sheet of lined paper, which rustled in
my front pocket as I sat.

"Smell that?" Jasper asked, as he and Bo claimed the folding chairs on either side of me.

"Lentils?" I guessed.

"Fear. We should set up a Mylanta stand at one of these. Probably make serious bank."

Jasper was right. Nervous tics were out in full force, from finger twitches to compulsive throat-clearing. Even our parents looked tense, though they visibly relaxed when Cam slid into her spot.

Mom peered past Cam, clearly expecting to see the twins. "Where are your sisters?"

Cam shrugged. "No idea."

Deep vertical furrows appeared between Mom's brows. "Then how did you —"

"I caught a ride with a friend." Cam stared fixedly at the table. I looked where my sister hadn't, spotting Jeff leaning against the wall with his muscular arms crossed. Fortunately for my sister, Mom had bigger concerns than Cam's method of transportation. Her fingers fumbled to unfasten her watch, setting it on the table in front of her as though it might read differently from that angle.

Dad squeezed her shoulder. "They must be running late." While he scanned the crowd, Mom closed her eyes, slowing her breathing to yoga mode. They always took it in turns to panic.

"If you had cell phones, you could call them," Jasper said helpfully.

"Phones are against the rules," Neill informed him. "That

said, it *is* rather late." I couldn't bring myself to seize the conversational opening. *Isn't it? And by the way, are you seeing anyone?*

"Teams, to your tables," said the announcer. "It's match time." There was an immediate flurry of movement. Dr. Pressler had taught in the theater department before her promotion to dean and knew how to command a room.

Mom finished her exhale before opening her eyes. "Mary," she said calmly, gesturing at the empty spaces where the twins should have been. "Neill."

Neill was up like a rocket, all but leaping into his seat while I hesitated, casting a last look at the entrance. When the twins did not magically appear, I dropped onto the bench between Cam and Neill, barely registering Bo's thumbs-up.

"Don't worry," Dad said, twinkling at me. "It's all in good fun." Cam snorted under her breath.

There was no time to explain that the pressure of the competition was only one of the reasons I'd begun to perspire. Was Addie still talking to herself in the bathroom, perhaps in need of sisterly support? And where was Van? Maybe she was having her own breakdown, in the parallel fashion of twins. Not to mention the absolute impossibility of making chitchat with Neill under these conditions. It would be like holding a tea party on a tightrope.

I rolled my head from one shoulder to the other, trying to stretch some of the tension from my neck. My eyes opened in time to watch Anjuli, seated with her mother and several other members of the psychology department at the Psy Fry table, turn away without acknowledging my existence. Good to know I was still a nonentity. There was nothing like a snubbing from your ex-best friend to warm the cockles of the heart.

"I see you," Neill whispered, apparently for my ears alone.

I assumed he was referring to my silent standoff with Anjuli. Then he winked.

"I get it." His tone was even more patronizing than I recalled. "Everything about me screams 'eligible bachelor.' I knew one of you would be unable to resist."

"One of who?"

"You Porter-Malcolm girls. Judging by the way you've been staring all night, it's obvious you're nursing a *tendre* for me. Hoping to be the Zelda to my F. Scott, the Vera to my Nabokov. To be honest, I'd hoped it would be one of the blondes. No offense. It's an aesthetic preference."

I stared at him, speechless. So much for changing my hairstyle.

"Just try not to get too flustered. I'll handle the questions." He nodded at the judges' table.

"First round," intoned Dr. Pressler, who also hosted a weekday classical music program on the campus radio station. "Our topic is 'sailing the seas.'"

Excited whispers crested and then hushed. Trivia Night themes were a closely guarded secret, though heated speculation abounded in the days leading up to the match. Mom and Dad had already started tossing names like Melville and Defoe back and forth, the way athletes jogged in place on the sidelines.

"Question number one." Dr. Pressler paused to survey the room. "Name three of the four shipwrecked sons from the novel originally published in 1812 as *Der Schweizerische Robinson*."

Doug's hand shot up. "Fritz, Franz, Ernest, and Jack," he said in a rush.

"Technically I asked for three, not four, but we'll let it stand," Dr. Pressler replied. "And of course, the novel in question is better known as *The Swiss Family Robinson. The Swiss Family Robinson*," she said a second time, an affectation my parents said she'd picked up from watching too much "Jeopardy."

At the Psy Fry table, Anjuli rolled her eyes. Ignoring her, I smiled my congratulations at Doug. Unfortunately, he was too busy staring wistfully at Noreen to notice.

"Our second question is about the artist Paul Gauguin." Smug looks passed among the members of the Humanities team. "Before his more famous sojourn in Tahiti, Gauguin spent time on which island?"

"Martinique!" yelled a young visual arts professor.

"He was on his way home from Panama," one of his teammates added, not to be outdone.

Mom leaned closer to me. "They're both up for tenure this year."

The next question, about the HMS *Beagle*, went to an emeritus member of the biology faculty, who name-dropped Darwin as though they were personally acquainted. A history professor claimed a question about Sir Francis Drake. Then a brief scuffle broke out between two archaeologists over land versus sea routes and the peopling of the Americas.

"Last question for this round," Dr. Pressler said loudly, allowing another few seconds for the contretemps to subside. "How many *e*'s are there in Queequeg?"

"Three," Mom and Dad shouted in unison, before looking sheepishly at Cam, who was technically the family Melville expert.

"No problem," she said mildly, sipping her tea. In truth it had been more of a speed question than one of knowledge; I could have answered too, had I not been distracted by the sound of the door opening and the shuffling of feet as several new arrivals squeezed inside.

"It's Van," I said eagerly. Neill cursed under his breath. As Van made her way to our table, I waited for Addie to appear behind her. Then I caught a glimpse of cascading ringlets. She'd brought *Phoebe* to Trivia Night?

"Round one is officially over," Dr. Pressler announced. "Please complete any substitutions or other team business during the five-minute break." The timekeeper checked his watch.

"Hey," said Van. "Sorry we're late." I felt my eyebrows lift at the collective pronoun. Maybe it was some kind of cast bonding exercise. "How's it going so far?" She glanced at the score sheet, nodding at the even spread of points—typical at this stage of the evening. The action always heated up as the evening progressed. Her gaze shifted to Neill. "Thanks for keeping my seat warm."

What she couldn't see was that he had his legs wrapped around the base of the table and was holding on for dear life.

Removing him would have required the application of both brute force and an industrial-strength lubricant.

"Here." I extricated myself from the bench, one leg at a time. "Take my spot." Part of me hoped Van might protest, but she merely patted me on the head before seating herself in my place. Her concern was reserved for Phoebe, whom she pointed to the chair between Bo and Jasper I'd been planning to claim.

"I guess I'll circulate a little," I said to no one in particular. Anjuli sniffed pointedly as I passed her table.

The line for refreshments was six or seven deep, but since I wasn't really thirsty I didn't mind.

"That was something," the person behind me said in a confidential tone.

I spun, confirming the impossible: Alex Ritter, at Trivia Night. "Why are you—" I began, before answering my own question. "Phoebe."

He *hmm*ed an affirmative, gazing across the room at her. "Did you know she was an actual cheerleader, before she discovered her inner artiste?"

It might have sounded like a boast — *I'm dating a cheerleader!* — if not for the spark of amusement in his eyes. "I . . . did not know that."

"She keeps it on the down low. One of the many phases of Phoebe. Although that was middle school, so I don't know if it counts. Before the dance conservatory."

The offhanded manner in which he relayed these facts seemed to presume that I was either a) already acquainted with the broad strokes of her biography or b) desperate to know more because Phoebe was so incredibly fascinating.

Unless it signified that c) Alex regarded me as a confidante. I hadn't considered that as a potential consequence of asking him for advice. The prospect should have been alarming, yet I was mostly conscious of a flush of warmth. He could have been talking to anyone but had chosen *me*.

He nudged me with his elbow. "Let's hope she doesn't get fired up and start turning handsprings."

I looked down, swallowing a laugh. "It's definitely not that kind of crowd."

"No joke." He leaned closer. "These people are scary. I was afraid someone was going to be strangled with their own bow tie."

"Wait until the third round. It's a free-for-all."

"Are we talking *Game of Thrones*–type stuff here, Merrily? Should I not have worn white?" He batted his lashes, leaving me temporarily at a loss for words. Which was probably for the best, as I might have commented on the fact that for once he wasn't wearing blue, and that *could* have given him the impression that I made a study of his wardrobe.

Dr. Pressler clapped her hands. "Please take your seats, everyone. Round two is about to begin."

The crowd in front of us dispersed, leaving a clear path to the refreshments. I reached for one of the chunky plastic tumblers lined up on the table, then hesitated. "Would you like a drink?" I asked, turning to Alex.

"Just the one. I'm driving."

I handed him a room-temperature cup, then grabbed another for myself before threading my way through the tables to a vacant spot near the kitchen. To my surprise, Alex followed. Before I could ask why he was trailing me instead of sitting with his inamorata, Dr. Pressler's voice cut through the chatter.

"The theme for our next round is Sex and Censorship."

Shaking his head, Alex passed me his drink, placing his freed hands over my ears. "You're too young to hear this." We stood that way for a moment, his hands warm against the sides of my face. "You do have curls, you know." One of his hands shifted so that the thumb brushed my temple. "Right there."

I twisted out of his grip, afraid he would feel the pounding of my pulse. "Here," I said, handing his cup back to him.

The first question was about *Lolita*. I kept my eyes fixed straight ahead, but it wasn't enough to block out the teasing glance Alex slid my way. Still grinning, he took a sip of his drink, only to gag loudly enough to interrupt a question about erotic imagery in classical sculpture.

Half the room turned to stare, more affronted than concerned for his welfare. Alex raised a hand in mute apology. As soon as everyone looked away, he spit into his cup.

"That's disgusting," I said.

"No, disgusting is what I just drank. Are you trying to kill me?"

"It's water. With a little raw cider vinegar. It's supposed to be good for you."

"Define 'good.'"

"Something about the immune system. I think."

He shook his head. "How could you do this to me, Merrily? I thought we had something. Here, feel my throat." Taking hold of my wrist, he raised it so that my fingers brushed his neck. "Is there a hole?"

The skin was, of course, perfectly intact. Also warm to the touch and very much alive; I could feel his pulse beat against my fingertips. Swallowing hard, I repossessed my hand. Was he actually flirting with me while his significant other was in the same room? That struck me as reckless, even for him.

"Cat got your tongue, Merrily? Or did you fry your vocal cords with this stuff?" He raised his cup before setting it in a gray plastic tub of dirty dishes.

"Why do you keep calling me that?"

"You said you didn't like your name." He edged around to the other side of me, putting distance between himself and the abandoned drink. "It suits you. Merrily, merrily, merrily, as in, 'life is but a dream.'"

"I'm familiar with the reference."

"You don't like it?"

"I'm trying to listen," I replied, evading the question.

"Which of these common items was *not* used as a vehicle for Victorian pornography?" Dr. Pressler read in stentorian tones. "A. Trading cards. B. Snuffboxes. C. Pocket watches. D. Tussie-mussies."

Neill bounced a foot off his chair. "D. D. D," he chanted, waving both arms.

"Correct," said Dr. Pressler. Neill looked so pleased with himself I was surprised he didn't run a victory lap.

"Who's the guy?" Alex asked, following the direction of my gaze.

My mouth made a moue of displeasure, or at least what I imagined a *moue* to look like. "Neill."

"You two have a history?"

"What?"

"You keep looking at him."

"Yeah, no. There's no history there—and definitely no future." Breaking the news to Arden would be hard, but still preferable to feeding the inferno of Neill's ego.

"Sure, Merrily. Whatever you say. Two-time me all you want."

"Believe me, he's way too much of a Casaubon. Full of himself," I explained, before he could ask. "And threatened by anyone else with a brain. Why Dorothea ever married such a withered old windbag I'll never understand."

Blue eyes studied my face. "Dorothea?"

"From *Middlemarch*."

Alex nodded. "Of course." He was silent for a moment, watching Neill drum the table with both hands. "Is a tussie-mussie one of those fluffy things French maids carry around?"

"It's a small floral arrangement."

He considered this in silence. "Then that was a pretty obvious answer?"

"Yes," I agreed, pleased he'd pointed this out.

"Do you think they'll ask about that dirty book you told me to read?"

"I never—"

"*Dangerous Liaisons,*" he reminded me. "Because you'd be all over that one."

"I'm not in this round," I reminded him.

"Lucky for me." He leaned closer, nudging me with his shoulder. "What was the guy's name again?"

"Neill?"

"No. The one who wrote the book."

"Choderlos de Laclos."

"Say it slowly."

"Cho-der-los de—" I broke off, realizing he was toying with me. "Shouldn't you check on Phoebe?"

"Why?" He made a show of looking around. "Did someone give her one of those drinks?"

The innocent act was cut short by the end of the second round. The noise level jumped as teams and spectators began to move around the room, heatedly discussing the recent action.

"Excuse me," said a voice from behind me. I tried to move out of the way, but the only place to go was closer to Alex. I mumbled an apology while bumping against him. The contact was only slightly more intimate than the time I'd measured him for a costume he didn't want. When I looked to see whether whoever it was had enough room to get by, my eyes widened.

"Anjuli." The last thing I'd expected was for her to seek me out, especially after looking right through me before—

Her arm jutted toward Alex. "Anjuli. From Psy Fry."

"Team name," I explained in response to his puzzled look.

Inching forward, she angled her body to block me from view. "Do you act?" She made a square with her hands, positioning it in front of his face like a viewfinder.

Alex looked from Anjuli to me. I thought I had schooled my expression, but whatever he read on my face made him turn back to Anjuli with a thin smile. It was not one of his patented charm offensives. "We're kind of in the middle of something here."

"You're funny. How do you feel about surrealism?"

"Pretty much the same way Mary feels about me talking to her friends. It's a hard pass, I'm afraid."

"That's okay." Anjuli returned his regretful smile with a relieved one of her own. "We've grown apart lately anyway."

I scoffed at the euphemistic phrasing.

"If you're thinking I look familiar, it's probably from the article in the school newspaper. 'Rising Stars of Experimental Cinema.' I suggested it to the editor." Anjuli pressed a business card into his hand. "Let me know if you want to do a screen test."

As she walked away my stomach roiled, a bitter stew of disappointment and cider vinegar.

The door to Mung's swung open, ushering in a blast of cold air. It also brought Addie, whose face appeared both mustacheless and reasonably composed. Some of the tension in my spine dissipated. Now that she was here, everything could go back to normal. Someone (most likely Van) would tell Neill to shove off, and that would be that.

But as Addie approached, it was Van who stood, without acknowledging her twin. Turning her back on the team table, Van squeezed in beside Phoebe. It looked like they were sharing a chair, bodies pressed together from shoulder to hip. What was it about theater people and lack of personal boundaries? Always giving each other back rubs or flopping their legs onto someone's lap or . . . slowly drawing the pad of a thumb across the other person's palm.

I whipped my head around. It looked like . . . but maybe I was . . . only it had been so telling. The smallest of gestures, one hand touching another, yet even from across the room the intimacy of that covert caress rocked me back on my heels. I needed to compare notes with someone, make sure I wasn't reading too much into it. Except the person standing closest to me was Alex Ritter.

"Oh," I said, as curiosity gave way to chagrin.

"What?" He tried to see past me. Grabbing his arm, I spun him around to face the opposite direction.

"Have you seen the mural? It's like *The Last Supper* but with all these sci-fi characters." I pointed at the crude painting that graced the restaurant's back wall. "The owner is really into that stuff. Hence the name of this place."

"I thought mung was a type of bean."

I nodded much too eagerly. "Yes, but there was some bad guy named Ming the Merciless, so . . . you know. A play on words."

Alex looked from me to the mural. I wasn't sure he was buying my attempt to distract him.

"That's Spock," I continued with false cheer, "and Chewbacca and that robot guy—"

"It's a Dalek." His gaze shifted to my hand, still gripping his sleeve, but he made no move to break free. "You seem nervous, Merrily."

"No! Well, maybe a little. But only because of Trivia Night. Nothing else."

He shifted so that we faced each other. "Are you sure?"

"Take your seats, everyone," said Dr. Pressler. "It's time for the third round."

I seized on the diversion. "We better, you know—"

"Find the seats we don't have?"

"Yes," I agreed, too wound up to invent a better excuse. I led him to another corner of the room, from which it would be much harder to see Van and Phoebe's surreptitious flirtation. Whatever his past transgressions, Alex didn't deserve to be publicly betrayed. Especially after the way he'd taken my part with Anjuli.

"They call this the Melee Round," I told him. "If none of the teams know the answer, anyone can weigh in."

He favored me with one of his lazy smiles. "Madness."

I shrugged; he'd see for himself soon enough.

"Our theme for this evening's final round is popular culture." Dr. Pressler savored each syllable, as if she were licking the words off a spoon. Groans erupted from all sides.

Alex bent to whisper in my ear. "It's like their worst nightmare."

"Pretty much."

While he surveyed the unhappy faces surrounding us, I snuck a glance at Phoebe and Van. The handsy business seemed to be at an end, at least for now. I wanted to walk across the room and ask my sister how she could be with someone who was already in a relationship. It was such a blatant moral failing. That must be why Addie had been withdrawn lately: the weight of knowing her twin had become the Other Woman.

I was so busy making sure Alex didn't notice anything untoward, I barely heard the first few questions. We were standing close enough for him to nudge me with his elbow any time he found a response particularly amusing, such as Noreen guessing the Beatles when the answer was Justin Bieber.

"Even I knew that one."

I feigned surprise. "You have hidden depths."

He gave me another of those looks — pleased? intrigued? — that made it difficult for me to remember what we'd been talking about. Somewhere far away, a voice read the next question.

Suddenly I snapped to attention. "Wait, what?"

Alex shrugged, hands in his pockets. No one else seemed to know the answer either. Obligingly, Dr. Pressler repeated herself. "In this best-selling popular novel turned feature film, heroine Allie Calhoun suffers from which devastating disease?" She set down the index card, sliding her reading glasses to the end of her nose. "Bonus points if you can name the title of the work in question."

I turned to Alex. "I know this."

He started to raise my arm. "Shout it out."

"I can't." I pulled away. "The teams have to concede first. I'm sure somebody'll get it."

"My money's on you, Merrily." He moved to stand behind me, gathering my hair back over my shoulders and holding it loosely in one hand.

"What are you doing?" I half turned, but not so much as to dislodge his grip.

"You can't have a bunch of hair in the way when it's time to kick ass." He tapped his temple. "Sisters, remember?"

Of course I remembered. It was one of the disturbingly large number of Facts about Alex Ritter I had somehow collected. "I have to concentrate."

He nodded. "Eye of the tiger."

A professor of opera threw his hand in the air. "Tuberculosis!"

"Incorrect," said Dr. Pressler.

"Cholera," tried another voice.

Dr. Pressler shook her head.

"Scarlet fever."

"I'm afraid not," Dr. Pressler replied.

Desperation set in, shots in the dark fired at will:

"Putrid throat."

"Syphilis."

"Hemophilia."

"Typhoid."

"Diphtheria."

Alex's breath fanned my ear. "Interesting friends you have, Merrily."

"A wasting sickness!" That one was from my dad.

"There is a certain irony in your inability to find the correct answer," Dr. Pressler observed. I tensed, sure someone would get the hint.

"Electra complex," suggested one of the psychology faculty. "Fugue episodes!"

"One answer at a time, please," said Dr. Pressler. "Unless you're ready to concede, in which case we will open the floor." My hands clenched, fingernails pressing into damp palms.

When both kleptomania and scurvy had been shot down, Dr. Pressler surveyed the room. "Alternates, you may weigh in."

Heart thundering, I raised my hand.

"Yes." Dr. Pressler dipped her chin at me. "Do you have an answer?"

I nodded.

"For which team?"

"Let's Get Lit." I ignored Alex's snort.

"Go ahead," said the dean.

"Alzheimer's."

She smiled. "That is correct."

Over the ensuing hubbub, I added, "And it's from *The Notebook*."

"Also correct. With the bonus point" — she paused to glance at the scorekeeper — "Let's Get Lit takes the win."

Alex squeezed my shoulders. When I spun to face him, he held up both hands for a double high-five, linking his fingers with mine when I would have let go.

"Nice job, Merrily," he whispered, eyes never leaving mine.

Jasper whooped loudly, and someone called my name — the real one.

"I think they want to carry you around the room." Alex slowly slipped his hands from mine before nudging me toward my family.

"Wonderful," said Dad.

"We're so proud," added Mom.

As they accepted grudging congratulations from the other team captains, Neill thrust himself into the fray. "Lucky for you they asked something only a teenage girl would know."

Jasper shoved in front of him. "Don't get your panties in a twist. Mary just saved your bacon."

"Nice work, Mare-Bear," said Van. At her side, Phoebe offered a smile I couldn't quite return. "Mary's the baby of the family," Van explained with a poignant sigh. "They grow up so fast."

"Actually, I'm the *second* youngest," I corrected. "And sixteen isn't a baby."

Van frowned at me. "You're not sixteen."

"Almost," said Addie, who had come up behind me. "Her birthday's next Saturday."

Bo sketched a check mark in the air. "Marked that date on my calendar a long time ago."

"You should come for dinner," Van said to Phoebe, as though the rest of us were a convenient backdrop to their flirtation.

"Will there be cake?" Phoebe asked, eyelashes fluttering as she pretended to mull it over.

From anyone else, it would have been charming, but I refused to be swayed. "Sometimes I ask for pie."

"You do not," Van argued. "You've never once asked for pie for your birthday."

"I could change my mind."

"Pie is also good," Phoebe murmured.

Neill grinned obsequiously at her. "I like it both ways, too. Maybe I'll stop by." He winked at me before mouthing the words *you're welcome*.

Dear Diary,

I can't remember the last time I was this excited about my birthday. Not the presents, or even turning sixteen. I just keep imagining the party, and having this perfect, candlelit evening with my friends and family to celebrate all the changes in my life over the last year. A very civilized, elegant affair that says to the world, "See? She's becoming such a refined young lady."

M.P.M.

CHAPTER 22

The rule of birthdays in the Porter-Malcolm household was that for twenty-four hours, you got to choose all your favorite things, and no one was allowed to complain. In practice, this applied mostly to food. Picking a menu without editorial comments from six other people was a luxury — as I'd explained to my friends when asking them to join us for dinner.

Though I had yet to forgive Van for inviting her illicit girlfriend to my party without so much as a by-your-leave, my general mood was upbeat. The changes in my life since last year felt satisfyingly dramatic: a milestone worthy of celebration. Plus my grades were good, my skin reasonably unblemished (knock on wood), and I had real friends — the kind who seemed genuinely excited for me, instead of complaining that I was too hard to buy for because I only liked books, and since I'd read everything they had no choice but to forgo the giving of presents altogether, as Anjuli had done last year.

By contrast, Arden, Lydia, and Terry had been whispering

about my birthday for weeks, with a dramatic uptick once I mentioned Neill's probable attendance. I knew perfectly well he was only coming to gorge himself on free food, but rather than spoil the festive atmosphere, I decided to let them discover the truth firsthand. As soon as he regaled them with a few choice anecdotes about papers he was thinking of writing, or the pithiest comments he'd made in class that week, my friends would beg me to run the other way.

The day swept onward, and I sailed happily in its wake until it was almost six o'clock and the house smelled pleasingly of fondue. My triple-layer yellow cake with chocolate frosting was waiting in the kitchen. At last the doorbell rang.

"I'll get it," I yelled, hurtling down the stairs. When I yanked open the front door, Anjuli glowered back at me. My smile crumbled to dust.

"What are you doing here?" I asked, after rapidly discarding my first theory (a rupture in the fabric of space and time).

Anjuli gave a huff of annoyance. "Your mom called my mom."

"Why didn't you say no?"

"She would have asked too many questions." Her eyes shifted sideways. Was that a flash of guilt? "Don't worry. I won't stay long. There's a Maya Deren retrospective at the Orpheum later, so obviously everybody from EFS is going. We might get coffee after."

Speaking of mothers, mine chose that moment to step into the hall. "Come in, come in," she said, beckoning to Anjuli. "Why don't you go on into the living room? We have snacks."

As soon as Anjuli was out of earshot, I turned on my mother. "Why did you invite her?"

"I assumed you'd been too busy with school to worry about party planning." She patted my cheek. "Sorry if I undermined your independence."

This was so far off the mark I had no idea where to begin. Had she not noticed Anjuli wasn't coming over anymore? Did she pay *any* attention to my life whatsoever?

The doorbell sounded a second time. "I'll get it," I said, reaching for the knob.

I was so ready to turn to my mother and say, *See? These are my real friends!* that it took me several heartbeats to register that I was looking at Neill. He didn't wait to be invited in.

"Got something for you," he said, and I almost fell over from the shock. *Neill* had gotten me a present? Then I realized he was talking to my mother. He held out a thumb drive as if presenting her with a jeweled scepter. "My latest magnum opus."

Mom smiled thinly. Neill wasn't one to write twenty pages when forty-five (plus references) offered so much more scope for his brilliance. "Thank you, Neill. I'd better get back to the kitchen. There are things in need of . . . stirring."

"Is she here?" Neill asked as soon as we were alone.

"Who?"

"That girl you were talking to at Mung's. Your sister's friend?"

"I'm not sure *friend* is the right term. And no, Phoebe is not here." She was probably too glamorous to attend a sixteenth

252

birthday party. Even though I hadn't wanted her to come, I felt preemptively offended by the idea she wouldn't show.

"Great name. Perky." He made squeezing motions with both hands that I opted not to interpret. "Can't wait to further that acquaintance, if you know what I mean."

"Yeah, she's pretty busy. Lots of . . . commitments." Not that she was honoring them.

He winked. "That's what I'm counting on. Fits right into my plan."

Part of me considered putting my fingers in my ears and humming, but the rest was too curious. "What plan?"

"Have you seen my course load this semester?" When I shook my head, he snorted. "Let's just say it's *monumental*. Do I have time to manage a relationship? No way. But does that mean I have to be alone? No. It means I need to be smart. Which as you know is not a problem."

By pretending I was a statue, I managed not to gag.

"I figure anywhere between a third and a half will work with my schedule."

"A third of . . . ?"

"A girlfriend. Especially if there's another lady involved. The two of them can handle all the emotional business, freeing me up to devote the necessary time to my studies." He leaned forward, lowering his voice. "I'm on track to finish my PhD by twenty-two." He nodded, as if I'd made some expression of amazement. "Quite a feather in your parents' cap."

I shook my head. "Van will never date you."

"Not directly, but by extension —"

"No. And Phoebe already has a boyfriend, so you'd be looking at a foursome. At least."

Neill's foot tapped. "But is he an academic wunderkind?"

"He's not dumb. And he's *quite* debonair."

He thought this over, breath whooshing loudly through his nostrils. "You're just jealous."

Before I could assure him of my indifference, someone knocked at the door. "Snacks are in the living room." I waved Neill in that direction before turning to greet the new arrival.

This time I was braced for another unpleasant surprise, so of course it was my friends, the people *I'd* invited to my birthday party. They came in like springtime, soft and sweet-smelling and bearing flowers, as well as a helium balloon, gift bag, and giant box of chocolates. They took it in turns to hug me, calling me Lady Mary and telling me I looked great. (Anton had found me a vintage Liberty print blouse in rich autumnal shades.) Before I could explain about Anjuli, someone tapped the half-open door.

"Hello," said a deep voice. Apparently my mother had also invited Pittaya, who was holding a book-shaped present with an elaborate red bow. I wondered if he'd wrapped it himself.

"I thought you said Neill was short," Arden whispered behind her hand.

"This is Pittaya." I pointed out Terry and Arden. "Lydia you know." They nodded at each other, not quite smiling. "Why don't we ... go into the dining room?" I suggested, since the living room was now full of people I preferred to avoid.

We'd taken a few steps in that direction when the front

door swung open behind us and Bo staggered in, carrying a pot of mums so voluminous he could barely see over it.

"Oh my gosh," said Arden.

"I told my mom to get the biggest bunch they had." Bo's voice sounded strained.

"Would you like some help?" Pittaya asked.

"Thanks, man." Bo passed him the flowers, dusting off his hands before adjusting his tie.

"That is so sweet!" Arden looked like she wanted to pinch his cheeks.

"Yeah, thanks." I smiled at him. "Jasper would never bring me flowers."

He winked at me. "I'm not your brother. Can't say that enough times."

"Nice tux," said Lydia.

"This old thing?" He smoothed his lapels as he sauntered past us, leading the way into the dining room. "Why don't you put them in the middle of the table?" he told Pittaya.

"Actually, the fondue pot goes there," I said quickly, before the table could be turned into an arboretum. "How about here?"

As I arranged the flowers and gifts on the sideboard, Mom hurried in from the kitchen with a basket of cubed bread.

"Hello, Pittaya and Bo." She turned to the girls, smiling politely. "Are you friends of Cam's?"

Heat rushed to my face. "Mom, these are *my* friends. Arden and Lydia and Terry." They smiled politely at my mother.

"Hello, ladies." Jasper posed in the doorway, one hand to his heart. "You're a vision of loveliness."

While my friends laughed, I counted placemats. "Can we put another leaf in the table?" I asked my mother, sotto voce.

"Boys." She clapped her hands. "Go down to the basement. We need more chairs."

Jasper opened his mouth.

"Because you're standing there, that's why," Mom said before he could protest. Muttering to herself about extra skewers, she headed for the kitchen.

Voices approached from the other direction. My shoulders stiffened, while Arden's expression brightened. "Is it him?" she asked.

"Um," I replied.

Anjuli entered first. Neill followed, a bowl of cheese puffs clutched to his chest.

"Hi. We're friends of Mary's from school," Arden announced with a perfect cocktail party smile. "How do you know each other?"

Open-mouthed, Anjuli looked from me to the other three, and then at Pittaya. Her eyes narrowed. "I'm basically her oldest friend."

"From my old school," I hinted.

"Ah." Arden was temporarily at a loss for words. "How nice that we can all be here to celebrate Mary," she finally managed, placing a restraining hand on Lydia's arm.

Thumping and clattering, Jasper and Bo made their way up from the basement. "Excuse us," Jasper said, forcing Anjuli to dodge out of his way. "Oops," he added, disingenuously. "Didn't see you there."

"Is dinner ready?" Neill crunched as he spoke, his fingers scrabbling at the bottom of the mostly empty bowl.

"No!" Jasper sent me an accusing look. "You didn't tell me there were cheese puffs!"

"It's a night full of surprises," I replied as my brother stalked across the room to repossess the bowl.

He looked suspiciously at Neill's hand. "Have you been licking your fingers?" Neill shrugged. With a scowl of disgust, Jasper shoved the bowl back at him.

"You know it's bad when Jasper won't eat it," Bo whispered from behind me.

I could only nod, thinking how ill all this boded for the meal ahead. Food shortages. Petty squabbles. Poor table manners. Instead of seeing my family at its best, my friends would be treated to the kind of infighting that always broke out when resources were scarce.

Then I heard footsteps on the stairs and Addie appeared, bringing with her a ray of hope. If anyone could keep things civilized, it was my serene oldest sister.

She smiled at me as she placed a package next to the other presents. "Full house."

"Mm-hm," I agreed through closed lips.

Next to arrive was Cam, who took in the scene with a quick side-to-side flicker of the eyes but otherwise betrayed no reaction. Van arrived a few steps behind.

"Which one is from us?" she asked her twin, glancing at the pile of gifts.

"That depends," Addie replied. "What did you get her?"

"I assumed you were on top of it. You know the strain I'm under. Four extra rehearsals this week alone. I've barely slept."

"It really *is* a tragedy," Addie said, not quite under her breath.

Mom burst through the swinging door. "Hot stuff, coming through."

"And we have fondue," Dad quipped, a few steps behind.

A pair of extra pans had been pressed into service as fondue pots; one cast iron and the other a cheerful red enamel. Hopefully the arrangement appeared semi-intentional, and not as though we were scrambling to accommodate unexpected guests.

"Grab a chair, any chair," Dad said. Anjuli and Neill reacted as though a piñata had burst open, leaping forward to seize what they could, while Jasper calmly pulled out a chair for Terry. Pittaya and Lydia reached for the same seat, but he immediately conceded, bowing her toward it. When the dust cleared, I tried not to mind that I was stuck with the worst folding chair, the wooden slats striping the backs of my thighs.

"That's certainly an impressive pile of gifts," my father remarked as the bread basket made its way around the table.

"And flowers," added Bo.

Jasper stabbed his fondue fork into the nearest pot of bubbling cheese. Neill, seated next to him, pulled out an empty skewer. He cast an accusing glare at Jasper, who smiled beatifically. Neill flushed, looking around for someone to whom he could tattle.

"More bread?" my father offered.

"Do you have any white bread?"

Mom gave Neill a look.

He gulped. "The crunchy kind is perfect." Careful to avoid Jasper's marauding skewer, Neill began covering cube after cube in cheese, filling his plate with gradually congealing lumps. Lydia stared, aghast.

"That's what you call a fon-don't," Bo whispered. He and Jasper fist-bumped.

Arden smiled at my parents. "This is delicious. You know what it reminds me of?" I wondered which part of the experience she was referring to: The fondue? The uninvited guests? Neill's gluttony? An eighth-grader in a tux? Her eyes gleamed. *Little Women.*

Everyone with the last name Porter-Malcolm froze.

"Because of the big family," Arden said into the fraught silence, her smile dimming. "Or ... not. I mean, obviously you're not all girls."

"I could be Laurie," Jasper offered. "The heartthrob next door."

Mom failed to notice that her youngest child had made a literary reference. "Alcott is a sensitive subject around here," she said grimly. "I lost a sister to that book."

Arden blanched. "Like Beth," she whispered, pressing a hand to her lips. "I am so sorry! I had no idea."

Jasper snorted into his milk glass. "Aunt Abigail's still alive and kicking."

Mom lifted her chin. "It was a question of interpretation."

"Our aunt is kind of literal," I explained.

"As opposed to *literary*," added Van.

Jasper tossed a chunk of bread into his mouth. "She's a reenactor, basically. They have this whole old-timey village, and they live there and pretend to be the Alcotts."

"The Marches, you mean," Addie corrected.

He shrugged. "Whatevs."

"They've turned that novel into a tourist attraction." Our mother quivered with righteous indignation. "Can you imagine?"

"Er, no," Arden said quickly, though I could tell she'd been doing just that.

"Cousin Jo loves her calico." Jasper jerked suddenly, then bent to rub his shin. I couldn't tell which of my sisters had kicked him.

Mom was eviscerating a chunk of bread with her fingers. "Some of us are more serious about literature than others."

"I'm sure you're the *most* serious," Arden said fervently.

Another silence descended on the table, making it easy to hear the light tapping at the door. Van went instantly alert, setting down her fork. "Come in," she yelled.

Phoebe floated into the room, pink-cheeked from the cold with an adorable knit hat over her abundant curls. She looked like a magazine ad for ice skating and engagement rings.

"Sorry I'm late." She offered no excuse beyond a glimpse of her dimples and a wave that took in the table at large. Something about her smile tugged at my memory, but before I could place it a more immediate dilemma presented itself. We were out of chairs. Van kept looking around the room as though additional seating might materialize from the ether.

"She can sit by me," Neill offered, though he had neither an empty chair nor space to add one.

Addie scraped the tines of her fork across her plate. "Maybe she should take my place."

Van frowned at her. "How would that help?"

"She obviously brings more to the table than I do." Addie wasn't looking at her twin, so she didn't see the way Van's entire body tensed.

"Seriously, Addie? What is your problem?"

"You have no idea, do you?"

"Obviously not, which is why I *asked!*"

I snuck a glance at Phoebe, still marooned in the middle of the floor. In that moment, I almost felt sorry for her. Then again, it wasn't *her* birthday going to wrack and ruin.

"Girls." Dad spoke with a note of bewilderment. "Perhaps there's a more appropriate venue—"

Addie threw down her fork. "I'm tired of being ignored." Her voice was thick, as if she were on the verge of tears.

Van looked stricken. "I know we haven't been spending as much time together lately," she began, falling silent when her twin gave a bark of bitter laughter.

"You think I'm jealous because you're spending all your time with her?"

From the way Van's eyes met Phoebe's, I could tell they'd developed this theory together. "Maybe?" Van ventured.

"I wanted that part," Addie said quietly, her eyes fixed on her plate.

"You?"

Even without the air of incredulity, this would have been the wrong response. Addie threw up her hands. "Yes, me," she snapped. "Why is that so shocking? You think I can't do it."

"No—I just—you never said anything."

"I shouldn't have to tell you. You're supposed to *know* me."

"There are recorded examples of identical twins with—" Neill began, before our mother cut him off with a razor-edged glare.

"I thought you wanted to be Iago," I ventured.

Addie gave a small shrug. "I figured Desdemona was more attainable. It's a minor part. Nowhere near as challenging."

It was as though the twins had switched personalities, and kind, patient Addie was now the caustic one. Or maybe that side of her had always existed, but she'd been content to let Van supply the edge for both of them.

"You are such a snob," Van snapped, casting a worried look at Phoebe.

"At least I'm not a cliché," her twin retorted.

"Excuse me?"

"The director dating the leading lady?" Addie scoffed. "Spare me. *I think we should add a dance sequence.* I wonder where that idea came from!"

Van set down her fork. "You know, Addie, maybe the reason I've been avoiding you is that you're acting like such a shrew."

"Me? You're the one who goes on and on about how it's so hard trying to balance the life of an artist with your *relationship*, like the rest of us couldn't possibly understand."

Van lifted her chin. "I really like Phoebe. She's important to me." To her credit, Phoebe blushed.

Arden's fingers closed around my wrist. "*Like* like?" she mouthed.

I nodded. Her raised eyebrows posed the next obvious question — *what about Alex?* To which I could only shrug. Even if we'd been able to speak freely, I wasn't sure what to say.

Nor, it seemed, was anyone else. Aside from the sound of Neill chewing, the room was painfully quiet — until Yarb started retching from somewhere under the table. Feet jerked out of the way, though we were packed so tightly it was hard to move very far. The convulsive gagging went on and on, like a lawnmower trying to start.

Happy birthday to me, I thought glumly.

"Jasper," Mom said.

"What do you want me to do, reason with him? Hey there, Yarb, maybe you could yack up that hairball later, when we're not eating fondue?"

Arden, who had a sensitive gag reflex, clamped her lips together.

Jasper pushed his chair back far enough to peer beneath the table. "False alarm," he announced, straightening. "Far as I can tell. But I'd keep your shoes on, just in case."

Cam stood. "I have a boyfriend. We're going to Winter

Formal. He might stop by later for cake, if there's any left." She grabbed her plate and glass. "You can have my place," she told Phoebe.

Phoebe perched nervously at the edge of the chair. There was another awkward silence—almost long enough to make me wish Yarb would start hacking again.

"Winter Formal is a lot of fun," Arden said with a faint air of desperation.

"High-school dances," Neill scoffed, still working on his lukewarm fondue nuggets.

"You went to a lot of them?" Phoebe asked sweetly. Jasper grinned at her in open-mouthed delight.

"Jeff," I said, before another fight could break out. "That's the name of Cam's date. He's very environmentally conscious."

Mom's lips pursed with interest. "Hmm."

"We set them up," Arden confided.

Pittaya turned to Lydia. "Do you have a date?"

She folded her napkin before setting it down. "Are you asking?"

He nodded.

"Okay." Lydia tried to sound casual, but a smile was about to break free, despite—or perhaps because of—the death glare she was getting from Anjuli.

"But . . . just like that?" Arden looked as stunned as I felt, though I doubted *she'd* mentally penciled Pittaya in as a date for Terry. "After all the times I tried to set you up?"

Lydia moved a few leaves of salad around her plate. "Maybe I didn't want a pity date."

Oh no, I thought desperately, clutching the edge of the table. *Not them too!*

"We should go together," Terry said, throwing me a lifeline. "Since we don't have dates."

"That's hot." Neill spoke through a mouthful of bread and cheese, making the words even more distasteful.

My parents turned to him in unison, smoke all but billowing from their ears. "I was talking about the fondue," he choked, reaching for his glass.

"Well, this has been unexpectedly fun." Jasper folded his hands on the table in front of him. "Is it time for cake?"

Dear Diary,

I wish I could afford to visit a **modiste** to design the gown for my first dance. She would hold up the fabrics one by one — shot silk, crushed velvet, sprigged muslin — until she found the perfect material to transform me into a more radiant version of myself. But then I'd also need a maid to do my hair, and a carriage to get me there. Not to mention a dancing master to keep me from making a fool of myself.

M.P.M.

CHAPTER 23

I thought the aftermath of my birthday would resemble a war-torn landscape: the rubble of buildings, scorched earth, hollow-eyed survivors staggering through the ruined streets. Instead, the ensuing weeks were marked by a climate of remote politeness. It was as if the annual quota for soul-baring had been met and exceeded in that one night, leaving everyone shaky and subdued.

Arden made no further mention of Neill, beyond adding an entry about Egocentric Scoundrels with Poor Table Manners to our guide. Nor did she press Terry and me to find other dates, or demand details from Lydia about her plans with Pittaya. I attributed Arden's diminished enthusiasm to the pressures of school and being on the dance committee, plus the general frenzy of December, all of which must be exacerbating her scheduling difficulties with Miles. It was no wonder she seemed distracted.

At home, the rest of the family tiptoed around Addie and Van. Mom filled the tea cabinet with herbal blends that

prominently featured words like *soothing, harmony,* and *peace.*
When there were no further explosions, and Cam didn't rat-
tle the household with additional revelations, we cautiously
resumed our normal routines. Dad said hopeful things at the
dinner table about clearing the air, prompting Jasper to volunteer, "That wasn't me."

This was followed by a gaseous noise we all knew and
dreaded.

"Wait." My brother held up a finger. "That one was."

We all covered our noses.

❯✠

Despite the surface calm, it was not without trepidation that
I mounted the stairs to the attic the night of the dance. Partly
this was selfish; the twins had promised to do my hair and
makeup for the evening, and I wasn't sure how sublimated
aggression would translate to cosmetics use. My vanity was a
small thing, however, compared to the deep-seated need to see
the twins restored to their former place as pillars of my world.
They were supposed to be capable and mature, not sharp-
tongued and falling apart.

I knocked on the door of their bedroom already wearing
the dress Anton had helped me select from the Baardvaark costume department. The cocktail-length black number hailed
from a recent production of *Henry V,* set during the late 1940s.
It cinched in at the waist and poofed wide over the hips; according to Anton, this was a signature of Dior's New Look, and thus
perfectly suited to the Parisian theme. When I removed it from

the dry-cleaning bag, I found a note pinned to the shoulder in Anton's spiky cursive: "Try not to break too many hearts."

"What do you think?" I asked diffidently, when Addie opened the door.

She beckoned me inside. "Turn around." I made a slow rotation, holding the sides of the skirt as though about to curtsy.

My sister nodded in satisfaction. "You have such a tiny waist. It's perfect for this dress."

I looked down at myself in surprise. Where the twins and Cam were willowy and narrow-hipped, a look I'd always envied, my figure had a lot more ins and outs. Maybe that wasn't a bad thing, in this dress anyway. I swished experimentally from side to side. It was like wearing a cloud, only scratchier.

Van got up from her bed to adjust my neckline, which was relatively high-cut but wide enough to expose my collarbone. She twisted my hair into a coil so that we could check the effect in the full-length mirror. "Up or down?"

"Up." I liked the way it looked: dark dress, pale neck, dark hair.

Van turned to her twin. "Should we give her a beauty mark?"

"People will just think it's a weird freckle," I pointed out, not without a modicum of self-pity. My sisters all bronzed in the sun instead of speckling like a springer spaniel.

"It's winter," Addie said as she removed the last bobby pin from her mouth and slid it into my hair. "Your freckles hardly show. Anyway, I like them."

"Addie used to want freckles so badly she Sharpied herself," Van told me.

"It would have looked better if I hadn't used red."

"One of the grading pens?" My voice dropped to a scandalized whisper. We were strictly forbidden to borrow them, as our parents required a steady supply to mark student essays and they tended to slip through our father's fingers like grains of sand.

"Mom thought she had chicken pox," Van said.

"But then she realized that was impossible, because you would have had them too." Addie looked at Van as she spoke. When their eyes met in the mirror I held my breath, lest I disrupt the fragile rapprochement. Van offered a tremulous smile, but Addie's expression had already shuttered.

"I'm going to check the curling iron." She kept her eyes on the floor as she hurried from the room.

"What?" Van asked, catching me looking at her. "You think it's all my fault."

"I never said that."

"You always side with Addie."

"No I don't!"

Van gave me a look that reminded me of our mother. I supposed she had a point. When battle lines were drawn, I defaulted to Team Addie, in the same way that Jasper and Cam had an unspoken alliance. I'd never thought about where that left Van.

"I'm just surprised," I said, in lieu of answering her directly.

"That I'm dating a woman?"

"Nobody cares about *that*."

Van looked disappointed. No doubt she had a speech prepared.

"What bothers me is that you're having an *affair*." My heart pounded as I waited for Van to respond.

Her brow furrowed. "Except neither of us is married."

"That doesn't mean it's not cheating."

"I'm not—wait, you think Phoebe's with someone else?"

It should have been a relief to discover Van didn't know, but she looked so crestfallen I almost wished I'd kept my mouth shut.

"Who?" she whispered.

I braced myself. "Alex. Alex Ritter. I saw them together at auditions."

Van was silent for a long moment. Then she bent forward, gripping the edge of the dresser. Her shoulders shook.

"It's okay!" I patted her with both hands. "You'll meet someone else, and they'll be so much better. You deserve someone faithful and true . . ." My voice trailed off as I realized my sister was laughing, not weeping. Had she succumbed to nervous hysteria? Maybe I should slap her.

Addie walked back into the room shaking a bottle of red nail polish. "What's so funny?"

Van wiped her eyes before taking a deep breath. "Mary just informed me that Phoebe is dating someone behind my back."

Addie's arm fell to her side. "I'll kill her."

"Wait!" Van waved her to silence. "You haven't heard the best part. Guess who it is?"

"Who?" Addie directed the question at me.

I sighed. "Alex Ritter."

Addie looked away, pressing a hand to her lips, but not quickly enough to hide that she was laughing at me too, albeit with more restraint. How wonderful they'd finally found something to agree on. I was sorely tempted to walk out and leave them to their mirth-filled reconciliation.

"I'm sorry." Addie gasped for breath, clutching her ribs. "I shouldn't laugh. You didn't know."

I looked from her to Van, who appeared to be on the verge of another fit. "Know what?"

"Alex is Phoebe's *brother*," Van said, clearly relishing the word. "Not her boy toy."

Phoebe was Alex's sister? I thought of their slender frames and curly wheat-blond hair, the dark lashes and blue-gray eyes. It was . . . not impossible.

"But he came to Trivia Night." This was not a protest so much as a question—the first of many circling my brain like moths around a porch light.

"He heard me telling Phoebe about it. Said it sounded entertaining." I felt Van's eyes on me. "Maybe he had another reason for showing up?"

Addie set down the nail polish. "Is there something you want to tell us, Mary?"

"Me?"

"Who else would he have gone there to see?" Addie asked.

"You. Van. Random strangers. How should I know?"

"Pretty sure he knows I'm spoken for," Van pointed out.

I sniffed. "That didn't stop him before."

Addie frowned. "What do you mean?"

"*Antony and Cleopatra,*" I reminded them. "With what's-her-name? She had a boyfriend at the time, and then Alex came along and suddenly people were sobbing in the prop room and slamming doors."

Van made a noise of disgust. "Oh please. Julia and Tad were like the low-rent Heathcliff and Cathy, way before Alex Ritter showed up. We ordered sandwiches after rehearsal once and somehow it led to this huge crisis with Tad locked in the bathroom and Julia rolling around on the stage yelling 'hey nonny my ASS.'"

"Over condiments," Addie recalled. "She was *not* a mustard person."

I must have missed that day. "But what about you guys? Didn't he, you know—"

"Flirt with us? Oh yeah. It was adorable. He was like a baby Lord Byron, without the sleaziness. Or the incest." Van grinned at me. "Too soon?"

"It was harmless," Addie put in. "Flattering in a way. You could tell he didn't really mean anything by it."

"Oh." It must be nice, to be able tell things like that.

"He wasn't the best-looking guy in the world, but he made you think he was." Van picked up a brush and began running it through her hair. "That's the power of charisma."

"Magnetism," Addie agreed. "The sparkle in the eye that hints at inner life."

I huffed in disbelief. "You're kidding, right? Alex Ritter is extremely handsome."

The twins exchanged a glance. Addie spoke first. "Are the two of you—"

"Dallying?" Van finished.

"No! Not at all." I looked at my hands, twisting in front of me. "That would be stupid."

"Why?" Van asked.

"Wouldn't you guys warn me away from someone like that?"

"I would never tell you who to love," Van said loftily. "I trust you to follow your heart. If it ends badly, so be it. You have to be open to new experiences. What's the point of living otherwise?"

There wasn't enough room in my brain to process what she was saying. "It doesn't matter. He's not really interested."

Van waved a finger at me. "Don't sell yourself short, Mare-Bear. I thought the same thing about Phoebe, but we Porter-Malcolms are not without attractions of our own."

"Be true to yourself and other people will see your worth. *If* they're worth your time." Addie's words seemed directed to her twin as much as me.

While Van smiled, a thread of unease settled in the pit of my stomach. They made it sound so easy, like riding a bike— but I had come late to that skill, too.

Dear Diary,

Even a Victorianist like me is not immune to the spell of the Cinderella trope. Is it humanly possible to attend a dance without thinking you might magically turn out to be the belle of the ball?

M.P.M.

CHAPTER 24

My rational mind was aware that Winter Formal wouldn't be a ball in the traditional sense. Nevertheless, I'd envisioned a certain level of elegance. If not crystal chandeliers, silk gloves, and a full orchestra, then at least a style of dancing that didn't involve the use of butt cheeks as hand grips.

As I stepped through the doors of the Millville High gymnasium, I was forced to scale my expectations down, and then down again, at which point I began to appreciate the effort that *had* been made. The streamers and balloons gave off a metallic sheen that went some way toward disguising the battle-worn state of the gym, and the giant Eiffel Tower projected on the wall was certainly on point, thematically. My classmates had also taken on a surface gloss, sporting hair as stiff and glittering as their new clothes. Eventually I might even get used to the groin-rubbing.

"It's a lot, isn't it?" Terry whisper-yelled at my side. "There's your sister."

She pointed to the dance floor, where Cam and Jeff were bringing a uniquely athletic flair to their spins and turns. Their moves had more in common with boomerang throwing than the minuet.

"Hey," said Lydia, stepping in front of us. She wore a sleeveless pink dress with a sweetheart neckline and smattering of sparkles across the bodice. "What are you looking at?"

"Mary's sister," Terry replied. "Cam."

Since the twins weren't at Winter Formal, the clarification seemed unnecessary. I felt a *ping* of curiosity as the music changed tempo. Lydia's shoulders twitched in time with the beat.

"Have you guys seen Arden?" she asked.

As I shook my head, it occurred to me how odd that was.

"Let me text her." Lydia slipped her phone from her beaded clutch. "Probably her dinner ran long." The ding of a response was immediate. "In the bathroom. She'll be here in a sec."

My inclination would have been to seek out a dark corner from which to wait and watch, until I remembered that Lydia was here with a date.

"Pittaya's helping with the sound system," she said, correctly interpreting my covert surveying of the crowd.

At last Arden appeared, dressed in the red gown she'd tried on at the mall. Her movements lacked their usual bounce, but I attributed that to the stiletto heels. A bold choice considering the height differential with her date.

Lydia peered over Arden's shoulder as they hugged. "Where's Miles?"

Arden's response was swallowed by the music. Was it my imagination, or had she flinched before answering?

"Huh?" said Lydia.

"He's not coming," Arden replied. I edged closer, thinking I must have misheard.

"He bailed on Winter Formal?" Lydia's hands balled into fists on her sequined hips.

Arden shook her head. "He bailed on *me*."

The three of us stared at her in shock until Lydia managed a hoarse, "What?"

"It's fine." Above her lock-jawed smile, Arden's eyes were bright with unshed tears. "I'm over it."

"Over—what are you saying?" Lydia sputtered. "Did you and Miles *break up?*"

"I don't really want to talk about it, but yes."

"Was it that girl?" Lydia demanded.

"No." Arden looked at the floor. "That wasn't the problem."

"What was it?" Terry asked.

Arden shrugged. "Me, apparently."

"That prissy little jerkwad," Lydia started to say, grinding each word between her teeth.

"I literally cannot do this right now," Arden said, holding up a hand. "I want tonight to be fun, and that means no crying."

Lydia pressed her lips together in an angry line, nostrils flaring. I suspected she was counting in her head. "Can you at least tell us what happened?" she said in a more measured tone.

"Fine." Arden bowed her head. "I'll give you the short

version. You know at Mary's birthday, how everyone was so brave, laying all their feelings on the line?"

I gave a reluctant nod, not sure I would have characterized the evening in quite that manner.

"It made me realize it was time to talk to Miles about some things, so I decided to do what Mary said, and last weekend I drove to the conference center where he was having his tournament."

"I said that?" I pressed a hand to my chest.

"Like the lady in the book," Arden reminded me. "The one who goes to surprise her husband, but then he thinks she's someone else?"

My stomach landed in my shoes. The last thing I'd intended was for Arden to use *The Tenant of Wildfell Hall* as a blueprint for her own life. Even by Brontë standards, that plot was over the top.

"And?" Lydia prompted. "Did he know it was you?"

"Yeah. Only he wasn't very excited to see me—especially after I let it slip why I was there. He wasn't happy about me not trusting him. Or the part where I was trying to trick him."

"What happened then?" Terry asked.

"He had to go to his next session." Arden bit her lip. "I felt bad because he was obviously upset, and he didn't exactly get to look over his note cards."

"Boo-freaking-hoo," Lydia cut in.

"Miles said he'd call me later," Arden offered. I couldn't tell whether she meant it as a defense of his behavior or was simply relating the next step in the story. "So I went home and tried not to completely fall apart."

"Why didn't you text me?" asked Lydia. "I would have come over!"

"Because I was hoping everything would be okay. I figured I could tell you when there was a happy ending." Arden blinked hard. Caught up in the blow-by-blow, I'd forgotten we already knew how this story finished.

"Did he call?" Lydia pressed.

"Yeah. The next day. That's when he said it was too much, and he couldn't keep me happy and fulfill his other quote-unquote *obligations,* so maybe we should take some time apart."

"But that's not the same as breaking up," Lydia said eagerly. "It's temporary."

Arden pressed her palm to her stomach, inhaling in a series of staccato breaths, each one accompanied by a tiny squeak.

"Are you hyperventilating?" Terry asked.

She shook her head, lips fluttering as she released a long exhale. "Lamaze breathing."

A nearby chaperone jerked her head in our direction. Oblivious, Arden continued her respiratory exercises. Lydia gently steered her toward a deserted corner.

"What are you doing?" Arden gasped between breaths.

"Going where none of the teachers will assume you're in the middle of a Lifetime movie." Satisfied we were out of earshot of any adults, Lydia crossed her arms. "Okay. Go ahead."

"I lasted almost three days, and then I couldn't stand it anymore, so I called him back and told him to go ahead and do it if he was going to break up with me." Arden paused. "That was . . . a pretty long call. I was a tad emotional."

"Because you're not an android," Lydia said at once.

"Tell that to Miles," Arden sniffed. "He said he couldn't handle the drama." She shrugged. "That was that."

Terry's mouth moved as she counted under her breath. "So you broke up with him on Wednesday?"

Arden lowered her chin in a shaky nod. "I thought he might change his mind. But he hasn't."

There was a beat of silence before Lydia grabbed her by the arm. "Let's get out of here. We'll put on pajamas and eat junk food and you can scream and jump up and down, because I freaking love your drama — "

"No!" Arden pulled away. "You don't understand. This" — she gestured at the crowded gym — "is the only thing keeping me going. What does it say on my list? *The Big Dance*. Not Break-ups and Ugly Crying!" Her hands twisted. "I can't lose Winter Formal on top of everything else."

The four of us stood there in fraught silence until Terry said, "Are you sure?"

"Yes. I don't want to end up like that freaky lady Mary told us about who got dumped at the altar and spent the rest of her life staring at a rotten wedding cake."

"Miss Havisham," I supplied.

"If that's what you want." Lydia's voice was heavy with reluctance.

"It's not like I'm completely alone, right? I still have you guys." Arden lifted her chin. "But I'm not going to get sappy right now, because this is a party." Squaring her shoulders, she beckoned to a guy in combat boots and mad scientist glasses. "Hey, Michael. Do you want to dance?"

"Totally." He held out a hand to Arden, and the two of them disappeared into the crowd.

"Wow," said Terry.

"She's got skills," Lydia agreed. Catching sight of Pittaya threading his way toward us through the throngs of people, she started in that direction. "See you on the dance floor," she tossed over her shoulder in parting.

Terry and I exchanged sheepish smiles. So this was how it felt to be a wallflower, another circumstance I'd read about but never experienced for myself.

"Do you want to sit down?" I indicated the scattering of small round tables and folding chairs, which were meant to approximate a Parisian bistro (the paper napkins had pictures of croissants).

Terry turned to follow me, coming to an abrupt halt when a boy I vaguely recognized from my English class stepped in front of her with a hopeful smile. Terry sent a questioning look my way; I shrugged helplessly. If there was a graceful way to decline such an invitation, I had no idea what it was.

As my last companion joined the swaying mob, I set off in search of a less obtrusive place to be alone. Skirting the edge of the dance floor, I passed a line of bored-looking teacher chaperones. At the other end of the gym there was a long table draped in blue plastic, topped with a smattering of glittery snowflakes and a mostly empty punch bowl. I picked up a paper cup, wincing as the sugary flavor hit my tongue. The tragic fate of Arden and Miles was still sending shock waves through my system, and this wasn't going to do my already unsettled stomach any favors.

"Is it that vinegar stuff?" asked a familiar voice.

I spun to face Alex Ritter. "What?"

He nodded at the cup in my hand. "You're giving it a really nasty look."

"It's not about the punch. Though it is pretty gross." I tossed the half-full cup into the nearest garbage can.

"So how did it work out?" He waggled his fingers at me. "Your scheme?"

"Not so great. I mean, your advice was fine, but there were unforeseen complications." To put it mildly.

"You're here alone?" It was hard to pinpoint his tone. Not surprised, but not entirely blasé either.

"Sort of, but not really." I frowned as a new thought crossed my mind. "Who did you come with?"

"Apparently I should have asked Phoebe, since the two of us are so close."

I squeezed my eyes shut. Of course they'd told him; the whole cast and crew of *Othello* was probably laughing at my expense, not to mention their friends and extended family. After an agonizing few seconds, I managed to look him in the eye. Or rather, the chin. "I felt bad for you. I thought you'd been cuckolded."

"That sounds painful."

I opened my mouth.

"I know what it means, Merrily. And I appreciate your concern."

"It's all so confusing," I said heavily.

"My family tree?"

"People. Relationships." As so often happened in his company, my words leaped ahead of my brain. "Why do couples break up?"

"In my vast experience, you mean?" He shrugged. "Lots of reasons. A person changes. Or loses interest. Or meets someone else."

"But doesn't that mean they should never have been together in the first place, and the whole thing was a mistake?"

He regarded me thoughtfully, head tipped to one side. "You know, my mother is a real estate agent."

"Okay."

"She says the only way you learn what you really want in a house is by living in a few that miss the mark—no en suite master bath, or a detached garage. That's how you know what to look for the next time around."

I blinked at him. "That's your metaphor for love? Buying and selling houses?"

Alex shrugged. "It's more realistic than thinking the first person you date is going to be your soulmate."

However reasonable on its face, this sounded suspiciously like a justification for playing the field. Not to mention the high probability of personal unhappiness. "I think it would be less painful if everyone waited until they were really, really settled in life, like maybe in their thirties, to get into a serious relationship. Just to minimize the odds of heartbreak."

"But you'd miss out on so much." He fixed me with one of his patented stares: half smolder, half amusement.

"Like what?"

"Meeting new people. Hearing their hot takes on relationships. Dancing." He held out a hand, palm up. "Shall we?"

I frowned. "Are you being serious right now?"

"I never joke about dancing."

I cast a desperate look at the maelstrom of bodies. If I said no, he'd think I was a coward. But if I said yes . . . I had no idea what would happen. If only my friends were here to advise me.

My friends! What if they looked over and saw me swaying in Alex Ritter's arms?

"I can't." The words were aimed at my feet. When I risked a glance at Alex, he lowered his chin as if reaching a decision.

"Come on." Taking my hand, he led me through the crowd, carving a winding path toward the far end of the gym.

When we reached the exit, I hesitated. "Where are we going?"

He gave me one of his rakish grins. "There's only one way to find out, Merrily."

I didn't let myself think about the fact that he'd probably used that same smile on dozens of girls before me, or that I'd read far too many cautionary tales to be taken in by such an obvious lure. Alex leaned against the door, and I followed him into the darkened hall.

Dear Diary,

Why do people in books always let themselves do things they know they'll regret? It's like they've never heard of self-control. I just want to yell at the page. **Stop! Before it's too late!**

M.P.M.

CHAPTER 25

He backed past the glass-walled trophy case, tugging me gently in his wake. The sounds of the dance were muffled, like the distant thump of a clothes dryer.

"Ready?" he asked.

I said nothing, unwilling to expose my ignorance by asking, *For what?*

"It's easy." He stepped nearer, placing one of my hands on his shoulder while his other arm circled my waist. "Just follow my lead."

My full attention was on the feel of his palm against my back, so it came as something of a shock when he started counting, *one-two-three, one-two-three,* stepping forward on the second *one.* I had no choice but to move with him, stumbling slightly in my heels. Alex tightened his grip to steady me.

"You know how to dance." It came out slightly breathless, as we rounded the corner at the far end of the hall. *Really* dance, I meant. With a partner. Not like the scrum I'd witnessed in the gym. At the same time part of me thought, *Of course he can dance*. Alex could probably work up a decent sonnet or arrange flowers, too — anything that fell in the broader *wooing* category.

"My sisters made me take lessons with them at the rec center. There weren't enough guys signed up for the class." He pulled me to a stop. "I can just about fake my way through a waltz."

I blurted the first piece of information that popped into my head. "It used to be considered scandalous — the waltz."

"You sure you're not thinking of the Lambada?"

I shook my head. "Back then the dances had a lot less contact." My hand sketched the distance between our bodies, until I realized what I was doing and dropped my arms to my sides.

"I wonder what they would have said about the junior high sway."

Seeing the blankness of my expression (my old school had not gone in for dances), he drew my hands up to his neck. Placing his palms at my waist, he pulled me closer.

"Nice dress, Merrily." His gaze was warm across the bare skin at my shoulders and neck.

I pretended to be fascinated with something behind him, though the only thing on the wall was a tattered poster about the importance of hand-washing during cold and flu season. "We just rock back and forth?"

"Yep. It's like a hug set to music." He crossed his arms behind me, narrowing the gap between us even further.

"This is a lot closer than a waltz." My voice sounded as wobbly as our side-to-side movements.

"Shocking," he agreed as his cheek came to rest against mine.

"*My* sisters let me come to their stage combat class," I said, when the silence was too much.

He leaned away far enough to look at my face. "Is that your way of telling me to back off?"

"No. It's just an anecdote. About sisters."

Although we were no longer dancing, neither of us moved away. At this distance, he hardly had to raise his voice above a whisper. "You know, if your sister marries my sister, we'll be related."

"I already have a brother. One is plenty."

He gave an exaggerated sigh. "And here I was dreaming of family holidays. Group photos. Summer vacations." I rolled my eyes, which only seemed to encourage him. "You and me, Merrily. Roasting chestnuts in our matching holiday sweaters."

"Have you ever actually roasted a chestnut? They're impossible to peel and you end up stabbing yourself in the cuticle about a hundred times. It's a nightmare."

The corners of his mouth twitched. "So much for that fantasy."

I squeezed my eyes shut. "I can be a little bit of a wet blanket sometimes."

When he didn't respond, I took a breath, thinking maybe I should explain what I meant—and then his mouth touched mine.

My eyes flew open. He was already pulling away, the contact

so fleeting it was over as soon as it began. "Why did you do that?"

He seemed bemused by the question. "You tell me, Merrily."

"Um, shock value?" I racked my brains for another possibility. "Or maybe because I was being pathetic, and you wanted to change the subject?"

Alex smoothed the hair back from his forehead. "I can't say I gave it that much thought."

"So it was like an accident."

"I didn't trip and land on your mouth, if that's what you're asking."

"An impulse, then," I suggested. "Like walking past a bakery and thinking, 'Hey, I could go for a doughnut'?"

"Are you calling yourself a doughnut, Merrily?"

I was too busy wondering which kind I would be to answer. Apple fritter? Jelly-filled? No, wait: an old-fashioned.

"You're frowning, Merrily. Was that . . . not okay?"

"Hmm? Oh. No, it was fine." Except I wished he'd given me a little notice, so I could have concentrated. The whole experience had been so abbreviated that when I tried to summon the memory, all that came to mind was a hint of softness, followed by a mild heart attack.

"Fine?" he repeated.

I lifted a hand to rub the lower half of my face before remembering my lipstick. "You know what I mean."

"I don't actually."

"I wasn't offended," I assured him, since that seemed to be his primary concern.

"Uh-huh. So it was 'fine' and also inoffensive?"

"I'm not saying it was *bad*," I clarified. "Just different. From what I expected. Not that I expected you to—you know. But if I had, I would have thought it would be more, you know." I broke off, searching for the right word. "Elaborate."

Without breaking eye contact, he raised my hand to his lips and placed a kiss above the knuckles. "More like that, maybe?"

I swallowed. "Maybe."

Turning my hand over, he pressed his mouth to the center of my palm. "Or this?"

I gave a microscopic shrug, not trusting myself to speak.

"What about this?" he murmured, brushing a kiss against my cheek. "Is that how they do it in your books?" He dipped his head, breathing a feather-light kiss at the base of my neck.

I was too busy enjoying the feel of his slightly roughened skin against my throat to reply. He pulled back, watching me. I got the distinct impression he wouldn't go on until I answered.

"They don't go into a lot of detail. You have to read between the lines."

"For example?" He was watching me with an expectant air. It occurred to me that Alex often looked at me that way, as if I might at any moment say something delightful and surprising.

"Like two characters go on a carriage ride and end up taking a detour through the woods. She lets him kiss her and the next chapter she's having a baby and naming it Sorrow."

"That's terrible."

"Tip of the iceberg. She ends up stabbing the guy later."

His hand came to rest on my shoulder, thumb lightly

brushing my collarbone. "The good news is you can't actually get pregnant from kissing."

"I know that."

"Just making sure. I wouldn't want you to shank me."

I glanced down the darkened hallway. The music from the dance was faint as a lullaby.

"Should we go back?" he asked, following the direction of my gaze.

"Why?" I was frowning up at him as though he'd proposed a barefoot walk over broken glass. My reaction seemed to please him. Bending forward, he brushed his lips against my earlobe, making me shiver.

The entire situation felt dream-like, free from the rules of ordinary life, so I let myself act without thinking, stretching up on my toes to kiss his neck, and then his ear. His hands tightened at my waist, which I took to mean I was doing it right.

I stepped back just far enough to see his face, my palms resting on either side of his shirt buttons. "Alex."

"Merrily."

We looked at each other for a long moment, not quite smiling. When he kissed me again, I wrapped my hands around the back of his neck, both to hold him in place and because I'd secretly wanted to touch his hair forever. It was silkier than I'd imagined, the texture softer than mine.

Aha, said a distant part of my brain. *So* this *is why people make a big deal out of kissing*. It was like the first sip of a milkshake, dizzyingly sweet and delicious in a way that made you want to keep drinking forever.

We were both breathing unevenly when we broke apart. He leaned his forehead against mine.

"Is it always like that?" I asked.

"What do you mean?"

"Like if I kissed someone else—"

"Why would you want to do that?"

"I wouldn't."

"Good."

"It was, wasn't it? Good, I mean."

"It was fine."

"*Fine?*" I repeated, outraged. "You're kidding, right?"

"Not at all. Why, did you have any doubt? I knew the two of us would be a solid B-plus."

I shoved his shoulder.

"Ow." He rubbed that spot. "You have to leave something to aspire to, Merrily. For next time."

I didn't have long to wonder if he was speaking hypothetically, of some future occasion that might never arise. When he kissed me again my lips were slightly parted, which led to the revelation that French kissing was neither slimy nor gross.

This discovery was so absorbing I didn't hear the gym doors clank, or the footsteps heading in our direction. It wasn't until a voice called my name—not, I suspected, for the first time—that the world came crashing back into focus.

Dear Diary,

I used to think the term **pathetic fallacy** referred to a poorly constructed argument, but it's actually about the weather, and making it seem like nature has human emotions. Which is why it's always stormy in **Wuthering Heights**, because even the wind and the rain are caught up in the tempest of dysfunctional behavior.

M.P.M.

CHAPTER 26

Arden was the first to reach us. She yanked me away from Alex. "Are you okay?"

No. No, no, no. It was the only word my brain could form. My lips must have moved, because Arden rounded on Alex.

"How dare you?" Wrapping an arm around my shoulders, she pulled me to her side. I felt like a mannequin, stiff and unwieldy.

Alex rubbed his forehead. "I'm not sure what you think is happening here. Mary—"

"Don't even think about it." Lydia shoved between us.

Alex leaned sideways, trying to catch my eye. I knew he was waiting for me to explain. But what could I say? *It just happened.* Part of me hoped if I stayed very quiet, everyone would forget I was there.

Unfortunately, they were all staring at me. I put a hand to my cheek, certain it must have hardened like clay inside a kiln from the heat of my embarrassment.

"It's okay, Mary." Arden stroked my shoulder. "We're here now. You're safe."

"Mary," Alex began, and I cringed at the entreaty in his voice.

"She doesn't have to talk to you." Arden waved a hand in his face.

"I think she does, actually. Mary," he said again.

Forcing my eyes open, I took a deep breath. "It's not . . . ah mmm." I bit my bottom lip and was briefly lost in the memory of what that mouth had been doing mere moments ago.

"You don't have to explain," Arden said soothingly. "We know how men are. *Especially* him."

My mouth opened. It was imperative to tell them it wasn't his fault, that what they'd seen had not been a case of the hardened seducer leading the naive young maiden astray. But I couldn't make the words come out.

"Stockholm syndrome." Terry's voice was heavy with sympathy.

Lydia glared at Alex. "It's lucky we got here in time."

There was an agonizing half minute during which I might yet have spoken up, telling my friends the truth. And then my time ran out. Alex raked a hand through his hair. With a last disbelieving look at me, he shoved his hands in his pockets and walked away.

"And don't come back," Arden yelled after him.

The only response was the heavy door to the outside slamming shut behind him.

Arden wrapped her arms around me. "I'm so sorry you had to go through that. We shouldn't have left you alone."

To my horror, I felt my eyes well with tears. My friends surrounded me, murmuring reassuring words, but their kindness only made me feel worse.

Gently, Arden turned me in the direction of the doors. "Let's get you home."

"I'm going to grab our coats," said Lydia, still scowling ferociously.

"I'll let Cam know we found her." Terry turned to follow Lydia.

"Cam?" A fresh wave of horror washed over me. "Don't tell her about the . . . other part."

My teeth chattered as we stepped into the parking lot.

Arden squeezed my shoulder. "We're almost there."

"But the dance . . . you don't want to leave. And Pittaya?"

"Lydia can catch up with him later. Or he can suck it up. I don't really care."

When we reached her car, Arden opened the back door, closing it behind me before hurrying around to the driver's side. She glanced at me in the rearview mirror as she fiddled with the temperature controls. Terry and Lydia arrived a few minutes later, handing us our coats as they climbed inside. They looked from me to Arden, waiting for a cue. I turned my face to the window.

As we left the lighted parking lot, the air seemed to grow heavier, weighing me down. What was I doing? It was like I'd stumbled into an alternate life where everything I did was backwards and wrong.

Arden angled a vent so the hot air hit me full in the face. "Are you warm enough?"

I nodded, though in truth I was flushed and perspiring. Could regret make you sweat?

Lydia twisted in her seat to look at me. "You don't have to talk about it if you don't want to."

Arden flicked on her turn signal with more than necessary force. "I bet he found out it was your fault Terry wouldn't go out with him, so he decided to target you next. Men are the *worst*. They shouldn't even be allowed out of the house."

Had it really been an elaborate revenge plot? Everything in me rebelled at the thought. "No," I whispered. Even to me, it sounded weak.

A light rain had begun to fall, mixed with sleet; Arden switched on the wipers. "You don't have to make excuses for him," she said. "That's how they get away with all their crap. 'Oh, he didn't mean it. He's just so busy and important, and you're too silly to understand the *pressure*, wait quietly and maybe he'll remember that you exist if he has an extra five minutes to spare!'"

She was breathing heavily when she finished. Lydia stared at her, eyes narrowed, before speaking. "Pull over."

"What?" Arden checked her mirrors. "Why?"

"Because I don't want to argue with you while you're driving."

Frowning, Arden steered the car to an empty stretch of curb a few blocks from my house. As soon as she was parked, she turned to Lydia. "Why would you argue with *me*? I'm not the bad guy. I think we all know who that is. Starts with an *A*, ends with an *X*." She made a slashing motion with her finger.

"Are you sure? Because it sounded like you were talking about Miles just now."

"All guys are the same," Arden retorted. "Ask Mary."

Lydia shook her head. "This has always been about Miles, and you."

"What are you talking about?"

"Your obsession with getting everyone coupled up, because romance is so great! Dating, dating, dating, guys, guys, guys." Lydia fluttered her fingers. "No wonder Mary fell for Alex's BS. What if we hadn't found her in time, and something even worse happened, just because you didn't want to deal with the fact that your relationship was over!"

"Excuse me? What have I been doing for the last two days?"

"It's been going on a lot longer than that." Lydia set her jaw. "You didn't want to admit it, because you couldn't stand the idea of not having a boyfriend. What could be worse than being single!"

"That's not why—"

"And now you're miserable, and you wasted two years of your life, and for what?"

"I didn't waste my life." Arden's voice quavered. "We were happy for a really long time."

"Until you weren't, which you refused to acknowledge, so instead you created this big distraction." Lydia circled a hand in the air, taking in the four of us. "Way to model healthy lifestyle choices."

A choking sound emerged from Arden's throat. "Thanks for the judgment. I really needed that tonight."

"I'm just saying, did you ever stop to ask yourself if *you* still wanted to be with Miles, instead of putting up with his crap? Maybe you should have dumped *him*."

"You would have liked that, wouldn't you?" Arden said bitterly.

Lydia squinted at her. "What's that supposed to mean?"

"You've always resented Miles. You never liked it when I spent time with him instead of you. Do you know how hard I had to work to keep you from getting jealous? Like I needed the extra stress!"

I caused this, I thought, ribs tightening like a vise. If the argument escalated much further, their friendship might never recover, and how would I live with myself then?

"It was me," I said, before either of them could accuse the other of something worse. "This whole thing is my fault."

"No, it's not." Arden rubbed her eyes. "This started way before we met you."

"I mean with Alex."

Lydia's mouth compressed into an angry line. "You physically overpowered him and forced him to stick his tongue down your throat?"

"He asked me to dance, but that was just being nice. Since I was alone."

"Some guys can smell weakness," Lydia said. "They always go after the vulnerable ones."

"Why were you in the hall?" Terry asked quietly.

"He thought I was shy about dancing in public."

"And then?" Lydia said in her courtroom voice.

"We just kind of . . . kissed."

Lydia didn't hide her skepticism. "Out of the blue, Alex Ritter asked you to dance and kissed you and you decided, why not?"

"We talked once or twice. Before tonight."

Arden frowned. "You never mentioned that."

I looked at my hands, knotted in my lap. "I wasn't sure what to say. It felt awkward."

"Talking to Alex?" Lydia asked.

I shook my head.

"Talking to us." Arden's hands tightened around the steering wheel. "But we trusted you, Mary. *I* trusted you." She broke off, shaking her head. "I broke up with Miles because of what you said. And the whole time, you were seeing Alex Ritter behind our backs?"

"I didn't mean to," I said miserably.

Excuses crowded my brain. I didn't realize! I was too naive to understand what it meant when he teased me, or touched my hair, or stood close enough to whisper in my ear! But it was too late to play the ingénue, when I'd been pretending to know it all. Nor could I stomach another half-truth. Every time I'd kept Alex a secret, I'd deceived all of us—myself included.

"He had lipstick on his neck." Terry didn't present the information as a gotcha, but it was damning nonetheless. "Forensic evidence," she added, sounding almost apologetic.

"I don't believe this," Lydia said.

"I'm sorry." Choking on a sob, I threw open the car door and ran.

Dear Diary,
Whenever I heard the phrase **dark night of the soul,**
I used to imagine Christmas Eve, when you're too
excited to sleep.
Now I know better.

M.P.M.

CHAPTER 27

I cut through a side yard, heels sinking into the wet grass. The street, when I darted across it, was slick with sleet, but I managed to stay upright long enough to reach my house. Shivering, I hurried up the steps and through the front door.

I stood on the rug in the entryway, arms limp at my sides, aware of nothing but my own misery and the hot streaks coursing down my cheeks. After several minutes of this, the increasingly urgent need for a tissue forced me to move. I'd taken a few steps toward the downstairs bathroom when I noticed the soft jazz wafting from the living room. A glance in that direction revealed flickering candlelight, empty wineglasses—and my parents.

I stared at them in horror. They looked back at me with equal dismay. On top of everything else, I'd interrupted date night.

"What's wrong?" Mom asked, pulling her legs from my father's lap and leaping to her feet. She crossed the room to wrap an arm around me.

"Nothing," I said thickly, wiping my nose and cheeks with the back of my hand. "It's raining."

They exchanged a look, silently debating whether to call me on the world's most transparent falsehood.

"Come sit down," Dad said, patting the couch cushion.

"That's okay." I tried to sound stoic. "I just want to go to bed."

Mom led me to the couch. "What happened?"

I shrugged as I settled between them. It was easier not to cry if I kept my mouth closed.

"Mary." She lifted my chin to get a better look at my face. "You're worrying us."

"I did something ba-ad." A hiccupping sob split the last word before I managed to clamp my lips together. Mom's hand tightened on my shoulder. I caught a flicker of panic in her eyes before she schooled her expression.

"Talk to us," Mom said. Dad pulled the afghan off the back of the couch and draped it around my shoulders, as if that would help.

Strangely, it did. I let out a shuddering breath. "I was at the dance," I began, not sure how much backstory to give them. "And there was this guy—Alex."

Dad scratched his chin. "The one you spoke to at Trivia Night?"

I blinked at him in surprise before nodding.

"Handsome fellow," he observed. For a second I lost control of my face, mouth wobbling as my eyes wrinkled into teary slits.

"Why don't you make us some tea?" Mom suggested, patting Dad's knee.

He looked from her to me. "That might be for the best."

Mom waited until the kitchen door swung closed behind him. "First of all," she said, pressing my limp hand between both of hers, "there's nothing to be ashamed of."

I gave a sputter of disbelief.

"The early stirrings of love can be confusing, particularly in their physical manifestations. But as long as both partners share a mutual respect and consideration . . ." She trailed off, jaw tightening. "It was, wasn't it?"

She'd lost me. "What?"

"A joint decision." She enunciated the words carefully, watching my face. "You didn't feel compelled, or coerced, to do anything you weren't ready for?"

I stared back at her with mounting dread. "What are you talking about?"

"I'm talking about whatever you want to talk about. In a spirit of openness and acceptance."

"I kissed him, Mom. That's it."

"Oh, thank God." She covered her eyes with one hand. "You're much too young. I was trying to be broad-minded, but I don't think either of us is ready for *that*." Leaning forward, she yelled, "You can come back. It's not about sex."

I closed my eyes as the last word reverberated through the house.

Dad stuck his head through the doorway. "It's not?"

"Just a kiss," Mom assured him.

The kettle whistled. "I'll be right there," Dad promised, ducking back into the kitchen.

Mom patted my hand. "We've been meaning to have the Talk with you, but to be honest we assumed we'd have more time. Or that you'd ask one of your sisters," she added hopefully.

"It's not about that. I mean, it is, but it's not." Could I even form a sentence anymore? I closed my eyes to stop another gush of tears.

Dad bustled into the room, setting a steaming mug on the coffee table in front of me before handing one to Mom. "What did I miss?"

"It is and also isn't about the kiss," Mom recapped.

I wrapped my hands around the hot mug, pulling it close to my face. The steam eased some of the stiffness. "I shouldn't have done it."

"Because?" Dad said leadingly.

"Because I told everyone he was a bad person. But now I think maybe—" I drew a ragged breath, "I'm the bad one."

Once I started talking, the words poured out. From Alex liking Terry and how I'd kept them apart, somehow kicking off three wonderful friendships, to our vexed efforts in the dating arena, including the misguided setup with Jeff.

"Your friends encouraged you to pursue your sister's boyfriend?" Dad interrupted.

"That was before we realized. And now I think maybe Terry likes Cam too. And Miles and Arden broke up because of something I said! It's a catastrophe."

"It is a bit melodramatic," Dad agreed, which did not strike me as a helpful observation.

The tears flowed anew. "I ruined everything. They'll never want to be friends with me again."

Mom's brows drew together. "Because you kissed the boy your friend wasn't dating?"

"No! Because it makes everything I ever told them look like a tissue of lies!" Part of me hoped they would argue the point, but that wasn't my parents' style. They took their time mulling my words, making contemplative sounds—a lingering *hmm* in Mom's case; head scratching for Dad.

"Can't you tell your friends what happened?" Dad asked at last.

I shook my head violently. How was I supposed to explain to them when I didn't understand it myself? It was as though I'd discovered a hidden door inside my own home, one that led to a dank and cobwebbed basement I'd never known about. Only the door was in my head, and the basement was a side of me I'd never seen—a selfish, sneaky crawl space.

"Now, now," Dad said as I began sniffling again. "I'm sure things aren't as dire as they appear. Friendships have survived worse."

I couldn't tell him that in my world, friendships were brittle things that could be shattered with a few words. How lowering to think I'd alienated all my friends for the second time in the span of a few months. Not to mention Alex.

"There's something else," I said. "*Someone* else."

I felt Mom stiffen beside me. "Another boy?"

"The same one," I sighed. "Alex. I kind of . . . threw him to the wolves."

"How so?" Dad asked.

"I let my friends think it was his fault. The kissing. Like I was just an innocent bystander."

For several endless moments, the only sound was the ticking of the grandfather clock. "That was unfortunate," Mom said at last.

"I know! And I feel terrible about it." I raised my head far enough to glance hopefully at my parents. "I sort of confessed the truth on the way home."

"To your friends," Mom clarified. I nodded.

"And your fellow?" Dad asked.

I shook my head, not bothering to point out that he certainly wasn't *my* fellow anymore — if he ever had been.

Mom took a meditative sip of tea. "You know, Mary, there is no version of this story where you don't make mistakes."

"What story?" I rubbed my forehead to smooth the lines I could feel forming. I'd probably wake up with gray hair, too. "My first dance, you mean?"

"Your life," she corrected. "It's the nature of existence. To err is human. We screw up, and then screw up some more."

"But I don't *like* being in the wrong." I jabbed a hand at my midsection. "This is the worst feeling in the world. I *hate* it." Dad's warm hand landed on the back of my head. I took a deep breath before continuing. "I tried really hard not to do all the dumb things you're not supposed to do, and I *still* messed everything up. It's not fair."

"We all have to face our fallibility at some point," Mom said. "If we didn't, it would be too easy to turn into sociopaths." Dad cleared his throat, their private shorthand for *take it down a notch*.

She took a deep breath before continuing. "Remorse forces us to take a hard look at ourselves. It gives us the strength to grow, and the courage to do the right thing next time—or at least try. Speaking of which." Mom sat forward, smacking the arm of the sofa with an open palm. "I think you know what you have to do now."

I scowled at her. Unlike my mother, I couldn't flip the switch from despair to resolve at the drop of a hat.

"Sometimes we have to admit our mistakes," she went on, brimming with conviction. "However painful that may be."

Dad and I gave her matching *come again?* looks.

"What?" she asked. "It's good advice."

"Yes," Dad agreed. "Although a bit . . . *mmm*."

"If you have something to say, I wish you'd say it."

He coughed. "I suppose I was thinking . . . 'physician, heal thyself.'"

Mom started to puff herself up like a turkey.

"It's true," I said quickly, relieved to be discussing someone else's flaws. "Apologies are not your strong suit." We all knew when she was sorry; there was a very particular look her face got, sort of chastened and uncomfortable. But it was always implicit. She wasn't one to say the words.

"Nonsense." Mom made a shooing motion with her hand. "I'm woman enough to admit when I'm wrong. It just doesn't happen very often."

"Or ever," Dad said, not quite under his breath.

"That's ridiculous. You just don't recall." Dad's faulty memory had long been her argumentative ace in the hole.

He set down his mug. "By all means, refresh my memory."

"I can think of one right now." She gave him a smug look. "On our second sabbatical in England, when we took that side trip to Yorkshire."

"I remember the trip," Dad said. "We carried the twins in packs on our backs."

"Then you should also remember the argument we had about visiting Haworth. I said it was too late in the day to set out and we'd never make it in time, because it was the off-season and they were sure to be closing early. You insisted we go anyway." Mom crossed her arms. "The rest is history."

"I'm afraid I don't recall the argument," Dad said mildly. "It was a lovely afternoon, though. Didn't we stop for a cream tea afterward?"

"Exactly." Mom inclined her head. "Because you were right, and I was wrong."

His brow furrowed. "And you acknowledged that fact, in so many words?"

"Of course!" She gestured at me. "Mary heard me."

"I wasn't born then," I reminded them.

Mom cast her eyes to the ceiling. "I'm talking about *right now.* I believe my exact words were 'you were right, and I was wrong.'"

"Just to be sure I'm following," Dad said, "you mean to tell us that this evening you apologized for something that happened twenty years ago?"

"More like eighteen," she corrected. "I was pregnant with Cam at the time. Which is probably why I wasn't thinking clearly."

Dad nodded slowly, lips pressed together as he tried not to laugh.

"There's no need to be petty," Mom huffed.

"Certainly not," he agreed.

"You see, Mary, it's never too late to put things right." Mom smoothed the hair at my temples. "Finish your tea, take a nice bath, and get some sleep. Things will look better in the morning."

I sincerely doubted that. Then again, the thought of waiting two decades for the situation to right itself was not particularly appealing.

The phone rang in the front hall. After a quick look at me, Mom rose to answer. "Yes," I heard her murmur. "She's here. No. It's fine."

I held my breath as she walked back into the living room. "That was Cam," she said. "Making sure you got home safely."

The last ember of hope died. Of course it was my sister. Who else would be calling me, ever again?

Dear Diary,

I'm not going to write anything down because I will never ever want to remember this time in my life. Maybe I should just throw you in the fire.

No offense.

M.P.M.

CHAPTER 28

I f there was any justice in the world, I would have
caught a dramatic illness on my dash through the freezing
rain. Then at least I would have an excuse to spend the next
few months lying pale and wasted in my frigid garret, coughing
spots of blood into a lace hankie. Instead, I woke with nothing
worse than a headache and swollen eyelids to betray my inner
turmoil.

Overnight the precipitation had turned into a solid layer of
ice, coating branches and sidewalks. Or so it looked through the
window of my bedroom, where I spent most of the day. I would
have taken to my bed on a more permanent basis if I thought I
could get away with it, but my mother didn't believe in malinger-
ing. There was no way she'd let me skip school just because I'd
laid waste to my entire existence in a single miserable evening.

Thus it was that on Monday morning I dragged myself out
of bed and dressed in an appropriately gloomy brownish-gray
sweater.

"You look very *Winter of Our Discontent*," Van commented

when I walked into the dining room. Jasper watched this exchange with interest, no doubt waiting to chime in with a helpful observation of his own.

"Don't forget your father and I are having dinner with the provost," Mom said, casually stirring a pat of butter into her hot cereal. "There are leftovers in the refrigerator."

On cue, my siblings began arguing about who got the lentils and who got the stew. I suspected the diversion had been deliberate, especially when Mom flashed me an encouraging smile. Which was all well and good, except that the real challenge was yet to come, and unless I could think of a way to bring my mommy to school with me, I'd be facing the rest of the day on my own.

⟳

There was no dramatic confrontation. I avoided my friends, and assumed they were doing the same. Even amid the noise of the hallways, silence surrounded me, slowly thickening until it felt like a solid enclosure, cutting off air and light.

This was how it happened to a fallen woman: once your transgressions came to light, you were walled off from polite society. Invisible. Forgotten. They might as well set you on the SS *Disgrace* and shove you out to sea. By the end of the week, I could count my social interactions on one hand.

Monday, someone in my English class asked to borrow a pencil.

On Tuesday, I was so hungry by the last bell (having skipped lunch for the second day running) that I found myself detouring to Tome Raider on the way home. Every time a car passed I stiffened, forcing myself not to whip around and check whether it was Arden's. The balance tipped back and forth between wanting to see them and dreading the possibility. What if they cruised right past me, pretending I wasn't there — the *cut direct*? Or gave me dirty looks and whispered behind their hands? Or maybe they would mournfully shake their heads, regretting every second they'd wasted in my company.

"Hello, Mary," Doug called as I stepped inside, stomping the slush off my feet. "Table for four?"

My bottom lip quivered. "Just one today." *And probably forever.* But no, that wasn't fair. Maybe I could send my former friends an anonymous note, deeding them the rights to Shaggy Doug's. I would hang out at home instead. In my room. With the curtains drawn.

"No problem," he replied, a little too heartily. "One is fun!"

I attempted a smile as I slouched across the room. Judging by Doug's anxious expression, it wasn't a success.

"I'm doing my *Anne of Green Gables* menu," he said, wiping his hands on the towel tucked in his waistband.

All I could think of was ipecac, which Anne gives to some sick kids to make them throw up their phlegm, thereby saving their lives. That was where I'd learned the word *expectorant*.

"Raspberry cordial," Doug said, filling the silence. "And mousy pudding. It's a marzipan mouse. From the scene where Miss Stacy comes over for dinner and the mouse accidentally gets into the dessert?" He looked hopefully at me.

"Sounds great," I said bleakly, pulling my backpack onto my lap. "Do you mind if I eat my lunch first?"

"Go ahead. I'll just" — he pointed behind him — "be in the kitchen."

I inhaled my sandwich so quickly it gave me the hiccups, which made me think the ipecac might not have been such a bad thing.

"Here we are." Doug bustled over to the table, handing me a goblet of dark pink juice. I swigged the whole thing at once, hoping to rid myself of the hiccups.

"It's just juice," he said uncertainly. "Nonalcoholic. Not like in the book."

He was referring to the scene in which Anne and Diana, her best friend, accidentally get drunk on what they think is fruit juice. Diana's mom blames Anne, forbidding the girls to see each other. It's one of the worst tragedies of Anne's life — losing her dearest friend.

To my horror, my eyes filled with tears. Then I hiccupped. Loudly.

Doug tactfully looked away. "Is there anything I can do?"

"Why, have you been talking to my parents?"

He shook his head. "I simply noticed that, ah —"

"I'm alone?"

"Yes, that and also —"

I closed my eyes. "I look like I've been crying."

"Er, no. Well, yes. But it's more than that. You seem . . . blue." He gestured to an empty chair. "May I?"

We sat in silence, Doug with his hands threaded in front of him on the table. I would have liked to eat the apple in my lunch, but it seemed rude with an audience. Also, I was still hiccupping.

"Here's the thing, Mary. I'm not going to tell you it gets easier, or pretend you ever stop missing them," Doug said. "Because it's miserable to be alone. We both know that."

"Uh, okay." I wondered if that was the extent of his pep talk.

"But you have to keep hope alive. Like me and Noreen."

This wasn't the first time Doug had brought up his relationship woes in front of me, but usually one of my parents was around to serve as a buffer. I thought of reminding him that I was barely sixteen but had a feeling it wouldn't make much difference.

"I made up my mind a long time ago to stand firm. Keep the dream alive. Whatever it takes, that's what I do." He sniffled and I desperately hoped it wasn't a precursor to tears. If he started, I was sure to crumble, and I still had to walk the rest of the way home.

"Like what?" I asked, hoping to shift the conversation onto less mawkish ground.

"I wrote her a letter. Put my heart on the line. Told her I'd be here, faithfully, waiting."

Many people would have been swayed by that level of devotion. Sadly, Noreen was not among them. In my experience, displeasure was pretty much her defining characteristic. "What did she say?"

He became very interested in a crusty blotch on his half apron. "Don't know. I'm still waiting."

"How long has it been?"

Doug sighed. "Coming up on six years."

❧

Wednesday it snowed all morning, big fluffy flakes that blanketed the world in white. Unfortunately for me, there wasn't enough accumulation to cancel school. On the way to third period I caught a glimpse of Arden in the distance, wearing a burgundy scarf I'd never seen before. It clashed wonderfully with her hair. I would have loved to tell her so, instead of concealing myself behind a bank of lockers until she passed out of sight. Had she and Lydia mended the breach in their friendship? Perhaps they'd united against a common enemy. Namely: me. I would probably never know.

Later that afternoon, I was slipping along the haphazardly shoveled sidewalks of my neighborhood when a door closed on the opposite side of the street. Dropping to a crouch, I peered around the bumper of a parked car as Alex exited his piano teacher's house. He paused to adjust his winter gear. Had everyone in the universe gotten a new scarf except me? His was black. Like his mood, perhaps.

A breeze swirled icy crystals into the air, and his cheeks reddened in the cold. Suddenly I thought of Anna and Vronsky on that winter evening before their affair began, when their train stopped in the middle of nowhere and they found themselves alone in the snowy dark, staring longingly at each other.

Not that Alex was looking at me.

He stopped suddenly at the bottom of the stairs. I shrank farther out of sight, hunching down until I was practically squatting in the snow. Had he sensed my attention? Or was he thinking about the fact that my house was down the block? Maybe today's piano playing had been suffused with melancholy grandeur, a storm of angry notes with an undercurrent of yearning? Holding my breath, I risked another peek. A sign, however small, that he hadn't forgotten me would mean so much.

Frowning, Alex glanced behind him. Then he looked down, shuffling through the stack of music books in his hand. Near the bottom of the pile, his brow smoothed.

Apparently he'd found what he was looking for.

⌒

Nothing happened Thursday. Not a blessed thing—unless you count *dwelling on unhappy thoughts* as a pastime.

By evening, the loneliness was suffocating. It shouldn't have been possible to feel that way in a house full of people, but I wasn't just at-home Mary anymore. I'd had a taste of another life, and it was this version of me—the one with my own friends, separate from my family—that was starved for contact. Did that Mary still exist, or was I a tree falling in a forest with no one to hear?

After everyone else went to bed, I crept into my parents' office and booted up the desktop computer. It was hard to say what I hoped to find: a peek at my friends' lives? That they'd continued the Scoundrel Guide without me—or worse, taken it down, erasing all trace of our shared existence? A shard of ice lodged in my chest.

No, there it was, loading at last. I stared at the screen, questioning the evidence of my eyes. How could there be a new entry, without me? It felt like a betrayal, even though I knew I had no right to complain. Why should they leave it frozen in time like a sad memorial to our past? It was obvious they didn't need me anymore; they didn't even *miss* my presence. Their lives had carried on, as if I'd never been part of them.

Even as these thoughts crashed over me in sickening waves, my brain skimmed the text. It was about Miles; I knew that much. It hadn't been so long that I'd entirely lost track of their affairs.

Another Way to Break a Heart, read the scrolling cursive at the top of the page, superimposed over a black-and-white photo of a girl staring through a rain-streaked window. Off to one side there was another caption, in a different font:

When they decide extracurriculars matter more than you do, because no one is going to give them a trophy for being a good boyfriend.

Ouch. Did Miles know about the Guide — and if so, had he recognized himself? Then again, he might not be sitting at home digging for crumbs of information about what Arden and her friends had been up to lately.

I scrolled down a little farther. There was a picture of a book, lying open on the ground in the middle of a forest. A single black feather had fallen onto the page. Holding my breath, I read the final note:

Maybe there's a story like that. It's impossible to know, when the person you trusted to tell you those things is gone, and everything you thought was true turns out to be an illusion.

With shaking hands, I closed the browser and logged off.

⁓

On Friday, I found someone else to offend.

Dear Diary,

The thing I hate most about **Pamela** (the book **and** the character) is that she's so helpless. It's all, "Oh no, I can't climb over that stack of bricks," and, "Woe is me, there's a cow in that field!" If she really wanted to escape Mr. B, she would have done something about it instead of wringing her hands for five hundred pages — and then marrying him!

M.P.M.

CHAPTER 29

When I walked through the door of my house at the end of that long, miserable week, my body sagged like a puppet whose strings had been cut. For two whole days I could hide from the world. The muscles of my face might finally relax, now that I would no longer be forced to pretend I wasn't aching on the inside. And if any of my family members asked why I looked so dismal, I had only to blame it on a book—something French. Or Russian. Or German. There were plenty of depressing literary options.

"Hey, Mary," said Bo's voice, startling me from this pleasant daydream.

"Oh. Hi." Pasting on what I hoped was a reasonably normal expression, I started to move toward the stairs.

"Homework?" he asked, arresting my progress.

When I mumbled an affirmative, he nodded as though he'd expected as much. "Must be a busy time. Jasper said you've been coming straight back from school every day."

My hand flattened across my belly; it felt like I'd been kicked in the gut.

"Do you want a snack?" Bo asked, misreading the gesture.

"No thanks." Our substitute teacher had shown a movie during American history, under cover of which I'd eaten most of my lunch. I tipped my head in the direction of the stairs. "I just need to—"

"How was the dance?"

At first, I thought he was grasping at conversational straws. Then I noted the tension in his posture and wondered if he hadn't been working his way around to this subject all along.

"Did you have a good time?" he added, when I failed to respond.

I looked at the floor. "No."

"Good. I mean, not good, but you know. Because I would hate to see you get caught up in all that superficial high-school business. Like dating, or boyfriends. Committing yourself too young. Before you explore all your options."

I sniffed despondently. "No danger of that."

Bo nodded several times. I thought maybe that was the end of it when he suddenly said, "Because I like you the way you are."

"Oh. Thanks." *That makes one of you.* Still, I was grateful for the positive feedback, even if my fan club consisted of a lone thirteen-year-old.

"You're very nice," he continued.

"I'm not, actually."

"Yes, you are! And smart. And really pretty."

A warning light flashed in the recesses of my brain, but I was too preoccupied to pay close attention. "That's very generous of you to say." Too generous, in fact. "Did someone put you up to this?"

"Up to what?"

"Trying to make me feel better." I watched his face for signs of guilt. "Because of what happened at the dance. With *Alex*."

He gulped audibly. "Alex?"

"Alex Ritter, the one who—" I broke off, shaking my head. "It's complicated."

Bo's shoulders slumped. "Complicated is bad."

Softened by this unexpected display of sympathy, I crossed the room to join him on the couch. "I just never thought he would be interested in me, you know? I assumed he was playing around because he's so far out of my league." For the hundredth time, my memory replayed certain moments of my acquaintance with Alex. Sitting on the bench in the backyard. Trivia Night. Dancing . . . I shut down that memory before it could go any further.

Bo cleared his throat. "When you say he was *playing*, does that mean the two of you were, ah, what you might call *together*?"

"No! Well, not exactly. At least, I don't think so." I rubbed the back of my neck with one hand. "I would have known. Presumably." I glanced at Bo to see if he had any insight on the matter.

"Presumably," he agreed, not meeting my eyes.

"It's not like he asked me to the dance," I reasoned. "Though he did ask me *to* dance while *at* the dance. But that's not really the same thing."

"I would have asked you way ahead of time. And taken you out to dinner and gotten you a corsage. Orchids." He touched his wrist, indicating the imaginary flowers. "Did Alex wear a tux?"

"No."

"I would have worn a tux."

I didn't point out that he would have been the only one in formalwear. The fervency of his words suggested the tuxedo mattered a lot to his overall vision. Which was remarkably vivid.

"This *Alex* character." Bo's nose wrinkled. "He's older?"

"A senior."

"Damn it!" His fists clenched. Slowly he eased back, expression lightening. "Like you and me." Bo waved a hand between us. "You'll be a senior when I'm a sophomore."

"I suppose that is . . . technically correct."

"It's not impossible then." There was a stubborn edge to his voice, as though we'd had this argument before. "We could go to the dance together."

From the whirring blender of my brain, I seized the first semicoherent thought. "I didn't go to the dance with Alex."

"You would have."

I opened my mouth to deny it, then closed it again. An aching throb had started in my skull. "The thing is, Bo—"

"I know. That's a long way off. A lot can happen in two years. Don't you think?"

He had backed me into a rhetorical corner. "In theory," I allowed.

The front door flew open. Jasper stomped inside, kicking snow off his shoes. "There you are," he said to Bo. My brother fell silent when he spotted me.

"Mary and I were just discussing the future," Bo explained. Jasper raised his eyebrows. Bo stretched his arm along the back of the sofa, not quite reaching my shoulder. "I don't know what you're doing two Decembers from now, but I've got my date for Winter Formal locked down."

I whipped around. "What?"

"You didn't say you *wouldn't* go with me," Bo pointed out.

"I thought we had tabled the issue."

"Potato, potah-to."

Jasper caught my eye. When he was sure he had my attention, he mimed yanking something. I frowned to show I didn't understand. He cut his eyes at the floor lamp—or more specifically, the cord attached to the outlet.

Pull the plug. How was I supposed to do that? Hopping to my feet, I moved to the doorway. "Listen, Bo," I began.

He stuck fingers in both ears. "Can't hear you."

"I'm just trying to say that while I obviously esteem you greatly"—at this Bo flinched, before remembering he wasn't supposed to be listening—"it's in a purely platonic way. You're like a brother to me." I pointed to Jasper, as though the concept required illustration.

Bo started to hum loudly.

I had the queasy feeling I'd gone back in time to the night

of the dance and was once again faced with the impossible task of telling people I cared about something they didn't want to hear. It was so much more pleasant to have a clean, simple answer. *No, I didn't want to kiss Alex Ritter! Yes, I might suddenly develop romantic feelings for a boy who's like a sibling to me!*

Jasper sketched a circle in the air with his index finger, signaling me to get on with it.

"The thing is, I could maybe go with you—" I broke off when Jasper sighed loudly, shaking his head. Bo had stopped humming, though his fingers were still in his ears. "But I'm never going to another dance. Ever. That sort of thing is . . . not for me. I plan to concentrate on schoolwork. My studies. And so on."

I gave a decisive bob of the chin. And then I ran away—but not before seeing the hurt in Bo's eyes.

⁓

Late Sunday afternoon I was creeping up the stairs with a mug of tea and a handful of cashews when Addie came running down from the attic with a sheaf of acid-green paper in one hand. The twins had been ghostly figures of late, their existence hinted at by midnight creaking from the attic and the random movement of objects from place to place.

She held out the stack of pages for my inspection.

I glanced at the *Othello* poster, forcing a smile. "Cool."

"It is," Addie agreed.

I looked at her more closely. She seemed . . . excited. Not withdrawn and brooding, the way she'd been the last few months. "The play's going well?"

"I think so. It's maybe not for me to say, but it feels like it."

"That's good." I tried to make my voice hearty and bright, the way it would have sounded a week ago, but I was having trouble summoning that version of me.

"Yeah." She smiled like her old self, which was to say with the unshadowed brightness of a summer afternoon. "I can't wait for you to see it."

It warmed me, both the smile and the fact that she wanted *me* to be there. For a shining instant, I wasn't persona non grata. Even Yarb had given me a wide berth, with a cat's instinctive distaste for neediness.

"Here." She handed me a few flyers. "You can give these to your friends."

And just like that, my spirits plummeted back to earth. "I don't need that many." One would be plenty.

But Addie was already halfway down the stairs, singing under her breath. At least one of us was happy.

❧

That night, I was staring at the cracks in my bedroom ceiling when someone scratched at my door. "Yes?"

"I can hear you moaning from across the hall," Jasper informed me, shutting the door behind him.

I rubbed the end of my nose. "I must be coming down with something."

"Sure you are." Crossing to my desk, he availed himself of the room's only chair, turning it to face me.

"How's Bo?" I asked, guessing at the purpose behind this unexpected visit.

"Since your very special get-me-to-a-nunnery speech?" He shrugged. "He'll survive. But I didn't come here to talk about Bo."

"Is there something bothering *you*?" I asked hopefully.

Jasper ignored my diversionary tactic. "Listen, Mary. You're my sister." I nodded; thus far we were on the same page. "I can't watch you drowning and not throw you a rope." He fixed me with a serious look. "What I'm about to say stays between the two of us. No ratting me out to Mom and Dad."

"As long as it's not dangerous. To people *or* property." Many years' experience had taught me to lay out the fine print before agreeing to one of Jasper's propositions.

He straightened his shoulders, exhaling in a determined way. "Okay, here it is. W-W-J-A-D."

I waited for illumination to strike, to no avail. "Huh?"

"What. Would. Jane. Austen. Do." He sketched a question mark in the air.

I pushed myself up to a sitting position. "*Jane Austen* Jane Austen? *The* Jane Austen?"

"Yes." He waved at me to lower my voice. "Obviously."

"How is it obvious?" For years he'd been flaunting his lack of literacy, particularly where the classics were concerned. And it didn't get much more classic than Austen.

"Because maybe I've read one or two of her books."

I continued to regard him skeptically.

"Fine. I've read all of them." He picked at a loose thread on his pajama bottoms. "Including *Sanditon*."

"*Sanditon*? Seriously?" Even mega fans often eschewed the

partial manuscript Austen had left unfinished at her death. It was the equivalent of reading Brontë juvenilia.

"What I read is my business. Let's not get distracted from the main issue."

"If."

"Huh?"

"*If* you read. Because according to the line you've been feeding Mom, you'd rather poke yourself in the eye with a sharp stick."

"Low expectations can be a blessing. But that's not the point. The important thing—"

"Besides you being a closet Janeite?"

"Whatever, *Emma*."

"I'm not an Emma!"

"Really, back-seat driver?" He looked me up and down. "No puppet-master tendencies? Trying to run other people's lives?"

I flinched; if it wasn't a direct hit, he was at least prodding the vicinity of a sore spot. Because of course my epic screwup was even more embarrassing given the way I'd handed down judgment on everyone else, with nary a thought for complicating factors such as the animal instinct to keep doing something that feels really good. Like being in close proximity to Alex Ritter, as often as possible.

But did that make me an Emma Woodhouse, blithely dispensing advice while ignoring the truth of what was going on all around her, and in her own heart? Surely I wasn't that blind.

"So you're saying Alex was my Mr. Knightley?" That would be a far more comfortable interpretation. And Alex *was* an older man, though our age difference was about a tenth that between Emma and her neighbor/love interest.

Jasper shook his head. "I'm not talking about Lover Boy. Though it does sound like you've basically been going around telling everyone how mean he was to poor, misunderstood Wickham."

"Wait." I held up a hand. "Does that mean Alex is my Darcy? Because that would make me —" I couldn't bring myself to say it aloud. Who didn't secretly dream of being compared to Elizabeth Bennet, the witty and vivacious heroine of *Pride and Prejudice*? As for Mr. Darcy . . . I shivered pleasantly.

"Simmer down there," Jasper tutted. "I wouldn't go that far. A wee bit fixed in your opinions, though? Quick to rush to judgment?" He tapped his chin, pretending to consider.

The sad part was, I couldn't even argue. I felt his words seeping through the cracks in my memory, altering my vision of the past. Had I been hasty? Unfair? Certainly to Alex.

"Then again," he went on, "you might be more of an Anne Elliot, trying so hard to be a good girl you end up sad and alone. Or one of the Dashwood sisters, caught up in your own drama. Perhaps a Catherine Morland, whose mind is warped by *reading too much?*"

I cast him a baleful look. "Now you're showing off."

"That's what you think. I'm just getting warmed up —"

"If you compare me to Fanny Price I will scream." Of all Austen's novels, *Mansfield Park* is the only one in which it's hard not to root for the villain over the milquetoast heroine. Fanny would never have passionately embraced Alex Ritter in the school hallway. She didn't have the backbone for it. And despite everything that had followed, that was one part of the evening I couldn't bring myself to regret.

"Your words, not mine. But since we're on the subject, I've always thought Fanny missed out when she sent Henry Crawford packing. He was way more interesting than Edmund."

Rakishly interesting. A would-be seducer who ends up falling for the target of his attentions, only to be cruelly rejected when she chooses the stick-in-the-mud instead. Except Alex wasn't actually much of a scoundrel, as it turned out, despite my preconceived ideas about him. I shook my head. Stupid Fanny. Stupid *me*.

"Let's say I believe you," I began. "For the sake of argument. All it tells me is what I've already done wrong, which I sort of already knew." Jasper gave me a skeptical look, but I hurried on. "What I need help with is figuring out what to do *now*."

"I don't know. Go tour his palatial country estate with our least embarrassing relatives?"

"Forget Mr. Darcy. What about my *friends*?"

My brother frowned. "I thought you were pining for a dude."

"That's not pertinent," I said, dodging the question. "He won't — it was never going to happen anyway."

"Huh."

To my extreme frustration, I couldn't tell whether he was agreeing with me or not. "I guess I could do a reread of the major Austen novels, take some notes . . ." My voice trailed off as Jasper gave me a thumbs down.

"No way. It's time to act."

"Act?" I pictured a darkened stage with a pool of light in the middle, and me giving a dramatic monologue.

"Shake things up, instead of sitting back and waiting for someone else to call the shots. I bet you'd still be following Anjuli around if she hadn't kicked you to the curb."

I flinched but couldn't deny it.

"And now you're just letting your friends go without a fight." He shook his head, as if my lack of nerve was a grave personal disappointment. "When's the last time you took a risk? I'm talking IRL, not in your reading material."

At first, I couldn't summon an example. Then I remembered that day at Toil & Trouble. I'd put myself forward to warn them about Alex Ritter—and reaped the rewards of that impulsive decision, far beyond anything I could have imagined.

Until it all fell apart.

"I don't know, Jasper. It's like you're asking me to stick my hand back in the fire."

He rolled his eyes. "I'm asking you to get close enough to roast a freaking marshmallow." Standing, he scratched his belly. "What about that?" He pointed at the Baardvaark flyer on my desk.

"What about it?"

"Ask your friends," he said through an open-mouthed yawn.

"Just walk up and invite them to the play?"

He shrugged. "Will it work? Maybe, maybe not. But you know what I hate?"

I shook my head.

"The part in books where supposedly smart characters screw up their lives because it's *just too hard*" — he made a cry-baby face, fists twisting in front of his eyes — "to tell someone the truth."

"The truth," I repeated.

"I love you, I miss you, I can't live without you." Jasper yawned again. "Whatevs."

"You're right." My cheeks puffed as I blew out a heavy breath.

"Try not to sound so excited."

"It's a little demoralizing," I admitted.

Jasper cocked a brow. "Getting schooled by your little brother?"

"Being as dumb as the people in books. I always thought I'd be smarter. Make a better choice at the moment of crisis. Take the road less likely to screw up my whole life."

"Yeah, but those people weren't reading about themselves. They couldn't, like, peek ahead to the end." He mimed flipping pages. "It was all happening to them. Boom! In your face!"

I pressed my fingers over my eyes. "Okay, I get it. You can stop saying smart stuff now."

Dear Diary,

You go your whole life thinking you know exactly which kind of character you are. Virtuous. Loyal. Full of integrity. Brave if the situation calls for it, which hopefully isn't too often. The hero, not the villain.

But what if the bad guys feel the same way? Maybe they aren't sitting around cackling evilly and twirling their mustaches; they just cut themselves too much slack when it comes to doing what they want.

M.P.M.

CHAPTER 30

Like a dream that fades upon waking, the optimism I'd felt after talking to Jasper was hard to sustain by the light of day, especially when I walked into school and found Anjuli waiting next to my locker. My first instinct was to pretend she was invisible, or that I was, but that didn't fit with my new unflinchingly honest approach to life.

"You actually did make friends," Anjuli said by way of greeting. "With those girls. Assuming that was for real." She chewed pensively at her thumbnail while I struggled to pull the metaphorical dagger out of my chest.

"Yeah. It just sort of happened." It felt both strange and not strange to be talking to her. The weight of habit *almost* balanced the months of estrangement, like we were on a teeter-totter temporarily holding level.

"So I guess you are capable of changing. When you want to."

"Maybe I didn't have to. They liked me the way I was, old books and all." I hoped she didn't notice the past tense.

"Sure. It's all my fault. Perfect Mary never does anything wrong."

I tried not to betray myself by flinching. "I didn't say that."

"Please. Everything just falls into your lap."

I stared at Anjuli, the coddled only child whose parents bought her the latest everything, sent her to expensive camps, took her on trips all over the world. "What are you talking about?"

"New friends, a cute guy." She crossed her arms, fixing me with an accusing scowl. "I bet you even went to the dance."

"Yeah. And that turned out so well. Lucky me."

Her eyes lit with curiosity, but I had no intention of giving the "it was the best of times, it was the worst of times" speech before first period.

"What about you?" I countered.

"What about me?"

"You have a whole new group of friends. And a fancy hobby."

"Stamp collecting is a hobby. Experimental film is a *passion*."

I had a sudden inkling of how my conversational style must sound to Anjuli. The way it might make her want to beat her head against the nearest hard surface. "Right."

Anjuli looked down, adjusting the strap of her backpack. "Listen. We both know it wasn't working. You're not a risk-taker, so you expected me to stay the same too. Like there was this box labeled Anjuli and I was supposed to sit there quietly and be your sidekick. And watch PBS with you on the weekends."

This was a palpable hit, but I didn't think the fault was *all* mine. "Why didn't you say something, if I was so horrible to be around?"

"Not horrible, just . . . not what I wanted." Anjuli blew a breath out the side of her mouth. "It's not like I was what you wanted either. You moved on fast enough once I was out of the picture."

It almost sounded like her feelings were hurt. But there was a trace of smugness too, like she'd done me a favor. Maybe I'd never really understood the way her brain worked.

"So it wasn't about Pittaya?" I asked, relieved to think we hadn't fallen into that particular cliché.

"That was a side thing. The icing on the cake."

"Or maybe the straw that broke the camel's back?"

"Whatever, Word Girl."

It was something one of our teachers had called me years ago, though I couldn't recall Anjuli ever using the nickname before. Somehow in that moment it wasn't uncomfortable to have the weight of so much history behind us.

I felt a shifting in my brain, pieces of the past rearranging. All this time I'd been thinking in absolutes, like it was an either/or proposition: friends versus not friends, and if it ended badly, the whole thing must have been a lie. But maybe it was more complicated. There could be different types of friendship, and different stages within each one. Deep bonds of loyalty and affection, or ties that have more to do with convenience. Relationships that hold you back, and ones that grow with you.

I thought of something Arden said weeks before, when only

Lydia's size had been available in a pair of boots both admired. "A true friend is happy for you when good things happen. They don't get jealous and petty."

Instead of which, Anjuli and I had cast each other as villains. As obstacles to be overcome. It was a weak move, pretending it was all someone else's fault—like they had the power and you were a waif tied to the railroad tracks.

I took a deep breath, feeling a weight lift. Now that the hurt and shock had faded, I could admit that Anjuli and I had been rubbing each other the wrong way long before the Shunning. And even though getting to this point had been graceless and painful, we were probably better off not pretending, or trying to force each other to become different people and resenting it when we couldn't.

"What you said about me, that day?" I looked her in the eye. "It wasn't completely wrong. I could have put myself out there more, instead of hiding behind books."

Her sigh spoke of exasperation, but maybe also relief. "And I guess I could have . . . used my words better." She grimaced. "Can we be done talking about this now?"

"Okay," I said, and it was. This ending I could live with.

℘

When lunchtime rolled around, I hovered near the cafeteria entrance. Fever-like symptoms had set in: flushed skin, trembling limbs, a fog that muddled my conscious brain. The pervasive aroma of boiled hot dogs didn't help. Perhaps it would be better to lie down somewhere dark and quiet instead.

Alas, it was too late. They had spotted me. I eyed the three of them warily as I moved in that direction, alert for signs of anger, or disgust. When I reached the table, no one spoke.

"Hello." My voice sounded rusty. The pause that followed stretched on and on, a century or two at least. I gripped the back of a chair to hold myself upright.

"Hi," Arden said at last. Lydia gave a stiff nod. Terry's mouth moved in what might have been an attempted smile.

I drew an unsteady breath. "Could I talk to you?"

Arden's narrow brows arched. "I don't know, Mary. Can you?"

It took me a second to realize she wasn't being sarcastic. "I hope so? I mean, I'd like to. If that's okay."

The three of them looked at each other before nodding. With a shaking hand, I pulled out the chair and sat down. The others fidgeted in silence, their lunches forgotten.

It was nothing like old times. The starkness of the change drove home the enormity of what I'd lost. I tried to swallow, but the saliva stuck halfway down my throat. The tickling sensation made me want to cough; I cleared my throat instead. It sounded like I was gagging.

"How come you're not avoiding us anymore?" Arden darted a glance at me before returning her attention to the water bottle she was turning in circles.

"What? I wasn't. I mean, I was, but not because *I* wanted to."

"You bailed on us," Lydia blurted.

Arden snapped her fingers. "Just like that."

"Like you didn't care," Terry whispered.

"No! It was the opposite. I care a lot. A really lot." Why did words always desert me at the most inopportune moments? My mother would have had the perfect quote for the occasion.

Lydia hooked a finger under the chain of her necklace, rolling the enamel daisy pendant back and forth. "Then it wasn't all part of a master plan?"

I looked at her blankly.

"A plot," Arden put in.

"Because if getting with Alex was your goal, then it would make sense that you dropped us as soon as you had what you wanted." Lydia's tone fell just shy of accusing.

"No," I said quickly. "It wasn't like that at all. That would be diabolical. And incredibly complicated. What made you think that?"

"We're kind of in the habit of looking for the deeper meanings behind things," Arden reminded me.

"Psychology," said Terry.

"Hidden motives," added Lydia.

It dawned on me that they were talking about *my* influence. I had trained them to see everything as a twisted reflection of something that once happened in a book.

"I wanted to be friends with you," I said slowly. "That was my only secret agenda. Except not secret. If anything, I was using him to impress *you*." Not the actual Alex, of course, but the Vronsky I'd conjured.

"Then why have you been ignoring us?" Blotches of color appeared high on Arden's cheeks. "I kept thinking, 'We need Lady Mary to lay down some truths, because this sucks,' and then it was like, 'Oh wait, that's not going to happen, because she ditched us!'"

Startled by this unexpected outburst, I was slow to respond. "I didn't think you'd want to see me."

"You're the one who jumped out of my car and ran away!" Arden reminded me.

"Do you have any idea how long we spent cruising your neighborhood?" Lydia asked. "It's a miracle nobody called it in."

I bowed my head. "It was my fault, so I figured I should be the one to suffer. I didn't want to offend you with my presence."

Arden exhaled loudly. "That's not how it works."

"It's probably because of what happened with her other friend," Terry said.

"Or maybe it's from a *book!*" Lydia jabbed a finger at me.

My mouth opened and then closed again, cutting off the denial I'd been about to issue. There *was* something highly literary in the idea of succumbing to a fatal, solitary misery, like working myself to death making hats.

"Maybe," I allowed. "I can't tell anymore." When it came to my own behavior, I felt less insightful all the time.

"If those books were even real." Arden lifted her chin. "Some of that stuff sounded way over the top. Like the one where they find that lady's exact double and then put her in an asylum so they can get the other lady's inheritance?"

"It's a real book," I assured her. "They all are. In fact, there's one that's really apropos, about a dying heiress and this couple that wants to get married, but they don't have enough money." I broke off when Lydia held up a hand.

"No books."

Arden nodded her agreement. "Let's stick with the people at this table. IRL."

I took this as my cue to launch into the remarks I'd painstakingly prepared. "Okay, first I want to apologize to all of you. Not just for ruining Winter Formal, although I also feel really bad about that." I looked at each of them in turn. "I'm so sorry. You're the best friends I've ever had, and I feel terrible that I repaid you by being underhanded. And I betrayed you most of all." I turned to Terry.

She stiffened. "Why me?"

"Because I talked you out of dating Alex, when it turns out he's actually a nice person." A better woman might have enumerated his sterling qualities, but even that much of a concession made me want to roll around on the floor gnashing my teeth. There was a difference between selflessness and masochism.

"That's okay," Terry said. "I didn't want to go out with him anyway."

My first reaction—profound relief—was followed by a paradoxical urge to argue. "Why not?"

"I'm just not interested." She shrugged. "In any of them. I never was."

"Why didn't you say anything?" Lydia asked Terry.

"I was going along with the crowd, since you guys were into it."

Arden gasped. "This is like that story about the girl who cut off all her hair but then the guy sold his watch and they

343

had nothing for Christmas. Not that we're talking about books right now." She mimed zipping her lips. "New rule. From now on, everyone has to be straight up about what they want, or don't want. Like with me and Lydia, and how I secretly felt guilty that I had a boyfriend and she didn't, because I kept thinking it would bother me if it was the other way around."

"It did bother me," Lydia admitted. "Which made me feel stupid. But I felt even worse when it seemed like you were totally obsessed with me being single, like it was a massive head wound."

Terry nodded. "And the boyfriend would be like stapling your scalp, so you don't bleed out."

"That is one hundred percent not how I thought of it," Arden assured us.

Lydia shrugged. "I know that *now*."

"Because we got it all out in the open," Arden concluded, with the same inflection typically given to the phrase *and they all lived happily ever after.*

"And—you and Miles?" I crossed my fingers for another miraculous reconciliation.

"He sent me an email." Arden lifted a shoulder. "I don't know what will happen. I'm not sure I like the way he made me feel like a burden. I want someone who wants me."

"And who you want," I said, easing into my next point. "Whoever that might be. Because it's okay to want things that *aren't* the things you think people want you to want."

Lydia squinted at me. "You lost me there."

"Sometimes people want someone . . ." I searched for a tactful way to phrase it, "unexpected."

"Like you and Alex?" Arden suggested. "Because I did *not* see that one coming."

I winced. Naturally I knew he was beyond my reach, but did we have put it out there so baldly?

"I pictured you with someone way smarter," she continued, and now I felt bad for Alex. People probably underestimated him all the time because of his looks. Or maybe that was just me.

"Actually, I was talking about Terry," I said, demonstrating my newfound commitment to full disclosure. "And I hope I speak for everyone here when I promise that if she ever wanted to tell us about feelings she might have for a certain someone, we would fully understand. Even if it was more or less hopeless, at least for now."

Lydia looked questioningly at Terry. "Do you have any idea where she's going with this?"

Terry shook her head.

"Let's just say I've noticed you admiring this person," I hinted.

"Oh my gosh, are you talking about yourself?" Arden imitated my eyebrow-raising.

"No," I sighed. "It's obviously not *me*."

"Obviously," Lydia echoed. "Crystal clear."

I smiled gently. "It's Cam, isn't it?"

"Your sister?" Terry shook her head. "I'm not in love with her." It was a simple, forthright denial. No blushing, no cringing, no looking away.

"I didn't say *in love*," I amended, thinking it might be a semantic issue. "I just meant you might be carrying a torch. Because of how you talk about her."

"I do admire her," Terry said. "She's so cool. Great poker face."

It wasn't exactly an ode to romantic love. "Then you don't want to date her?"

"Not really, no."

"Huh." My eloquence seemed to be fading along with my ability to read people.

"I thought it was because of your mom." Arden lifted her chin in Terry's direction. "Like you were afraid she'd feel bad if you found someone before she did."

Her mother! A classic thematic wrinkle. Why hadn't I thought of that?

"I do worry about her being lonely, but that's not why." Terry looked at us through her lashes. "I've never really had a crush on anyone. Or if I did, I didn't notice. I'm not sure what it's supposed to feel like. Is that strange?"

"Strange is someone who picks off pieces of their own skin and eats it. Your feelings, and nonfeelings, are just part of who you are." Arden smiled encouragingly. "Maybe you just haven't met the right person yet."

"Or maybe she'd rather be alone," Lydia countered.

"Or a nun," suggested Arden, snapping her fingers.

I pointed at Terry. "Who's also a forensic pathologist."

Lydia looked impressed. "I'd watch the crap out of that TV show."

The first bell rang. We still had five minutes to get to class, but lunch was technically over. I felt a frisson of panic. Was everything settled? Had they forgiven me? Were we friends again, or merely in a state of détente? These didn't seem like the kind of questions I could verbalize.

Arden stood, looking down at me. "You know what we need to do now?"

"Oh. Sorry." I stumbled to my feet.

"What are you doing?" Lydia asked.

"I meant to leave after the apology. Not overstay my welcome."

"That was your plan? Show up, apologize, take off?"

"Kind of? I thought maybe you'd want to discuss things — without me."

"What I was *going* to say," Arden cut in with a trace of impatience, "is that we should celebrate. Preferably someplace that is not the cafeteria."

I looked down at the scarred tabletop. "Then you're speaking to me?"

"*We* never stopped," Arden pointed out.

Sighing, I added this to my list of recent blunders.

As we wended our way through the cafeteria, I felt Arden watching me. "I guess they didn't cover this in any of your books," she said when I looked up.

"This?"

"Friendship."

It was true that the driving force in novels was more often a romantic arc: the so-called marriage plot. Unless it was a story-of-my-life bildungsroman, but those seemed to be the exclusive province of boys. (*Quelle surprise,* as my mother would say.)

"You're right," I said. "Most of what I know about friends I learned from you guys."

Dear Diary,

Jasper, if you're reading my diary again, I have one word for you: thanks.

M.P.M.

CHAPTER 31

M ary!" Doug cried as I walked through the door of Tome Raider that afternoon. "And you're not alone!"

I was too incandescent with relief to mind being exposed as a pathetic loner. If the shoe fit, and all that.

Arden shrugged out of her coat, draping it over the back of a chair. "What's on the menu, D?"

"Snow Queen meringues. A fluffy outside with glassy shards of spun sugar in the middle."

Terry's hand shot up. "Make mine a double."

Doug paused on his way to the kitchen. "Did you bring posters for the show, Mary?"

"Uh, yeah." My cheeks reddened as I extracted the flyers for *Othello* from my backpack. "You're all invited to the dress rehearsal on Thursday. It's friends and family night."

"How cool." Arden grabbed a flyer from the stack. "Very VIP."

"It will be," I agreed. "Doug's doing the refreshments."

"I'm trying something new," he chimed in, returning from

the kitchen with a plate of meringues. "I call them Desdemona's Pillows. But just between us it's basically a *pastelito*."

Terry reached for a meringue. "My mom makes those."

"Really?" Doug rocked forward on the balls of his feet. "I don't suppose she shares her recipes?"

"Yeah." Terry held a hand in front of her mouth to hide the chewing. "Why not?"

"Great! Would she be willing to email me? I can give you my address." He patted his pockets, searching for a writing implement.

"Or maybe she could stop by?" Arden suggested.

"I wouldn't want to impose," Doug demurred.

"We'll set it up," she assured him.

"If you're sure it wouldn't be too much trouble, that would be wonderful!" There was a definite spring in his step on the way back to the kitchen, Birkenstocks notwithstanding.

Arden watched the door close behind him. "Are you thinking what I'm thinking?"

"About the pastelitos?" It was hard for Terry to concentrate on other things when dessert was involved.

"About your mom. You've been saying she needs to get out more." When Terry looked at her blankly, Arden jerked a thumb toward the kitchen door. "Why not him? He's single, he's like a big gentle bear, he can cook—she could do a lot worse."

Lydia swiped at the corner of her mouth, brushing off meringue crumbs. "I thought we were getting out of the matchmaking business."

Arden flashed her a look of bewilderment. "Why?"

"Because of . . . everything?" Lydia reminded her. "We can't just assume people want to be fixed up."

"Of course not," Arden said easily. "We won't *assume* anything. Terry can ask her mom first." She bit into a meringue, catching the pieces that crumbled in her cupped hand. "Now that's settled, let's go back to that fateful night. What did we miss, Mary?"

"That's not a very interesting story." Picture me lying next to a pile of damp tissues: The End. "I'd rather hear about you guys."

"I'll go." Lydia sat up a little straighter. "Pittaya's a gentleman. Very nice hands. I might see him again. Not that I'm looking for anything serious."

Arden took a deep breath, visibly restraining herself from demanding details. "Your sister slow danced with Jeff, to a fast song."

"And I wasn't jealous of either of them," Terry assured me.

"That's everything there is to know about us." Arden inspected a meringue it as though all her attention was focused there, instead of on me, fooling exactly none of us. "Which leaves you, Mary. And your dance partner."

"You guys don't want to talk about that." I hesitated. "Do you?"

The three of them exchanged looks. "Um, *yeah*," Arden replied for the group. "Feel free to skip to the juicy part. What's going on with you two?"

"Nothing." It should have been a relief to report this with

a clear conscience. Instead I felt a distinct hollowness in my stomach, despite the meringue I'd just inhaled.

"You ghosted on him too?" Lydia asked.

"It's not like we had a relationship. He's probably moved on by now." I tried not to make it sound like a question. Lydia shook her head, meaning either *no* or *I can't believe how insipid you're being right now.*

"If I can quote Miles for a second, I'm noticing some inconsistencies in your logic." Arden bit her lip. "It barely even hurt to say his name. Progress!" She allowed herself a small fist pump. "What I'm saying is, if he's not a player, he's not a player."

"I think maybe he's not." This was a bittersweet admission, to say the least.

"Ipso facto, he's into you," Lydia summarized.

Arden wagged a finger at me. "I had my suspicions a long time ago, after Terry told us how he chatted you up at that party. But then I figured, 'No, if he was hitting on Mary, she would know.' Since you're all about hidden agendas."

"Ha," I croaked, for lack of a more cogent response.

"You haven't talked to him at all?" Terry asked.

"Are you saying I should?" I'd assumed cutting off contact with Alex would be a condition of restoring their faith in me. The punishment must fit the crime.

"We want you to do what you want to do," Arden said evenly. "As long as it's the right thing."

"But I messed everything up," I reminded her. "Think about your list, and all the work you put into it!"

She placed a hand over her phone, which was resting face down on the table. "Actually, you didn't go that far off course."

With exaggerated slowness, Lydia turned to frown at her. "Say what?"

"First kiss," Arden whispered.

"How was that supposed to be a group outing?" Lydia demanded.

Terry looked thoughtful. "Maybe if it was spin-the-bottle."

"I didn't say we all had to be there watching," Arden retorted. "It's just one of the milestones of a high-school experience, so I jotted it down. For Mary. Just in case. Totally optional, obviously. She didn't *have* to kiss anyone."

"Which brings us to the real question." Lydia sat back, arms crossed. "What do *you* want, Mary?"

My hands knotted under the table. "It doesn't matter. That bridge is burned. As in, ashes and dust."

"There's only one way to find out." Arden tapped the stack of Baardvaark flyers.

"Put on a thinly veiled dramatic reenactment of our story and see how he reacts?" I guessed, thinking of *Hamlet*.

Lydia frowned. "I'm pretty sure she means he'll be at the play to see his sister. On Thursday."

"Think of it as a do-over," said Arden. "You say, 'You know what, I'm kind of into this guy' and we go, 'Okay, interesting, tell us more.' And we take it from there."

I bowed my head. "Is that really how it would have been?"

"If someone said to you, 'I have the hots for Alex Ritter,' what would you say? 'Ooh, that's so freaky, I have no idea what you see in him?' No," Lydia continued, answering her own question. "You wouldn't. Because we're talking about *Alex Ritter*."

"Actually, I did say that," I reminded them. "To Terry. The first time we met."

Arden patted my hand. "You're special, Mary."

Pushing her napkin to one side, Lydia leaned her elbows on the table. "What's your move?"

"I don't know."

"What would a person in your books do?" Terry asked.

"One where they don't all die," Arden amended.

"I thought I was supposed to stop relying on books to figure things out."

"Mary." Arden's tone was solemn. "You're still you."

"Don't change yourself for a dude," added Lydia.

"There is one thing," I admitted. And it was pretty literary, in the WWJAD sense. "I've been writing him letters."

"And?" Lydia circled a hand in the air. "What did he say?"

I shook my head. "Nothing."

Terry sucked in a breath.

"I haven't actually sent any of them. It was more for me—just to have a way to express things I was feeling."

Arden nodded slowly. "A love letter. I like it. Old-school romantic."

"It was really more of a long, detailed apology." My wrist cramped at the memory. "Pages and pages."

There was a brief silence.

"Yeah, no," said Lydia. "That's not going to work."

"Think short apology, then straight to the sappy stuff,"

355

Arden advised. "I don't suppose you know calligraphy?" I shook my head.

"She's still going to have to talk to him," Lydia said. "Mano a mano."

"That means hand to hand," Terry told her.

"Huh. You get what I'm saying. The letter is like your deposition—"

"Only on beautiful stationery," Arden cut in. "And maybe you should spritz it with a little perfume."

"And send him something sweet with it, like cookies," suggested Terry.

Lydia cleared her throat. "As I was saying, you can start with the letter, but you'll still have to take the stand eventually."

"And we'll all cross our fingers the verdict goes your way." Arden gave an exaggerated wink. "Because I'm pretty sure Mary checked off another item on my list."

"Colossal screwup?" I guessed.

She shook her head. "First love-slash-crush. Because you really fell for him. Am I right?"

I nodded. *Guilty as charged.*

Dear Alex,

I know you don't remember the first time we met. You talked to me backstage, but when we ran into each other a few days later, you had no idea who I was. Which is part of why I had a hard time trusting you. I was afraid you'd forget me again.

You know that day we were sitting in my backyard and the leaves were falling and you were telling me what it's like to have a crush on someone? I get it now. To tell you the truth, I knew then. I was just too much of a coward to admit what I was feeling. Which is why this letter will never be sent. And I'm the only one who'll know that the times we had together were the closest my life has ever come to the kind of moments that could be in a book.

~~Love~~

~~Affectionately~~

~~Cordially~~

~~Yours Truly~~

~~Regards~~

Mary

CHAPTER 32

I f ever an enterprise cried out for poetry, it was this one. Unfortunately, in our house all the romantic verse was stored on a bedside shelf in our parents' room, which for many reasons discouraged casual browsing.

Two days and a dozen failed attempts later, I bent my steps toward the public library. Nodding a quick hello to the librarian on duty, I made a beeline for the Literature and Poetry section. There was no one else around. My finger traced the many-colored spines until I hit the word *romantic*. Pulling the heavy book from the shelf, I rested it on my knee. From my pocket, I withdrew the latest draft of my letter to Alex, using the flat of my hand to smooth it. It needed to be better. Perfect. Irresistible.

Time passed, and I kept turning pages. I didn't want a poem that was obviously talking about getting it on. Nor did I want one of the really saccharine odes to rosebuds and cherubs (which were probably also about sex). It needed to be something that felt like me, and my feelings for Alex, in a non-cheesy way.

I rolled my shoulders. Maybe the whole thing was hopeless. I'd tell my friends I'd tried, but it was no good.

Tucking the book under my arm, I climbed stiffly to my feet. I needed to walk around, drink some water, get the juices flowing. Preoccupied by my own thoughts, I was oblivious to my surroundings until I stumbled into the study area. It was packed with people of all ages, including a healthy sprinkling of faces I recognized from school. Apparently that was the kind of thing that happened when everyone had final exams the same week.

Since I had no desire to talk to anyone, particularly while in possession of a book of love poems, I kept my head down and hurried on. A pair of legs entered my field of vision. I looked up to avoid a collision.

"Oh," I breathed, coming to an abrupt halt. "Oh, no!"

"Hello to you, too," said Alex Ritter.

"I didn't mean it like that," I whispered, conscious of our audience. "It's just—the timing."

"Well, don't let me keep you." He stepped around me, heading for a table with a single empty chair, and three very pretty girls obviously awaiting his return.

"Oh," I said again. "I see." My gaze fell to the book of poetry in my hands. Talk about a wasted effort. How stupid of me to think he wouldn't have found someone else by now.

"What?" Alex stopped with his back to me.

"Nothing."

With obvious reluctance, he turned around. At the same moment, the letter slipped from my grip. I stood frozen with horror, watching it float through the air. Then Alex reached for it.

I lunged, plucking the page from the carpet and holding it out of his reach.

His eyes narrowed. "It's obviously *something*." Realizing he was trying to read the title of my book, I twisted aside. A white-haired woman cleared her throat, then pointed to the sign on her table: QUIET, PLEASE!

I took a tentative step to the left, sending a questioning look Alex's way. He sighed but followed me into the cookbook section. When we reached the remotest end of the aisle, I pivoted to face him. My heart was beating so hard, I wasn't sure I'd be able to speak.

"What?" he asked, arms crossed.

I glanced at the page half crumpled in my fist, then back at him. "It's a letter."

"Okay." He shrugged angrily. "I wasn't trying to read your mail."

My toes curled inside my shoes as though gripping the end of a diving board. "It's yours, actually."

"You stole my mail?"

I closed my eyes. This was going so well. "It's *to* you — from me."

His gaze fell to the page in my hand. "Do I get to read it?"

"It's not finished." In fact, I suspected it might never be finished. I'd keep writing forever, never quite getting it right, until I was a withered crone, and he was a well-preserved movie star with a house on the Riviera and dozens of linen shirts in varying shades of blue.

"You said it was mine." Uncrossing his arms, he held out a hand. "What does it say at the top?"

"'Dear Alex,'" I admitted, unable to stop myself from glancing at the telltale words. "But that's not—"

"Yes, it is." He locked eyes with me, and even though he wasn't doing the Smolder or any of his other signature looks, I melted. It felt like centuries since we'd been close enough for a staring contest. Before I could think better of it, I handed him the letter.

"Thank you," he said stiffly, as though I'd passed him the pepper grinder at a dinner party. "You can read your love poems while I look this over."

I choked, and not just because he'd spied the subject of my book. "You can't read it now!"

"Why not?" His thumb stroked the edge of the page, where a translucent spot marred the white paper. "Is this grease?"

"It certainly is not." I scoffed at the very idea.

"Then what is it?"

"I'd rather not say."

His nose wrinkled. "Something worse than grease?"

I pressed my lips together, looking away. "They're tear stains, okay?" Instantly, my face went up in flames.

"Why were you crying?" Alex asked, after a lengthy pause.

My eyes cut to his face, checking for signs of mockery and finding none. "Because . . . you were right, and I was wrong."

His brows rose.

"About everything. You. Me. My sister . . . s. My friends. The past. The present."

"I get the idea," he interrupted. "Is that all?"

I looked down. "I missed you. And I wanted to see you so much, but I knew it would never happen because I screwed up so badly. Ugh!" My foot stomped like a toddler's. "That was supposed to be way more eloquent." I gestured helplessly at the letter.

He looked at the page in his hands. "Maybe I better read it at home. If it's a tearjerker."

"You should definitely wait. I could make you a clean copy," I offered, leaping at the chance of a reprieve. "This one's really messy. I should fix it for you."

"You're just trying to steal my letter."

"Look, that's a blob of avocado," I said desperately, pointing to another spot.

Alex blinked at me. "You were eating avocado while you wrote this?"

"Guacamole is my comfort food."

"I like warm milk," he confided. "With honey."

"That's — a really good one."

"You sound surprised."

I shook my head, wanting to smile but not sure I had the right. We were drifting toward a semblance of our old rapport. The desire to have him look at me in that teasing way again, to call me Merrily, was a physical ache.

"I'm sorry, Alex." In the letter, I'd devoted three paragraphs to the subject, naming everything I'd done wrong. Standing here in front of him, the simplest words felt truest.

His jaw tightened. "What about your friends? Do they still think I'm the devil?"

"Not at all. I made a clean breast of it." An uncomfortable silence ensued, during which we both studiously avoided glancing at my chest. "I told them everything, I mean."

"They got a letter, too?"

The heat rushed back to my face. "Only you." I took a deep breath. "You don't owe me anything, obviously, and you're probably still mad, but if you do read it, instead of ripping it up or setting it on fire, that would—I would be grateful."

When I risked a glance at him, his expression revealed nothing.

"I better get back to my group," he said at last. As he turned to go, he folded the letter and tucked it in his pocket.

Dear Diary,

Sometimes people are surprised that so many classic books have sad endings. Other people are shocked when they don't. I guess it's a glass-half-empty versus glass-half-full kind of thing.

And also a good way to keep people guessing.

M.P.M.

CHAPTER 33

W hat were the exact words again?" Arden asked, leaning across the armrest. It was Thursday evening, and we had arrived early enough to claim most of the theater's fourth row.

"I wrote, 'I'll save you a seat,'" I told her. "But it's the very last line of the letter, so he might not even read that far." And not because it was as long as *Jane Eyre*.

"He knows it's tonight?" Terry confirmed.

I nodded.

Lydia tapped the program against her knee. "I thought you'd go more heart-eyes-emoji for your closing argument. Oh my darling, blah blah blah."

"It was a rough draft," I reminded them. "I was planning to polish it later."

"I'm sure it was a very good letter," Terry said. "You worked really hard on it."

"Hours and hours."

Arden squeezed my wrist. "Then there's no way he'll be able to resist."

I was glad to see she'd recovered her natural optimism, however difficult I found it to share the sunny outlook. From where I was sitting, it seemed Alex was having no trouble resisting the invitation to join me here. No doubt I'd done it all wrong, never having asked anyone out before.

"Did I mention how great you look?" Arden nudged me with her elbow.

"Seriously," Lydia chimed in. "Your makeup game is on point."

"That was all Anton. But thanks." He'd offered to do my hair, too, but I'd been too anxious to sit still long enough for hot rollers. Baardvaark's final dress rehearsals always fizzed with nervous energy, but tonight I felt the tension at a cellular level.

As the minutes crawled past, and more and more people found their seats, all color and brightness seemed to bleed from the world, circling the drain along with the last dregs of hope. Then I realized the darkness wasn't metaphysical; the house lights were dimming. I surveyed the auditorium one last time, on the off chance he'd slipped past me unseen.

Cam was sitting with Jeff in the same row as our parents. Bo manned the video camera in back; he gave a dignified nod when our eyes met. To my right sat Arden, Lydia, and Terry, the latter of whom didn't seem to mind Jasper's whispered commentary. Mrs. Larios would be there soon, to help Doug serve the pastelitos at intermission. The two of them were talking about seeing the show together a different night.

All the principals were accounted for — except the one I most wanted to see. Maybe this was my bittersweet denouement. The chastened young woman facing the future with her friends at her side, sadder but wiser in the wake of life's travails.

A spotlight flared to life and Van strode confidently toward the center of the stage. She was wearing her I'm-the-director outfit: slim black pants and a white button-down with the sleeves rolled up. The paisley scarf was a new touch; I suspected Phoebe's influence. After running through the standard litany of thank-yous and warnings about cell phones, she paused, hands steepled in front of her, until she'd captured everyone's attention.

"It's my pleasure to announce a change to the program. Tonight, the role of Iago will be played by the one and only Adeline Porter-Malcolm." Scattered whoops and hollers greeted the news, gradually building to a sustained round of applause.

Arden poked me in the shoulder. "Did you know?"

I shook my head. No wonder Addie had been so cheerful of late. She'd found the courage to stand up for what she wanted, and now her dreams were coming true. It was nice to know that worked out for some people.

After Van left the stage, the spotlight winked out, plunging the theater into darkness. The twins said this was one of their favorite moments of any production: the dividing line between regular life and the heightened reality of the stage, when everyone held their breath, balanced on the knife-edge of anticipation.

The velvet seat shook beneath me. Someone had dropped

into the empty place at my side. *Don't get your hopes up,* I cautioned myself.

"Alex?" I whispered, taking a chance.

"Merrily."

I closed my eyes. He was here. And he'd called me Merrily. My hands gripped the armrests to keep my body from puddling on the floor.

"Glasses." His voice was low, barely audible over the crinkling of programs and squeaking of springs. At first, I thought I must have misheard.

"What?"

"I got an eye infection, so I couldn't wear my contacts, but I was too cool for glasses." He paused. "If I acted like you were invisible, it was because I couldn't see past the end of my nose."

A few seconds passed before my brain caught up. He was talking about that day years ago, when he'd looked right through me backstage and I'd been so sure he was giving me an epic brushoff. "So you weren't being fickle," I said slowly. "It was just vanity."

"Exactly. You should definitely put that in my next love letter. I could get into this whole literary girlfriend thing."

I turned to face him as faint lighting began to illuminate the stage. It was just bright enough for me to see the smile playing about his lips. With the kind of reckless abandon that would surely have led to my imminent death in a nineteenth-century novel, I leaned in and kissed him.

It was a little disconcerting when the entire audience broke into applause, until I realized that Roderigo and Iago had just made their entrance. My eyes went immediately to Addie. Her mustache was much more convincing this time.

"So what's the deal?" Alex murmured in my ear.

"You mean with us?" It surprised me he was asking to define our relationship. I'd been led to believe modern men were commitment-shy.

He tipped his head at the stage. "The play. I only know the basics."

"Like the part where my sister conspires to get your sister murdered?

"Yeah." He reached for my hand, threading his fingers through mine. "Outstanding first date, Merrily. Very on-brand. Who needs happy endings, am I right?"

Me, I thought, squeezing his hand.

Only not endings, because this didn't have the feel of a finale. The shivery, hopeful, heart-pounding certainty that something good was about to happen: It was like starting a new book, with countless pages left to turn. Except better, because this time I didn't have to imagine myself into the story. It was all happening to me, right now, each moment indelible as ink on paper.

For once I wasn't worried about trying to predict how everything would turn out. There was a lot to be said for the unexpected adventures that happened along the way. A twist of fate. A lucky break. The part of a tale everyone recognizes as

THE ~~END~~ BEGINNING

THE SCOUNDREL SURVIVAL GUIDE, APPENDIX I: WORKS CITED

Which Tragedy Was Which?
Or: A Brief History of Mistakes That Have Been Made, Literarily

By Mary Porter-Malcolm

The One about the Eponymous Governess, Her Much Older Love Interest, the Madwoman in the Attic, the Ghostly Voice Echoing across the Moors, and Alex's Essay Test:

All that and so much more can be found in *Jane Eyre,* by my favorite Brontë sister, Charlotte.

(NB: The story does NOT end with Jane fighting off her husband's homicidal first wife.)

The One about Codependent Drama Queens Heathcliff and Cathy, Who Inflict Their Relationship Issues on Everyone around Them:

That would be *Wuthering Heights,* by Emily Brontë (a.k.a. the more twisted Brontë sister).

The One about the Cruel and Philandering Husband Who Has No Skill at Subterfuge:

The Tenant of Wildfell Hall is by Anne "The Perpetually Overshadowed" Brontë. The scene in a moonlit garden that Arden recreated with Miles goes something like this:

"My darling, you love me again! Does this mean you'll stop carousing with your vile friends and corrupting our son?"

"Helen!" (roughly shoving her out of his arms) "What are you doing here? Go inside at once!"

"Oh . . . okay." My, that was odd! One might almost think he was expecting someone else, like the beautiful lady who's been staying with us for months, giving me mocking glances. I wonder what it could mean?

The One Where She Names Her Baby Sorrow and Later Turns Stabby:

Tess of the d'Urbervilles, by Thomas Hardy. There are actually two bad guys here: one coerces Tess into single motherhood, and the other (not-so-aptly named Angel) judges her for having a checkered past, even though he's not exactly pure as the driven snow himself, thereby driving Tess to violent despair.

The One in Which Being Poor but Pretty Is a Recipe for Disaster, Especially When Your Friends are the Worst and Society Is a Shark Tank (but More Vicious):

The House of Mirth, by Edith Wharton.

The One about Whales, Obsession, Testosterone Poisoning, Phrenology, and Ten Thousand Other Digressions That Will Test Your Patience to the Breaking Point:

Moby Dick, by Herman Melville.

The One about the Innocent Abroad Marrying the Sleazy European Fortune Hunter with the Mistress, Even Though Isabel Archer Had Way Better Options:

Henry James had a thing for stories in which the virtuous are punished. The most famous is this one, *Portrait of a Lady*.

The One about Cecil the Snobby Fiancé and the Au Naturel Guy She Goes for Instead, with Bonus Italian Scenery:

A Room with a View, the most cheerful of E. M. Forster novels.

The One about a Pretentious Geezer Named Casaubon Who Tries to Hide That He's Full of It by Browbeating His Much Younger (and Cleverer) Wife, Dorothea:

That would be *Middlemarch*, by George Eliot, the pen name of one Mary Anne Evans. Happily, Dorothea eventually sees the light. And a handsome, age-appropriate love interest who respects her.

The Ones with Sleepwalking, Doppelgangers, Secret Societies, Cursed Jewels, and the Birth of the Detective Genre:

The Moonstone and *The Woman in White*, both by Wilkie Collins.

The One with the Slut-Shaming Double Standard and the Scarlet *A* That Is Not a Monogram:

The Scarlet Letter, by Nathaniel Hawthorne.

The One Where the Handsome Mill Owner Sees the Object of His Affection at a Train Station with Another Man Late at Night and Assumes the Worst, but Everything Turns Out Okay in the End:

North and South, by Elizabeth Gaskell. (Spoiler alert: the guy at the station was really her brother.) The miniseries gets top marks, too.

The One with the Tragic Waste of a Wedding Cake:

Great Expectations, by Charles Dickens. And yes, it's really about Pip and Estella and a thousand other characters, but

Miss Havisham casts a long shadow. Hell hath no fury like a woman abandoned at the altar.

The One in Which the Heroine Is TSTL:

How dumb is Pamela, heroine of the eponymous novel by Samuel Richardson? She can't climb a low wall without injuring herself. She's afraid of cows, because she thinks they are bulls. And when the horrible Mr. B climbs into bed with her disguised as a housemaid, Pamela doesn't have a clue. (With thanks to Lydia for teaching me the phrase *too stupid to live*.)

The Collected Works of Jane Austen:

Ask Jasper. He's the expert.

ACKNOWLEDGMENTS

If you have read my book, as opposed to turning directly to this page for mysterious reasons of your own, it won't be a surprise to learn that I grew up in a big family. I would not be the person I am today (bossy, sarcastic, possessive about desserts) without my beloved younger siblings, Dan, Luke, Claire, and Joe. Thanks also to their significant others, Lindsay, Beth, Ahmed, and Leelanee, for making holidays an even bigger party, and to the next generation (Coulson, Gabriel, Elias, Pablo, Marie, and Amael) for keeping us all laughing.

My parents, Peter and Sharon Henry, took me seriously as a reader and a writer from a young age. Mom gave me Jane Austen and Madeleine L'Engle, and Dad supplied me with Anne McCaffrey and Ursula Le Guin. Thank you both for laughing at my jokes, even if it was partly the hysteria of moving five kids back and forth across the country.

To Amy, my best friend of thirty-five years and a living reminder of my YA self, you are still the funniest person I know. Remember when you asked me to summarize *An American*

Tragedy on the way into class and then you aced the test except for misspelling the main character's name? You should tell your students that story.

On the publishing side, I am indebted to my agent, Bridget Smith, for being a kindred spirit and consummate professional, plus that whole making-dreams-come-true thing. My editor, Lily Kessinger, brought abundant warmth and intelligence to this process at every stage. Thank you for your patience, enthusiasm, and unflagging good cheer. Additional thanks to everyone else at HMH and beyond who helped make this a book, including Monique Aimee for the swoon-worthy cover art, designer Andrea Miller, publicist Sammy Brown, and copyeditor Megan Gendell.

To my film agent, Kristina Moore, and all the other industry gatekeepers who gave me a thrill of hope along the way, thank you.

Speaking of crucial encouragement, I am grateful to everyone who read this book in some form and offered feedback, including Randi Hacker, Gwendolyn Conover, Laura Huffman, Janet Lukehart, Korey Kaul, Melissa McCrory Hatcher, Heather Cashman, Darci Falin (also a photographer and graphic designer extraordinaire), Trenna Soderling, Beth Henry, and Melissa Zinn. And to Claire and Mom again, because no one on the planet has been forced to read the first chapters of this book more times than you two. Good news: I'm finished changing them!

I am fortunate to have a bunch of amazing writers in my general vicinity. For advice, editorial notes, encouragement, and interpretive dancing, I am especially grateful to Natalie Parker and Tessa Gratton (sorry I went to your wedding on the wrong day); Megan "Effervescence Incarnate" Bannen; and mystery maven Julie Tollefson. And to Miranda Asebedo, Rebecca Coffindaffer, Sarah Henning, Dot Hutchison, Adib Khorram, Christie Hall, and the rest of the local writers gang: you are the only group I've ever wanted to be part of, with the possible exception of the Super Friends.

To all the writers I only know through their books, whose words have rocked my world and put down roots in my brain: I hope one day I can give someone else a taste of the deep happiness I found in your stories.

On the home front, I am grateful for my *belle-fille* Lucile, who has inspired me with her grace and generosity of spirit, not to mention her skill at accessorizing, since she was a little girl.

To my not-so-little Gilly Bean, thank you for talking through plot points on long walks, asking for the Trivia Night scene as a bedtime story, and telling your kindergarten class all those years ago that your mom was a writer. To which they replied, "She's probably just sitting at home, eating chocolate and watching TV."

My husband, Fred, has kept the faith throughout the long journey to publication. For bringing music to my life and believing I'm a great writer even though my books are notably light on war and science and existential dread, *merci beaucoup*. (I totally pronounced it right in my head.)

Finally, to my fellow readers: I hope you never run out of good books. And thank you for giving this one a try.

Don't Miss

Belittled Women

by Amanda Sellet

Lit just got real.

Jo Porter has had enough *Little Women* to last a lifetime. As if being named after the sappiest family in literature wasn't sufficiently humiliating, Jo's mom turned their rambling, old house into a sadsack tourist attraction. Now Jo, along with her siblings, Meg and Bethamy (yes, that's two March sisters in one), spends all summer acting out sentimental moments at *Little Women Live!*

But when Jo gets a little too real about her frustration with the family biz, she will have to make peace with it before their livelihood suffers a fate worse than Beth.

"I thought every story should have some sort of a moral, so I took care to have a few of my sinners repent."

– Jo March, fictional character,
Little Women

"New rule: The next person who quotes *Little Women* gets slapped."

– Jo Porter, actual human and
not-so-little woman

Contact: Abigail "Marmee" Porter, <u>marmee@litlady.net</u>

FOR IMMEDIATE RELEASE
Coming Soon: The Seventh Spectacular Season of
Little Women Live!

———————••●••———————

New Concord, KANSAS—Mark your calendars! The area's most literary attraction, *Little Women Live!*, kicks off a seventh spectacular season this June.

Our one-of-a-kind destination offers visitors a magical opportunity to see their favorite characters come to life in an intimate and family-friendly setting. Watch the March sisters grow up before your very eyes as our talented cast acts out classic scenes including: a Christmas with no presents! Amy bringing limes to school! Jo and Laurie getting into "scrapes"! And, of course, Beth's emotional farewell!

Brand new this year: Meg's wedding!

While here, take a seat in the parlor. Try your hand at making jam. Enjoy a picturesque stroll through our landscaped grounds. Discover your inner Little Woman! Bring your own costume or buy a pinafore and bonnet in the gift shop.

Ample parking, modern restrooms, dining at our quaint Tea Shoppe, and souvenir shopping at the Concord Mercantile are all part of your Living Literature Experience.

For group rates, school tours, or to inquire about holding your next special event at *Little Women Live!*, contact Abigail Porter (a.k.a. "Marmee").

"My child, the troubles and temptations of
your life are beginning, and may be many."

—Little Women

CHAPTER
ONE

It doesn't matter how fast you run, or how far. There are
things in this life you can't escape.

Like your family.

At least not during track season.

If this had been a cross-country workout, my sister would
be eating my dust right now. Unfortunately, it was spring,
which meant circling the asphalt loop behind school like ham-
sters with delusions of NASCAR. It also gave Amy a chance
to trail after me wailing, "Jo! Wait!" like she needed my help
defusing a bomb.

When I sped up, she cut across the end of the field to catch
me coming around the bend. By now the rest of the team had
probably recognized that the freak in street clothes pinballing
around the inside of the track was my sister, so there was no

point pretending not to know her. Plus, Coach Solter blew her whistle, beckoning me with one finger. Fun time was over.

"Didn't you hear me calling?" Amy panted, when I jogged to a stop beside her.

"People in the next state heard you." I hadn't been ignoring her. Well, not the whole time. When I was running, my mind spun out into the future. Today I'd been imagining a college campus somewhere far, far away. Walking slowly across a grassy quadrangle. Autumn leaves. Lots of wool. I could almost smell the crispness of the air, until Amy bulldozed through the middle of my daydream.

"Why are you here?" I resisted the urge to yell. Coach probably thought all the drama signaled a legit emergency, as opposed to Amy's standard attention-seeking behavior.

My sister pressed a hand to her belly as she drew in a shaky breath. You could have made a sandwich during the pause that followed, because apparently no crisis was too urgent to keep her from grandstanding. "We need you at home, Jo."

"I have practice until four thirty."

"Whatever. You're not even on the team."

It was a cheap shot. The only reason I didn't run track was that I'd have to miss half the meets—including state championships—due to the demands of our family business. Though the word "business" was a stretch. Tragic obsession would be more accurate.

"Coach wants me here." A minimum of three weekly workouts was mandatory, so those of us who only ran cross-country didn't lose all our conditioning in the off-season. That was the official reason; unofficially, we were demonstrating our commitment, team spirit, and extreme dedication to the cause. All of which were crucial if I wanted a shot at being cross-country captain next fall. Not that Amy would care about that.

Coach pushed her sunglasses to the top of her head, clipboard balanced against one hip. She was already getting the distinctive ski-goggle tan line around her eyes. "Why didn't you tell me there was a problem at home, Jo?"

"It's not—" I pressed my lips together, doubting I could make her understand. "Everything was fine this morning. They were singing at breakfast."

"When the red, red robin goes bob-bob-bobbin' . . ." Amy began, falling silent when I glared at her.

"We need to be able to communicate." Coach squinted at me, and I caught the unspoken message: *if you want to be a leader.* And since I had yet to secure more than one provisional offer from a college team, there was a lot more riding on next year than another varsity letter.

Amy grabbed Coach by the arm, leaning in like she was paying her respects at a funeral. "Thank you for understanding," she said in a totally fake rasp. Straightening, she jerked her head at me. "Let's go."

"I have like three laps left—"

Coach shook her head. "Family is important, Jo. We'll see you next week."

"Such a beautiful message," Amy murmured. From her backpack she produced a crumpled piece of paper, which she handed to Coach with a smile. "Take one of these. I did the design myself."

Also known as "typing," if you weren't full of yourself. Although the blocky paragraphs were printed in simple black ink, certain phrases leaped off the page, sizzling behind my eyelids. *Family-friendly. Pinafore. Ample parking.* Because if you had to brag about the parking, didn't that say it all?

I tried to snatch it away, but the damage was done. Coach scanned the press release like there might be some hidden message, as opposed to the same tired promotional language we used every year.

"That time already, huh?"

"Not really. It's still March." For a few more days, anyway. If the clock wanted to stop right here, it would be okay with me.

"You know what they say. It's always March at our house." Amy sent Coach a hopeful look that with the slightest encouragement would turn into a wink.

"No one says that. Ever."

"I can send you a countdown widget," my sister told Coach Solter, as if I had myself on mute. "So you can *track* exactly how long it is until the big day."

Ha. Not the words I would have chosen to describe our annual pageant of humiliation. *Waking nightmare,* maybe. *A living hell.* And this year would be even worse.

"It's like watching the time tick down until Christmas," my sister blathered on.

"Or an asteroid on a collision course with Earth," I countered, not quite under my breath.

"The anticipation builds and builds." Amy squeezed her fists in a pantomime of excitement. "And then, bam! It's finally May."

"May Day," I said grimly, like the distress signal it was. *Mayday. Mayday.*

"We're so pleased to be able to offer an exclusive sneak preview for the local schoolchildren." Amy spoke like she was hosting a charity telethon. "Giving back to the community is hugely important to the entire *Little Women Live!* family."

"Did you take too much allergy medicine?" I tried to see if her pupils were dilated.

"All this"—she fluttered her fingers toward the track, ignoring me—"is such a valuable part of Jo's process." It sounded like she was throwing Coach a bone. Because three consecutive Class 4A state titles couldn't possibly compete with the personal validation of contributing to a third-rate tourist attraction.

"It's really not," I assured Coach.

"The Other Jo was always scampering about—"

I stepped on my sister's foot to shut her up. Her elbow caught me in the rib cage before I could dodge sideways.

Coach tucked the press release under the other papers on her clipboard. "You should hang one up in the locker room, Jo."

I made a noise that passed for agreement, even though what I really meant was *That would be tricky since my copies are at the bottom of the recycling bin outside the cafeteria.* By now they were probably drenched in Smurf-colored Powerade. Or worse.

"Thanks again," Amy said, like they'd just completed a professional transaction.

"I know school tours are a big deal." *For your sad, impoverished family.* Coach didn't say that part out loud; it was written in the sympathetic pinch of her expression.

My sister yanked me by the arm before I could disagree. We'd only gone a few steps when she let go, wiping her hand on the front of her shirt. "Is that sweat? Gross."

"I just ran four miles."

"I'm surprised you didn't flood the stadium."

That reminded me. "I think I left my water bottle by the bleachers." I gestured with my thumb. Amy glanced back at me, eyes widening.

"No way." This time she grabbed the hem of my T-shirt. "You're not going back there."

"It'll take me two seconds."

"That's not why," she hissed.

I was briefly distracted by a series of weird eyebrow contortions, like her face was using Morse code. "Are you glitching out right now?"

Although there was no one else within twenty feet of us, she got right up in my space. "David," Amy said through gritted teeth. "He's over there."

My shoulders lifted in a shrug I was only halfway to feeling. "So? The guys' team has practice too." I stole a quick glance in that direction, easily spotting David's lanky form among the knot of runners getting ready to hit the track. He was the tallest by several inches, but even without the extra height I would have recognized his posture: hands on hips and head down as he listened to someone else talk. It was a neat trick for someone his size to make himself so unobtrusive.

Amy smacked me on the shoulder. "Will you stop staring? He looks the same as always."

"He got new running shoes." In happier times, I would have known all about them: brand, model, how he was breaking them in. We might have even gone shopping together.

"Whatever, perv. Quit ogling. What if he looks over here?"

"I don't know. We'll wave at him, like normal people?"

"We can't do that." From the look on her face, you would have thought I'd suggested sawing off a limb.

"Why not? It would be way ruder to ignore him."

"News flash. David doesn't *want* to talk to you."

"And you know this how?"

"Because, unlike you, I'm capable of understanding delicate emotions." Amy placed a hand over her heart. She probably thought that was where feelings lived — the Hallmark version of human anatomy.

"What's your point?"

Her head tipped back as she heaved a sigh. "It's too painful for him to see us. A reminder of what he's lost."

I resisted the urge to glance at David. Not that I'd be able to read signs of devastation from this distance. Even up close he had a pretty good poker face. "I'm sure he's realized he's better off by now."

"Wow. Disloyal much? Meg is our *sister*."

"Which is how I know she was a terrible girlfriend."

Amy pressed her lips together. Even she couldn't pretend our space-case older sister was an ideal romantic partner.

"David's too nice for any of us," I continued.

"Except you, right?"

"I said *us*, dumbass. As in our whole family."

"There's no *me* in *team*, Jo." Amy glanced at Coach, like she was thinking of repeating this bit of sporty wisdom to her. "But that still doesn't mean he wants to be around *you*."

"We were friends before. There's no reason that has to change." I'd been a little afraid to test this theory by actually talking to him, but I wasn't going to share that with Amy. "It's not like I'm the one who dumped him."

"He doesn't need you to run in circles with him, Jo. He has a whole team for that." She flung an arm in that direction, which of course made David look our way.

I froze, painfully aware we'd been busted. Had he gotten even taller, or were his shorts shorter than usual? Right as my brain sent a signal to my face that this would be a good time to smile instead of staring at his legs, Amy jumped in front of me.

"Nope." She held a hand in front of my face to block my view. "You are not going to charge over there like a wrecking ball and make him hang out with you. Let him grieve in peace."

"I wasn't going to *make* him do anything."

"That's right, because we're leaving. Mom needs us." She shoved me forward with both hands. I thought about turning around and slide-tackling her legs out from under her, but there was a chance Coach would see. Plus David probably thought we'd been talking about him and then deliberately given him the cold shoulder, which was like choking down a chili dog of awkwardness on top of the deluxe shameburger of Amy's earlier performance.

"Why exactly do we have to go home?"

"She'll tell us when we get there."

I gave a small yet eloquent huff.

"You're going to feel bad when it turns out to be something major."

"Somehow I'll survive."

As we stepped past the chain-link fence that bordered the track, Amy spotted a gaggle of her equally loud and show-offy sophomore friends, who of course she had to greet with squeals and hand-grabbing and hopping in place. It had probably been under ten minutes since they'd seen one another. I could have won the lottery and made less of a production.

Crossing my arms, I gave Amy a look.

"What?" She was faking it for her friends, pretending not to understand my silent warning. The one that said, *you are standing on thin ice.*

"I have to go," Amy told them, cutting her eyes at me. A chorus of "Bye-ee!" and kissy noises erupted. They hugged like it was a contact sport, swaying side to side. It was all very *notice me,* as evidenced by the way they kept stealing glances over one another's shoulders, hoping for an audience. I stared back, stony-faced.

"Could you *be* more of a downer?" Amy muttered as she joined me.

"You dragged me away from practice. I'm not going to stand there and watch *The Amy Show*."

"Sometimes I think that's my true medium." She stared dreamily into the distance, head cocked, before glancing at me to see if I was impressed.

"Acting fake in public?"

"It's not fake. I just *enhance* things. Make them more vivid. And beautiful."

"Then it's definitely not like your art." Our house was littered with Amy's failed experiments in everything from origami to bottled sand. When your own mother asks if you've considered paint-by-numbers, it's probably time to find a new hobby.

"At least I'm actually creating something." She stuck her tongue out. "Besides stanky puddles of sweat."

"Being dramatic is not an art. Nobody gasps that much unless they're being strangled. Which unfortunately hasn't happened."

Amy sucked in an outraged breath, not exactly disproving my point. "You wouldn't understand."

"The pathological need to be stared at? True."

"If anything, I'm more honest than other people because I express myself openly. Which is way better than trying to hide your feelings and then turning all sour and twisted on the inside." She side-eyed me while pretending to cough.

"Congratulations on being an exhibitionist." We'd reached the car, an ancient station wagon lacking any hint of vintage coolness. Amy thrust the keys at me without a word.